Praise for *The Legacy*

'[Kirsten Tranter's] first novel, *The Legacy*, shows her to be a novelist with a commanding talent – a tough plain-stylist who can people her fictional world with characters of great vivacity and vigour ... Full of suave and stunning evocations of Sydney and Manhattan, this sparkling and spacious novel captures the smell and sap of young people half in love with everyone they're vividly aware of, and groping to find themselves like the answer to an erotic enigma'

Peter Craven, *The Monthly*

'This hypnotic debut from Australian author Tranter pays homage to Henry James's *A Portrait of a Lady* while offering a suspenseful story line worthy of Patricia Highsmith ... While Tranter's sedate pacing avoids typical thriller antics and conventional crime plot twists, she raises some wickedly keen questions about art world wheeling and dealing'

Publishers Weekly

'An intelligent and engaging novel that is dense, intricate, detailed, acutely observed, and beautifully written in a voice that is measured and consistent from start to finish.'

Debra Adelaide, author of *The Household Guide to Dying*

'*The Legacy* never lacks self-assurance or narrative drive'

Sydney Morning Herald

'[Tranter is] an innovative revisionist unafraid of challenge and more than up for the risks, tempering the satisfaction of the known with the surprises of the new ... *The Legacy* is an entertaining literary thriller that skilfully describes the almost pleasurable pain of love and life denied'

Weekend Australian

Kirsten Tranter grew up in Sydney and lived in New York from 1998 to 2006, where she completed a PhD on English Renaissance literature at Rutgers University. She has published fiction, poetry and literary criticism. This is her first novel. She lives in Sydney with her husband and son.

To Robin,
Best wishes
Kirsten Tranter

2011

The
LEGACY

KIRSTEN
TRANTER

FOURTH ESTATE • _London, New York, Sydney_ and _Auckland_

The author gratefully acknowledges the support of
the Literature Board of the Australia Council for the Arts
during the writing of this novel.

Fourth Estate
An imprint of HarperCollins*Publishers*

First published in Australia in 2010
This edition published in 2011
by HarperCollins*Publishers* Australia Pty Limited
ABN 36 009 913 517
harpercollins.com.au

HarperCollins*Publishers*
25 Ryde Road, Pymble, Sydney NSW 2073, Australia
31 View Road, Glenfield, Auckland 0627, New Zealand
A 53, Sector 57, Noida, UP, India
77–85 Fulham Palace Road, London W6 8JB, United Kingdom
2 Bloor Street East, 20th floor, Toronto, Ontario M4W 1A8, Canada
10 East 53rd Street, New York, NY 10022, USA

National Library of Australia Cataloguing-in-Publication data:

Tranter, Kirsten.
  The legacy / Kirsten Tranter.
  ISBN: 978 0 7322 9081 8 (pbk.)
  Missing persons–Fiction.
A823.4

Cover design by Natalie Winter, adapted by Mark Thacker
Cover images: 'Whisper' © Samantha Everton; branches by Shutterstock.com
Author photo by Steve Baccon
Typeset in 11/16.5 Baskerville BE
Printed and bound in Australia by Griffin Press
50gsm Bulky News used by HarperCollins*Publishers* is a natural, recyclable product made
from wood grown in sustainable plantation forests. The manufacturing processes conform
to the environmental regulations in the country of origin, New Zealand.

5 4 3 2 1   11 12 13 14

In memory of departed friends,
Josh and Kirstin

Well! And what if she should die some afternoon,
Afternoon grey and smoky, evening yellow and rose;
Should die and leave me sitting pen in hand
With the smoke coming down above the housetops;
Doubtful, for a while
Not knowing what to feel or if I understand
Or whether wise or foolish, tardy or too soon...
Would she not have the advantage, after all?
The music is successful with a 'dying fall'
Now that we talk of dying –
And should I have the right to smile?

T. S. Eliot, 'The Portrait of a Lady'

Prologue

Fleur knocked on my door and I must have been asleep because it seemed to wake me. I guessed that she had heard something of the argument the night before. It hadn't sounded very loud at the time, but that morning it occurred to me that the whole world was dimmed and muffled. The light was very faint, just leaving night behind.

I let her in. We looked at each other.

'I'll be back,' she said, and came back a few minutes later with tea in a cup on a saucer. The delicacy of the china was somehow wonderful, transparent even in the dull light. Strength, fragility, all at once.

She sat down in the chair at my desk – I was sitting on the chaise longue – and lit a cigarette. 'Sorry,' she said, 'I know you don't like it, but too bad.' She smoked it half down. 'I'll go with you. To the hospital.'

I sat there, quite still. 'No,' I said.

'Have you looked in the mirror?' she asked.

I smiled at her, or started to. It hurt.

She finished the cigarette and stubbed it out in a dented metal saucer she had brought in with her. 'OK,' she said. 'I'll call Carl.'

I didn't complain.

She went downstairs and shut her door. The sound of her voice came very faintly through to my room, only because I knew to listen for it.

My dress from the night before lay on the floor in a pool of silk. It was pale oyster grey, with a split up the side that had shown the bruise on my upper leg like an ugly pressed flower. Gil had stayed by my side all night to shield the view. His fury when we walked in the apartment door had been fast and strong, a striking snake.

I'm being dramatic again.

Fleur came back up carrying the newspaper and handed it to me. She had a magazine as well, and she sat down with it. She picked up the little amphora on my desk and held it in her hands, turning it over, then set it down again.

'I don't like him coming here. I wish you would go to the hospital this time.' She sighed, a short sigh, a sort of huff. 'He's coming anyway, and he'll stitch you up.'

I must have flinched at that.

She narrowed her eyes at me, then picked up her magazine and put her feet up on the desk and started to read. She was wearing striped socks, three colours repeated. I spent a while studying the contrast they made against the white surface.

'I'll wait here,' she said, without looking at me. She turned a page. 'Dad's gone to the gallery already. His bag is gone so I think he'll stay upstate.' The statement caused her visible effort.

I hadn't heard him leave.

There are no mirrors in my room, so I didn't need to look. Carl was Gil's cousin, a plastic surgeon with a practice a few blocks away. He faxed through prescriptions for Gil, antibiotics or whatever, and I suspected that he faxed a few for Fleur too.

The morning suddenly had some structure: I was waiting for Carl to arrive. Then I would wait for him to finish. Then he would leave. That was about all I could think through.

He seemed to take a while. I'd read through the whole style section but couldn't remember a word of it, I found when I came to the last page, except a vague sense that black and white together were in vogue. I closed and folded it when the buzzer rang and Fleur went to answer it.

I heard them talking. There was the sound of water running in the kitchen sink. Carl came into the room carrying a brown leather case, an old-fashioned-looking doctor's case, and Fleur stood behind him holding a basin. Steam rose from it. Carl was wearing a white shirt and the pants of a grey suit. His teeth were very white when he smiled at me.

'Ingrid, Ingrid,' he said, chiding me.

I started to smile. It hurt, but I kept it up as well as I could. I tried to arrange myself with confidence. My limbs moved stiffly. He dragged the desk chair over to the chaise and sat himself down. Fleur put the basin on the desk. It sat right where her feet had been before. I looked down at them. She had put on soft black ballet slippers that were scuffed around the toe.

Carl smiled his white smile at me and shook his head ever so slightly. 'Those stairs!' he said, turning his head an inch and giving me a sideways look. 'A real nuisance.' His voice shook a tiny bit and I glanced at him quickly.

3

'Oh, yes,' I said, keeping it vague.

The muffling that had been there earlier was gone, and I didn't like the new sharpness in the sounds I was hearing. I frowned. He gave me a tiny medicine cup full of bright red liquid and I drank it. It felt warm.

'Now,' he said, drawing out the word, and got to work.

It was only three stitches in the end, tiny little strips of sticky tape that held my face together in a line just above my eyebrow. I knew that because I did look up at the mirror later that afternoon in the bathroom, brushing my teeth. I looked away quickly but I saw them.

Carl kissed my hand gently when he was finished. Once his bag was closed he stood up and became very chatty, telling me how much he was looking forward to having us all round to dinner next week.

I nodded. 'Thanks, Carl,' I said, 'thanks for coming over.' It sounded wrong. 'For coming by.'

'You've got everything you need?' he asked. 'Can I send Fleur out to get anything?'

Fleur raised her eyebrows sarcastically. She was back, leaning in the doorway with folded arms. 'We're fine,' she said. I nodded again.

'Rest,' he said. 'You must have one hell of a headache.' His sideways smile again. He left, taking the stairs quickly, in a rhythm, da-dum, da-dum.

A small bottle of the red liquid sat on my desk, its medicine cup showing the trace of what I'd drunk earlier. A little Alice-in-Wonderland drink, I thought, and reached for it. *Drink me.*

4

Fleur poured herself one too after I'd finished. 'Cheers,' she said, and drained it down.

I lay on the chaise and closed my eyes. It didn't hurt. I heard Fleur laughing at something she was reading in her magazine, and I smiled.

'Aren't you supposed to be at school?' I asked her.

She laughed at me, the same laugh. I opened my eyes. 'Aren't you supposed to be at school?' she echoed, mocking me.

'Well, yes,' I said. 'No. I don't have to go today.'

'I'm not going today either,' she said, and flicked a page. 'Mondays are a waste.'

A minute passed. 'I'm going to the studio later though,' she told me. 'Not for long. I'll be back for dinner. We can order Thai.'

We ate that night sitting at the island in the kitchen, only because she refused to bring the food upstairs to me and once I was down there in the kitchen I wanted to stay with her.

'You're looking after me,' I said to her, only realising it was true as I was saying it. She chewed and swallowed and didn't say a thing. 'It's supposed to be the other way around,' I said.

'Sometimes it is,' she replied.

I'm not sure what she meant, whether I sometimes looked after her, or that stepmothers in general sometimes looked after their stepdaughters. At the time it sounded comforting. The muffling came down again as I went to sleep on the chaise in my room but one of my thoughts was sharp through it for a moment. I knew both that she was too young to be looking after me and old enough that she would not be prepared to do it for much longer. I wondered how far she would go to protect me. I wondered how much I had looked after her, and what kind of loyalty that had bought me.

Our shared cup sat on the desk, line of red against the plastic. Not at all like blood or rubies, although it suggested those. Like liquid plastic, unmistakably artificial cherry red. The amphora on my desk was back exactly as it had been before she picked it up, at the same angle, the same spot. She was clever. I knew that already.

I knew that trusting her laid burdens on her that were unfair, but I let myself be unfair. The sounds of the traffic outside and far below floated up softly, cars coming and going and sirens wailing in a fading cry. I lay there with my Alice bottle and thought about the story I could tell, the curse that I could lay, the scrolls that I could fill. I could engrave it all on plates of steel, as tall as my body, stacked up against the walls.

Those mirrored, shining doors dissolved and I fell into a dream that was all about escaping on a boat across a river. The island city dropped away behind me. I felt a joyful sense of freedom until I saw the man at the stern of the ferry, his hand held out for payment. Then I knew that the river we were crossing was the one no-one ever crossed back from, and I grasped his outstretched hand in supplication. He smiled at me, a cruel smile I knew well, and coins fell down around me, welling up around my knees, golden in the shadows.

Part One

I.

There were three letters addressed to me on the kitchen counter when I arrived home that Thursday afternoon in August, white and cream envelopes bright against the blue tile. One stood out as I looked through them: a long envelope, thick with paper contents.

The notepaper inside was a heavy stock, its creaminess matching the envelope. It bore embossed initials: RH.

A message was there in Ralph's scrawling hand, challenging any reader to make out a word. I took out the envelope's other object, a plane ticket. One way, business class, Sydney–New York. I laid them both out on the counter.

Julia –
   There's a return waiting for you here. I hope you'll listen to an idea I have.
   Please do come. Saturday? I hope you're well.
   My love,
   R.

It was an overly theatrical kind of gesture, even from Ralph. The address was printed on the back of the envelope but I knew it well. Garden Court. Kirribilli. I ran my fingers over the inked-on letters, their imprint on the paper's surface.

The house was quiet and empty. The kettle began to screech and the sound turned into a song note. I turned off the gas but as my hand moved to do it I fought an impulse, quick and lively as fire, to pick up the paper and touch the corner to the flame. It would have burnt nicely. The note drew out all the old, warring feelings. To burn it or to cherish it, keep it safe in a drawer forever. I left it there on the counter for the moment and gave in to blaming myself for being so instantly unsettled.

Outside the window the lawn sloped down to the shade of the trees at the end bordering the fence. Its vivid green defied the drought; Jenny, my aunt, swore that it was the toughness of the breed of grass, but I suspected her of extreme over-watering. Beyond the trees the hill began to drop down to the sea. I went out onto the verandah. The grass seemed to hold the twilight like a pair of hands, the light seeping through them and away like water. Or sand. The fine, white grains of the beach. The letter from Ralph was making me think in overdrawn metaphors.

Down at the bottom of the lawn where the trees marked the border there was a stone Diana, half the size of life. At least, I had always thought of her as Diana. As she faded away into the twilight I supposed that she could be any classical woman figure, a girl or a goddess, appropriately robed for the purposes of garden art. She might have been part of a fountain once. Beyond the trees the line of the horizon showed, the sea standing up like a wall of water, beginning to lose its distinction from the sky as night came on. I had come from the city across the water and the smog was still there on my clothes, a fine grit on my skin.

My aunt, who owned the house, was sitting a little way over on the lawn in a wooden folding chair. In a second chair was Keith, the owner of the gallery that showed her paintings. The lawn glowed green. They both held cups of tea, and they were talking quietly. Jenny, grey-haired, sat tall in her chair. Keith leaned forward, elbows on his knees. He raised his hand in a questioning motion, gesturing into the distance. My aunt nodded. Words drifted up faintly, muted by the grass and space. I went back inside.

The walls of the house were filled with paintings, Jenny's work as well as others, most of them gifts exchanged over the years. They made an odd mosaic, small frames hung next to and underneath large canvases. My aunt's work stood out with its signal blue, abstract and devoted to line. The house had been a precious refuge when I had been smaller, and still felt like one at times. Some people have family homes that their parents have lived in forever, that they can always go back to. My parents weren't around – father long dead, mother far away – and had moved frequently anyway, but this house was one of the true constants in my life.

Jenny came into the kitchen from the verandah. The sound of Keith putting the chairs back in place against the wall clattered in, and then he stood in the doorway and said hello.

'We've been discussing the next show,' he told me, one hand clasped over his other arm, tall body bent against the door frame, slightly hesitant as usual. He had a warm, open face that smiled easily, intelligent eyes. 'Your aunt here seems to think she needs a whole six months to prepare.' His tone was friendly, not seriously impatient.

'I don't paint as fast as I used to,' she said.

We all laughed at that: Jenny had always worked very slowly, in contrast to the finished effects of her paintings with their swift flashes of colour.

My aunt rubbed her hands a little at the joint of her thumb as she said goodbye to Keith. The quip about her speed of painting had some truth to it. The beginnings of arthritis had started to slow her down.

'So you have the time you wanted?' I asked her after Keith had left.

She sighed quickly and pulled the screen door so that it was really shut. 'Oh yes. More or less.' She didn't sound satisfied. Her hair was cut straight and blunt just above her shoulders, and she ran her hand through it, as if planning to tie it back, and stopped.

I held the note in one hand. 'It's from Ralph,' I explained to Jenny. 'He's asked me to go see him, on Saturday. So I think I'll go.'

Even as I said it I knew that the invitation was not like water to a thirsty soul, the way it felt, but more like a slug of whisky to a recovering alcoholic. Was there a difference, after all? That's how it went, my self-rationalisation.

'OK, good. It's been so long, hasn't it?' Her voice was carefully casual.

'He's sent me a ticket to New York. I don't know what he's thinking.' I had some idea, of course, but didn't want to put it into words.

She put her hand out and rested it on my forearm. I covered it with my own for a brief second. 'New York?' A troubled look crossed her face. 'Let me know how it goes.'

She finished her gesture with a brief pat to my arm, picked up the mug of tea I had poured, and wandered slowly back down the hall to her studio. The biggest room of the house, during the day it was always lit with sun through its many windows and a skylight in the ceiling. The door was panelled in glass patterned to blur the view of what was inside, as though someone had pressed their fingers all over it while it was still drying. She closed it behind her. The glass panels showed smudged pieces of colour and light. It looked like the Bonnard painting of his wife in the bath, one of the only reproductions my aunt had in the house. In the painting, each tile of the bathroom wall glowed with wet, iridescent colour, the rainbow of an oil slick.

I looked back down at the note, resolving to put it on the dresser in my room, determined that it would not go into one of the drawers where I would treasure it even if I pretended otherwise. Instead it would probably sit there for months gathering dust. That looked more like not caring. The difference was not much at all but, I told myself, I had my pride.

It seemed like a long drive to Kirribilli, even though it was only a few miles. I managed to take a couple of wrong turns on the way. I'd driven there many times, but always from another direction, never from my aunt's house. It was around eleven on Saturday when my car pulled into the driveway. The house looked paler, peach walls more bleached by the sun. The frangipani trees around the front were bare and ugly. I knocked. A beautiful boy of about eighteen opened the door. A fuzz of golden hair was cropped close to his head. His feet were bare, and he was wearing a black sleeveless shirt and a sarong in bright batik colours. He had the calm smile of a Buddha.

'I'm looking for Ralph –'

Before I could finish saying his name, the boy cut me off. 'Julia, yes, of course, come in.' The way he spoke over Ralph's name made it sound as though he thought I was looking for myself.

'Ralph,' I repeated, and went inside.

It was warm in the house. The familiar hallway stretched away dimly, staircase sweeping grandly up to one side. Light from the stained-glass panels on the door made patterns on the floor. The boy had disappeared. I waited. He emerged from a door off the far end of the hallway, and held it open for me. 'In here,' he said. There was a brightness showing through the door, and I caught the sound of running water.

We walked through into a large space of greenery, a glass-roofed conservatory. When I had been to the house before, the family had never used this room, although Ralph's father had liked gardening. Plants were everywhere in shades of dark green, lightened in some places by paler ferns, delicate against the larger, stronger leaves of what looked like huge aspidistras. The sun shone through the glass but was caught and dappled by the plants, some of them growing tall towards the roof. The light seemed to have had the warmth bleached from it, while a thick, humid heat came from some other source. The sound of water came from a fountain over towards the far corner, half-obscured by plants, a large stone urn decorated with garlands of stone flowers. My skin softened with the dampness in the air.

Two cane armchairs sat in front of a black, lacquered table. Ralph was seated in one of the chairs, his legs crossed. All the contours of his body, the angles of arms and legs, were dear and familiar and brought about a dull ache in my chest. I'd seen him sit like that a thousand times, in this house, at mine, on a dining table next to a spilt glass of wine late at night in some forgotten kitchen, in the seat next to me in class, across from me at the campus bar. I had missed him and it consumed me now like a sudden thirst. At that first sight of him it seemed impossible that I'd gone without seeing him for so long. It had always been like that when I saw him after a long break, I reminded myself warily.

The boy walked to a trolley near the chairs and put ice from a silver bucket into two glasses with a clink.

'Ralph,' I said.

He lifted his arms and said my name in reply, the rest of his body still and cross-legged in the chair. I kissed his cheek, his high cheekbone against the skin.

'It's good to see you,' he said. 'Sit down. I'm so glad you could make it.'

I sat.

'Won't you have a drink? Wine? Or do you want some whisky?' He gestured towards the boy and smiled. 'This is Aaron.'

Aaron fixed a gleaming smile on me and brought me a glass. It smelled like brandy. I was already feeling light-headed from the heat. The glass was very cold in my hand.

I asked him how he was. It couldn't be a casual question anymore. He had always been thin, never quite filling his clothes. His clothes now were as expensive and well-cut as ever, and they hung from him loosely. A beautiful, coffee-coloured shirt. He gave me a smile with one side of his mouth, lips closed. His eyes had the same brightness, brown filled with light.

'The new drugs have done wonders for me, although you may not be able to see it. A couple of months ago I was a lot worse.'

He had inherited this thing with his heart, a kind of arrhythmia that made it sometimes beat too slow or too fast, out of its proper pattern.

'And you're still working?' he asked, as though it were a peculiar hobby.

'Yes, in the bookshop. It's going well.'

'And you're still living over in Mosman with your aunt?'

'Still living there.'

'And Mark?'

'He's still around.' I waited. 'I am thinking about moving,' I said, not sure how many details I wanted to offer. The topic of moving in had been raised again recently with Mark, without much real intention.

'Oh. I'm sorry.' He looked thoughtful. 'Moving,' he repeated, with a faint disgust. 'It's always so … unsettling.'

I waited. 'It's hot in here,' I said. My dress was sticking to the seat, and my legs sweated inside tights. I remembered reading his note in the kitchen and my urge to burn it and felt the satisfying heat of the flame against my hand as surely as if I had done it after all.

'I've asked you here to talk about Ingrid,' he said after a minute, as I had known he would. 'I want you to go to New York. I can't, you know.'

And he explained his idea to me.

'I'd just like to know some basic things. What was she working on? What's the place like where she was living? What did she like to do there? Maybe you can meet some of her friends. You can give my, you know, regards to Maeve and Gil. I'd appreciate that. It's just been very hard ...' He paused, and started again. 'I have a lot of regrets, you know, about not being part of her life for the last few years. I just thought that if I could know a bit more about it, it might be easier to let go.'

I looked at him.

'Does that make sense to you at all?' he asked.

'Yes,' I said, and it did. I'd thought similar things myself over the past eleven months. It was coming up for a year since her death.

'So you want a kind of report on Ingrid's life?' I asked.

'Anything you can tell me,' he said. 'I don't expect a whole dossier. I know it's sort of voyeuristic. But I don't mean it to be like that.'

Aaron moved around the green room behind us, watering plants from a watering can and spraying the leaves with a fine mist from a bottle.

Ralph looked away. 'Gil won't tell me anything. No-one's been any help.'

'What about Eve?' I asked, meaning his mother. 'Isn't she going there for some reason or other anyway?'

'No,' he said. 'She's not travelling so much anymore. She spends more time in Sydney.'

I asked if she was there, at home, at the house. He said she wasn't.

'We've swapped in a way. It's funny. About six months ago. She was sick of the house. I was sick of the flat. She's always loved it – she had owned it for years before I took it. So she moved in there and I moved back here. It's just me and Aaron now.'

Aaron looked over briefly at the sound of his name, turned back to the plants.

I'd brought the ticket with me with the idea that I might have wanted to give it back. It was in my hands now.

'It's not refundable,' he said. 'I knew you would hate to waste it by not going.'

I laughed.

'I can't put you up at the Plaza,' he said apologetically. 'But I have a place for you to stay.'

It was an apartment that his uncle, Robert, owned in the West Village and stayed in every now and again – he lived most of the time in London, where he ran a couple of restaurants. I had spent some time in New York years earlier, in a year I had spent travelling after finishing high school. It was one of the usual extended around-the-world trips that Australian eighteen-year-olds did: the States, Europe, London, home. In England they had called it my 'gap year', as though it were an empty space. More recently I had visited New York with Ralph for a couple of weeks, not long after Ingrid had met Gil Grey, when we were all still friends.

I thought about the city: the subways, the park, the long, straight avenues and little streets downtown. It took some courage. I thought about the hole in the ground down there at the end of the island.

'I know you're not back at law school,' he said. I didn't ask how he knew that. 'I'm sure they can do without you at the store for a little while. Just go for a couple of weeks if you like. Take a walk around the Columbia campus. Take a camera. Tell me what's new in the Prada shop. Or wherever she shopped at. J. Crew. Who knows. Do what you like.' He shrugged, but he kept his eyes on me.

'Aren't you curious about Fleur?' he asked. 'We never did meet her. I'd love to know what she's like. Did you know she's taking photographs now, no painting?'

He was persuasive. It might not have worked if a range of factors hadn't been in place. I was tired of the pattern my life had fallen into: not tired of Jenny and her house, which I couldn't really imagine leaving for Mark's flat. I was tired of Mark. I'd taken on more hours at the bookshop after deciding to take the semester off with the dim idea of doing some writing, a script, an outline, something – it was a love story, a mystery, it changed every month – in reality knowing I couldn't face the mountain of reading and assignments for each week's class. It was quiet at the shop and Martin often let me go home early. Not much writing had happened. It was another kind of gap year, not like the deliberate coming-of-age overseas journey I'd taken at eighteen, but a kind of hiatus that might never come to a close, a drifting sense of purposelessness.

It wasn't much to do with Ingrid, my decision to go. She had been shut away into some cupboard of memory by then and the thought of opening that door wasn't all that interesting. It was just the idea of leaving that was appealing.

But all that might have been irrelevant. On the drive home I tried to remember just one other time that I'd said no to something Ralph had asked me to do. None came to mind. My flight left in three weeks' time.

Just a few days earlier Mark had noticed the thing that made me realise that I really was tired of the way things were going. He was wearing a towel around his waist, and rubbing at his hair with another towel to dry it.

'It's been weeks since you've taken anything, Julia,' he said. He threw the towel in his hand over his shoulder. 'I'll start to think you don't care anymore.'

He walked into the kitchen in his bare feet. Cups and plates clinked together. The hallway he came from was in shadow, fighting the sunlight at the only time of day when any light would get remotely close. The morning sun shone brightly through the windows behind me. I stayed sitting in the big old leather chair, the possession of his I coveted most wholly.

He was right, and I hadn't even noticed. It had been weeks since I'd taken anything.

Mark and I had literally run into each other two years earlier in a bar in Potts Point not far from the bookshop where I worked. He had managed to spill half his beer down the front of my dress, bumping into me by accident; he bought me another drink and hung around while I sat there looking like a wet T-shirt competitor, which he seemed to like, and I didn't mind. When he turned his head a certain way after the second round the light had caught his dark brown hair and made it look just like Ralph's. My heart had skipped, guilty and alert.

The first time he stayed I'd taken a big thing – keys – without thinking about it, and realised later that I'd meant for him to come back for them. I had been happy to see him at the door the next day, standing there framed against the evening. He had stayed again, taking his keys with him this time when he left. And leaving behind, unintentionally, a pen I had removed from the pocket of his jacket. It was a small thing. I'm not sure if he ever did notice that it was gone.

It started early with me, not like most girls who begin shoplifting when they turn thirteen and get shamed out of it when their parents have to collect them from the store security office or, worse, the police station. It began with playing with the objects on my mother's dresser, the fascinating arrangement of perfume bottles, boxes, powders, the silver-backed hairbrush and mirror. That was back in the days when she still wore French perfume and brands you could buy at the chemist, before she switched to jasmine oil and clary sage. I stood there when she was out and examined them all in detail, and made sure I always put them back in precisely the same position. It was a kind of puzzle. One day she came home unexpectedly before everything was back in place. The front door opened and shut. A bracelet of blue beads was in my hand. My fingers closed over it. Everything else was as it had been. I thought about hiding under the bed – why was I so afraid of discovery, I wonder now – but instead slipped out and joined her in the kitchen where she was taking off her coat and opening the fridge.

'Darling!' she said when she saw me, as though she was surprised to find me home. She hugged me briefly and the beads pressed against me through the fabric of my dress where they sat in my pocket. They were open pockets, two of them sewn onto the outside of the dress, with a rounded shape and a large button on each one. I was afraid the bracelet would fall out. It didn't.

She didn't say anything about the lost bracelet. I thought about putting it back but I didn't want to, and I was afraid of being caught in the act of replacing it. It had come from a box containing many bracelets, and it wasn't one she often wore.

It was months before she mentioned it.

'Have you seen that bracelet of mine with the blue beads?' she asked my father one morning. She had just finished dressing, and she was putting her earrings in as she spoke. She pulled the second one through her ear. 'Do you know the one I mean?'

My father hadn't looked up from the paper. He made a noise that might have signalled a negative answer.

Peter, my brother, looked at me accusingly from the floor where he was lying stretched out with a book in front of him. My mother stalked back to her room and came out again with nothing on her wrists. She didn't mention the blue beaded bracelet again, and I enjoyed the victorious feeling of having got away with something.

It turned out that I was good at taking things in a way that people didn't notice, and good at not giving myself away on the occasions when they did. It became a rare event as I grew older.

Mostly I took books from Mark's house, just occasionally – that wasn't so pathological – and always left them in a pile in the corner of my bedroom where he'd pick them out and take them home again when he was ready.

Ralph gave me things so often that it didn't feel necessary to take anything. Whatever it was I wanted from him was so big and so impossible that taking an object would have only made the desire more mortifying.

I took only small things from Ingrid – a pencil from the pocket of her bag, a hairclip – but my heart was never in it and these tokens exuded no power. I put them back. The happiness she got from finding the hairclip I had replaced in her bag made me feel like a benevolent angel. That was new. Ingrid had snapped the clasp in and out when she found it, a piece of metal fixed against the plastic imitation tortoiseshell. It was shaped like a leaf, an autumn leaf. She fixed it into place, and the shine of the plastic showed against her gold hair. I regretted returning it then. The beauty of the object emerged when it was on her, once it was joined to her, something I had missed when I had taken it and viewed it alone.

Some part of me was waiting for something of hers to present itself that would be worth taking. It wasn't something that would be found by looking. After a while I forgot about it and the desire passed.

Mark handed me the paper when we said goodbye that morning, making sure I was taking something. It was still folded up in its place outside the door to the flat, freshly delivered. I hesitated before taking it. Mark wasn't good at giving things. He was writing a thesis, a doctorate in Philosophy that was all about revising late twentieth-century theories of gift and exchange. Doing all that reading had screwed with his own ability to give anybody anything without being overwhelmed by anxiety about what kind of moral and ethical structures he was condoning or violating. So even the newspaper was weirdly extravagant. At birthdays the issue with gifts became irritating, but most of the time it was OK with me; it encouraged a very minimal sense of emotional obligation, which is what I suppose he intended in a way. Our involvement was like that – always tentative, both afraid of risk in our individual ways. From the most cynical angle I was continuing on with it to prove something to myself or the world: that I was over Ralph and capable of sustaining an adult relationship. Or a semblance of one.

He kissed me goodbye, still wearing the towel. I put the paper on the back seat of my car and didn't look back at it.

2.

Before Ingrid became our friend, Ralph liked to tell the story of his first meeting with me. I was working in a video shop up at Kings Cross back then, a shift that started in the afternoon and went through until late at night. The shop was on the border of the Cross and the less sleazy neighbourhoods surrounding it, the only video place within a mile that wasn't dedicated solely to pornography. It was late on a weeknight and quiet. I was eating a bar of chocolate I had taken from the stack for sale on the counter and watching a Humphrey Bogart movie on the TV set up high on the wall, with the sound turned down low.

The shop was a cavernous space with low ceilings and shelves placed too close together. You entered it by walking down three steps from the street. A red neon sign blinked in the window: 'VIDE MANIA'. The 'O' in 'VIDEO' flickered on now and again. Seen from inside, read backwards, the sign always suggested a Latin exclamation to me. Ingrid saw it too, when she was there. 'Video, videre, visi, visus!' she would chant triumphantly, reciting her principal parts.

'What about mania?' I asked her once. Ingrid paused for a moment. 'Maneo, manere, mansi, mansus!'

Ralph was sitting in the corner reading, and he rubbed his forehead and observed her doubtfully. 'You can't form "mania" from that word.'

Ingrid frowned and looked back to the window. The fluorescent light made her yellow hair unusually dull and her red coat was redder than ever. The 'O' on the sign winked and surged. Her face was reflected for a moment perfectly in the window – beautiful in its classic way, features made harsher by the light – and mine behind hers, dark hair and brows, blur of white skin and vermilion mouth.

At high school I had been teased for being a goth by the girls who looked superficially like Ingrid – tanned and blonde – because of my colouring: hair so dark it was almost black, and skin that only burned, never went golden brown. And I wore black in the same way that they wore pink or light blue. It didn't quite make sense to me as an insult – I lacked the black eyeliner and masses of silver jewellery that the real goths wore. Ingrid wasn't like those girls, which I didn't see right away; I worked out after a while that the same types at her school had come up with reasons to exclude her too, and that she looked down on them fiercely.

I knew 'video' as Latin for 'I see', dredged up from some mental warehouse of etymology. I looked up 'maneo' later in my aunt's battered old Latin dictionary. *To stay, remain anywhere. To wait. To await one's fate.*

But neither of us had ever met Ingrid that night Ralph first came into Videomania. It was late 1996, towards the end of second semester, a warm October night. Ralph came in just behind another, older guy who dumped a stack of videos in the return slot. They slid down in a jumbled pile into the box below. Ralph was wearing a brown jacket made of velvety corduroy, his hands deep in the pockets, and tortoiseshell-framed glasses. His brown hair was damp and he ran his hand through it. He watched the screen above for a moment. There were two other customers in the shop, two girls together, and they came up to the counter with two movies. I glanced at them – comedies, new releases – and fetched them from the shelf in the back. They giggled with each other. When they left, Ralph leaned towards me on the counter and tipped his glasses forward so that he was looking over them at me.

'Would you happen to have a *Ben-Hur*, 1860, with the duplicated line on page one-sixteen?'

I smiled and held his gaze for a second. He was quoting from the movie on screen, a scene that had passed a moment before he'd come in. I reached down to flick the pages of the telephone-book-sized volume on the counter, a big reference list of movies that you could use to look up any film and any actor, pretending to search.

'Or a Chevalier Audubon 1840?' he asked.

I closed the book with a slap. 'Nobody would,' I said, playing along. 'There isn't one.'

He smiled with his lips closed and looked down, tapped his fingers lightly on the counter.

'Isn't this the part where I tell you it's going to rain and you bring out a bottle of whisky?' I asked.

He looked up. 'I can pop around the corner for that,' he said. 'Or we could try *The Maltese Falcon*. That's the film I'm meant to be watching for class tomorrow.' He stood up straight and began to pull his shoulders back, gave up and slumped.

'You begin to interest me. Vaguely,' I said, and he blinked, hands back in pockets, and gave me a sidelong look.

I bent down to collect the stack of returns. Soft porn with an Arthurian legend theme. A large, jewelled sword featured prominently on the first cover alongside a woman with very long and thoughtfully placed blonde hair and a knight with his visor up who was either tying her to a tree or undoing her bonds. It was from the refined end of the section over in the far corner of the shop. When I straightened up, the little bell on the door rang as it opened and closed and Ralph was gone.

An hour later it seemed unlikely that he would return. I was stifling a yawn and watching the start of *The Maltese Falcon* when he walked back in, soaked a little by the rain and more rumpled than he had looked before. 'Sorry,' he said. 'Got distracted.' He was holding a bottle in a brown paper bag and there was a soft packet of cigarettes crumpled in his top pocket.

'Come on back,' I invited him, and opened the section of the counter that came up like a drawbridge.

He grinned, and showed his teeth for the first time. One of his incisors overlapped the other teeth at a crooked angle. There were a couple of chairs behind the counter, cracked vinyl that could have started out any colour and were now greyish green, and he took one. His legs were long and thin and he crossed them at the knee with a practised motion, wound close around each other.

When Ralph told the story at parties and in the campus bar he was usually quite drunk but could always remember the names of the films we watched in the store and back at his flat around the corner after my shift finished. At one point we started *Sir Galahard*, the returned Arthurian porn that I hadn't got around to shelving, and stopped in fits of laughter after ten minutes as the second band of maidens entered the knight's chamber. Mostly we had stuck to noir, and better-tailored damsels in distress.

I remembered the movies too, but it was never me who told the story. By the third time I heard him tell it, to some people who had probably heard it already the first or second time, I stood up and went to get another drink when he got to the part about me inviting him back behind the counter. The next time I stayed to hear it, and it didn't feel so bad. Ralph and I couldn't have told this part of the story the same way. The hopeless flip my heart had made when he'd smiled and ducked through the drawbridge of the counter, and pushed a cigarette into his mouth as he grabbed one of the small glasses I had pulled out. What would he have said to that?

He didn't strike me as exactly good-looking at first, although his face was intelligent and interesting. Usually I fell for conventionally attractive men with evidently damaged personalities and psychic wounds, against all my better instincts. I had been in love before, or so I had thought: a long high-school romance that ended in boredom on my part and chronic infidelity on his; passionate, short-lived flings in various places in the year I had spent travelling before going to university. But I'd never believed in love at first sight, so I dismissed the sheer clarity of that feeling when he smiled and joined me. I didn't understand it or reflect on it; it was a note in a new key, unknown, pure-sounding. It made more sense to me later to believe that my feelings for Ralph grew over time like a friendship – like our friendship actually did – but in reality the dark heart of it, complete and complex as an old city, was there from the very start.

Occasionally, in Ralph's retelling, he included a brief version of the story of what he'd been doing in that hour before he came back with the bottle; it involved something anonymous in the laneway behind the bottle shop.

'I've never seen *Ben-Hur*,' the guy next to me said the fourth time I heard the story, sitting on a sagging couch that seemed determined to swallow us all over the course of the evening. We were at the campus bar.

'The book, not the movie,' Ralph said to him scornfully. 'We're talking about *The Big Sleep*.'

The point of the story seemed to be mainly to display the extent of his ability to quote film dialogue on the spur of the moment, and to exhort admiration for my own abilities in that respect. I agreed that *The Big Sleep* was worth knowing so well, although not that many people did. In this sense I did feel that we had found a soul mate of sorts in one another. But that wasn't what Ralph showed by the story. By that fourth time his seemingly endless displays of cleverness were beginning to grate on me. I grabbed the knee of the guy who hadn't seen *Ben-Hur*. He was wearing black jeans. 'Maybe we could watch it sometime,' he said, and kissed me. I sank further into my seat and felt Ralph get up from his place on my other side and leave.

*

The night Ralph and I first met, I'd fallen asleep on his couch and woken up in the morning to the faint buzz of static on the television screen in front of me and violent sounds of smashing glass outside as the recycling trucks trundled by. We had made bacon and toast for breakfast together, with strong tea. Ralph lived alone in a small flat with high ceilings and lemon-coloured walls in one of the art deco apartment buildings in a street at the back of the Cross as it sloped down towards wealthy Elizabeth Bay. It was only about a ten-minute walk away from the video shop down narrow, unevenly paved laneways and doglegged streets.

I sometimes dreamt about living on my own, the pleasure of a space that was entirely mine, but the expense meant it was out of the question for me. I'd finally graduated up to the best room in my house, the balcony room at the front, after living there for a year. It was a crumbling Victorian terrace in Newtown a few blocks away from the south side of campus that I shared with two other students in fields that were mysteriously alien to me – speech pathology and medicine. The balcony sagged alarmingly in one spot, but that was easy to avoid, and I loved to lean on the iron-lace railing with a drink in the evening, watching the smog hanging dense in the sky through the leaves of a tall eucalyptus tree at the front of the house and the fizz of the streetlights starting up for the night.

After that night Ralph came to sit with me at the video store most Wednesday nights and we would watch whatever he'd been assigned to see in his Film Studies class, or a Humphrey Bogart film, or whatever was on top of the return pile that we hadn't seen. We watched *The Big Sleep* together every now and again. For some reason Ralph hated *Casablanca* and left in a bad mood the one night I wanted to watch it. I watched it to the end, and was crying into a tissue when the last customer of the night came in and wanted a list of every film with any of the Baldwin brothers in it, and rented them all. There had been stranger requests.

It turned out that we were both students at Sydney University, the old, gothic sandstone campus in the inner city, miles west from the Cross – I was in my second year and Ralph was in his third – and had somehow never wound up in the same classes, although we were both studying Arts and taking classes in English and Art History. Ralph's schedule was chaotic, with courses in every department from Russian to Archaeology, Philosophy and Linguistics while he tried (unsuccessfully, it turned out) to decide on a major.

I used to tease him that he chose a subject determined by the beauty of the building it was housed in, always avoiding the ones stuck in the ugly modern extensions around campus. Ralph stuck with Philosophy much longer than he should have simply because he loved the winding stone staircases in the old quad and the worn gargoyles that jutted out from the gutters, vomiting water when it rained. That, and the fact that the classes were filled with more thoughtful, good-looking boys than other subjects. The big concrete library was a source of constant disappointment and disgust to him, and whatever time he spent studying on campus was based in the small Art History collection in the Mills building, with its whitewashed, mossy exterior walls, next to the dilapidated tennis courts. We shared a fascination with the Transient Building across from Mills, a huge, rust-edged structure of corrugated metal that had stood there since the nineteen forties and was almost beautiful in its bleak simplicity, fluorescent strip lights winking through the aluminium windows.

We met every Friday in the bar on campus where my other friends went and played Trivial Pursuit in the corner over beer, sitting on one of the dirty red couches until it was dark outside. It turned out Ralph knew some of my friends in the scene there and slotted right in. There was an intensity to our connection right away that was different from the rest of my friendships – most of them people I had met in class, and their friends who hung out in the bar and coffee shops in the student union buildings. These had never quite managed to turn into closeness. I found something with Ralph that I had been longing for without even realising it, a rapidly formed version of intimacy. My social circle expanded to include his other friends as well and we trudged from one party to another over the weekends, from Newtown – where I lived – to Surry Hills in the east, another neighbourhood bordering on the Cross with a high proportion of students. Once or twice we made it out to Bondi, where I ended up alone one night, freezing, waiting for the late night bus, after Ralph disappeared downstairs with someone I vaguely recognised from my English tutorial (all I remembered was that he was very enthusiastic about Keats).

I started going to lunch with Ralph at his family's house every couple of weeks, a meal that went on for hours into the late afternoon and invariably included roast meat of one kind or another. The big old mansion sat on the north shore of the harbour and had a rambling garden filled with frangipani trees, poinsettias and climbing jasmine. It was solid and squarish and beautiful with a red-tiled roof and walls painted a dirty peach colour that had faded over time and showed through more brightly in little patches under the windowsills. Inside it was all burnished wood and bronze and antiques, a wide carpeted staircase and rooms with perfect proportions and tall windows.

The day I met Ingrid it had been several weeks since Ralph had visited, and I was meeting him there. His mother was around, back from one of her frequent long trips, and he had been avoiding her. She was a buyer for some kind of high-end boutique, a job that she didn't seem to need but liked. It seemed mainly to involve flying all around the world looking for pretty things to take home.

Ralph's father, George, was good-natured with a kind of surface crankiness that he performed happily, embracing the role of grumpy old man in his late middle age. When I visited he liked to start half-hearted fights with me. He was tall like Ralph and always wore the same checked shirt in a slightly different colour, sometimes with a grey cardigan. His wealth came from his work in finance, trading stocks and lending money, but he seemed to be now mostly retired after a bad heart attack the year before. Every now and again I heard him on the phone yelling at an office underling or talking intently, advising a colleague. The heart condition was serious but he hated any mention of it; he waved his arms, glass of wine in hand, and argued when

Ralph made any suggestion at the table about something he might want or not want to eat or drink.

'No damned difference!' he would shout. 'It's all damned genetics! Now pass the bottle or I'll get up and fetch it myself and give myself a cardiac arrest.'

He had it in his head, wrongly, that I was a film student, having put that together with studying art history and working in a video store. I wondered sometimes if he was a little deaf. 'How's the opus?' he would ask every time, studying me attentively. By this he seemed to mean my own film, or possibly a film script or long essay. 'Eh? How're the studies? Studying hard, I hope!'

Ralph was subdued around him. He made more thoughtful displays of cleverness, hoping to get his father's attention, but there was real affection between them. It was always Ralph who fetched the bottle and poured from it in the end, or passed the potatoes, and handed him his cup of tea at the end of the afternoon.

It was Ralph's mother, Eve, who answered the door that Sunday. I was late. Eve kissed me and covered me in a cloud of Chanel. 'Come in, darling. I'm so glad you've come. Come in and let me introduce you to my niece. You'll be thrilled to meet her.' Their little greyhound, Racer, came with her and sniffed me disinterestedly, and loped away.

We passed through the hallway. It was wallpapered in dark red and black, wooden coat racks and side tables shining. The living room we stepped into was dominated by a large bay window. A velvet armchair was facing away from me as I entered, showing above its back the dark-blonde head of the figure sitting in it. It was flanked by George on one side, sitting in his usual worn club chair, and Ralph's friend Ed on the other, in a chair that looked as though he'd dragged it across the room to be closer to the velvet one in the centre. Racer had gone to sit next to it too. Ralph himself stood, one foot crossed over the other at the ankle, gazing down at the woman in the chair with rapt attention. He glanced up and gave me a brilliant smile.

'Julia!' he said. 'Come and meet Cousin Ingrid.'

Ingrid looked then, showing the full beauty of her profile as she turned towards me, and the solemn eyes, hair gathered at the back.

Eve was busying herself with tea and coffee on the other side of the room. She wore an emerald green shift of shot silk, the brightest thing in the room, and no shoes. Her toenails were painted a perfect, bright red. She was small, a full head shorter than Ralph. I had never seen her exchange more than a sentence with Ralph's father. Their antagonism was rooted in some ancient feud that Ralph couldn't even remember the source of. In front of me they just seemed to ignore each other as much as possible, but, according to Ralph, without visitors around, whenever they did talk to each other there were arguments.

'I've been telling Ralph for weeks now to come home and meet Ingrid,' Eve said. 'You know I brought her back from Perth, from Western Australia. Ralph, get some more milk. Julia, Ingrid's at university, she's just started – maybe you know her too.'

Ralph disappeared into the kitchen. Ingrid remained in her seat. We said hello. She was wearing a dress that looked as though it was covered in squashed roses. Her thick blonde hair was drawn all over to one side of her neck and forward over one shoulder. She pulled at the ends of it. There was a delicate silver oval frame that looked as though it had once held a cameo, now empty, hanging from a chain around her neck.

She looked at me, a trace of reserve. I recognised her: two rows in front of me in the big lecture theatre the week before, a lesson on Robert Browning's 'My Last Duchess' and some other poems. She had been wearing a red coat, shrugged off to sit crumpled behind her on the seat. There was something solid to the shape of her shoulders, the look of a frequent swimmer. Her chin had been cupped in her hand for the whole hour, elbow on the little fold-up desk, other hand busy taking notes. The boy sitting next to Ingrid had noticed her too, and I had watched his little glances to the side, his swift smile upwards when he dropped his pen and bent to pick it up. Ingrid had barely turned her head then but had chatted graciously with him when the lecture ended and they filed out, red coat clutched in her hands. I had looked down at my own sparse notes at the end of the hour.

Neptune???

How we know

Command he can't refuse

Secret – spot – stain of feminine sexuality – smile

Image – something to be possessed – statue, power

Speaker/audience

They went on like that, a telegram with no finished clauses.

I looked at her now. Up close the squashed roses on her dress looked as though they had been painted on, brushstrokes of red against old silk. Eve started talking to her, continuing a conversation that my arrival must have interrupted.

'I'll help Ralph,' I said, and retreated.

He was pouring milk from a carton into a silver jug.

'Cousin Ingrid?' I asked him.

'Half-cousin. But yes.' He closed the fridge door and leaned his arms on the counter. 'You know Eve was over in WA after her brother-in-law died, to help close up the house or sell it or whatever – it turns out that Ingrid was his daughter, she's my cousin. Her mother was Eve's half-sister. She died years ago. Eve didn't see that much of her sister to begin with, and didn't like her husband, so we never had anything to do with those cousins – I'd forgotten I had cousins on that side to tell you the truth – and now she's staying here.'

I rubbed my finger on a spot of tarnish on the jug. Ralph's hand brushed mine as he grasped the handle. A drop of milk spilled over the side.

'We've even been in class together. I hadn't been paying attention to anything Eve said to me. I thought she'd been talking about a Cousin Margaret. Ingrid says she just didn't guess. Maybe she's shy. You like her, don't you?' he asked. 'She's brilliant, you know.'

'I like her,' I said. Why did it sound as though I was protesting? 'I don't know – I'm surprised, that's all.'

He cradled my cheek for a second with one hand, his thumb just to the side of my mouth. I could hear Ed's voice, enquiring, Ingrid's voice, responding. It was a nice voice, slightly hoarse and light at the same time. Ralph dropped his hand and walked back to them all.

Ingrid was the centre of attention at the lunch table and bore it with a detached kind of ease. It wasn't clear whether she was aware of her own beauty. It wasn't exactly modesty although it was something like that. Ed made attempts to impress her. He was a friend of Ralph's from school, and Ralph looked pale and thinner than usual next to Ed's muscle. He was a rower with a square jaw and extremely good teeth, studying Economics, probably destined to be a conservative politician. I had met him a few times with Ralph on campus. He was always expressing frustration with his apparently Marxist tutor. Ed was the only person I knew who lived on campus, in one of the wealthiest and oldest residential colleges, built of stone with picturesque, leadlight casement windows set deep into the walls. All my other student friends were still at home, or had moved into a shared student house like mine if they could afford it. As well as being the most privileged, Ed's college had the worst reputation on campus for debauched parties at which women students were routinely date-raped. He didn't strike me as someone who would take part in that aspect of college culture, but I maintained a kind of prejudiced wariness of him for a while all the same.

My hair was newly cut in a short, straight bob with a high fringe and George took to calling me 'Pandora' over lunch, saying I looked like Louise Brooks in *Pandora's Box*. There was a poster from the film on the wall of the video store in a cheap plastic frame, Louise staring down with her heavy-lidded gaze and rosebud mouth.

'Yes …' Ralph said, happily. He was sitting next to me.

'Yes, well, you can't quote a silent film at me,' I said.

'That's true.' He looked disappointed.

'I was going for a kind of flapper-ish Lois Lane,' I said. 'Try that.' But he had turned back to Ingrid, across the table.

Ingrid looked over and caught my eye and gave a small smile. We didn't talk much to each other over lunch. She was monopolised by the men at the table.

Eve looked admiringly at what she had brought home with her, pleased at her success. She shared with me her impressions of Perth. 'It's such an innocent-looking place,' she said. 'So dull really.'

Ingrid ended up in the kitchen with me after the meal, clearing the remains of roast chicken and preparing plates for the enormous pavlova that Eve had bought for dessert.

'I'm sorry about your father,' I said.

I ran my fingers across the paintwork on the plates in front of me, gold paint over black-and-red-painted designs on the borders. It looked as though it would scratch away with a fingernail, but it didn't. She turned off the tap – she had been rinsing plates in the huge porcelain sink.

'Thanks,' she said evenly. She dried her hands on a red-and-white-checked towel. 'You'll meet Victoria if you come over next week,' she said. 'My sister.'

'Your sister?'

'Oh, she's the pretty one.' Ingrid smiled.

'Really?' I wondered what that made Ingrid.

She answered my thought. 'I'm the one, I suppose, into books.'

I steadied the dessert plates in their stack on the counter. She leaned back against the sink. 'Do you want to go and get a drink after this?' she asked. 'Back over on your side?'

'OK,' I said. I was curious about her. And something even then told me that she was destined to be part of Ralph's life in a way I couldn't ignore. 'Where do you want to go?'

'I don't know!' Ingrid laughed. 'I'm new in town, remember? From innocent old Perth.'

She took a large knife and started to slice the pavlova with some clumsiness. 'Let's do this at the table.'

Eve had flown over to Perth just after the death of Ingrid's father, 'to help take care of things,' she told me as we sat in the living room after eating. Ingrid had been alone there in the house, trying to decide what to do with it after her sister, Victoria, had gone back to Queensland following the funeral. Eve arranged for the house to be put on the market. 'It was in good shape,' Eve said. 'In a good area. Too far out from the city but near the beach at least. They'll do well with it.' Real estate was one of her many areas of knowledge and expertise. Ingrid had been thinking of applying to the University of Sydney in any case – she was in her second year at the University of Western Australia then, studying Classics and English – and Eve helped to 'speed up the process' so that she could start this semester, even though it was a week or so into term. Eve was good friends with someone on the University Senate and not afraid to call on them. 'It would have been nonsense for her to have been stuck over there.' She grimaced. 'So I brought her back with me. It's not bad to have some company here in this big old house anyway.'

Ingrid didn't seem to be listening to any of this. She was talking to Ed and Ralph, and George was watching them.

Racer sat up beside her, his grey jaw on her knee, and she stroked his head gently. George seemed older than he had the last time I'd seen him; his greying, sparse hair was thin, swept back from his face, and his cheeks were sunken. He was wearing slippers instead of his usual battered loafers. Despite his look of tiredness there was a light of interest in his eyes, turned on Ingrid.

He looked over at me and winked. 'The dog thinks he's hers now,' he said cheerfully. 'No loyalty.'

Ingrid protested, smiling. Racer stayed next to her, his body stretched along the floor and paws out in front of him. Ralph stood up and stepped over the dog carefully and came over to me.

'Come on outside,' he said. 'I've hardly talked to you.'

We stood outside the back door and he smoked a cigarette.

'Dad's happy,' he said. 'He adores her.'

'That's good.'

'It's good, isn't it?'

'It's really good.'

The grass of the back lawn was darkening as the light went and the air smelled damp.

'Ralph,' I said. 'Are you sick too?'

I don't know what made me ask it. His arms were folded across his body. He didn't look at me.

'It's all in the bloody genes, isn't it?' He ground his cigarette under his shoe. 'Well, not exactly. Let's go in.'

'Ralph.'

'No. Julia, I don't want to talk about it. I mean, I'm fine.'

He took my hand quickly, just the fingers, and let it go, and went back inside. My pulse raced and slowed. I followed him in.

It took a while for the gathering to wind down. George was drinking sherry by then, Eve eyeing him grumpily, Ralph fussing over him, finding him the particular glass he liked, the one with the gold rim. Ralph and Ed were staying at the house to 'watch the game' with George, a ritual that revolved around tennis on television.

'See you next week,' Eve said to me, and kissed my cheek.

When Ingrid and I left, Ed insisted on driving us to the ferry stop in his newly bought car, a vintage Jaguar, just to show it off. The car was sitting in the driveway next to the house, green with dark green seats and the little leaping cat on the front. The body was a bit knocked around, a dent in the driver's door, and the paint was wearing thin. I fought an urge to take hold of the cat, to see how firmly it was stuck there, to see if it would break off in my hand.

'It's nice,' Ingrid said.

She opened the door and sat in the driver's seat. Ed looked nervous. He was holding the keys in his hand and looked unsure about what to do with them. His other hand rested on the roof of the car. Ingrid put her hands on the wheel.

'I need a car,' she said. 'I like this one.'

For a moment Ed looked as though he was going to hand the keys over to her right there. If she'd looked up at him just then I think he might have. But she gazed ahead and dropped her hands and got out of the car.

'You can help me buy one,' she said. 'I don't know anything about cars.'

'Sure, great.' Ed sounded relieved. 'I can help you find one.'

'I'd like a Karmann Ghia,' she announced. 'Or a bug. One of those old ones but it has to go well. Do you think I can find one of those?'

Ed said he thought that would be possible. Ingrid opened the back door and sat down, hands on the back of the driver's seat. 'It's so strange to have money,' she said, almost sadly.

Everything today was strange, I reflected. Even more than usual the North Shore felt like another – much richer – planet compared with the city I knew across the bridge and I felt suddenly impatient to leave. I went around the other side of the car and sat down in the front passenger seat.

Ed took us down the hill, driving too fast, and returned to the house. As we waited there the sky turned into night over the water. On the ferry we sat outside and shivered. Ingrid looked at the city hungrily as it came closer. I didn't know whether they had ferries in Perth. It seemed like a stupid question.

'Do you like Sydney?' I asked.

'I love it. It's great to finally be here. I've wanted to come east for so long.'

Everyone from Perth who made it east always seemed happy to have left. The salt and spray hung in the air, and the dank smell of the ferry itself, metal and wood. Fireworks started to explode in the sky over Darling Harbour in the distance, followed by a series of muffled bangs as the sound travelled across the water. Showers of orange and green fell and disappeared. We looked at one another, wondering what they were celebrating. I shrugged.

Her cheeks were pink from the cold, eyes shining. We

talked about buses and trains and which one we would catch next. The ferry pulled in and we stepped across the swaying deck onto the pier.

We wound up at a pub near my house in Newtown and drank steadily until closing. Ingrid played pool well and beat me three games in a row. 'There's not much else to do in Perth,' she said.

'I thought you were the bookish one.'

'Oh, I am,' she insisted. She shot a red ball into its pocket with a neat clack and chalked her cue.

She drank and talked with me with a kind of obscure determination, as though she were practising for a part or fulfilling an obligation to its furthest extent. It was hard to tell some of the time whether she was actually enjoying herself. It wasn't that she was ill at ease. Her composure was the same as it had been all that day. It was a sense of presence that conveyed a strange lack of depth, although her cleverness was obvious. Or it was that whatever depths there were seemed entirely unguessable, unplottable. A dark flash of sadness and seriousness crossed her face now and again, cloud across the sun, and then was gone just as fast. 'She's brilliant,' Ralph had said. She probably was. It was easy to imagine her being a very good student and turning in all her work on time. The jealousy I had felt when she appeared with her empty necklace and pretty hair was a little stone in my heart. It never went away; I feel it still, sometimes, pushing gently against my insides.

But that wasn't all there was to it. I reminded myself that she was grieving, and recognised the robotic aspect it could produce, the need to concentrate harder than usual to perform everything normally. Perhaps this was behind the earnest way she questioned me about life in Sydney, curious about the neighbourhood we were in, how long I'd lived there, the girls who shared the house with me.

I told her what I could about Leah and Joanna. We didn't all hang out together outside the house, preferring to keep our lives separate. Joanna seemed to spend all her time either studying, or partying hard on drugs mixed up by some chemical-whiz med student friends, two boys with permanently bloodshot eyes who dropped over once a week and managed to seem competent and smart despite their obvious addictions and insanely risky hobby. It was a different recipe every time, some version of ecstasy or cocaine in little misshapen pills that I tried once or twice but never enjoyed much. Leah was wrapped up with her boyfriend, an intense and silent guy who tried not to stare at my legs if he ran into me coming out of the shower, or making breakfast in the morning.

'It sounds like living with two sisters,' Ingrid said.

I blinked in surprise. 'No,' I said. 'I don't think so, anyway. But I guess I wouldn't know.'

Ingrid nodded thoughtfully. She finished her drink at exactly the same time as me, went to the bar with our glasses in hand and fetched fresh ones, lined up the balls neatly and shot them down, never faltering when she missed, smiling brightly when she won. Losing to her didn't worry me, and I felt a glow of satisfaction about her skill, pleased and somehow proud to be with someone who played so well. She wasn't competitive in any straightforward way; it seemed that her pleasure was in the game well played, the difficult shot achieved, rather than in simply beating me. She wore her superiority in the game calmly, but I couldn't help wondering how she would react if I suddenly pulled off a string of successful shots, as occasionally happened after my second drink. My winning streak didn't arrive that night and I didn't get a chance to find out.

She put her hair up into a ponytail that snaked over her shoulder and sank the black with fierce concentration, staying bent over her cue for a second. I raised my glass to her.

'Oh, cheers,' she said, and hurried over to the table to pick up her glass and clink it against mine. 'Cheers!'

She gave a happy glance around as though she expected the whole pub to celebrate her victory. There were several people looking in our direction – admiring men, all of them – and her radiant smile seemed to include them all. She finally seemed a little drunk and silly then, and I liked her more. I realised that we had spent many of the past twelve hours in each other's company and it wasn't bad.

She got into a taxi when the pub closed and we said goodbye. I called Ralph when I got home, wanting to tell him about our evening, but he wasn't answering at the Kings Cross flat. He was probably staying with his parents, where she would be in a little while.

The semester finished and a new one began; the course Ralph was studying now included a lot of science fiction and we watched many aliens on screen. He came into the video shop one night and put *The Story of O* into the machine. I asked whether there were aliens in this that I had forgotten about.

'No,' he sighed, and watched the credits glumly. 'It's for English. I thought I'd see the movie before I read the book.' He pulled a crumpled syllabus out of his bag and inspected it. 'Servitude, Sex and Subjectivity. Next week, *Jane Eyre*! I love Orson Welles. OK. Is there a film of *Wuthering Heights*?'

I turned the sound down and shuddered. 'If there is, you can't watch it here.'

Ralph tilted his head slowly to the side as he followed the action on screen.

'I don't think that part is in the book,' I said.

'I bloody hope it is,' he murmured.

'The second one is actually closer to the original,' offered a woman at the counter, waiting with a cassette in her hand.

I had invited Ingrid to come and visit me at the video shop, and that was the night she first came. She was wearing her red coat, which swung open over a yellow dress, the necklace on again, locks of hair forward over one shoulder. She said hello. Her eyes went to the screen, where O or one of the other girls was thrashing around. A flush rose from her throat up across one side of her face.

I smiled and kept my gaze forward.

'Is that *The Story of O*?' she asked.

'Were you interested in renting it?' Ralph asked her.

Ingrid laughed, a full-throated laugh, and her cheeks glowed as the flush faded away. Her skin was the tan that comes with a whole life spent outside in the summers. 'No!' she protested. 'I recognised it because I'm reading it for class. The one I'm in with you.' She studied the screen. 'I do need to finish reading it,' she said, and looked back and forth between me and Ralph. 'Do you mind? Is there space back there?'

Ralph slid from his chair, his eyes on her.

'What do you want to see now?' Ralph asked Ingrid blurrily, later, when we had finished *The Story of O* and had a serious discussion about its narrative departures from its source and were casting about for what to watch next. The store was busy that night, a Saturday, and I was up and down fetching films and reshelving returns.

'Oh ...' Ingrid trailed off. '*Casablanca.*'

'Let's watch it,' Ralph said.

I rolled my eyes. The cover was right there on the top of the returns. Ingrid had obviously just seen it before she'd said the name. I put it in the machine.

'Why don't I get us something to eat?' Ralph said when the film had started, just as I had expected. 'There's great sushi down the road.'

He left. I finished putting a stack of cases back on the shelves and came back to the counter.

'What would you really like to watch?' I asked, flicking the pages of the big movie reference book.

Ingrid gave me a look that asked for sympathy. 'Well – you know what I thought of when I came in – it's stupid – I would love to see *St Elmo's Fire.*' She inspected her fingers, short, bitten nails, and laughed, embarrassed. 'Is that terrible? I've been having a nostalgic moment today.' She looked at me. 'Now I've told you, I'll have to kill you.'

I laughed too. 'No, we'll have to watch it.' I came back under the counter. 'After *Casablanca*.'

Ingrid's chair creaked and she settled in. 'What other classes are you taking?'

I stared at her blankly for a moment, unable to remember, drawn to the empty silver oval around her neck.

'Art history,' I said, recovering. 'Film – modernism. A class in English on the city in literature.'

'Handy,' she said, waving her hand vaguely at the shelves around us. 'For studying. For film class.'

'Uh, yes,' I replied, looking at the stacks of crappy Hollywood romantic comedies and action movies with their faded covers. We had a small foreign section and a better 'classics' shelf than a lot of places, but it wasn't what you would call an art house collection. 'Sort of.'

She smiled as though I had just agreed with her wholeheartedly.

'Do you love *Casablanca*?' she asked.

'Yes.'

'Who doesn't?'

I smiled and reached over to press PLAY on the machine.

We were still talking in that broken way conversation works when you are watching a video with a friend – a comment here and there, a reply, a shared groan at the action on screen, a shared sigh – when Ralph returned an hour and a half later with food in a plastic bag. I had grown used to the long periods of time it took him to do simple errands. By then Ingrid and I had made a start on *St Elmo's Fire* and were discussing the doomed career of Andrew McCarthy, and how James Spader had never done anything better than his role as Steff, the villain in *Pretty in Pink*. Ralph brought the warm night air with him from the street, but I shivered suddenly.

'Judd Nelson!' he said happily. 'Thank god I missed *Casablanca*.'

3.

The following Sunday I went to the house again with Ralph. He'd been there much of the last week but had stayed at his flat the night before after a late night out. We had started the evening at a party in a huge house in Redfern, one of the sketchier neighbourhoods close to the University where students lived alongside housing commission flats and blocks of Aboriginal families, a Victorian mansion that had somehow escaped being made into flats and was now occupied by at least six students. Ingrid had been with us but had disappeared some time after midnight. At one point I saw her kissing Ed in the corner, and saw some other girl walk up to them and slap Ed angrily on the shoulder. They had stopped kissing then, and Ingrid had looked up at the girl, tilted her head to the side, then pulled her hair absently over her shoulder when Ed got up and walked after the angry girl. I never heard her talk about it.

By the time we wanted to leave Ed was gone too, and I supposed that Ingrid had left with him – the angry girl was still there, now dancing with someone else in the front living room, all trace of fury gone. Ralph was worried about Ingrid. He spent half an hour looking through the house before he came downstairs. The music was terrible and I wanted to leave.

'This place is big,' he said.

He was wearing a black T-shirt with 'Cos cheap is how I feel' written across it in another shade of black. It was worn and soft to the touch – a sudden memory of my hand against his back arrived and wouldn't leave – but I didn't touch him now. He was edgy and his eyes moved around the room, away from me. He didn't want to hear about Ed.

'That's ridiculous,' he said.

'No, it's not. Come on. She's not here.'

He hung back and chewed his lip. I put on my coat. One of the people who lived in the house, a girl with stringy hair, stopped on her way past us. 'Your friend Ingrid?' she said. 'She left a while ago – she was with a couple of people? Sylvia and Dave?' Everything she said sounded like a question. 'She tried to find you to say goodbye, I think …'

Ralph nodded and followed me out the door. We walked a long way alongside the abandoned railway yards before finding a taxi that dropped me home and drove away with him. In the late morning on Sunday when I went to his flat he looked grey and gaunt. I wondered if he had come home not long before I got there. He brightened up after food and ate many pieces of toast, stacked up in a tall charred tower on a plate.

My car was working that day. It was an old bug, probably like the one Ingrid wanted, except it didn't go well most of the time. We drove over to Kirribilli, sky halcyon blue through the struts of the bridge.

Ingrid met us at the door this time, Racer close to her side. She leaned against the frame for a second before coming forward to kiss us both.

'Here you are – I lost you people last night in that huge house.' She smiled and gave a little shrug. 'Victoria'll be here soon. There's a friend of Aunt Eve's here too, from America. She's – you know her, Ralph! She's amazing.'

The smell of lamb roasting filled the house. The living room was connected to another room at the front and was usually closed off by two big sliding oak panel doors. Now they were open. There was a piano in the front room, sparse chairs and lots of books in bookcases around the walls. Rugs were layered on the floor as they were in all the rooms. Eve was the pianist in the family. Ralph refused to play for me, ever. The piano was being played now, although at first I took it to be a recording. It was softer than the piano ought to have sounded. Then I looked and saw a woman, seated, playing. Her back was very straight, her body still and her hands moved gracefully over the keyboard.

'That's Maeve,' Eve said, looking through to the piano room. 'An old friend.'

'Play some more Beethoven,' George demanded from his chair irritably. 'Can't stand that Debussy.'

It sounded beautiful to me, delicate and somehow dampened as the sound made its way to us, as though over a great distance. The piece came to an end, or she brought it to a close, and she rose and came in to join us.

I had thought before, at other times, that Eve was like a bird, and she was like one again today in bright ultramarine. Maeve was another kind of animal, something more than human as she moved across to us with a smooth, unhurried kind of walk. The long, simple dress she wore was black as a pelt. She shook my hand. I looked again and the fabric was green like a mallard duck's neck and deep blue, dense feather-dark. Her hands were perfect, white and ringless.

'It's so lovely to meet you,' she said in her pretty accent, New York and something else – faintly European – as though she were congratulating me. Her hair was blackish brown and fell to her shoulders with a stripe of grey running through it from her temple. In that moment her attention was very strong and then it was gone. She sat down in the velvet chair that I thought of now as Ingrid's, and Ingrid stood beside her.

'And how lovely for you, Ralph, to finally meet your gorgeous cousin,' she exclaimed.

He leaned down and kissed her cheek and she held his hand briefly.

'Half-cousin,' he said, reflexively.

'Half-cousin,' she repeated, faintly mocking. 'Well. I can't believe she's been hidden away all these years.'

'I haven't been hiding,' Ingrid said.

'No, of course not,' Maeve replied. 'I'm just delighted that you've … made it across.'

Eve looked a little smug and pressed her hands together. 'We're happy to have Ingrid here.'

The doorbell rang then, a set of three chimes, and we all looked up. Ingrid went to answer it.

'Victoria's coming from the airport,' Eve said, turning to Ralph. 'She's been working on a project – a shoot? In Queensland, I think. The Gold Coast?' She made it sound like an obscure foreign country. I suppose to her it was. Eve's travels took her overseas in the direction of Europe and the States, but never to Australia's north. 'Victoria's a model,' she told me.

When the two of them came in together, Victoria looked like Ingrid put through a magazine makeover – long blonde hair a shade lighter and hanging unnaturally straight. Her dress was a kind of peach colour that matched her lips. I saw it a few days later on a magazine cover, on a woman that looked a lot like her. She had eyes just like Ingrid's, blue and perceptive, but with the lashes heavily mascaraed black. She was the elder by just two years, and seeing them together like that – Ingrid's hair coming loose from its medieval-looking braid, the lace hem on her skirt torn and ragged but still somehow regal – seemed to show me everything that Ingrid had worked to distinguish herself from.

Victoria sat across from me at the lunch table. Once she established that I worked in a video store we had a topic of conversation. She liked movies and had thought about acting.

'Have you thought about applying to drama school?' I asked. 'Like NIDA?'

'Oh, that would be so great,' she said, without enthusiasm. 'It would be so hard to find the time though. My agent is looking into some roles for me.' She smiled at me compassionately.

Victoria's fork moved and the food on her plate shifted around but she didn't seem to chew or swallow very often. 'I'm just lucky that way,' she said out of nowhere. 'I can eat and eat and just don't put on weight. Not like Ingrid!' Victoria wasn't much thinner than her sister. 'It's all that sitting around, Ingrid,' she scolded her, imperiously.

Ingrid ignored her. The way she did this, with casual control, made it look as though the whole thing was a game – a cruel one – they had played since childhood. It made me wonder about the forms that Ingrid's retaliation would take, if it ever came.

'I love aerobics,' Victoria said then, and smiled around the table.

Maeve's eyes widened. My initial feeling for Victoria had been aversion, but her sheer disregard for what any of us thought of her somehow made me like her more. Eve came in with a large fruit tart in her hands. It glistened with a heavy sugar glaze: apricots, strawberries, blueberries under gold. We were all quiet as she passed slices around and Victoria didn't talk again as we ate.

'I'm so impressed that Ingrid knows Latin so well,' Maeve said to George when we had finished eating. 'I had no idea you could come across that kind of education here, in high school! Although of course I should have known.' She smiled across at Eve. 'With my brilliant friend here. I've always thought how wonderful it would be to read Virgil in the original. The *Aeneid*.'

George murmured his approval. 'She can quote it for you. Just ask her.'

'No,' Ingrid said.

When the table was cleared Eve said she wanted to hear Maeve play more. 'Go on and play some Mozart for us. Or whatever you like.'

Maeve stood smoothly. 'Will you come and turn the music for me, Ingrid?' she asked.

They went together into the piano room. It was dark in there now – the day had turned overcast – and Ingrid switched on a standing lamp next to the piano. She stood next to Maeve as she played, turning the pages quietly. The music had the same dampened sound as it had before. When the piece came to an end Maeve looked up and smiled at Ingrid.

Eve seemed happy, observing them. She was sitting next to me on the couch. 'Maeve's from New York,' she explained to me. 'She runs a gallery there – spectacular, a really wonderful space over in Chelsea. She's travelling from here to the desert to look at some paintings. Some Aboriginal artists out there that she's thinking about showing. Maeve!' she called out. 'Where is that place you're going to? With the paintings?'

'Utopia,' Maeve said, without turning fully around.

'Utopia,' Eve repeated, satisfied. 'Incredible.'

'And somewhere called Well Twenty-three.'

'Beautiful work,' Eve remarked. 'In the middle of nowhere.'

'Utopia,' Ralph said. 'I hardly imagine it's that in reality.'

I tried to imagine Maeve out there in the desert and found that I could, more easily than I could imagine any of the rest of us. Except Ingrid – I could see her with a backpack and sunscreen across her nose and a look of perseverance in the heat and sun, red dust on her skin.

Maeve kept talking with Ingrid, who was sitting beside her now on the long piano stool, looking down and picking something off her skirt. Maeve was inspecting her in a quiet, drawn-out way. She nodded at what Ingrid was saying, and didn't take her eyes off her for a second.

'Are you an artist too?' I asked Maeve when she and Ingrid came back to join us. Ingrid looked to her, expectant.

'No.' She smiled at me ruefully. 'I have to recognise talent in my job. And I realised pretty young that I don't have any.'

Ingrid frowned.

'I love what I do,' Maeve said to me. 'It's a joy, to nurture talent, to see it rewarded.'

Maeve stayed for a week before she left for the desert, and a week afterwards before she went back to New York. She took Ingrid out with her during the day to galleries and for long afternoon teas at elegant places in the city, sometimes with Eve and sometimes just Ingrid. Ingrid was in awe of her, and deeply flattered by the older woman's interest.

'She *knows* so much,' she said to me, a couple of nights after Maeve got back from the desert. 'Maeve says that your aunt is really good.'

'She is really good.'

We were behind the counter at the video store, early in my shift.

'Well, I saw some of her paintings in the gallery the other day. They are amazing.'

'I like them.' I wondered when Ralph was going to show up.

Ingrid sat with her chin in her hands, looking out the window. 'I wish I'd learnt to play the piano,' she said sadly.

'You know Latin,' I said, although clearly this was no compensation. She sighed.

Ingrid took to stopping by the video store most Wednesday nights from then on. She also started drinking with Ralph and me at the campus bar on Fridays. Scrabble and Monopoly were her games, and we played them at our corner table sitting on the same red couch and chairs. It had been the two of us before then, and now it was three.

4.

It became clear to me after knowing Ingrid a month or so that she knew more about Ralph's state of health than I did. There was something solicitous every now and again in the way she acted towards him, a kind of concern that reminded me of the way Ralph bent over his father, handing him his glass of water or wine, cautioning him, watching him. One day at the house after lunch we were sitting in the lounge drinking, already slightly drunk, and Ralph came in with several old tennis racquets in his hand.

'Who's up for a game?' he asked, bouncing a yellow ball up and down on the carpet. It made a kind of dull thud and didn't rise very high. His face was alight and there was a silly, manic edge to his actions, a little too expansive and tense. It was late afternoon, mid-April, and warm outside. I yawned. George laughed and wheezed. Ingrid squinted at Ralph.

'Where did you pull those out from?' she asked.

'Under the stairs.'

Racer regarded the bouncing ball with a bored look and stayed by Ingrid's side. She was holding a pack of cards, shuffling them between her hands.

Ralph tossed the ball to her. She raised her hand too late and missed, and the ball rolled into the corner. They both waited, poised, for the other to go and fetch it. Racer raised himself slowly and walked with a stiff gait to the ball. He pushed it with his nose and eyed Ralph resentfully, and picked it up and brought it to Ingrid's feet. She patted his head.

Ralph reached down for the ball. 'Julia, you come and play then.'

There was a tennis court down in a level of the grounds that I hadn't been to before, only seen from above.

'Ralph, why?'

He took my hand and pulled me up. 'Let's go.'

Ingrid spoke to him then. 'Ralph, don't be ridiculous. You don't play tennis.'

'What would you know?' he asked. 'How would you know?'

She looked to George. He shrugged and sat further back in his chair and called Racer over to sit with him. Ingrid stood up. Ralph let go of my hand. She pulled him by the elbow out the door, into the hallway near the stairs, and I heard her whispering urgently to him, and his replies in a low voice. 'I'm not a fucking invalid,' he pronounced. They reached some kind of agreement.

'We'll go for a walk outside,' Ingrid announced when they came back in, her eyes on Ralph. 'Julia, will you come?'

We walked down the terraced garden, down to the lower level overgrown with stringy ferns, and down a set of mossy steps, small concrete slabs full of cracks and breaks, to the tennis court. Morning glory vines and jasmine had taken over down here, and one long tendril snaked all along the ragged net, bluish-purple trumpet flowers blooming. Ingrid was wearing a white shirt of almost transparent cotton, cheesecloth or muslin with tiny dots all over it – Swiss dots, I heard her say once – and strings that dangled from the open collar, never tied. The light showed right through it and created a purplish penumbra around her. Stray hairs floated as though raised by static electricity. She held the old tennis racquet in her hand, turning it over and over, fingers on a loose thread in the weave. The frame was worn, showing the remains of yellow paint, wood underneath the colour of dry grass or old wicker. The surface of the tennis court was faded by the sun until it looked like a dried-out version of the moss on the stairs, blackish and hard. I didn't want to step onto it.

'What are we going to do?' I asked, bored with being part of a plan I hadn't been involved in making. 'Are you going to play?'

Ralph shrugged. Ingrid had clearly won the argument. He tossed the ball to her and she hit it across the court, not hard, her arm a smooth arc through the air. The muscles in her shoulder and upper arm flexed. Ralph looked over at me. I couldn't read his face. I picked up the other racquet – he had only brought two with us; the other one with practically no strings left remained in the house, watched over by Racer – and went to get the ball. I was no tennis player. Ingrid and I hit the ball back and forth for a while, lazily. I missed half the time. She never did. Ralph dragged up a battered old chair from the corner of the court and sat on it, leaning back with his arms folded behind his head, his feet in canvas tennis shoes crossed in front of him. He called out a random-sounding score to us every once in a while. My feet started to hurt. I was wearing flat black leather shoes with two side buckles and a skirt that didn't leave much room for running or sudden movement. Ingrid's feet were bare. Her toes flexed against the ground.

'OK.' I hit the ball one last time and it collided with the net. 'I'm finished.'

Ralph came over to me and took the racquet from my hand and leaned down to pick up the ball. Ingrid didn't seem to mind. She didn't look at him directly for long, just in glances, but she seemed to be watching him closely in her peripheral vision. Ralph threw the ball up in the air a few times, catching it, and bounced it. He tossed the racquet once or twice, spinning the handle around. He grinned at me, showing his teeth and that one overlapping incisor. I stood there. Ingrid was standing still, waiting. He tossed the ball up suddenly and served it to her, graceful and fast. She didn't move much, just one foot to the side, and reached out and caught it lightly in her hand.

She started strolling back to the house and he moved fast to catch up with her. They walked up the stairs and across the next terraced level close together, shoulders almost touching. Ingrid swished her racquet backwards and forwards against the grass and ferns on the ground. I watched them from behind. They were the same height and for a moment they looked like brother and sister, the blonde and the brown, and I was reminded that they were cousins. I felt a kind of detachment even then from my own sense of displacement, for surely it ought to have been me walking closely beside him, watching over him. This feeling of exclusion was painful in its own way but also had such an aura of inevitability that it was hard to hold on to any resentment; it wavered and flickered. At times like this it was hard to remember that Ralph and I had been friends first, before Ingrid, especially when she so often seemed to make a show of including me so graciously, as if she were politely extending an invitation to join a longstanding family. They both turned their heads at exactly the same moment towards me.

'Are you coming, Julia?' Ingrid said, still smiling at something Ralph had said.

She kept her eyes on me but he turned his own towards her, where they rested on her face. I quickened my pace and caught up with them, not walking beside them but one step behind.

I wanted to ask Ralph about it later, the whispered conversation in the hallway, the protests against tennis, but decided that he would tell me if he wanted to.

This knowledge Ingrid seemed to have about Ralph's illness was part of the sense of a quickly growing intimacy between them. His fascination with her only seemed to grow stronger. He stayed at the house a lot now, enduring the cold war between his parents that had been part of his original reason to leave a year before.

'It's much better at home with Ingrid there now,' he told me one night at the video store. 'They both love her so much. Dad loves her even more than Eve does.' He always called Eve by her first name, and sometimes 'Mother' to her face. 'I think he wants to adopt her. If he could legally I think he would.'

'They both love *you*. It never made any difference,' I reminded him.

'That's true. But she's come to us ... fully formed – she didn't have to grow up with us, did she?'

I thought of Ingrid. She seemed to present a state of being in formation, with a contour all her own and yet not fully formed at all, and eager to take shape. It was this sense of vivid potentiality in her that was so attractive to George, I knew, seeing the end of his own life and hers just really beginning.

'Anyway, they both love her and it makes them nicer to each other. She breaks the ice somehow. Maybe because she doesn't pay attention to them and the arguments, you know. All the tension. She's so ... focused on herself and what she's doing. And she loves the house. She takes the dog for walks and she cooks.'

'She cooks?'

'OK, she cooked last night and it was terrible – I didn't know you could do that to pasta. My god. But it was a nice effort.'

He squinted at the TV screen. 'Anyway, don't worry, I'm not giving up the flat.'

'I'm not worried.'

I hadn't been, and now I wondered if I ought to be.

I pictured them at home together – for some reason I could only imagine them sitting on a bed together, in Ralph's old room or the guest room that had now become Ingrid's, with her framed prints up on the walls and her yellow crocheted bedspread too small on the big bed – drinking cups of tea and whisky, smoking with the window open, talking into the night, yellow lamplight around them.

I spent a night like that there myself with Ingrid, one evening when I'd gone over to meet them and go out but Ralph hadn't shown up. We had waited for him and eventually given up. I made an omelette for us at about eleven o'clock and Ingrid watched me very carefully, as though I were performing a mysterious operation.

'What did you eat, growing up?' I asked her.

'The microwave was a big thing in our house,' she said, with a little smile. 'There was someone to cook, a nanny, sort of, after our mother died, for a while, and then a lot of microwave food or takeaway.' She picked up a fork and inspected it. It was a minuscule thing, designed for oysters or something like that. 'What is this for, do you think?'

'I don't know.'

'Cake?'

'A very tiny cake.'

I wanted to ask about her dead mother and father but couldn't bring myself to do it. This would be one of the things she talked about with Ralph during those midnight chats.

Afterwards we sat up in her room. I sat on the floor on the thick, sea green carpet and she sat on her bed just like I had imagined, and braided her hair and opened the casement window over the bed, a princess in old, washed-out jeans.

'It's very different here to the house I grew up in,' she said. 'That was very ... suburban.'

She looked at me. 'Your father's dead too,' she said.

I straightened. My father had died in a car accident when I was eight. I didn't have many good memories of him – moody, distant, rarely affectionate. He had kissed me sometimes before I went to bed, on the side of the head, with his hands on my shoulders pulling me towards him. That was the good memory.

'Ralph told me. Sorry.'

'No, it's OK.'

'And your mother's away.'

'What else did he tell you?' I laughed, uncomfortably.

'She's some kind of hippie. Or a Buddhist.'

I sighed. My mother, Rachel, was a source of embarrassment. 'I'm not sure what she's doing now. She's living up north in a commune or something. I'm not in touch with her much.' She sent me postcards every once in a while. 'You've met my brother, though. Peter.'

We had run into him one night at the pub. It had been a little bizarre, since his world usually didn't cross with mine. He was four years older and finishing his medical residency. The way we had grown up – dysfunctional, uncommunicative parents – hadn't created a close bond between us like it seemed to do with some brothers and sisters. We had each retreated to private worlds that excluded others. But we liked each other well enough. Jenny, my mother's sister, brought us together every once in a while, for her birthday, Christmas, an occasional lunch when she wanted to try cooking something that only worked when it was made for at least six people, like paella. She wasn't exactly like a mother, at least in the fraught, critical way of mothering that was my only guide from experience. But for as long as I could remember she had been the only constant, caring presence in our lives. We relied on her to keep us glued together.

'I'm close to my aunt,' I told Ingrid. She nodded.

'I always wished for an aunt,' she said. 'We barely knew that Eve existed. But I wished for one when I was little. I thought it was a nice idea.' She picked at the bedspread.

'We were lucky like that.'

Ingrid had gone back to looking out the window with her hungry gaze. From this room you could just see the water, a piece of blue in the daytime framed by trees. It glittered out there in the night.

She changed the subject and told me bits and pieces about what it had been like to grow up where she did, the particular horrors of her girls' high school. She made tea and brought it upstairs on a tray, using the good china with cups and saucers and a jug for the milk. The cups were old and thin, traced in a pattern of roses and vines. I saw the care she took with them, with the whole process, and thought about the suburban world of microwaved food and whatever else it was she was escaping. The way she had folded herself into this life of old money and heirloom china made more sense. I loved the house too – it was like coming to visit a place in a novel, the sense of another world of beauty and wealth taken entirely for granted by those in it – but she had managed to move in and make it her own. Her quiet pride in possessing the thing sat alongside a sense of wonder that she had actually accomplished it.

She shrugged gently and handed me my cup. 'Aren't these beautiful?' she said. 'The whole place is so … beautiful.' She twisted the teapot around by its handle. 'Ralph is so lucky.' She looked up at me. 'And you.'

For all I knew she saw me as part of it, belonging here, here first.

'It's all pretty far away from the way I grew up,' I said. 'We were more with the microwaved food, like you said. It's only in the last few years that my mother has given that all up.'

Ingrid talked a little about how much she liked living with George and Eve. Her mother had been dead for a long time, since she was a little girl, and her father hadn't been around much. An engineer with a mining company, he had spent long periods away from Perth. It sounded like a kind of freedom in one way, but it was clear that Ingrid had found it lonely and liked being in a house where family were more present.

'Isn't it tough sometimes?' I asked. 'You know – with how they don't get along?'

She frowned at me, as though confused. 'No,' she said, 'not really.'

George loved her especially, and lived in exaggerated awe of her brilliance. Ralph had always been an average-achieving student, and happy enough with that, but Ingrid came first in all of her classes, with high distinctions every time. I wondered sometimes if Ralph was resentful of the attention George paid to Ingrid and the way he would extol her intellectual accomplishment. But he didn't seem to be – he wasn't ambitious in that way, and George seemed to accept that.

They had money, but even so there was surprisingly little expectation of Ralph finding something useful to do with himself after university, some kind of work or creative pursuit. There didn't seem to be anything like that. At the time I didn't understand how potentially serious Ralph's illness was, but George and Eve did, and now when I look back it's as though I can see them consciously deciding not to push him. But they also just adored him, and seemed to take as much pride and pleasure in his elegance, his charm and his wit as they would have in any other kind of achievement.

George had his own ambitions for Ingrid, and it was he who first hatched the idea of her going over to the States to study. He had paid a brief visit to a schoolfriend at Harvard once, years before, and had come away with a lifelong respect for the American Ivy League universities. 'They know what they're doing over there,' he'd say. 'Energy. New ideas. Great stuff.' It didn't seem as though he had any frustrated academic desires himself – he was not a man of letters, he informed me once, but a man of numbers, and proud of it, but happy that someone was doing the intellectual and creative things that he appreciated. George saw himself as an old-fashioned patron of the arts and loved to see his name in theatre and concert programs on the list of 'special supporters' or included in the 'producer's circle' reserved for the most generous donors. Eve brought the programs home from performances and George left them out not-so-discreetly for us to see. Ingrid wasn't creative herself, however much she admired artists, but George seemed to see her life itself as a kind of work of art in progress – fascinating, unpredictable, an enthralling performance – and wish for a role for himself as enabler or producer. 'She'll make something of it,' he said to me once, with a knowing wink. 'She'll go far.'

Ingrid was already making plans for her honours year and thinking about following that with graduate study. 'Harvard! Princeton!' George would exclaim. 'Why not!' Ingrid sometimes talked about Oxford or Cambridge, and of these possibilities George was scornful in his cantankerous way. 'They'd be lucky to have you. Bloody stuffy old Brits. They'll treat you like a colonial – never anything but that.' The sound of some old injury to pride came through whenever he talked about the snobbery of the English. 'But the Americans. They'll love you. You'll knock them dead, my girl.'

Ingrid often brought her books down to the dining table when she was working on an essay or a translation for class. She and George would both be sitting there sometimes when I came over, Ingrid sucking on a pencil, hunched over a notebook, and George reading the newspaper at the other end of the table, strolling over every once in a while to pick up one of her books in Latin or Greek and peer at it through his half-moon reading glasses, chin tucked in. 'Marvellous,' he'd sigh, and chuckle or shake his head, and rest his hand on Ingrid's shoulder. He could recite a few lines of Virgil from memory but knew no languages other than English.

The tea kept us awake that night in Ingrid's room – strong, fragrant Earl Grey – but we were both yawning by 2 am.

'You should stay here,' she said.

I went to sleep in Ralph's bed. It was freshly made, the sheets stiff and clean.

When I went downstairs in the morning, stupefied with oversleeping, he was there in the kitchen in a T-shirt and old pants, making toast.

'What are you doing here?' I asked.

He laughed and offered me some burnt bread. 'I didn't want to wake you up.'

Ingrid came in then, rubbing at her eyes. 'Put the kettle on, will you?' she asked, and reached up and pressed her lips to his cheek. His hand rested briefly on her hair, her neck, full of hesitation and restraint as he dropped it back to his side.

These moments between them were strange to watch. All his adoration and desire seemed to slip off her like water and she showed no sign of recognition, or reciprocation or rejection. She simply seemed to accept it, like a just offering. I could never tell whether what I saw was a carefully modulated public performance, or how it related to the way they were together when they were in private. Those evenings spent talking into the night on her bed over tea and whisky. There was no missing her love for him, but no telling how far it went. That could have been something to do with the fact that they were cousins and there might have been some kind of incestuous boundary she didn't want to cross, but it didn't quite seem like that. I suppose I should have been more scandalised by the fact that Ralph was clearly in love with her, but he embraced other kinds of perversity with such ease that this particular one didn't stand out.

He refused to talk about it. For a long time I didn't bring it up. Then we were all out one night at the campus bar, not sitting at our usual low table with the couch but somewhere else, near the windows, and we were waiting for Ingrid to come back with our drinks. It was the week before the last week of class, mid-June, so close to the end we might as well have been already there. She was taking a long time and Ralph was cranky and impatient. He drummed his fingers on the table and lifted his eyes now and again to scan for her. We both saw her then, halfway to the bar, talking to a guy in a red shirt from our film class. He was good-looking, pushing his longish hair back behind his ears and nodding at something Ingrid was saying. Ralph's face was dark. It was unusual for him to show jealousy so openly and I grew brave.

'What's going on with you and Ingrid anyway?' I asked him.

'There's nothing going on with me and Ingrid,' he said without much expression. 'Don't be so fucking insecure, Julia.' It was the first time he had spoken to me with any real sharpness. To my horror, I felt a prick of tears and quickly blinked them back.

Ingrid appeared and put the three glasses awkwardly on the table, spilling some from all of them, and sat down. She raised her glass and clinked it against Ralph's, as if waiting for him to toast. He lifted his own glass and drank, silent. She raised her eyebrows and looked at me.

'Cheers,' I said. 'Here's to the end of semester.' She smiled. 'And happy travels,' I added. Ingrid was planning a trip during the break, to Venice. I put my bag on my shoulder and stood up. 'See you soon,' I said. 'I have to work on my essay. For class.'

Ralph caught my wrist in his hand. 'No, don't go.' I tried to pull my hand away. 'Don't,' he said, voice low. 'Finish your drink.'

'You're hurting her, Ralph,' Ingrid said, steadily.

He released me. I picked up my glass and left.

The guy in the red shirt was in front of me when I was halfway to the exit.

'Hey,' he said. 'I was just talking to Ingrid. She's your boyfriend's cousin, right?'

'She's his cousin – half-cousin – he's not my boyfriend –' My drink started to spill as someone bumped my elbow. It was crowded.

'Steady,' red-shirt guy said, and put his hand against my shoulder. 'Is he gay then? I wondered.'

I remembered his name. 'Tom,' I said.

'Yeah! Hey, how's class going for you? Have you finished your essay?'

We stood there for a while, talking. He bought me another drink and we stood at the bar, being jostled by people. I looked to my side and Ralph was there, asking the bartender for a drink. I looked away but he had seen me.

'Julia,' he said in a rush. 'I'm sorry –' He looked across and saw Tom. 'OK, forget it.' He took his two drinks and dropped money on the bar.

Tom had a lot to say about the French New Wave. I was happy to hear it. We went to see his friends play in a band in a basement somewhere in the city. I didn't think any more about Ralph.

Ralph showed up two nights later at the video store. He brought a tub of good ice cream and a bottle of top-shelf gin and tried quoting Bogart at me again when he came in the door. I ignored it.

'Is Ingrid coming?' I asked.

He shrugged. 'She's doing something else. Theatre? I don't know.'

I brought out two paper cups. The glasses had all broken

in the cramped sink out the back the very week before; Ingrid, trying to be helpful.

'It's just you and me, kid.' He leaned on the counter on his elbows. 'Are you going to ask me back?'

I opened the counter for him and he stepped through. He went to pull up a chair. I opened the bottle and the seal cracked. I felt his mouth on the back of my neck – I flinched with surprise and pulled away – and he was behind me, standing there. I couldn't tell whether I had imagined it. He took the bottle from my hands, his eyes on me, and poured.

'So how's Tom? What's he like?' he asked.

'Oh, he's great.'

'You have a huge hickey on your neck.'

I pulled up the collar of my dress.

'Good for you.' He drank his drink.

'Do you have a problem, Ralph?'

'No, no.'

I looked at him and saw a dark pink, bruised mark on his own neck near the line of his collared shirt. 'You have one too!' I gasped in mock horror and laughed. He laughed too, but he didn't meet my eyes. He finished his drink and poured another.

It was that very night that the shop phone rang and it was Ed calling.

'Hi! Ed. How are you? How did you get this number?'

'I've been trying to find you for a while – I knew you worked at some video place in the Cross – Look, it doesn't matter – is Ralph there?' His voice was strained. I knew it couldn't be good news.

'He's here. I'll get him.'

I held the receiver against my chest. Ralph was absorbed in reading the back of a video case and chewing a piece of chocolate. I didn't want to give him the phone.

'Ralph?'

'Hmm?' He looked up.

'It's Ed. For you.' I held the phone out to him. 'On the phone.'

'Ed?' he asked. 'Hi, Ed. What can I do for you?'

His face went pale as old ash. He listened and nodded and said, 'OK. Thanks ... No, it's OK, thanks.' He hung up.

'It's Dad.'

I nodded.

'He's at the Royal North Shore.' He gathered up his coat and his books.

'Do you want me to come with you?' I asked. He shook his head. I handed him his bag as he left.

I caught a cab to the hospital a couple of hours later and looked through the doors into the waiting room. Ralph was there, sitting in one of the uncomfortable-looking plastic chairs, next to Ingrid, his head resting on her shoulder. It looked as though he was asleep. She was sitting up calmly, reading a book.

If they're waiting there, sitting there like that, I told myself, it must mean that it's OK. For now, at least. Nothing was happening. I don't know what I was thinking. Eve was nowhere in sight. I couldn't bring myself to go in. I went home.

Ed had called by the house that night looking for Ralph – or Ingrid; I always wondered – and found George at the end of a bad heart attack. He died early the next morning. I went around to the house later that day and, standing before the front door, went through some of the feelings I had experienced in the hospital the night before – a repulsion, an exhausting physical sense of rejection – but I made myself knock. Ed answered the door and let me in.

Ingrid and Eve were sitting on the couch together with Racer at their feet. The dog was alert and worried. Eve had a grim look of resignation on her face. Ingrid rose when she saw me. 'He's upstairs,' she said simply, and sat down again.

Days passed. A week later, the day before the funeral, Ralph and Ingrid were together in the living room when I arrived. She was back in the velvet chair and he was sitting where Eve had been before. I could hear Eve on the phone in another room. They had just come back from the reading of the will, at their lawyer's office in the city. Ralph was smoking, something I had never seen him do inside the house before.

'I wish you wouldn't,' Ingrid said to him. He ignored her and stared at me. I sat down next to him.

'How did it go?' I asked.

Ralph looked at his fingernails. There was a kind of electric charge to the air, similar to the one I had felt before when I came upon them alone, but subtly different. Ingrid had a new kind of seriousness in her face. She was wearing all grey, a formal silk shirt and wide-legged, tailored pants that reminded me of Katharine Hepburn. No-one spoke. Eve's voice continued, muffled, from beyond the room.

Ingrid cleared her throat. 'Well, George left me some money,' she said.

I waited.

'Quite a lot.'

Ralph seemed to come back to life somehow, and I hadn't realised quite how still he had been. 'Oh, I've got my share,' he said. 'And Eve. There was enough to go around.' He put out his cigarette. 'Alright,' he said. 'I'm starving. Julia, can you make us something to eat? Please don't let Ingrid near that stove again.'

A sense of happiness for her inched up on me but I felt apprehensive, seeing her own awed discomfort. George's knowing winks to me, his sense of satisfied pride in Ingrid's achievements, made a whole new kind of sense. With this inheritance he really had bought a role for himself as the executive producer of whatever she chose to do next, the glamorous production he had always imagined she would make of her life. There was something selfless about it – he wouldn't be around, after all, to enjoy the show he had enabled – but it nevertheless felt like an act that bought gratification for himself at least as much as for her. Ralph seemed unsettled by the news, but not surprised. It was clear that he had known what was going to happen. It was only later I guessed he had been instrumental in achieving it.

In the kitchen the good cast-iron pan rested in the sink with something charred onto its sides and base. There wasn't much in the fridge apart from eggs and some old lettuce. I sniffed the milk. It was OK. There was a moment, when I saw myself standing there about to cook and care for them all, that I felt vaguely like a servant; a shadow that passed across my sense of myself as their trusted friend. It was the money, I told myself. I was more than ever the only one who didn't have any. But the feeling passed. I opened the cupboards and pulled out a mixing bowl, put it back.

'I'm driving to the deli,' I called to Ralph, pulling my keys out. 'Back soon.'

Ingrid had been well off after her father's death. Now, she was incredibly rich. George had left her enough capital to finance any adventure she desired, in the world of Ivy League PhDs or whatever else. They never discussed any actual figures but I knew that Ralph had enough to live comfortably without ever working for money – at least – and her share had been equal to his.

'How much is it?' I asked him once, after the funeral. 'Could she buy a house if she wanted to? Could she buy a house like this?' It was the only way I really knew how to measure money.

He snorted. 'Yes,' he said sarcastically. 'She could buy the whole block if she wanted to.' This might have been an exaggeration.

It became clear soon enough that he wasn't bitter about the money – it had never seemed that way to begin with – but he was anxious about what Ingrid's plans would be. It turned out that there had been conversations about the money before George's death – at least one with Ingrid, and one with Ralph – in which George had declared his desire to enable Ingrid to pursue her interests and 'explore the world'. But none of them seemed to have known how much money there was, except for George, or how much he would settle on Ingrid.

Eve had the house and, as Ralph had told me, she had her share. She didn't seem openly resentful about the money George had left to Ingrid, but I noticed her treating Ingrid differently after that, with a thoughtful kind of reassessment, perhaps contemplating the results of what she had set in motion by bringing her niece into the family. I sat at the table one morning with her over coffee while Ralph and Ingrid were upstairs dressing. She was subdued, not wearing the jewel-like colours that she had always favoured but a pale pink knitted top with long sleeves.

'Do you know,' she said, hand resting on her cup, 'I told Maeve the news about Ingrid's inheritance. She offered her congratulations and said it was "well done" on Ingrid's part.' Eve raised her eyebrows. 'That was going a bit far, I think. I told her so. To suggest that it's some kind of achievement — I'm not saying she isn't entitled — but it's not as though she had it in mind as some kind of goal. It's an absurd idea. And Ingrid's obviously shocked by the whole thing. George was so eccentric. Who could have known.'

Was she asking me for reassurance, to agree that Ingrid had found her way into George's affections with purely innocent intentions? I believed that she had, and it seemed as though Eve really did as well. She was saying something to me, to herself, about Maeve, I realised, more than about Ingrid.

Ralph had little enthusiasm for travel — he was strangely opposed to it, and fiercely attached to his homes, the house and the flat, and his little routines. But Ingrid was wild for it. Having managed to get out of Perth, she wanted to see the world. The trip she had planned to Venice for the semester break was still going ahead and she was now planning to extend it, to spend more time in Europe and in England.

'Rome,' she said to me, her eyes bright and focused. 'So much is there.'

Eve had been planning to go with her but had changed her mind. She had travelled so much while George was alive and now her energy seemed depleted. It turned out that Maeve was attending the Venice Biennale with an artist from her gallery and she offered to show Ingrid around and take her to all the parties.

Eve came off the phone with Maeve one night about a week after the funeral. 'She's delighted that you'll be there, Ingrid,' she said, clasping her hands together. She sounded relieved. 'I'm so pleased. She's going to call again tomorrow morning to speak with you – she wants you to stay at her hotel and she's trying to arrange a room for you.' The vague mistrust of her friend that she had communicated to me a few days earlier seemed to have dissipated.

Ralph watched these plans take shape with a kind of grudging resentment.

'She's only going for six weeks,' I reminded him. 'She'll be back.'

'Oh, I know,' he said. 'And then she'll be off again.' He smiled wanly.

You have me, I wanted to say, pathetically. Instead I put my arms around him but he didn't embrace me back; I pulled away and saw his solemn face.

'It's a good thing for Ingrid,' I said. 'She's obsessed with getting away. It will … expand her horizons.' It sounded even to myself as though I were quoting from some debunked text.

'I know,' he sighed. 'We'll have a lovely break, together. Won't we?'

By the time Ingrid left for Venice the money was starting to weigh more heavily with her. The seriousness that had been there in her face the day of the will remained. She sat with me in the video store one night reading her Italy and Europe guidebooks, stacks of them. She looked worried.

'There's so much to see,' she said, and made it sound like a cause for terrible concern. 'There's a lot to know. I don't really know anything.'

'You're going to have a good time,' I reassured her. 'And you know lots anyway – right? Don't you know about all those, you know, ruins from class?'

She turned the pages of a blue-covered book. 'There's just such a lot there.'

'You can always go back next time and see whatever you don't make it to this time,' I said. 'Think of it as a fact-finding mission.' I picked up one of her books. A 'Shoestring' guide. 'You won't need this,' I said. 'And won't Maeve show you around anyway?'

'She's been going to the Biennale forever! I can't wait to meet some of the artists.'

Ingrid had a romantic fascination with artists; she'd shown a kind of awed respect for my aunt the few times they had met. 'I've never met an actual artist,' she'd told me after their first conversation. 'It's fascinating.'

A lot of things were fascinating, and wonderful, and new to

her in those first couple of months in Sydney. Thai food was amazing. The cocktail bars and art galleries of the eastern suburbs were cool and incredible. The crowded Oxford Street markets full of clothes and candles and junk were fantastic. It was a kind of willingness to be pleased and delighted that made it a lovely thing to take her somewhere new – there was always something fascinating about any place. She was self-conscious about her own enthusiasm – 'I'm so uncool,' she would laugh. 'I know! OK, I'll calm down.' And five minutes later would be enthusing again – 'It's amazing! How old is this place? What is in this food? What is this drink called? Oh my god!' After a while she adjusted to the city and stopped remarking so much on every new thing and I could see her working hard at being 'cooler' as she called it.

'But I'm so uncool,' I would say to her. 'You won't learn anything from me.'

'No, Julia,' she would protest. 'You have no idea. I learn it all from you. Like … your steely gaze.'

'My steely gaze?'

'Yes.'

'That is ridiculous.'

'See, that's it, right there! Your withering stare! I love it!' We were at a nightclub near Ralph's flat, late at night, and she had to shout over the music. 'OK – I'll stop. I'm going to go dance.'

'Go on.'

I didn't dance. It was one thing Ralph didn't join her in either, to my surprise. He would watch her from wherever we were sitting or standing, and eye off whoever she seemed to be dancing with, but he didn't ever interrupt.

5.

If I thought much about what Ingrid would be doing with herself in Venice and Rome and wherever else in Europe she was going on that trip, I imagined her seeing a dozen ruins a day, exploring every piece of the Colosseum, spending hours with the paintings in the churches in Venice. My own memories of Rome from visiting there in my 'gap year' were very hazy. The Colosseum had nauseated me. I couldn't help thinking about the gladiators dying in a slick of blood, the horrors of the basement levels of the building that were now exposed to view. There had been a lot of good pasta, and good-looking men on the streets, seemingly everywhere, and scooters and little red cars. Bookshop windows filled with elegant arrangements, boxes of jumbled books on the street outside. I imagined that Ingrid's experience would be a lot more studious and enriching than mine had been. I sometimes imagined a holiday fling for her.

In her studies, her readings of the ancient texts and poetry she loved, she was intrigued by the idea of love and its potentially overwhelming power. The semester she studied *Antigone* she became obsessed with it, confused and fascinated by the story. 'He's already dead, her brother,' she would say, her eyes distant. 'So why? What is she going to prove?' She sighed. 'But what else could she do? What else was left to her?' She pored over Ovid, the stories in the *Metamorphoses* of young women and men destroyed by their own desires, and she had a kind of awed respect for the grand passions of Edwardian romance. We read *The Age of Innocence* in the same class together and cried over the movie, watching it twice, once at the video shop late at night and again the next day at the Kirribilli house with popcorn made on the stove. She couldn't stand the end – wouldn't watch it the second time. 'No!' she said. 'Why doesn't he go in? It's unbelievable. Why doesn't she go down to him?'

'OK,' I said. 'Leave the room. I want to see it.' She went out and banged things around in the kitchen.

But she didn't import this romantic view of things into her own love life. The only attachments she seemed to form were fleeting and half-hearted. She was always the one pursued, and when she did give in to the pursuer it was with a kind of distant interest that never seemed to grow into real feeling or desire. I suppose now that I can't make any judgements from what I could see though; and I wondered even then how she changed when the doors were closed and the lights were off with these boys she sometimes went out with (but rarely seemed to sleep with), when there was no-one else to see. And I wondered endlessly about the time she spent alone with Ralph.

She didn't ever seem surprised by the attention she got, the interest from men, and when she did respond there was often the sense that I'd had with her the first time we went out, that she was exploring an experience with a scientific determination rather than real, lived feeling. It was a strange counterpart to her very real enthusiasm for life in general.

There were times here and there when I grew tired of being the face that was overlooked whenever I was out with her, and then I let myself call her narcissistic, but in fact it was strange how little it bothered me in general. I was pining after Ralph in those days and it was that competition with her that wounded me most. She won it without even trying, of course, and it wasn't a victory she ever held over me and I couldn't hate her for it.

It seemed as though she probably wanted to fall in love, but hadn't. So, when I thought about it, I wished for her a happy Italian romance with some exotic backpacker or art fan. Perhaps she would respond with more interest to men outside her familiar sphere, men from the world that she was so interested in exploring. Foreign accents were always very impressive to her; she loved hearing Maeve talk and she attended to the little differences in the words that Maeve used for familiar things. 'Cream,' Ingrid would say, 'but she means milk really. Doesn't she?' 'Bicycle. Motorcycle.' If she could start falling in love with other people, I thought, instead of just appearing to entertain herself briefly with random admirers, maybe Ralph would leave off brooding after her. Not that I imagined that he would turn to me; I knew very well that she was a unique exception to his usual interests, which were men, especially ones who seemed straight, and occasionally women, but always anonymous, or so casual as to be virtually that.

Her Ovidian fascinations did make me think sometimes that when she did fall in love it would be dramatic and intense and that she would embrace the role. The role? The surrender to feeling, when it finally came. Of course I had no idea that when it did come it would be like it was.

The excitement that had been there around the trip before George's death was muted now, but Ingrid's restlessness grew. The stillness that had characterised her when she had first arrived had been replaced by a kind of constant, subtle, internal agitation. She was always running her hand up and down her arm. She even tried smoking cigarettes.

The days of being at the house around her and Ralph and Eve had made me tired of her company and more solidly jealous of her relationship with Ralph than before. Ralph was sunk pretty deep in quiet most of the day, watching daytime TV and reading, and when he did snap out of it and look up from what he was doing it was her he watched, anxiously. She seemed aware of it for the first time. I left them each night sitting together on the couch in the little TV room upstairs, her legs curled up on the seat beside her.

By the time Ingrid left, two weeks after the funeral, Ralph was doing better. No more daytime TV. He spent a lot of time on one of his final essays for class that was extremely overdue; his teacher had given him a long extension because of his father's death but he was pushing the limits of it. He was back at the Kings Cross flat more frequently, always reading at the kitchen table, a giant stack of library books in front of him that seemed to grow by the day. It was something to do with Malory; or it began that way. His latest addition to the stack of books when I stopped by on my way to work was an ominously large collection of titles on Freud and Carl Jung. The retreat into books and the essay appeared at first to be his way of withdrawing himself from Ingrid before she went away, so that her absence when it came would be less painful. But the essay dragged on after she left and his absorption in it became an even more intense kind of distraction. He looked terrible, his stubble grown into an uneven kind of short beard, and the laundry room in the flat was piled with clothes. He came into the store regularly when I was working, but would stand there moodily, elbows on the counter, not watching whatever I was playing on the video machine. Or he would bring one of his books and sit in the back reading it, scribbling on little Post-it notes he would then stick in the pages. Every now and again he would look up and bring me slowly into focus.

'Venice. What's the weather like this time of year anyway?' he would ask. Or, 'What did you like about Rome? Where did you stay, again?' Or, with his Jung book in hand, 'If you were an archetype, what would you be?'

'I don't know.'

'Go on, pick one.'

'You pick one.'

He eyed me critically. 'Alice in Wonderland. The Lady of Shalott.'

'That's not an archetype. And those are two completely different things.'

'I suppose so.'

'What about you?' I asked once.

'Peter Pan,' he said brusquely, and got back to reading.

I tried to be patient.

Then one night he didn't come when I was expecting

him, and I was relieved. A cute customer struck up a conversation with me and I found myself wishing he would ask for my phone number. I thought about giving him a card from the little stack on the counter, but I would have had to have written my name and my own phone number on it, which seemed a bit laborious and desperate. The phone rang and it was Ralph, calling to tell me that he had finished the essay. He wanted to go out and celebrate. His voice sounded different and I realised how much I had missed the humour in it since George had died.

The good-looking customer had picked up a card of his own accord and held it in his hand. I smiled at him and took it and wrote my name and phone number on it and gave it back without thinking much. 'See you,' he said and left with his French movie with subtitles.

Ralph didn't answer my knock. I waited. I tried the handle after a minute and it opened. He was there on the couch, asleep. Ingrid's abandoned collection of guidebooks lay scattered on the coffee table. The stack of library books was gone from the kitchen table and now sat in two tall piles next to the front door. The kitchen table itself was strewn with papers and something that looked like an essay with a cover sheet, neatly stapled. It was about 1:30 am. His face was unbearably unguarded in sleep, dark hollows under the eyes, sadness not quite wiped away. I stepped back out the door.

A few days later the library books were all gone and the guidebooks were gathered together low on the bookshelf against the wall. The weekend papers were on the coffee table. Ralph's face was covered in tiny cuts.

'Never let me go that long without shaving again,' he said. 'I can hardly stand to go out like this. Is it cold outside?' He looked out the window. 'I haven't been out for days.'

We went over to Kirribilli for lunch. Eve had bought a roasted chicken from the local deli and made a salad. She and Ralph bickered the whole afternoon with no real enthusiasm until she seemed to just run out of steam. She showed us her postcard from Ingrid proudly – a collection of panoramas of Venice. Ralph was sullen. There was no card for him.

We got back into what felt something like old routines. I don't think I was naive about it; I hadn't expected things to go back to being exactly the way they had been before Ingrid had come along. And there was a lot to like about the way things were with her around. I missed Ralph's showy cleverness around her, his extra efforts, which weren't turned on for me nearly as much. I missed Ingrid herself and her catching enthusiasm. Ralph was happier than he had been a couple of weeks earlier, but he didn't have the brightness he had once had, when I'd first met him, and it was impossible to distinguish between the effects of grief over his father and missing Ingrid. He was cross with me at times, never really sharp, but snappy. I began to look forward to her return.

She called early one morning.

'I've called you once or twice,' she said. 'I couldn't reach you.'

She hated leaving messages on answering machines. I'd overheard her try to do it once or twice; she went on and on without getting around to what she was trying to say, talking until the machine cut her off.

'Everything's fine,' she said now. 'I just wanted to say hi. I miss you all!'

'Ingrid, it's really early here.'

'Oh, sorry, sorry, I can't ever get that right.'

'That's OK. I was awake. How was Venice?'

'You were? Venice – so great, beautiful, I'm so glad I came. Julia, I have to tell you – I'm in love.' She sounded very serious.

I smiled. 'I'm really happy for you.'

'Thank you.'

Her voice grew very quiet suddenly, a fault in the line, disappearing into the miles between here and there.

'Hello?'

'... a friend of Maeve's.'

'Sorry, I didn't hear you.'

'What? Oh, I was telling you about Gil. Gil Grey.'

'He's a friend of Maeve's?' It was hard to put Maeve, with her dark plumage and smooth walk, together with any of the young, easy, nicely accented types I had imagined for Ingrid's holiday romance.

'Yeah, from New York.' Her voice was swallowed up again into silence. It came back in suddenly. '... in Florence, a palace!'

'I can't hear you. Something's wrong with the line.'

'Oh, too bad. Look, I'm in Florence, I'm staying here a week longer and I've changed my tickets.'

'OK, that sounds great.'

'Can you tell Ralph?'

'Tell him what?'

'I'm staying longer?'

'Why don't you call him?'

'I've tried Eve's place …'

'OK, OK. Have fun.'

'I can't wait to tell you about it.'

'Bye.'

'Ciao, ciao!'

I fell back to sleep almost immediately and woke up when the phone started ringing again. I reached down to pick up the receiver from the table next to my bed but there was no-one there, just a dial tone that gave way to a long beep, beep. The ring had been a dream. It rang again, for real this time. I had a strong idea that it would be Ingrid again, and a feeling of dread came over me. It rang and rang. I answered it. It was Ralph.

'Are you just waking up? It's late!'

'I'm awake, I'm awake.'

'Yeah. Sure.'

'Ralph, Ingrid called me.'

'Really? When? Is everything OK?'

'Fine, she's just staying a week longer.'

'Oh, alright. She's going to miss the start of classes.'

My fingers felt clammy against the phone.

'I suppose she'll get here just in time for that. She said that she's in love.'

'Oh.'

'With some friend of Maeve's.'

'Ohhh. I wonder who.'

'Some guy called Gil.'

'Well, well.'

'I sort of thought that something like that would happen.'

'It would, wouldn't it?'

We were both quiet. He said goodbye. Seconds later the phone rang again and I picked it up right away. It was Ralph again.

He laughed. 'I'm an idiot, I forgot what I was calling you about. Before.' He wanted me to come to the bookshop with him to buy books for class. We were taking one together: Post-War German Film.

I lay back down. The next thing I knew Ralph was standing in my doorway. He said something in French and I recognised the word for sleep.

'*Merde*,' I said.

He closed the door and sat down on the bed and looked at the floor. The sun was high in the sky and my room felt airless, the window closed. I sat up, legs crossed on the bed. I was wearing a short cotton dress, yellow and white, that I liked to sleep in. It had a small hole near the hem. Had I been wearing it the day before? I shook my head. It wouldn't come clear. Ralph reached over – slowly, it seemed – and put his hand on my bent knee. I rose then, onto my knees, and put my arms around his neck, my head buried into his shoulder. We pressed ourselves together. His breath moved in and out, ragged like mine.

I struggled with an image – a picture in my mind of my dress lifted over my head, my arms stuck for a second, bound above my head as the dress caught. I closed my eyes. The room was all air, and then none, a vacuum, a knot of space.

He put his hand up to my hair, smoothing it away from my forehead. His face was bleak. He smiled. 'Get dressed,' he said.

I got up and went to the shower. When I came back he was sitting up on the bed with his back against the wall, ankles crossed neatly, reading a novel he had picked up from the floor. He kept reading it as I dropped the towel from around myself, dropped the dress I had been wearing earlier, and picked clothes out from the dresser. The yellow dress lay crumpled on the floor. I opened my wardrobe and took out a skirt. I stole a look at his mouth, thin and relaxed, as he read. For a second it took everything to stay standing up straight and not buckle over, a big dent right in my middle like a bent piece of tin. I wondered absently if this was what it felt like to be hit in the stomach. I pulled on my skirt and a long turtleneck.

We walked down the hill to the bookshop and bought our books. We must have talked on the way and when we were there – I can see his face now, against the shelves, pointing out a title to me and raising his eyebrows in an 'as if?' kind of look. He picked out two of all our texts and took them to the counter and paid for them.

'*Merci*,' I said.

'*De rien*,' he replied. It was all French that day for some reason.

6.

I first saw Ingrid after she got back from her trip in a class we were taking together, a course in the English department on the classics and English literature that I was taking to fill a requirement. She caught my eye across the room; Ralph was there next to her, looking tired and cross. We all went to eat lunch together afterwards. She was wearing a new shirt in a deep blue like a madonna's dress, with tiny pleats. Her tan was more obvious than ever next to Ralph and me after our wet Sydney winter.

She told me about Gil Grey.

'Well, he's an old friend of Maeve's. He used to be a partner in her gallery, you know. But you know who introduced us? Your aunt's dealer! Keith – I saw him there in one of the rooms, at the Biennale, and remembered meeting him at her house with you that time – and he was with Gil. I would have met him anyway because of Maeve, but it was Keith, after all.'

Ralph stared off into the distance. He had probably heard it already.

'Anyway – Gil was there in Venice with his daughter, Fleur. She's an artist – like, a child prodigy.'

'How old is she?' I asked.

'Thirteen.'

'And they were going to the Biennale too?'

'No – yes – well, she was showing there.'

'She was showing her art there?'

'It's amazing, isn't it? She paints these incredible abstract paintings – she's famous! She was famous when she was four years old. Her finger paintings – they're real art.'

Ralph hadn't spoken yet. 'It's true,' he said now, stifling a yawn. 'Eve knows all about her, through Maeve, I suppose. She was a kind of prodigy.'

'But she's not doing finger painting now?' I asked.

Ingrid pursed her lips. 'Well, her paintings that I saw all had some finger painting in them. It was hard to tell. Not just finger painting though – something else too …'

'And Gil runs the gallery with Maeve?' I asked.

'Well, no. He was part of it initially. He's a dealer now. But he's really a collector. He collects art.'

I wondered how old he was.

'We walked through Venice for days. And Florence. It's so beautiful.'

Ingrid's face was radiant. I looked down at my plate of lasagna from the caféteria and picked at it and remembered the good food in Rome.

Ralph pushed his plate away with an irritated motion. He hadn't eaten much. 'Why did you get the vegie burger?' I asked him. 'They're always so bad. Can I eat your chips?'

He shrugged and lit a cigarette.

'When did you start smoking Camels?' I asked. He offered me one and I turned it down. Give him a few days, I thought. He's happy she's back. But I really couldn't tell whether he was or not.

Ingrid studied even harder that semester than she normally did, while Ralph and I seemed to get slacker at our work. She was taking advanced Ancient Greek and lugged around enormous reference books and grammars. She stopped by the video store less often and didn't stay as late at the university bar on weeknights; she came out with us to parties on the weekend sometimes and seemed even less interested in men than she had been previously. Ed was still trying hard with her every so often, over at Kirribilli for lunch, taking her out to see potential cars to buy and giving her the occasional driving lesson.

'You know she had this big romance in Venice?' I asked him at a party one night. We were smoking in the backyard and Ingrid was inside, drinking a vodka drink in a bottle. I had one too. It tasted like lemonade and had some faux-Russian name.

Ed looked dispirited. 'Yeah, I know, I know. The artist from New York.'

'He's not actually an artist,' I corrected him.

'Oh, whatever, art collector, artist, dealer. I'm sure he was really great. And really smart. Fuck him.' He finished his bottle of beer and looked around for somewhere to toss it. 'American wanker. Old enough to be her father.'

Ralph came over to us then looking a little unsteady. He had taken a thin line of speed in my car just before we had arrived at the party, and it wasn't a drug he handled well. I hadn't wanted it, hating the jittery paranoia that it brought.

'Please tell me you're not talking about Grey,' he said.

Ed looked at me and didn't say anything. Ralph handed him a beer. 'Good.'

A few candles in glass jam jars were scattered around on the ground and the night was dark. It was a small yard, dead brown grass under our feet. Two guys I recognised from art history classes were trying to get a fire going in a metal garbage bin near the fence. Another guy came up and argued with them about the merits of wasting a cheap bottle of whisky to get it started and whether that would even work. 'I'll drink it!' 'There's heaps of beer!' 'Well, where's the lighter fluid then?'

'Let's go inside,' I said, and Ralph and Ed followed me in.

Ed stuck with me that night. He made a pass at me an hour or so later and I found it strangely annoying. Moments beforehand he had been still complaining about Ingrid.

'Look, I like you, Julia,' he said, after I'd pushed his hand away from my breast.

'I like you too, Ed.'

He was staring over somewhere away from me. I wondered if I had been too quick to get annoyed. He was wearing a polo shirt that had North Shore written all over it, but somehow he wore it with style. His face started to lose its set, frustrated expression as I looked at him. I wanted to reach out and smooth his troubled brow. The moment passed.

He folded his arms. 'You'll have no luck with Ralph, you know,' he said. He met my eyes with a bitter expression. It felt like a low blow, just as he had meant it to be.

'I don't want to be your fucking consolation prize,' I said.

It cut through to something.

'You might see it that way, Julia. No-one else would.'

Somehow that hurt me more than anything, and the sad reluctance in his voice. I walked away.

Ralph was arguing with Ingrid in a room off the hallway as I left. She looked bored. I'd never seen them argue before. It was a long walk home to my own house.

I didn't see Ralph and Ingrid argue any more but there was a tension between them every now and again that grew more frequent. Ralph spent less time at the Kirribilli house than he had before. I got another job, at the second-hand bookshop across the road from the video shop, and worked there every Saturday, cutting down to just a couple of shifts at Videomania. I found that I liked it. It made Ralph incredibly happy. Every time he came in for the first few weeks I worked there, he would launch into the routine from *The Big Sleep* again. 'Would you happen to have a *Ben-Hur*, 1860?' If I felt like it, I would go along.

'It was meant to be!' he would say with delight in his drawling, ironic way. I wasn't sure if he meant me working in the shop, or him and me together. I didn't ask.

'It must be nice, to have a job,' he said once, fingers tracing an invisible line along the counter, one day when he had stopped by with Ingrid. It was one of those times when things seemed to be back to a kind of equilibrium between them. I had just finished wrapping a stack of books for a customer. Ingrid glanced at him, alarmed.

'It must be nice, not to need one,' I said after a few seconds.

He looked up at me. 'Christ, I'm sorry. I'm an idiot.'

'You could get a job, Ralph,' Ingrid said, encouragingly. 'What would you like to do?' It wasn't clear whether she was being sincere or sarcastic.

Ralph never talked about what he wanted to do with his life; he didn't have to think about it and didn't want to.

'Right now I'd like to get something good to eat.'

'I thought we had decided that showering me with gifts was going to be our activity for the day?' Ingrid asked.

'That too,' he reassured her.

'It's my birthday next week,' Ingrid said to me. It was early October. She was going to be twenty-one.

They left arm in arm. 'See you tonight!' Ralph called over his shoulder to me as they passed through the door.

The bookshop was owned by Martin, a barely functioning alcoholic, and pretty much kept running by his assistant, Neil, who was a few years older than me. Martin mostly stuck to his tiny office out the back, doing the crossword and drinking from a flask in his bottom drawer. Neil was going over the procedure with me for closing the till at the end of the day when I heard a car horn sound outside. I looked up and a little BMW was there, a late 1980s model in dull silver with L-plates stuck on both ends, with Ingrid behind the wheel. Ralph was next to her and I could make out someone else in the back. She honked the horn again.

'OK, we'll go over it again next week,' Neil said and smiled at me.

'Sorry –'

'No, fine, go.'

I left.

It was a joint present from Ed and Ralph. As I rode in the car with them I wondered whose idea it had been in the first place. Ingrid was rapturous. She had been borrowing Eve's little Alfa every once in a while and mostly using George's old car, an ancient Mercedes that needed a new transmission. The BMW ran beautifully. It looked like something out of a very cool music video and it had a new stereo. The seats were dark red leather. Ed seemed very pleased with himself. We hadn't seen one another since the party where he had tried to grope me. I decided to make a truce and leaned in to kiss his cheek when I got into the car. His hand rested comfortably on my waist for a short second.

'Hi,' he said happily.

'Good one,' I told him, looking around at the car.

Ingrid drove fast but Ralph and Ed didn't seem to notice or to mind. It was the first evening that spring that we really noticed how long the days were getting. We drove for what seemed like hours, all the way out to a beach where we bought fish and chips and the most expensive champagne we could find – Ingrid bought it herself – and we ate sitting in the car, passing the bottle around. There was a fat white moon over the ocean.

'I'm going to sleep in here tonight!' Ingrid announced. 'I don't ever want to get out!'

'OK, but you'll have to let me drive now that you've drunk half the champagne,' Ed said.

She gave up the wheel grudgingly and Ralph joined me in the back.

'When did you do this?' I asked him.

'Last weekend,' he said. 'It's a good surprise, isn't it?'

'It's fantastic. Well done.'

We ended up back at the Kirribilli house, getting drunker and drunker, sitting in the car in the driveway listening to the radio as Ralph went back and forth to the house, bringing bottles of wine and water and glasses to drink out of.

Ed's car was there. He had been drinking less than the rest of us.

'Can I give you a lift home, Julia?' he asked when he was ready to go. I wondered if he was thinking of reviving his attempt.

'You're staying, aren't you, Julia?' Ingrid asked.

Ed looked at her with eyes full of regret. I think he realised that if his invitation to stay the night with Ingrid didn't happen now, it was never going to.

'You don't have to leave,' Ralph said to him.

'No, it's OK,' he said. 'Time to be getting home.'

Ingrid embraced him and thanked him again and again. They stood a few feet away from the car. Ralph fiddled with the radio dial. I saw her kiss Ed firmly on the mouth – once, twice; they were almost the same height, she didn't need to reach up much at all – and murmur something I couldn't hear. Ed walked away, his shoulders tight. I couldn't see his face.

Ingrid turned back to us, leaning her weight over onto one foot and swaying her arms a little. She was wearing a new version of the red coat, one she had tried on with me a week before, shopping on an expensive side street in Paddington. Buttons were falling off the old coat with regularity now. This new one was much like the old one, only with more swing as it fell from the waist. She had given a huge mock gasp when she had looked at the price tag in the shop, and twirled around in front of the mirror before replacing it on the rack. I supposed it was a birthday present to herself, and then I wondered if Ralph had bought it for her.

'Ed's so sweet,' she said. She wiped the back of her hand across her mouth, eyes shadowed. 'You could do worse, Julia.' She raised her eyebrow a little as she stepped over to the car and retrieved her glass from the dashboard.

Ralph turned to me with a disbelieving look. If she was flaunting some kind of power, I didn't know what she wanted to achieve with it. I decided that she was drunk and forgave her, but it was one of those moments when something in me hardened against her, instant scar over wound.

A little while later Ingrid showed me to one of the extra guest rooms upstairs. It was the room Maeve had when she stayed and it held a faint trace of her perfume. I had recognised it when I had smelt it on her because my mother had sometimes worn it, and my father hated it. Fracas, it was called. It was a dark, intense smell – I always thought of it as the same colour as its square, blackish-purple bottle – and it made me catch my breath.

Ingrid handed me a huge, folded towel. She was acting more and more as though she wasn't just at home in the house but as though it were really hers. I wondered if she was alone here much; Eve was away less than she had been before George's death but wasn't around all the time.

The bed was all soft down and cotton but I lay awake for a while. Voices sounded down the hallway, doors opening and closing, taps turning on and off, water running. I thought I heard the sound of the bath running and caught the smell of roses. Ingrid laughed in another room. I fell asleep at last and then woke again – I couldn't tell how long

I'd been sleeping – thinking I heard someone outside my door. The floor creaked but there was no knock, no door opening. When I woke again it was late morning and the smell of toast and bacon drifted up from the kitchen.

Gil's letter came a few days after that, the day after Ingrid's birthday. She told me about it when I saw her next on campus.

'He's invited me to New York,' she said. 'Fleur's having a major show there. There'll be a big opening and I can go. And I'll stay with Maeve.'

'Wow,' I said. 'When?'

'The end of November. I'll miss the exams but I only have one and I'm going to just take it early, before I go.'

'They'll let you?'

'Oh, yeah.'

I had forgotten Ingrid's special ability to get any kind of extension or exemption from her teachers.

'I was so hoping he would ask me,' she said. 'I was thinking of just going anyway, at the end of the year.'

She had been talking about going to the States but for some reason I hadn't put it together.

'Are you in touch with him?' I asked.

'A little – we've written, just once or twice.'

I wondered again how old he was. He must be in his mid-thirties – older? She had shown me a picture of him by then, slender and sharp-looking, leaning against a railing on a Venice canal. He could have been anywhere between thirty and forty-five. His hair was chestnut brown shot with silvery grey and he was wearing a beautiful linen suit.

We had arrived at the library. Ingrid was going inside and I was going to work. She was wearing the new red coat again – it was taking a while to really turn into summer – and her cheeks were pink and dusky tan. Her hair was pulled down inside the collar. Ralph hadn't been in class. I was about to ask her if she knew what he was doing when she said goodbye and walked into the building.

There wasn't the same tension as there had been before her last trip. Ralph seemed to accept it differently, and seemed more even-tempered when she talked about Grey. Then a week or so after the letter had come, he decided to go with her.

'Why not?' he asked when I met him at the campus bar in the late afternoon. 'We'd been talking about going somewhere together anyway, for the break. London or New York or whatever. I'll just spend a week or two in New York and then some in London. Maybe Paris. What do you think of Paris?'

'But Ralph,' I said. I didn't know how to continue. It seemed like a bad idea to put him in the same room as Ingrid's holiday romance, or whatever this thing now was. 'Are you going just to check him out?' I asked. This was verging perilously close to territory we did not touch on.

To my relief he smiled. 'Well, it wouldn't hurt, would it? Aren't you curious too? But look, he lives in New York. What's going to happen?' He tapped a cigarette on his hand. 'I'm looking forward to it.'

'Good.'

'Now.' He picked up the dice – we were playing Trivial Pursuit – and rolled them across the board. They were little coloured plastic things, mismatched from some other game. He counted up the numbers and groaned. 'Geography. Did we decide to leave that one out this round?'

'No. We're leaving out Sport this round.'

'I think if we're leaving out Sport and Leisure for you then we should leave out Geography for me.'

I picked up the card.

'Give me a clue at least,' he said.

I read out the question.

At the end of the second game, having won both easily, Ralph was content. I went to get another round of drinks while he packed the game away. The people on the couch next to us wanted a turn. When I came back, the Scrabble board was half-open and Ralph was smoking.

'Look,' he said when I sat down. 'Why don't you come as well?'

'Where?'

'Away. With me for the break. Come to New York. London. Paris. What did you think of Paris anyway? We could go anywhere.'

I folded the board out, and refolded it.

'I'll pay. It can be a birthday present,' he continued.

'You got me a birthday present already.' It had been a first-edition Chandler, *The Lady in the Lake*.

'Go on. Don't be stupid about the money.'

'OK, I'll think about it.' I didn't want to think about it, but it seemed better to end the conversation. 'Thanks. I mean, it would be fantastic, obviously – I just don't know –'

'Moral support,' he said wryly, his arm stretched out to ash his cigarette, the other folded across his knees. He was still smoking Camels, and I missed the smell of his old Marlboros.

'I thought you were just curious.'

He must have had some awareness of what he was asking from me, I thought, to support him in this preoccupation with Ingrid while I suffered through my own unrequited crush on him. I told myself that he didn't realise it was painful for me, that he didn't really guess, and at the same time denied the real destructiveness of it all to myself. I knew it was my choice to stick with him, so I couldn't blame him after all.

He didn't say anything. Outside, the long sunset was over and the lights over the footpaths were bright against the dark, the old sandstone buildings spotlit. The Trivial Pursuit game at the table next to us was getting rowdy; someone had defaced an Entertainment card so that the answer was illegible and an argument was taking place over what the right answer was. I knew the answer, and thought about interrupting. Ralph leaned his head over to them a second later. 'It's 1967, for Christ's sake,' he said to the player. It didn't help.

'Choose your letters,' I said, and unfolded the board.

He called me a couple of days later.

'OK, Julia, there's a two-for-one sale with BA so you can't say no.'

And I couldn't.

7.

Ingrid asked me to help her pack a couple of days before her flight, and I sat in her room working my way through a large chunk of brie I had found in the fridge while she pulled things out of her wardrobe and two enormous dressers. It wasn't like Ingrid to worry so much about clothes, and she seemed to feel as though she ought to care about what she wore on this trip but wasn't sure how to go about it.

'How much are you taking?' she asked.

'I don't know. I'm only going for three weeks.'

She looked at the pile of skirts on the bed in confusion.

'It will be really cold. But warm inside.' I went through one pile and put aside anything that wouldn't be warm enough. We wore the same size, but clothes looked different on her taller body. There was a few centimetres' difference or more between us in height, and sometimes I looked at her and wondered where exactly the extra height went – legs, waist, neck, all more elongated than my own.

'Thanks.' She sighed and sat down.

I went to work on the next pile. 'Don't you own anything black?' I asked her.

'Oh, one thing,' she said, pulling out a shirt. 'This would suit you.' It was pretty: eyelet lace with a round neck and three delicate crystal buttons in a closure at the back.

'It's New York,' I said.

'So I'll be able to buy all the black things I need.'

'Yes. In fact, you should pack light. Go shopping when you're there.'

'You'll have to tell me where to go. Oh! You can come with me!'

She looked at the piles of clothes.

'Let's stop. I'll finish it tomorrow. Are you going to eat all that cheese or can we go down and make something for dinner?'

It was a hot November, the smell of bushfires in the air already, and it was hard to imagine the cold streets of New York and the overheated interiors, the peeling off and putting on of layers, breath turned to mist in the air. From Ingrid's window the little piece of water visible through the trees glittered sharply.

Ralph and I left a couple of weeks later, the day after Christmas, and by that time we were glad to escape the summer. The bookshop was hot and stuffy by evening and the air on the street burned hot and dirty at the end of the day. My car broke down – sensitive to summer now, as well as winter cold – and ended up at the mechanics for days. I hated the long ride down the escalator into the train station to get home to Newtown, where the smog was even thicker. Ralph kept telling me to move over to the east – 'Why not, you're sick of that house anyway' – and I thought about it. But the old, thick brick walls of the terrace house in Newtown insulated it against the heat, and when I walked in the front door the coolness of the hallway always surprised me.

We finished our final essays and exams with time to spare before we left and spent it at the beach, drinking lemonade and beer into the afternoons. For some reason Ralph had decided he wanted a tan, and his already olive skin darkened. I applied sunscreen with improbably high factors of protection – '100 SPF? How is that possible?' Ralph would scoff. All the same, as the days passed I noticed what looked like the white imprint of a swimsuit growing whiter against my skin.

Our plane was hours late getting into New York and Ralph and I arrived at the brightly lit Plaza Hotel deep into a freezing winter's night. The room was a blur of warmth, all gilt and velvet. We bounced like children on the enormous beds when we first walked in the door. Minutes later I fell asleep on one of the overstuffed sofas in front of the windows, waiting for the heavy, strangely bright, grey clouds to start snowing.

Ingrid met us for an early dinner at a tiny Japanese restaurant on the Upper West Side on our second night. We reached the door just as she stepped out of a cab in front of us. She was wearing her red coat and some tall black boots I hadn't seen before, and a loose red beret with most of her hair tucked up inside it. She hugged us both and we went inside.

Ingrid and Ralph sat next to each other, with me across from Ralph. We all fidgeted a bit in the unfamiliar space. The whole place was decorated in pine, with lime green cushions and carpets. Grey was supposed to be meeting us there too. After half an hour of waiting Ingrid started making small excuses: he'd warned her that he might be running a little behind; he was probably caught up talking to one of his biggest clients who was visiting the city for just a few days, a wealthy Russian collector with a passion for American abstract art, she explained. After another half hour we started eating without him and I relaxed at moments when I forgot that he was coming at all. The food was artful, carved and shaped into precise and delicate arrangements.

Ingrid was staying with Maeve at her apartment in the Meatpacking District further downtown on the West side. There had been some issue of decorum over whether she would stay with Grey.

'With Fleur, you know,' she said, gently gripping her sushi with chopsticks. 'It might not have been appropriate with her.' We nodded. Fleur was still just a teenager. I imagined weirdly adolescent scenes of Ingrid going over to his place while Fleur was at school or with her friends, making sure that by the time she came home they were dressed and presentable, or gone, as though the roles were all reversed.

Ingrid's face glowed and I remembered the reverential tones she'd used when she talked about Grey on the phone that time from Florence, and when she arrived back in Sydney after that trip.

'I'm learning so much,' she told us now.

'You make it sound as though you're here for a study trip,' I said. 'Are you having fun?'

'Yes,' she said smugly, and smiled and sipped at her drink. 'It's all wonderful.'

Ralph was quiet, and exuded a possessive, careful attitude towards her that I recognised from the first weeks after he'd met her: handing her the menu, taking it from her to hand to the waiter, watching her glass to see when it emptied, draping his arm briefly over the back of her chair. She seemed as careless of it as she had always been.

Grey arrived when we were halfway through eating. Ingrid's face lit up, and Ralph looked at her and then at Grey, who was approaching from behind me, and back to Ingrid. He made as if to stand up and Grey motioned him down. 'No, no, don't get up.'

He kissed Ingrid quickly on the cheek and on the mouth, his hand on her shoulder, and then sat down next to me.

'I'm sorry to be running so late,' he said. 'I'd glad to see you've eaten, you're not starving.' A waiter appeared with a menu and he looked at it briefly then ordered, a complicated series of instructions.

He turned to me and shook my hand. 'It's good to meet you.' His smile was very charming. It was then that his name became really fixed for me — I could never think of him after that as Gil, as Ingrid called him, but only as Grey, as Maeve always referred to him, the colour I always saw him wearing and the colour of his serious eyes. He had fine-boned hands and the gentleness of his handshake surprised me.

He reached across and shook Ralph's hand. 'And Ralph. What a pleasure.' Ralph murmured a reply. 'What are you drinking? Let's have some wine.' He glanced at the wine list and ordered something as another waiter passed by.

Ralph looked on the verge of ordering a second martini but didn't. I wished for another one myself.

Ralph's little proprietary gestures towards Ingrid stopped. He met my eye only once for the rest of the evening and showed a mix of feelings — fear? Doubt? It was hard to tell.

Grey asked the appropriate questions about our flight and our hotel. 'How is it these days?' he asked, as though he were making enquiries about a mutual friend. I wasn't sure how to answer – to me it was an alien palace, another world of marble and gold edges from the New York places I had known in my time here before.

'I love it,' Ralph said. 'Great memories, you know.'

He had told me about staying at the hotel with his mother the one time he had been to the city before, when he was ten years old. Tea in the great dining room was a magical experience then, and he would look out onto the park for hours from their room, watching people making their way along the winding paths while his mother talked endlessly on the phone.

Grey had done some consulting work there, it turned out – 'Helping them find some actual art to put on the walls.' Whatever was hanging in our room was forgettable. When we arrived back there later I looked critically at the prints: sepia-toned images of flowers about to bud, gold frames against the thickly striped wallpaper.

I asked him whether Fleur was coming. 'I've heard so much about her.'

'She's out with some friends,' he said. 'Seeing some movie or other.' He smiled, raising his eyebrows in mock bewilderment. 'Something at the Antonioni retrospective downtown. *Blowup*?'

'I'm looking forward to seeing the show.'

'Excellent. Ingrid, you're going with them, yes? Later in the week?'

She nodded.

Grey seemed to know my aunt's work and asked me about her, and asked after Keith.

'We have a lot to thank Keith for,' he said, and met Ingrid's eyes. They shared a look, Ingrid's eyes wide and blue and in love.

There was an intimacy between them that it was more usual to see in couples who had been together for a longer time. It made Ingrid seem older, or brought out something more mature in her, as though she were doing her best to grow up for him. She was wearing a black dress that wrapped around and tied at the side, with a low V-neck and sleeves that came halfway down her arms like wings. It looked like angora. Her skin was golden against it, her hair dark gold as it fell in ropes over her shoulder.

'Do you need a cab?' Grey asked when we left and were standing on the pavement outside. A sharp wind had come up and the temperature had dropped.

I looked at Ralph. He said, 'Thanks, no, we're going to walk around a bit. Find somewhere to get a drink.'

Ingrid looked at him, hesitating. I wanted to ask her to come with us. I was about to, when Grey stepped out past me and hailed a cab. He put his hand on Ingrid's back and reached out the other to shake Ralph's hand – 'Again, a pleasure. See you again soon.' – and gave me a wave, a kind of salute.

Ingrid raised her hand, encased now in a fine, black, leather glove, and smiled at me, then grabbed my hand and embraced me quickly. 'See you soon. I'm so glad you're here.'

Grey shepherded her into the car. It waited for a few seconds before pulling out into the traffic. I watched them through the window – her hand reaching out to clasp his across the back seat, and then, swiftly, shockingly fast, the shape of him leaning across to kiss her, covering her body with his, hands disappearing into her hair and inside the red coat. I thought of that delicate hand of his, resting on her back, and saw the tension in it now, the desire to get her away, the desire. The car pulled out.

Ralph stood with his hands deep in the pockets of his dark brown overcoat, a long brown scarf knotted around his throat. He shivered.

'I'm freezing,' I said.

He gave a little smile with the corners of his mouth downturned.

'We're not really walking, are we?'

'No,' he said, 'of course not. Let's go and order something from room service. My sashimi tasted like nothing.'

We ordered hamburgers and ate in the big, dreamy living room back at the hotel with just one lamp for light. Ralph smoked and barely touched his food. The jet lag had killed my appetite and the food sat there mostly uneaten. We talked about Grey and Ingrid, trying to guess how old he was. Ralph said forty-five. He looked more like late thirties to me.

'Why isn't he involved with someone already?' Ralph kept asking. 'New York must be full of single women.'

He wasn't recently divorced; Ralph had found this out from Eve. Fleur's mother had died years before and he hadn't remarried. And Eve was sure that he hadn't been involved with Maeve, although she couldn't understand why. At that moment Maeve was carrying on some long, mysterious affair with an Italian tycoon who was still married but had been separated from his wife for at least two decades. 'It suits them all,' Eve would shrug.

According to Eve – according to Maeve – Grey was very dedicated to his daughter and to looking after her career. I asked Eve about it one day after lunch, while Ralph sat by looking morose, as though he'd heard it all before. It was a week after Ingrid had left for New York, a warm afternoon with the curtains all closed against the sun and the big French doors open onto the garden. Fleur's success was largely Grey's doing, his and Maeve's, Eve told me. He and Fleur had been living outside the city after his wife's death, in a small town on the Hudson filled with artists and antiques dealers. Fleur's mother had died from cancer, Eve thought, a swift and shocking kind of death, when Fleur was just a baby. Maeve was running a café with a gallery space with two other business partners in a building filled with artists' studio spaces. She and Grey struck up a friendship, and she was over at his house one day when she saw Fleur painting in the courtyard outside, the story went. Fleur painted for hours every day, outside on the flagstones of the yard in the summer and in a studio room inside when it was cold – big, colourful works on paper.

Grey had started buying better-quality paper for her by the time Maeve saw the paintings, but it was still basically those big sheets of construction paper that all kids paint on – they were having a hell of a time conserving those very early works now, Eve said – and Maeve knew when she saw them that she was seeing something special, something unusual. 'She saw that this girl had a kind of artistic vision that was more than what you would expect to find in a kid's finger painting. She had a sense of design, composition,' Eve said. 'Even then she was refining visual concepts, building on themes, expressing something – all with that kind of complete freedom from conventional form – all abstract, pure shape, pure colour, line ...' She stopped. 'They are very impressive pieces,' she said. 'Even those very early ones. I've seen them, at Maeve's gallery. You can see what she saw in them. But you can also see that it took Maeve's eye – she's so clever like that – to see that in them, to see what their real value and potential was.'

Maeve convinced Grey to show a few of Fleur's paintings at the café, and the response from viewers was extraordinary. 'Everyone wanted to know who this artist was – was it someone from town, was she showing someone from the city,' Eve said. At first they hadn't put up the pieces for sale, and then offers started coming in. There was a write-up in the local paper, and then a critic from the *New York Times* was there one day and saw the show, and that's when it really all exploded. A big collector from the area saw the paintings and wanted to buy them.

'For a while they weren't sure what to do,' Eve explained. 'Fleur was – four, five? I can't remember. I think she was a brilliant child, gifted artistically, obviously, but smart as well. They talked with her about it. It wasn't like they were taking her finger paintings away and seeing what they could get for them. She had some understanding of the process that was happening – she felt that if people liked looking at her paintings then they should be able to have them to look at. She could always paint more was how she looked at it. And she was so prolific – it's unbelievable, the consistency and quality and just the sheer amount of the art she produced in those years.'

The critic from the *Times* persuaded Grey to consider a larger show at a New York gallery. By then they had accepted offers from several collectors of well over ten thousand dollars each for some of Fleur's paintings – three of the works based around a red triangle that would become her most famous image.

'There's been some really nasty speculation about what happened to that money,' Eve said. 'But it went into a trust fund. It was a college fund. It makes sense when you think about it. You want to provide for your children however you can – you can't imagine what it costs to send a child to school over there – but there were a lot of people after that first New York show who said that Fleur was being exploited. I've met her,' – she raised her eyebrows at me – 'once, at Maeve's, and I don't believe for a second that that child was letting anyone push her around, even in kindergarten.'

Maeve went into partnership with the New York gallery, one of the first to make a name for itself over on the Chelsea side, and moved to the city. She became a kind of surrogate mother to Fleur, Eve told us – she never had children of her own – and was involved in decisions not only about Fleur's career as an artist but also about her life, her schools, her activities. Grey kept the house on the Hudson but bought an apartment in Manhattan as well, and Fleur started school there. By the time of her next show, when she was almost seven, she was an art-world sensation. Fleur stayed with the gallery. Maeve took it over, with Grey as a kind of silent partner or consultant as he built his own art-dealing enterprise.

'So, together they engineered her career,' Ralph said drily. 'A real team effort.'

'Well, she lasted the distance,' Eve said. 'She's still painting.'

Ralph looked at me. 'She's maintained a reputation, that's true. So has Maeve. And Grey – he made quite a career for himself out of it all as well.'

Eve watched him, her eyes shrewd.

'But you like him, don't you, Eve?' I asked.

'I can't say I know him all that well,' she said. 'But – yes – he's a brilliant man. And has amazingly good taste.'

Realising that this was the highest form of praise, Ralph seemed to give up. 'Yes, he does,' he said, 'obviously.' He set his glass down firmly on the table.

We saw Fleur's show at the Whitney with Ingrid a couple of days after the Japanese dinner. It was cold on the street outside the big concrete building but Ralph insisted on waiting for her out there. I went inside to look at the books on display in the foyer. They came in together ten minutes later, Ingrid in her red coat and hat and a long black skirt, pulling her gloves off her fingers one by one. She looked taller than ever, although her boots this time were almost flat. Her cheek was cold when she pressed her face against mine and I caught the faint scent of Fracas against the metallic smell of the winter air and Ingrid's usual smell that always made me think of tea and crushed grass. I wondered how much time she was spending at Maeve's.

We caught the lift up to the second floor where the show was hanging. The early finger paintings were there, framed behind glass, painted on long rolls of paper that stretched out, some of them for metres. The later paintings were on canvas, some in oils but mostly acrylic, large square canvases in strokes of bold colour. Although my aunt painted abstracts and I liked her work, I didn't like much other abstract art or know much about it. There seemed to be a lot of feeling in these square, spare images – handprints and fingermarks combined with heavy brushstrokes. In some the outline of letters, numbers, seemed to appear and then blur into something else.

'They seem ... angry,' I said to Ingrid, when she had finished talking in front of one of them. I hadn't been listening. But I looked at them again, and at the next series on the other wall, all purple lines drifting off into a white world, and I wasn't so sure. 'Some of them,' I said.

Ralph stared at the floor.

'She's the sweetest girl,' Ingrid said, turning around to look back at the wall next to us, and smiled a secret-looking smile.

Ingrid wanted to walk around the park after that – 'It's enormous. Julia, I had no idea how big it was. And so beautiful, even in the winter. I'd love to see it with snow ...'

She left with Ralph. Steam rose from manholes in the street, cloudy towers that dissipated as they rose and smelled faintly of rot, like the subway.

We met up again that night at Maeve's for dinner. She lived in a loft space over on the far West Side, close to the Meatpacking district with its blocks of butchers' warehouses butting up against designer shops and expensive brunch restaurants. Ralph and I walked into one huge room containing kitchen, living and dining spaces, big and white with polished concrete floors and windows that looked south. A long black table ran along one wall, and that was the first thing I saw. We had gone shopping together the day before – I had insisted on buying things for myself, although he wanted to pay for everything – and when we got back to the hotel he'd presented me with a bag I had decided against as being too expensive. I held it now, the softest leather with a trim along the edge of silver tweed, and wore the dress I had bought for myself: floating black silk with ruching on the front like a smock.

Maeve was wearing that duck's neck greenish black that I remembered from the first time we met. Tiny sequins glittered around her sleeves. Ingrid was already there, seated in a black armchair. Grey stood at her side, one arm resting on the back of the chair, looking as though they were posed for a portrait. She tilted her head up to look at him, showing her finely shaped profile. She stayed there when we came in, and it was Grey who came forward and shook Ralph's hand. Another couple was there as well, an artist and his wife. Fleur was supposed to be coming but she hadn't arrived yet.

For some reason the jet lag had hit me hard that day and all I could think about was getting through to the end of the night and lying down to sleep, knowing that when I did I would stay awake until three, listening to the faint hiss of the heating pipes.

The kitchen looked as though it was used only occasionally. Copper pans hung, gleaming, from a metal rack suspended over the stove. The refrigerator was shiny and black and I caught sight of a photograph stuck to the side of it with a magnet. It showed Maeve standing with a young girl.

They were in a large room filled with people, dimly visible in the background, while the faces of Maeve and the girl were brightly lit by the flash. It looked like a recent photo of Maeve. Her hair was pulled back, and her lips shone with gloss. The girl had an elfin face, hair pushed back behind her ears, and smiled warily at the photographer, an almost ironic expression. The pose suggested a photograph of a mother and daughter, but there was very little resemblance between the faces. The girl's face was familiar, but it was the contours of Grey's features that I saw there.

Maeve stood next to me, holding my coat, and followed my eyes. 'That's Fleur,' she said, as though explaining something obvious to a slow-witted person.

It soon became clear that Grey was courting the artist in some way. He had just moved to the city not that long before – he was English, and his wife German, or Swedish, a name I forgot as soon as she said it. He was showing at Maeve's gallery and was looking for a new dealer. I followed their conversation loosely.

Ingrid had a kind of languid air that I assumed came from long nights of passion, thinking of the kiss I had seen through the cab window. She seemed tired and I saw her covering yawns with the back of her hand. Grey looked at his watch and went to another room to use the phone. He came back looking dissatisfied. When the phone rang a few minutes later he shot Maeve a quick look and she almost hurried to answer it. She was gone for a couple of minutes – her voice came through, muffled, from the other room. It sounded like an argument; her contributions were alternately firm and cajoling. She came back in and nodded to Grey, and he went to the phone and was gone a while. He closed the door and talked quietly so we didn't hear any of the conversation.

He came back and stood next to Ingrid again. 'Fleur won't be joining us tonight. Sorry to disappoint.' He gave a quick smile to me and Ralph and his voice betrayed only a small hint of frustration.

The English artist seemed let down. Now the expression that Maeve had worn when she came in from the phone call made more sense; she had looked just like an exasperated parent fighting with their child, and the pieces of the exchange we had overheard sounded like that too. She was busy in the kitchen now, opening wine. Ingrid's face showed concern and she seemed about to ask Grey about his conversation with Fleur, but he looked away from her and started talking to the artist again. The food arrived from a local restaurant – the best modern French in the neighbourhood according to the artist's wife – and the man who delivered it stayed and arranged it all on the table for us.

It was a little while after that, just before we sat down at dinner, that I saw the look that passed between Maeve and Grey. I sometimes wonder if I hadn't seen that look whether I might have come to like him or trust him more. I only saw it the once. Most of the time in Ingrid's presence he and Maeve didn't look at each other much at all, even when talking; their glances slid away, quicksilver. Ingrid had risen to go to the bathroom. Her hair was falling down from its knot. She wore a short dress in a dirty purplish-blue, legs long in black stockings, and her hips twisted, rose and fell with her steps. Grey was watching her too, and then his eyes met Maeve's and I could see that she had been watching him look at Ingrid. They didn't actually nod at each other; they didn't need to. It was conspiratorial in a quiet, understated way. Maeve's eyes showed triumph – it reminded me of Eve, pleased with herself after she'd brought Ingrid back from Perth, displaying her to us. It was just as though Maeve had handed Grey a gift, and had been waiting for him to accept it. Grey seemed to be indicating his approval, his gratitude and a kind of pride in his own achievement.

It shouldn't have been strange, in a way; it was partly through Maeve, after all, that they knew each other. It was through her that the connection between them was consolidated by networks of acquaintance. It was natural, wasn't it, for Grey to feel grateful to Maeve for helping to bring a woman like Ingrid into his life, and to feel pleased with himself, I asked myself later when the memory of the look sat with me in the early hours. And in that sense of appreciation the look could have been more open – but there was something in it that couldn't have been spoken, an intimacy that was shocking in its depth and nakedness, in the same way I'd been shocked by the heat and speed of sexual passion that I'd seen when I'd glanced through the taxi window.

I seemed to understand then that if they ever had been lovers, Maeve and Grey, it was long in the past, and whatever it was that bound them now was more lasting and more complicated. It was a quick, silent look, and then Ingrid had left the room and Maeve looked over at the passageway Ingrid had just walked through, and Grey turned his eyes the other way, where they met mine and held my gaze for a long second without changing. He seemed to know that I'd seen the look, and calculated that it didn't matter, whatever I had made of it.

I broke the gaze and stood up, too quickly, almost knocking over my tall-stemmed glass. It shivered and rocked for a second before I picked it up. The others were all moving towards the table. Grey stood and waited for Ingrid, and when she reappeared he put his hand on her back, just as he had outside the restaurant, and guided her towards the table. It was a stiffer gesture than the one the other night, more expressive of control.

It was warm in the big, open room but I couldn't shake the chill that had entered me. The food was rich and delicious – plenty of roasted duck and buttery vegetables. Ingrid ate with her usual good appetite, more lively now, one hand always under the table on the side next to Grey, resting on his leg. This was how she had never acted with any of her admirers in Sydney; this was how I would have imagined her looking in love, right down to the slightly worshipful way she regarded Grey, ecstatically glad of his attention and approval.

At the end of the meal we stayed sitting at the table, drinking wine and picking at the remains of a flourless chocolate cake. The artist's wife glanced towards the window, and said, 'Look. It's snowing.' We all looked. Tiny flakes were drifting down, illuminated by the streetlights.

Ingrid's eyes were alive with excitement. 'Quickly,' she said, 'let's go down.'

She and Ralph were downstairs and out the door in seconds. I followed, struggling to pull on my coat. Ingrid turned her face up, eyes squeezed shut, and let the snow fall on her skin. The flakes stayed for a second on my hand, then melted to water. It was just the three of us down there, and for a moment it had the feeling of us being the children sent out to play while the adults stayed inside to talk. The snow fell more heavily. It wasn't cold enough for it to stick to the ground and it disappeared on the concrete path.

I left them together on the footpath, absorbed in a snowflake that had come to rest on Ralph's sleeve; back inside, all the others were gathered around the big windows looking out. I wondered why Grey didn't go down to Ingrid. She and Ralph came back up a few minutes later. The evening was over.

New Year's Eve was only a couple of days away. Ralph and I hadn't made it very far when we had talked about plans for what to do with ourselves but we had assumed that Ingrid would be part of it. So we were both surprised, and Ralph was visibly hurt, when she told us at the end of that dinner, just after they had come back in from the snow, that she was going to join Grey up at his place on the Hudson.

'He always spends New Year there,' she said to us. 'And we want to spend it together – and I want to see the house. So we're driving up tomorrow. It'll be for a few days. I'll see you when I get back.'

Ralph was silent and mutinous-looking.

'Well – I think it's really romantic,' I said.

'Yes,' she said with relief. 'Exactly, right.'

Ralph looked disappointed in me, and sighed, and then seemed to come around. 'We'll drink a toast to you,' he said, and kissed her cheek. 'Several.'

We said our goodbyes and went downstairs with the

English artist and his wife, who were walking home the other way. The street was quiet; a few busy cabs drove by and we walked a block or two until we found one to take us back to the hotel. It drove fast up the long, straight avenue. The snow was still falling, a white fuzz on our coats that disappeared as soon as we were inside the car.

Ralph was grumpy and unsettled. 'He's a cold fish,' he said, and played with his packet of cigarettes.

I thought of the decidedly hot kiss I'd seen between Grey and Ingrid in the cab.

'I don't mean –' Ralph started, and looked at me. 'I mean, emotionally. He's cold. Like Maeve.'

He put the cigarettes away in his pocket.

'I don't like the way he looks at her,' he said.

The look between Grey and Maeve was still with me, and the way that Grey had held my eye afterwards, indifferent.

I agreed. 'But did you see how she was looking at him?'

Ralph gave a little snort. 'What did you call it? Romantic?'

'It is romantic!'

I wanted somehow to be happy for Ingrid, to join in with her own clear happiness. I remembered Ralph's dismissal of the affair before we had left Sydney – 'He lives in New York, what's going to happen?' – and I thought of those two sets of looks, Grey's and Maeve's, and Ingrid's gaze at Grey, and felt a stirring of unease.

'She's really in love,' I said in wonder.

It hadn't meant to sound so sad, but Ralph nodded slowly and cast his eyes down with an expression of sorrow and resistance as though I had made the most tragic of pronouncements.

8.

We found a party to go to on New Year's Eve and got drunk on cheap sparkling wine at a tiny apartment in the East Village decorated with orange paper lanterns. Overcrowded little rooms – a blur of faces – Ralph's good suit rumpled the second we walked in the door – his kiss, hard and fast and passionless, at midnight in that second before the whole place went up in a roar. The rest of our time in New York was more shopping and days spent walking around Chinatown and the Lower East Side, eating enormous sandwiches piled with pastrami in the Jewish delis down there and working our way around all the bars in Ralph's guidebook. He made me go to the opera, *La Bohème*, and I surprised myself by loving it and crying all the way through – he smiled at me knowingly and settled far down into his chair – but I refused to go to the ballet and ate room service food instead.

I was falling asleep in front of the television when Ralph called from the bar downstairs. 'Come down,' he said. 'Ingrid's here.' We hadn't seen her since the dinner at Maeve's over a week before.

She was red-cheeked from the cold, some kind of dark red, velvet cloak on the seat beside her, and she and Ralph couldn't stop talking about how good the dancing had been. We drank Kir Royales, one after another, and there was happiness in Ralph's face as he looked at her. We didn't talk about Grey at all.

I grew tired after an hour or so and went up to bed, but for some reason I couldn't help myself before I left. 'How's Grey?' I asked her. Something slithered down inside me, a feeling as though I were pushing a pin into Ralph's arm, and disappointment in myself for doing it.

'Gil,' she said, smiling up at me. 'He's great. We had a really great New Year's.' Her eyes were warm. 'Goodnight! Sleep well!' And then she turned back to Ralph and picked up the conversation right where it had been before.

He flicked his eyes towards me. 'See you in a little bit,' he said.

He was there in the morning, heavily asleep in the second bed. I went out before he woke and spent all day in the Metropolitan Museum, getting lost over and over again, alone. Paintings, golden frames, bronze, stitched leather seats, acres of canvas and marble and wood. By the end of the afternoon I was wandering around the Arms and Armor section and found myself facing the four towering armoured warhorses for the third time after taking the wrong turn.

Tears of exhaustion started in my eyes and sat there. The room was filled with pale, wintery light from the skylights. I looked down at my map and turned it over in my hands and tried once more to plot a way from this room to the front entrance. The shape of the room didn't seem to conform to its image on the paper. I became aware then of eyes on me, and looked up just as a man on the other side of the nearest horse turned his head away. A few seconds later he was next to me, looking at the map I was holding.

'Do you mind?' he asked. I handed it to him. He studied it unconvincingly. 'Where are you headed?' His voice was English, low and neutral.

'I'm leaving. I'm looking for the exit,' I said. He nodded, slowly. The entire scene struck me as being very Victorian and ridiculous – damsel in distress, chivalrous knight. I waited for him to offer me a folded handkerchief.

He pushed his hair out of the way. It fell straight back into his eyes, the colour of wet sand with light blond strands. He looked as though he was struggling not to smile. The room seemed to empty itself of people as we stopped there.

He studied the horse in front of us carefully. It stood there, massive, not alive, one foot raised, prepared to charge into battle. Was it a real horse, I wondered, dead and stuffed, or a model they had made? A woman next to me was trying to restrain a small child from climbing up next to it.

'I'm going this way, if that's the way you're going,' he said. He looked down at the map and touched his finger to the room we were in, and pointed out through one of the doorways.

'Thanks.' I took back the map and held on to it. He paused, and I thought he was going to comment on my accent, but he didn't. Beside us the child – a little boy – was victorious and clung to the horse's hind leg, his face firm, exultant, as the woman tried to drag him back down.

We walked together in silence through several more rooms – medieval screens painted with weeping saints, sets of decorated china behind glass – and came to halls filled with classical statuary and Roman glass and coins.

'I'll leave you here,' he said, stopping beside a statue. It was a man – or a god, I couldn't tell – spearing a stag that lay fallen beside him. He looked straight at me for the first time. 'I mean, I'm stopping here. If you're going out, it's that way.' He pointed ahead. 'Or you can stay here and enjoy the wonders of Roman art.' He smiled ironically. His eyes were hazel green with fractured shards of brown.

He was being kind to me, but I had the uncomfortable sense of my embarrassment being a source of interest. It felt curiously like cruelty. I drew myself up to my full height – I was almost as tall as he was, but he remained slightly slouched. His eyes travelled swiftly over me, and then he turned back to examine the statue, and there was a small black notebook in his hand.

'Well, thanks again,' I said.

'Oh, it's all my pleasure,' he said, with a quick sideways glance at me.

The front entrance was just around the end of the hall, less than a minute away. The long, long set of stairs led down to the street, where vendors were selling pretzels and hotdogs from their carts. I bought myself a bagel and a grey coffee in a paper cup and walked for blocks in the cold to the subway, feet aching and my heart an oddly unfamiliar-feeling pressure in my chest.

The meeting in the museum disturbed me more than I realised at the time and I reflected on it often in the weeks after it happened: the intensity of my embarrassment, my attraction to him that might or might not have been returned. I tried to describe it to Ralph a day or so afterwards, but it was hard to explain the acuteness and singularity of it.

Instead it came out sounding clichéd, like the chivalrous scene it had briefly conjured up for me at the time.

Ralph made fun of me. 'You were too embarrassed to ask him for his phone number? That's not like you,' he said.

'Yes, it is,' I told him.

He chided me. 'Of course he liked you. I'm sure he fell madly in love with you.'

'Right.'

'You never know. And you don't know his name. The mysterious stranger. Now *that's* romantic.'

But it wasn't, somehow. It made me feel uneasy. His nameless face stayed with me, handsome and amused.

Ingrid agreed to come to Paris with us after all – she had decided that she had to see the Louvre – and was planning to go on to London with Grey after that. Her taking this time to spend with Ralph and I seemed in a way calculated to show that she wasn't enslaved to this new relationship; for Ralph especially it was an important signal that he still mattered to her. He seized on it with a desperate gratitude that he kept well hidden from Ingrid, pretending to her that he was simply pleased, and wouldn't have minded either way. But there was a triumphant shine in his eye, a confident straightening of his shoulders that extended into a hint of a swagger for days after the decision. Ingrid booked her own room in the same hotel we were staying at, an old building near the Jardin du Luxembourg enclosing a square courtyard. Her room ended up being across the courtyard from us, one floor below. The city was blue with cold, a frosting of snow on the old slate roofs when we arrived. Our room was really a series of rooms, all straight in a row with a bathroom at each end, then a bedroom next to that, and a long sitting room in the middle. 'It's like a palindrome,' Ralph said. The walls seemed to be papered in the same thick golden stripes as the Plaza, but the whole thing was on a smaller scale. Each room opened onto a balcony that ran the length of the apartment, little pedestals forming a railing. It was just wide enough to stand on, no room for tables or chairs, no plants. Our beds were covered with golden chenille bedspreads. Everything smelled a little like paint but none of the paint seemed to be particularly new.

I woke early the next morning and had breakfast sent up and stood with my coffee, wearing my coat and pyjamas, on the balcony. The sky grew bluer from its pale purple dawn colour. Ingrid appeared on her balcony across the way, a huge white bathrobe wrapped around her and her hair wet. She shivered and turned around to go back inside; I waved, and she saw me and smiled and pulled her robe tighter. 'Come over!' she called.

I wrote a note for Ralph on the hotel stationery on the desk in the sitting room − neat brown type and a little picture of the hotel that looked as though it had been traced by a child − and pushed it half under his closed bedroom door.

When I knocked on Ingrid's door she was still wearing the robe and white pyjamas. There was a tray on the table behind her filled with coffee and bread and pastries. Her apartment was just like ours would be if it were cut in half down the middle. Through the glass doors the sun was striking the opposite wall of balconies.

Ingrid pulled her fingers through her wet hair, easing out tangles. She sat at the table and started spreading butter on a croissant.

'Isn't this beautiful?' she asked, her mouth full.

I agreed, and poured coffee.

'Is your room gorgeous like this one too?'

I nodded again. I felt her eyes narrow on me. 'Except it's bigger,' I said. 'It's like this times two.' I spread out both my hands.

She nodded and seemed satisfied. I wondered if she was curious about our sleeping arrangements. She sipped her coffee and looked out at the balcony.

The coffee table next to us held a stack of several guidebooks and one hefty-looking art book, all of them marked with sticky notes. She noticed me looking at them.

'Oh,' she said. 'There's so much to see here in Paris. I thought we could start with the Louvre today?'

'OK,' I said. 'That sounds good.'

Ingrid's schedule was gruelling. I went with her for the first three days – the Louvre for the first two, Notre Dame and other sights in the Ile de la Cité the next – and by the fourth day was exhausted. It wasn't the sheer number of places she wanted to see; it was that she regarded her sightseeing as a serious educational experience and went about it with a kind of intensity that depressed me, despite her real pleasure in what she saw. Ralph came with us to the Louvre and stayed only long enough to see the *Mona Lisa*. We made our way together through the crowd to look at the painting behind its thick glass shield but after that he disappeared. He was back at the hotel that afternoon when I came back, reading *The Little Prince*, in English, with his feet up on the coffee table. He peered at me over his glasses.

'Don't let her drag you around the whole time to all these museums,' he said.

'Oh, I want to see them too,' I said, faintly.

He smirked at me. 'It's all Grey's doing. This European tour he's got planned out for her.'

I frowned. 'She was like this about Rome too.'

'Well, he's really brought it out in her.'

'Is she proving something to him, do you think?'

He closed his book. 'He's given her a bunch of places to tick off her list here before they go on their educational tour of London. There's restaurants too. That should be worth something at least. I'd like to eat at that one where Sartre used to always hang out.' His finger was still marking his place. 'Let's go there tonight.'

I had seen the notes in the eating sections of Ingrid's guidebooks. 'Actually I think she had somewhere else in mind.'

'Alright.' He settled into his chair and opened the book again. 'I'll call her in a little while.'

In Ralph's room, visible through the half-closed door, a bottle of whisky stood on the nightstand, half-empty. He was holding a glass of it as well. He didn't seem drunk. That was more worrying in a way, and made me wonder if he was drinking more than I realised on a regular basis.

He called Ingrid from the old-fashioned phone with its heavy, black handpiece. I wanted to take it home with me but couldn't quite see how it was going to work. In my bag was a cord from our room at the Plaza, a twisted golden rope with a tassel at either end that was used to tie the curtains back. That had been an easy one. He leaned back, standing against the wall, smiling and nodding and laughing a quiet laugh. He was wearing new shoes that he had bought in New York, brown leather brogues, and he looked down at them, bringing his feet together.

'Alright. See you shortly.'

He hung up and sat back down.

Things were easier between the three of us there in Paris than they had been in New York. It might have been a holiday that we had planned all together from the start. It was easier to forget that Grey was part of the picture, or to imagine that he wasn't, or to just leave him out of the conversation. I knew Ingrid talked to him every night or so but she didn't talk about him much. His name wasn't taboo as it had been in New York though; she dropped the occasional reference to a wine he particularly liked when we were eating out and choosing something to drink, or a highly regarded artwork that he personally despised and that we had seen at a museum that day. Ralph tended to roll his eyes a little at these statements about Grey's good taste.

I called Ingrid on the fourth morning to say I didn't want to go out to Versailles. She was happy to go alone. I imagined her taking careful notes on the train on the way back.

Ralph came out of his room as we said goodbye. 'So what do you want to do today?' I asked him. He smiled and rubbed his head, creating even more of a mess on the side where his hair was untidy from sleep. 'Pas de Versailles?'

'Non.' I had made virtually no effort to learn any French, relying on Ralph's fluency with the language and Ingrid's passable knowledge.

He said something else incomprehensible in French and smiled. The sun shone weakly outside through a thin layer of cloud.

He sat down in one of the armchairs and stretched his arms above his head. 'Well,' he said, 'let's go to that place on the corner down the street for coffee and something to eat. I'm trying to figure out how to ask for the number of the guy who makes the coffee.'

'Ooh la la.'

'That's right!' He laughed. 'One hopes.'

The coffee guy remained aloof and inscrutable, his back turned to us the whole time we were there, dedicated to the espresso machine. After dawdling for a long time over our coffee and croissants – and croque monsieur, croque madame, more coffee – Ralph left the hotel number on the back of the bill and we went on the Métro to look for the house Voltaire had lived in. We came up from the subway to find the day changed, the sky low with clouds and puddles already on the ground from light rain. We walked down a steep hill past short, narrow streets, around corners, up another hill.

'Shit,' said Ralph. 'I thought it was around here.'

'You don't know where it is?'

He shrugged. 'I didn't bring the guidebook. I thought I'd remember from reading it this morning …' He felt through his pockets and pulled out his copy of *The Little Prince.* 'But we have Saint-Exupéry!'

'Well, are we in the right area? Won't it have a plaque? Won't there be signs?'

'Maybe.'

We kept walking. It became clear that we had come out of the Metro at the wrong station and probably on the wrong line. We came to a short cobbled laneway running off to our right; Ralph squinted down it. 'I think I see a plaque down there on a house.' We walked towards it. The house was covered in yellow stucco and I couldn't tell how old it was. The cobblestones on the street looked ancient but the concrete under our feet on the narrow path was relatively new, covered in dog shit and gum stains. One sodden woollen glove lay in the wet gutter. Ralph read the plaque and told me that Henry Miller had lived there. We looked at the house. There was no sign of whoever lived there now. I pictured Henry Miller sitting at a table in a badly lit room, pen in hand, some woman or other sitting on his lap, glass in his other hand.

'I don't think I even like Henry Miller,' Ralph said.

'Me neither.'

The alley was a dead end. We walked back the way we had come and looked for somewhere to escape the drizzling rain.

When we got back to the hotel it was dark. We opened the door to find Ingrid in our room, sitting with her feet up on the sofa reading a novel. She put it down when we entered. I wondered how she had found her way inside. She was happy to see us.

'We went to Henry Miller's house,' Ralph said.

She tilted her head to the side a little.

'Is he a friend …?'

'No, no, a writer. A writer. And not Voltaire's house …'

'Oh, Voltaire's house! I would love to see that. Wait – did you go there – could we go tomorrow, after the d'Orsay – where were you, again?'

Ralph and Ingrid talked on, making plans. Ralph had admired the wineglasses at the bar we stopped at after Henry Miller's house, and I'd slid one into my bag before we left. When we entered our room I had reached for it, to show him, and my hand was still in there, inside the bag, fingers around the glass with its dark green, slippery stem, as I listened.

9.

Back in Sydney the three of us seemed to come apart so quickly, from those evenings in the hotel to the hot, long days of January and February where we hardly saw each other all together. Our schedules were all different that semester. The one exception was a film class I was taking with Ralph, which he rarely attended. The months passed slowly. Ingrid and Ralph came to visit on separate nights at the video store.

Ingrid drove me around in her BMW every now and again, long drives where she explored the city and the Saturday markets in every neighbourhood. She was in her honours year. I was taking longer, going part-time so I could work more hours at the bookstore, a job I had come to enjoy more than the hours I spent studying. On the drives she would tell me about her coursework and her thesis, on British appropriations of Roman divinities. I half-listened.

During the break she went back overseas to see Grey and came back engaged. She told me about it over at Kirribilli the weekend after she returned to Sydney. It was a cold July winter, rivers of rain streaming down the streets. Ralph was not around.

She wore an enormous diamond on her finger, emerald-cut in a long oblong shape. White-gold claws on each side held the stone in place. She explained to me that it had been Grey's mother's ring. It wasn't clear whether it had also belonged to his first wife. Marrying was the only way to make it possible for her to move there, to New York, and live with him, she explained, which was what she wanted more than anything. We were sitting on her bed like we had those months ago, with tea. She was wearing a mustard-coloured cardigan with sleeves too long for her. It should have given her a childish look but instead, as she folded the cuffs and pushed them up to her elbows, she looked older.

'And, it's what we both want,' she said. 'Well, you know,' – emphasising *you* – 'I love him.' She still had that look she had worn in New York when she and Grey were together: unmistakably in love, and a proud, determined set to her face.

I held her fingers – short fingers, hands squarish but pretty – and looked at the ring. The stone was so large it looked as though it would weigh down her hand. Little rainbows glinted from its facets like light from a crystal chandelier.

'He's so much older than you,' I said after I'd congratulated her. My feelings towards Grey had hardened over the months. At first I'd wanted to think well of him but that hadn't lasted. The memory of his shared look with Maeve was too strong. I never spoke to Ralph about the look. He hated Grey enough already, just as he had from the beginning.

'Oh, he doesn't mind that I'm so young,' she said. And it was clear that from her perspective he was the one bringing everything to the marriage that was really valuable: wisdom, experience, knowledge.

'Is Ralph coming?' I asked as we went downstairs.

'Isn't he?' She half-turned back to look at me. 'I thought you would know.'

We ate without him, Eve at the head of the table, and he showed up as I was finishing my coffee and getting ready to go. Ingrid stood there in the doorway into the living room, ready to receive him.

'Stay, won't you?' he said.

It was one of the last times that we were all together in one place. I left.

My aunt was making dinner for me that night. The rain drummed softly on the tin roof at her house and the kitchen was filled with the smell of tomatoes roasting in the oven. Keith was there, drinking wine with her in her studio. I told them the news of Ingrid's engagement.

'She's so young to be getting married,' Jenny said. 'But they're very happy together, aren't they?'

Keith looked at the floor.

'You introduced them, Keith, didn't you?' I said.

'Yes, yes. In Venice. Of course. Well, that's wonderful news.'

'They should invite you to the wedding,' Jenny said to Keith.

He glanced at me. His intelligent eyes looked guilty now, and serious, and for a second it seemed as though he was about to apologise for something. Then he smiled, and let my aunt tease him about being a matchmaker. They joked about finding collector husbands for all her artist friends. You don't like him either, I thought.

*

The time with Ralph and then with Ingrid seems so short when I look back on it now – the time when things were good, just beginning, the dynamic I seemed to spend forever trying to recapture and recreate afterwards. It was short in terms of the actual days, weeks and months involved. There weren't many, compared with how many there have been since then. But those months were so full of what felt like then, and looks like now, an almost perfect kind of intimacy and intensity that makes that time extend outwards artificially in the track of memory: technicolour, oversaturated with detail, compared with the dimmer pasts that surround it.

It was all very ordinary in a way, apart from our luxurious weeks in New York and Paris: in Sydney we went to class together and separately, and read our books and talked about them. There was some lounging around on the green lawn out the front of the sandstone quad and sitting under the shade of the jacaranda tree – a few of those conventional scenes of university romance – but it was mostly drinking together at the bar, finding each other at messy parties, recovering afterwards in late mornings, talking late at night, at home, at the video store, on the phone. Eve and George ignored each other frostily, but they welcomed me into the house, and compared with my own unpredictable, fractured childhood family experience it was a haven of stable, caring relationships. I loved the sense of discontinuity between the frantic, late-night urban world we moved through – winding inner-city streets strewn with garbage and seedy interiors and neon light – and the high-class opulence of Ralph's house at Kirribilli, the lamplight and soft carpet and good wine, the aristocratic kind of wealth of the North Shore. So many Sundays we wound up there for lunch, crystal glasses laid out for us, so hungover or strung out after all night up on beer and cocktails and badly cut drugs, feet sore from staggering down city blocks and narrow staircases, and I would sink into the big leather sofa in their living room as though it were a hot bath, listening to Ralph's father quoting Macbeth or Churchill and tuning the radio to the classical station.

And Ralph was my key between these places: he knew the dealers who sold the badly cut and well-cut drugs in tiny plastic bags, he knew the places open latest, down tiny laneways, where you could still get a drink after hours. He led me to the beautiful house across the harbour, and took me out to the theatre at the Opera House on the family season ticket when his mother couldn't make it, and knew the ferry as a way of getting around the city better than the rail line. Half the time at Kirribilli I expected him to disappear upstairs in his old jeans and corduroy jacket and reappear dressed for dinner in a tuxedo suit, descending the stairs like a figure from a 1930s film, completing the transition from low to high, depraved to refined.

Doing anything from the depraved range of our behaviour in that house seemed to make it at once more sordid and more sophisticated, full of audacious, gritty glamour: cocaine cut with a London postcard on a large, heavy book of Monet's landscapes in the upstairs bathroom, all gold taps and black tiles, while his mother set the table with all their silver; sneaking a bottle of good merlot into the garden and sitting out there smoking cigarettes and marijuana and drinking the wine from translucent china teacups. If we could have filled out the picture with covert, half-clothed sex in the black-tiled bathroom I think my happiness would have been complete, but it never came to that. Quite a few times I thought it would – his trembling hand against mine, closing the door behind us; other moments of unbearable proximity and almost-contact.

I suppose that feeling of remembered intensity is made keener by that sense of unrequited longing that suffused everything in those first months with Ralph, despair-inducing at first, and then fading to a background hum. He annoyed me, I adored him, I teased him, we had petty arguments and ones that seemed big but were really abstract and absurd, about whether George Eliot was better than T. S. Eliot, and were old movies better than ones now. We just seemed to love each other instantly, though evidently not in the same way. It usually took me longer to like someone, although he made friendships quickly and with ease. And then when Ingrid came along he loved her instantly, and I liked her too after my initial mistrust. That affection was fraught with ambivalence but there was a kind of harmony between us that still seems musical and beautiful when I remember it, even when I can see the notes of discord that made it often shot through with sadness and envy. A little operetta.

Those weeks and months weren't long but when it all fell apart I held a commitment to them and a flagging belief that something of the friendship between all of us could be resurrected. My faint struggle to achieve this lasted much longer in the end than that first happy time ever had. Right towards the end of the process, in the weeks before Ingrid left Sydney at the end of the year to marry Grey, I began to calculate it in those terms, and the act of calculation itself signalled that it was really finished.

I was living at my aunt's by then – I moved there just before Ingrid left. The lease came up on the Newtown house and my housemate, Leah, was leaving to move into a flat in Petersham with her boyfriend. Jenny offered one night when we went to see a film together.

'You don't talk about Ralph much anymore,' she said when we were waiting to buy our popcorn and soft drinks.

She had always liked Ralph, but had told me a couple of times that she was concerned about the extent of my feelings for him. They were awkward conversations that never failed to make me feel like a walking cliché: woman in love with gay best friend. 'I see other people,' I told her in response at those times, defensively.

'I'm not going to set you up on a blind date,' she would say, 'although I'd love to. But if you could start seeing people that you actually liked it would make me a lot happier.'

When Ingrid was still around those conversations were even sharper. 'You're a little in love with her too,' she said once, shocking me, when things were just starting to go onto the rocks.

'I'm not,' I had said, overcome by surprise that this would be her criticism of Ingrid; I'd expected her to say something else, that my friendship with Ingrid existed just to bring me closer to Ralph. Both possibilities, seemingly impossible to reconcile, made me so uncomfortable that I supposed there must be some truth in them.

The machine went on pouring popcorn and a hand reached in to scoop some up into a paper bucket. Jenny didn't sound as happy to hear less about Ralph as I thought she would be. I changed the subject by telling her about the end of the lease.

'There's room in my house for you,' she said, easily. 'It would be a break for you from paying rent. That would be good this year, with your studies, no? Less need to work. And I'll stay out of your way.'

I thought about it over the course of the movie and said yes to her at the end. I knew it signalled some kind of end of an era. Kirribilli was practically closed to me now. I'd hardly been there in the past three months, and Ralph fought with Eve or picked fights with me whenever I visited. No more surreptitious drug-taking in the bathroom, only extended drinking at the table. My aunt's house wasn't that far away from Kirribilli − it was in another North Shore suburb, looking out onto another part of the water that surrounded the city, a long walk from the same ferry line.

There was something soothing and alienating all at once about the anodyne upper-middle-class blandness of the neighbourhood. I wanted a break from the inner city, all the places there that were now wrapped up with exhausted friendships. It was a long drive over to campus, but I liked that, and crossing over the bridge on the way back to the house was a relief. Jenny's overgrown garden met me at the gate when I arrived, tendrils of flowering vines pushing their way through the wood and metal hinges, and I would snap them off, or pull them through and wrap them around the fence.

The house had always been a kind of sanctuary for me and Peter. When we were little we would stay there every other weekend, both in a room towards the back of the house with two creaky single beds in it. The fibro walls were still covered in patches with the stickers we had stuck there, faded blue Smurfs and animals, glittery ice-cream cones, BMX bikes, rainbows that ended in a starry cloud. There was a bookshelf too, stocked with paperback classics and old books from Jenny's childhood – boarding school adventures, horse stories – that I worked my way through. Even then, Peter was obsessed with medicine and science and gravitated towards the lower shelf, which held an incomplete set of the *Encyclopaedia Britannica* and a huge anatomy text, its thin, slippery pages covered with terrifying illustrations of the body's interior, secret places. In there he found a world that was knowable, bounded, that could be mapped and mastered, an antidote to the uncertainty we lived with at home.

Every once in a while Jenny would let us sit in the studio while she painted, and those were the most magical times. It was always at the end of the afternoon, with hot, late sunlight in the room, and she would talk to us while she worked, priming a canvas or finishing the corner of a painting. Most of the time the door to the studio was closed while she painted and she didn't mind us being noisy or watching television, which we were allowed to do for hours at a time.

It was quiet there, but in a peaceful way, not like the quiet of our house. That was the quiet of emptiness, waiting for our father to come home, and then the quietness that he enforced and demanded, punctuated by his raised angry voice, almost always aimed at Rachel, occasionally at Peter. I suppose he must have spoken to us directly once in a while, and he must have fought with her in front of us, but in my memory that sound always comes from behind a closed door, dampened but not silenced by the walls of the house.

Those weekends would sometimes end up stretching into weeks – we didn't think it was out of the ordinary, and there was something exciting and adventurous about making the long trip from Jenny's house to school. At the end of those times, when we prepared to go back home, I would often beg her to let us come and live with her. It's hard to remember how seriously I meant it when I was still not even eight years old. Then there was the car accident, and our father was dead, and Rachel was in hospital for a while, and Jenny came to stay at our house while Rachel got better and off the crutches. I remember thinking with that child's kind of superstition that I'd got my wish, that we could live with Jenny, but that it hadn't happened how I'd really wished for, with Peter and me (or just me, in the most selfish versions) at her peaceful house; instead, it seemed that with my wishing I had brought about a horrible set of events. It was difficult to miss our father, but for months our mother was even unhappier than she had been before, and Jenny seemed tense and unhappy at our house as well, not like she was at her own house where she was happily quiet, always relaxed and ready to smile at us, preoccupied with her work but patient with our questions and demands when she left the studio. That's how it seems from this distance anyway.

So when Jenny asked me to come and live at her house that night at the movies it was like a belated and transformed response to those begging questions from my very young self. My first thought was about the stickers on the wall, knowing I couldn't bear to live with them but equally couldn't stand to remove them.

'You can have the room at the side,' she said. 'Not that old one where you used to stay. There's a terrible patch of damp in the corner there now where the gutter pipes leaked. You have the one off the verandah. I've cleaned it up.' I had known this room before as a closed space filled with unused furniture and old canvases.

There was surprisingly little to take with me to Jenny's house. The room had been cleared of the old canvases, and there was a bed and a writing desk with a chair I liked already in the room, an ugly old wardrobe and a small chest of drawers of indeterminate age, painted white. I had mostly books to bring and a couple of suitcases of clothes and other things. Peter came over with a friend's borrowed station wagon and helped me load everything in the car, and we drove over to Mosman with boxes and lamps piled precariously in the back. He carried it all inside with me, and disappeared for a few minutes into the old room at the back with the stickers and damp corner. He came out looking solemn and I wondered what he had been remembering.

'There's room for me in there,' he joked. 'I'll move in next week and it can be just like old times. We'll have to update the encyclopedia though.'

My aunt had come into the room, where I was staring at a box, preparing to open it, and she gave Peter a vaguely alarmed smile.

'Not really,' he said.

'No, I know,' she replied. 'Come on. Sit down and we'll get something to eat. Julia – you too.'

In that moment it was just like it used to be, and the spell didn't break right away when we followed her into the kitchen and sat down at the table, but seemed to fade out gently without our noticing and getting suddenly sad about it.

My new bedroom had windows all along one wall looking out onto the verandah, rippled glass that muddled the light as it came through. The walls were white, with floorboards that had once been painted and were now bare and unpolished. An oval rag rug in a faded rainbow of colours covered the floor in the centre of the room. There was an oval mirror hanging on the wall over the chest of drawers, stylised flowers etched around the top and bottom of the glass. I stuck a postcard there, wedged it inside the metal grips that held the mirror to its back. My only card from Ralph – an old image of the Eiffel Tower that he'd bought in Paris and used to write a note to me in the hotel: *Back later, let's have dinner ma cherie! R.* That was it. I unpacked and it was home.

After Ingrid left for the States for good, I blamed George a lot. Sometimes Ralph agreed with me, and then he would change his mind and fight with me over it, and we would argue back and forth. A lot of his anguish went into those arguments, the grief over losing George, losing Ingrid, his own powerlessness, his own sense of culpability. The arguments pushed us further apart in those months after she left.

'You know it was George's fault,' I said to him one morning over breakfast, when we had managed to get through a whole night without talking about it – a quiet party for a new book by one of his teachers, followed by a long night of drinking with other academics and classmates at the pub around the corner. I had lain awake for hours that night on Ralph's comfortable couch, unable to keep my eyes away from the photograph of Ralph and George and Eve all together, taken years before, that faced me on the mantelpiece above the fireplace.

'It was all about the money,' I continued.

Ingrid had glowed with relief when she told us about the great uses to which her money would now be able to be put, in Grey's capable hands. Bequests. Purchases. The growth of his cache of modern art. His transition from dealer to collector. 'He's been building a serious collection for years but without the funds to fufil what he wanted. Now he will be able to really complete it. Well, we'll own it together. It's significant – collectors like Grey can really have a lot of influence. Not that he cares about that. He's so committed to nurturing new artists.'

My stomach quivered with sleeplessness. Ralph's moping was becoming tiresome. When she'd left it had seemed as though there was a chance that something of the old intimacy between us would return. Instead we saw each other even less, and his depression was impossible to shake.

'OK,' he said. 'If there hadn't been the money it might not have been the same. But you don't know. It might have been. She might have gone to Venice anyway, she would have met Grey. You may as well blame Maeve for encouraging them.

You may as well blame Eve for bringing her over to Sydney to begin with.'

'I do.'

'I thought you blamed Dad.'

'I do. I blame him. I blame them all.' He looked at the table. 'And you encouraged him,' I said, shocking myself.

'What?'

'About the money. I know you did.' I hadn't known this, but suddenly I did.

He twisted one side of his mouth, a habit he had when he was thinking.

'I thought it would be a good thing for her,' he said eventually. 'I didn't need all the money. Why not?'

'But you never wanted her to leave!' I protested.

'I didn't want her to leave but I knew she wanted to. That's the thing.' He turned his coffee cup around on the table by the handle, just like Ingrid used to do with the teapot. I remembered his dead stillness the day I was there after the news of the will. 'I didn't imagine that she'd never come back.'

'You made her …' I struggled for words. 'Like … like a piece of prey to him.' The words were horrible. I thought of Homer, the lines Ingrid loved to quote: *What words are these that have escaped the fence of your teeth?*

Like me, Ralph now put his forehead in his hands. 'Fucking hell.'

'I miss her too, you know. I feel bad about it. You aren't the only one.'

He didn't look up.

I said, 'Look, I didn't mean that – I mean, that you did that. She made her own decision about it. Stupid idiot.' This was a formulation we had argued through before, since she had decided to marry Grey. It was her decision, after all.

He said, 'Let's just not talk about it anymore.'

'OK, fine. Good.'

'I mean it. I don't want to talk about it anymore.'

'You shouldn't feel guilty, Ralph.'

'I mean it, Julia. I don't want to talk about it again, period. That's it.'

'OK.'

And so we didn't.

10.

Ingrid and Grey were married in New York in a small ceremony at Grey's property on the Hudson River in May the following year. Ralph and I were invited, but it was hard to tell how genuine the invitation really was; they held a party in Sydney a few months later that was meant for Australian friends and family who couldn't make it overseas, and it felt as though I belonged there rather than at the New York event. Financially it was close to impossible in any case. Ralph made up some excuse about needing to study for his Russian exams.

Ingrid sent a set of photographs of the Hudson wedding to me and Ralph, small prints tied together with a ribbon and a note, identical for each of us: *Here's Mrs Me! Wish you were here. Love, Ingrid.* The note was written on a square, pink card. I saw Ralph's when I was visiting one night. The photos were scattered under the coffee table and the ink had run in the note where the base of a wine glass had left a wet, red circle.

In these pictures Ingrid looked slightly drugged, stunned and happy. I examined the photographs for hours at night, turning their tastefully white-bordered edges. Few of the people in the background were familiar. All were good-looking and well-dressed. There was Eve, draped in a yellow scarf, and Victoria, Ingrid's sister, whose face in one picture was casting a resentful look at someone just outside the frame. I recognised Fleur in one shot, small and slim with her long, fine hair fixed in complicated braids. She stood between her father and Maeve, looking mistrustfully at the camera, refusing to pose or smile.

In one of the images Ingrid looked like a white ghost against a dark bank of trees, grass green under her feet. Strings of lanterns were visible in the near distance, little coloured blurs against the trees and twilight sky. One arm hung down, holding her bouquet as though she were about to drop it, flowers pointing towards the ground. Peonies and dahlias, flashes of scarlet, pink and rose. The diamond on her hand caught the light. Her hair was pinned up but had started to fall down. It seemed to be the end of the party. Her dress looked vaguely Roman, pleats in fine linen that reached all the way to the ground, obscuring her feet. Ivory-coloured cords snaked around her waist and around her shoulders, binding the dress to her body. The other arm stretched out from her side, holding Grey's hand. She faced the camera with her mouth slightly open. Grey wore a light grey suit, white shirt just open at the collar, no tie. There could be no mistaking his expression as he looked at her, handsome profile to the camera, just a hint of shadow along his jaw. I've got you, he was silently saying. I could hear his voice saying it. His hand gripped Ingrid's lightly. Their hands were slightly blurred, as though they were swinging their arms when the camera caught them. Ingrid looked as though she was walking, though Grey stood obviously still.

I held the photograph in one hand and a glass in the other. My thumb creased the paper. I was trying to prepare myself for the gathering in Sydney the following weekend. Ingrid's eyes shone, and now she looked like a slightly crumpled flower, a white gardenia just taken from the tree. I put the picture down with the others.

The party in Sydney was a bit of a disaster, although the evening probably improved after we left. I had spoken to Ingrid about the event only once on the phone, just before their New York wedding. Her voice had been easy until the issue of Sydney came up, and then the strain was evident.

'We'll have a celebration in Sydney, of course. It will be beautiful, a real celebration. It will be nice to do it that way, won't it? I think it will.' She talked fast, not waiting for an answer. 'Because you can't all make it, all of you, all my friends in Sydney, my family, you can't all make it to New York. And it's my home, I feel really that it is. New York will be my home now, but Sydney's home, it's so important.'

'Yes,' I said, and reflected that Ingrid could well afford to bring her friends to New York if she really wanted to. I was still half-hoping that she would press me to come and half-dreading it. The idea of being at the Hudson wedding seemed romantic, but my imaginings always turned cold – it would be chilly there in the spring evenings, I felt for some reason. Sometimes these ideas included a handsome artist friend of Grey's pouring champagne for me, but then I remembered that other people would be doing that, waiters hired for the occasion, and thinking about talking to a wedding full of strangers filled me with dread.

'You'll be there in Sydney,' Ingrid said. 'And Ralph will come if it's in Sydney. He'll have to.'

'He'll come,' I assured her. 'He'll be there. Don't worry.'

There was a short pause.

'Do you want me to tell him?' I asked, realising only then that this had been the real point of the phone call. 'Is that what you want?'

'Well … thank you so much, Julia! Thanks. I didn't … I couldn't see … Anyway, thank you.'

I didn't say I'd do it, I thought.

Ingrid talked on about the party, relieved to be done with the issue of Ralph. '… no speeches, just really want to see you all and bring you all together …' Her voice trailed off.

I began to understand that Grey didn't want to have the Sydney party.

'Doesn't he want to come all the way here? He's never been.'

'Oh, it's so far, I know, it's true. It's so far. But we won't be there for long. He doesn't want to spend all that time away – I mean, we'll be away for a few weeks, a honeymoon, but it's hard for him to spend more time away from his work, and Fleur's in school.' She was silent for a moment, holding in her breath. 'He's making a bit of a fuss. But it will be all right. It's important to me. Victoria's helping to arrange it all.'

I had to stifle a snort. 'That's great. That's really great.'

'Her PA, Meredith, is really so wonderful. She's so helpful. She's sending all these things over the internet, pictures …'

I thought about saying, 'I'll help you,' but didn't.

'That's great,' I repeated. 'Where –'

Ingrid cut me off. 'I have to go. The florist is calling on the other line. It's so hard to arrange for peonies right now for some ridiculous reason, can you imagine that?' I could hear Grey's voice in the background, talking to the florist on the other line.

I wished her luck. The line was dead.

I pictured Grey's house on the Hudson that had been there in the background in the photographs. It was a massive, untidy Victorian structure with turrets and many storeys. The river was down there below the grounds somewhere, beyond the trees. I imagined fields of peonies behind the house, pale pink and overblown, shedding their petals in the breeze.

After the Hudson wedding, with its flowers and coloured lights, they spent three weeks in Florence at an apartment belonging to one of Grey's friends. They were to make a short trip to Venice to visit the site of their first meeting, and Grey had someone to see there about the next Biennale. After my talk with Ingrid I heard nothing about the Sydney party for a while. The date originally planned came and went. She sent a postcard from London, worded briefly: *Still on for Sydney, August now, will call soon. London's so rainy and cold, Ingrid.* And two weeks later an ornate invitation arrived. Ralph called just a minute after I opened mine.

'It's me,' he said.

I waited, not wanting to ask. I had kept my sort-of promise to Ingrid and told Ralph – warned him, as though delivering a bad weather report – only a week before.

'Fuck,' he said now.

'We'll go together,' I said finally. 'It'll be OK. Are you home? I'll come over.'

'Fuck,' he muttered again, and, 'Great, great, come on over.'

We didn't mention the invitation until the end of the night, two movies and two bottles of wine later. Ralph had seemed sober when I arrived, though later it became apparent that it had been shock and the calming effect of gin. He cried at the end of *The End of the Affair*. I regretted my choice of film.

'We'll go together,' I told him again. He sniffed and smiled wanly. 'You'll have to help me find a frock to wear,' I warned. At this he brightened slightly.

I finished my wine and took the glass to the sink, a little unsteady on my feet. The invitation was there on the kitchen counter, tasteful RSVP card on top with boxes to tick for vegetarian or kosher meals, just like an airline. I found a pen and made a cross through the box marked 'attending'. Ralph's name was written at the top of the card in a careful, anonymous, calligraphic hand. I sealed the card into its little envelope and held it.

She's happy, I thought. He'll see. And then she can go back to bloody New York.

I touched my hand to the top of Ralph's head as I came back to the couch.

'I'll post this for you,' I said, and put the envelope into my bag. Ralph stared blankly at the television screen. 'Come on,' I said, and sat down. 'Let's watch TV.'

Five minutes later he was snoring. I left him there and went home.

*

They would stay for one week only, Ingrid told me on the phone two days before they arrived in Sydney. I offered to help this time, knowing it was too late.

'If there's anything I can do. Anything last minute. Did you get the peonies?'

'Oh, the peonies were for New York. Vicky's doing the flowers for there. I think there'll be orchids. Tropical something.' She sounded unenthusiastic. 'Ralph's coming, I'm so glad,' she said.

I told her that we were coming together and that I was bringing Mark. She hadn't met him yet.

'I'm married!' Ingrid said suddenly. 'It's really true!'

'Yes. Should I call you Mrs Grey?'

Ingrid laughed, and I liked the sound of it, and missed her suddenly.

Her laugh ended like a sigh. 'No Mrs Grey. Mrs Holburne-Grey, with a hyphen. Ms,' she said, buzzing the zed sound of the word. 'The hyphen is the thing here. I could have just kept it the same. But I wanted it to be different.' Her voice grew more intense. 'I wanted it to be something different, not just the same as it was before. It *is* a change.'

She sounded suddenly thoughtful. 'I'll have the same name as Fleur. The same last name, almost the same.'

'Is she coming with you?' I asked.

'No. She's with friends of hers in London, friends from school, they're here with their parents. She'll meet us in New York.'

'Oh.'

'It is weird to be a stepmother,' Ingrid said, exaggerating the word. 'But she doesn't hate me.'

'Good, I suppose.'

'She likes me.' Ingrid sounded surprised. 'I like her. We like each other. She's actually quite shy. And she's a total genius. A genius.' She laughed again. 'It sounds silly, doesn't it? But it's really true.'

I could picture her clearly, sitting and leaning against the wall as she did on the phone, twisting the cord around her fingers. It was probably a cordless phone over there. Static crackled down the line. I wanted to hear her laugh again, but couldn't think of what to say to evoke it. Say something, I thought, something to tell me you are happy. She sounded happy about Fleur.

'The line's quite bad, isn't it?' Ingrid said. 'I'm starting at Columbia just a couple of weeks after we get back. I can't believe it. I'll be a student again.'

It was late at night in Sydney, and early morning where Ingrid was calling from. I yawned.

'It's so late there!' Ingrid exclaimed. 'I'm sorry!'

I had been twisting the cord of the phone around my own finger in imitation of Ingrid's gesture. My hand stilled. I was sitting on the bed in my room, legs up on top of the covers. My dress for the party hung over the back of the old school chair at the desk. I reached out and ran the fabric between my fingers, the dark blue of midnight, the sapphire blue of a stone. It felt like water between my hands, covered in tiny black beads like little rocks.

'Did you like the teapot?' I asked.

The teapot had seemed like the thing that Ingrid would most like from among the many items on the extensive wedding registry. It was fat and round and blue like lapis lazuli.

'The teapot?'

'The blue one …'

'Oh, are you talking about a present? I haven't seen any of them. I can't wait – they're all waiting for us in New York. We can finally finish setting up the flat.' She corrected herself. 'The apartment. It's seemed quite empty since we moved in. That was ages ago, before the wedding. But the decorators will be finished when we get back and then we can move the presents in.'

It was the first she had said about decorators. She had told me about the apartment, a vast space overlooking Central Park on the West Side. It had levels – staircases within it, an unthinkable luxury. Ingrid talked now about antique tables as I wondered about staircases and how high the ceilings reached.

We said goodbye. The receiver clicked down at the other end and I unwound the cord slowly from around my finger. It had left faint marks.

Ralph wasn't answering the phone the night before the party. I tried a last time before midnight.

'Give up,' Mark said, pulling his T-shirt over his head, as I was leaving a message on the machine. 'For fuck's sake.'

'I am giving up,' I said. I looked at the phone. 'I give up.'

Mark's bedroom was small, a square with a wardrobe jammed in the corner and just enough room to walk around the bed. I lay down and stared at the ceiling. 'Let's get there early tomorrow, when we pick him up, in case.'

'Fine,' Mark grunted.

We got there just on time in the end. I was surprised to see him dressed and shaved when he opened the door.

'You're early,' he admonished me, and smiled. 'Where's Jenny?' he asked, tapping a cigarette against the back of his hand.

'Not coming.' My aunt was in Melbourne for the opening of some show.

'Oh. How is she?'

'Fine.'

'Nice suit,' Mark offered. He didn't much like Ralph, but had a grudging respect for his sense of style.

The suit was beautiful, pale like candied honey. It made me think of Ingrid's note that had come with the photos, stained with its circle of wine. It didn't look like a colour that would withstand much in the way of wine stains. Mark's own outfit was surprisingly good: a dark blue wool suit he had pulled with a flourish from a corner of his wardrobe. It was perhaps the first time I had seen him out of jeans. We matched, almost, with me in my midnight blue dress. The beads itched when I moved. Mark was admiring the stitching on Ralph's cuffs.

'Ralph, I like your dark suit better,' I tried.

He laughed, a quick bark. 'Hey, it's a party, not a funeral, right?' He winked at Mark.

He met my eyes and I felt a small chill seeing what was there, and then I saw the colour of his skin that the honey suit was doing its best to tone up. It looked as though you could push a finger right through to the bone. His hands trembled as he straightened his collar.

'How drunk are you?'

He smiled and took my arm, and spoke calmly. 'Would you like a Xanax? Mark?'

Mark turned his head, considering.

'No!' I slapped Ralph on the arm, harder than I had meant to. 'Ralph, you're a mess when you drink with those. Jesus.'

The apartment was in more disarray than usual, as though the site of a struggle or half-hearted burglary. Small shards of glass lay broken on the fireplace grate at the end of the room.

Mark's hand was already out. I sighed. 'OK, give me one.'

Ralph pulled the silver strip from his pocket and popped a small pink tablet into my hand. 'And one for later.' He winked again.

'Stop winking. The cab's waiting outside,' I said.

A piece of late afternoon light came through under the lowered blinds at the window as the sun moved to a new angle. The room brightened in that one corner. I smoothed my dress down.

'Tally-ho.' Ralph gestured widely to the door. Mark's hand in the small of my back pushed me out.

A chill wind was blowing as we arrived at the place, a vast glass restaurant at the end of one of the old piers on the harbour. By the time we all got out of the cab the drugs were working and my limbs felt smooth and slowed down, as though we were moving through a thick, viscous liquid.

The room was respectably full of people, gathered in small groups around a centrally placed long table. Ingrid's eyes were bright when she saw us, spots of pink high in her cheeks. She stepped away from Grey, leaving him talking to someone else, and walked towards us.

'You're all here!'

She embraced Ralph quickly before he had a chance to say anything. He had managed to get a glass of champagne before we had even crossed the room and he held it awkwardly, tipping it as one arm gripped her shoulder and the other arm circled her waist. His lips brushed her ear and paused to whisper something, and the look in her eyes was hard as she pulled away, her smile just slightly broken.

She moved towards me. Her eyes were brighter, with the start of tears in them, quickly blinked away. She pressed her cheek to mine. 'Thank you,' she murmured. 'Thanks for coming.'

In one corner a trio played mournful-sounding jazz: an upright bass, a muted saxophone and a black grand piano. The musicians looked at the floor or the instruments of the other players, and not at the guests.

I found myself talking to a former lecturer of mine and Ingrid's from art history, and that conversation seemed to melt away, and I didn't know the people in front of me, and wasn't sure if I was part of the conversation or not. Mark came into view at the edge of my vision. He was seated in a corner deep in conversation with a girl who looked almost too young to be drinking, and he was refilling her glass from a bottle. The girl said something, her eyes wide and earnest. Ralph appeared then in front of me, pulling a drink from a passing tray. A cigarette hung in his fingers and the waiter with the tray looked at it and said something cautionary, which Ralph ignored.

'How's it going?' I asked. My voice sounded as though it hadn't been used in a while. 'Do you want to go outside with me and smoke?' A long balcony stretched the length of the place, smokers dotted along it. The lights of the far shore blinked across the water.

'No, I'm fine,' he said calmly. His eyes had a sleepy glitter that scared me a little. He drew on his cigarette and wobbled slightly and looked away.

When would we eat, I wondered. Small pastry parcels and towers constructed of cucumbers floated on trays somewhere across the room. I looked at the long, white table and wondered if we would ever sit down or whether we would all stand here all night, eating tiny morsels and drinking until we couldn't stand up any longer. Apart from Mark, with his bottle and girl and chairs in the corner. A tall potted palm now hid him from view. I turned around and was soon explaining to a man with an undefinable accent how I had met Ingrid. The lift of his eyebrows made it seem as though he was unconvinced – by Ralph's relation to her, or my relation to Ralph, I couldn't tell. He looked at me in apparent disbelief – why, I wondered, did it sound so unlikely? Ingrid's sister, Victoria, walked past and I grabbed her arm.

'Victoria! I was just telling … just telling about how I met Ingrid.'

Victoria looked at me briefly with plain contempt and said, 'Yeah.' She flicked her long hair over her shoulder and turned a brilliant smile on the man with the lifted eyebrows. He kissed both her cheeks – they seemed to know each other – and I felt again as though I were standing at the margins. This was better than being the object of narrative doubt. Over in the corner behind the potted palm the bottle was there, empty on the floor under the chairs against the wall, but Mark and the girl were not. I saw him then, coming out of an unmarked door near the kitchen entrance, no glass in hand. By the time he made it over to me he had two, and pressed one into my hand, and kissed me on the neck.

He clinked my glass with a quick smile, and said, 'Hi, I'm Mark,' interrupting Victoria and shaking her hand vigorously.

'Your fly is undone,' I said.

He turned to me and clinked my glass again while zipping with the other hand. Victoria walked away, hand raised to summon a waiter with a tray.

'What happened with that girl just now?' I asked him.

Mark took a sip from his glass and met my eye for a second before his glance slid away, and as it did his arm went around my waist. 'You are way off,' he hissed. 'How much have you had to drink?'

I clinked my glass against Mark's again, and realised it was empty. 'Just get me something to eat,' I said, and turned away.

Ingrid stood near the musicians at the end of the room, talking with a group of people, one of them a young girl who looked only ten years old, her hair a shiny black curtain down her back. Ingrid's dress was a long shift of pale blue, thick watered silk, her hair golden against it. The summer sky, I thought, and smelled the smell of cut grass right through the air full of wine and the salt of the harbour. Ingrid stood with one arm bent in front of her, clasping the other by her side. I felt a twinge of memory, and thought of the days in the past when Ingrid would have stuck together with me at parties like this, when we would have been the ones with a smuggled bottle getting drunk and giggling in the corner, and I would have been the one to have fumbled sex with someone else's boyfriend behind an unmarked door.

Ingrid caught my eye and smiled, and before the smile there was something else, something of my own instant of sadness reflected there, and something else again. She came over and touched my hair hesitantly, and drew her hand back. Her mouth opened and closed and I finally made out words, about the party and the water outside, and nodded.

'Do you have a cigarette?' Ingrid asked in a pretend whisper. 'Let's go outside.'

I didn't have cigarettes.

'We'll find some,' Ingrid said, and pulled my hand along towards the doors.

'I have Xanax,' I offered, and Ingrid laughed.

The air was cold outside and Ingrid lit two cigarettes for us that she took from an older woman going inside, who kissed her cheek and pressed a hand to her face.

'Who are these people?' I asked.

Ingrid looked offended. 'A lot of people came over from Perth and WA,' she said. 'You know, friends of the family. You wouldn't know them.' She smoked as though she had been getting a lot of practice. 'And there's all these people from uni — not everyone could make it.'

I looked back inside and saw faces familiar from lectures and the university bar and the parties with Ingrid I had been thinking of earlier. Mark was talking to another woman with wide eyes. Where did he find them?

The balcony over the water stretched and wrapped around the building, made with big, uneven slats of salt-bleached wood.

'Do you remember those parties?' Ingrid asked. She looked over the water, away at something in the distance.

'Yes,' I said. 'I was just thinking about them.'

I reached out for Ingrid's glass, having lost my own between inside and outside, and drank, and handed it back. She was drinking water, cool and sweet.

My memories seemed very loud compared to the stillness of the night and the quiet between the two of us, and I wondered if Ingrid was thinking about the same times. There had been a tiny kitchen with fluorescent light in a house lit with candles, ferociously loud music coming from a stereo that managed to be noisy despite being moved out into the front yard. Every inch of counter space had been covered with coloured plastic cups, and a bottle of green liqueur with an unpronounceable name was the only thing left to drink apart from Guinness. There was the smell of toast. Ingrid, finding bread, and butter in the fridge (otherwise filled with Guinness), and buttering the toast, laughing breathlessly as she held the knife, her eyeliner smudged and running. The comforting taste of burnt bread, and our shudders at the green liquid.

'It's all a blur,' Ingrid said happily.

My memory clouded too, then sharpened. Ralph appeared in the fluorescent kitchen brandishing a bottle of gin. Applause. Blur.

'I remember it,' I said. 'Do you remember the kitchen, the time you made toast?'

Ingrid's face was doubtful, then she smiled. 'Oh, the toast.' She passed her cigarette from one hand to the other. 'I think so. There were a few nights ending with toast, I think. Are you talking about Terry's party?'

I frowned. There was a memory of sleeping in someone's bed and waking up with toast crumbs on the sheets but it may not have been Terry.

'No, it was me that slept with Terry,' Ingrid said, answering my thought. 'It was his house with the toast though.'

We were quiet as we finished smoking.

'What are you going to do here, Julia?' asked Ingrid, leaning back against the balcony rails with her arms folded.

I shivered. 'What are you going to do *there*, Ingrid?' I asked in turn.

Ingrid scowled and turned away. There was no possibility of a conversation like the others we had shared just after the engagement, when her face had glowed with excitement, about the marriage, art, love, study, the city, everything. All of it.

'I have to start preparing for Columbia, the fall term – this has all taken so much time and energy. Gil thought I should defer for a year but I don't want to.'

He appeared then before us, and took Ingrid's arm. 'We're missing you inside,' he said in his quiet voice, and kissed her. 'Hello, Julia. So good to see you here.' He kissed my cheek. His hand remained on Ingrid's back, the same proprietary gesture I remembered from seeing them together in New York. 'I love your beautiful city,' he said, moving his gaze to take in the whole harbour, the whole city.

'So much … natural beauty.' His thoughtful tone suggested disdain for whatever Sydney might have to offer in other, cultural terms. 'The water is really exquisite.'

We all looked at it, the waves slopping on the pylons below the pier, the winking lights of boats passing over the water, windows on the shore beyond.

'Julia loves New York, I've told you,' Ingrid was saying to Grey. 'You'll come and visit soon, won't you?' she asked.

'We'd love that,' Grey added. But his eyes on me were cold, the same dispassionate regard I had met before dinner at Maeve's apartment after I had seen the look between the two of them.

I realised that I was being farewelled. The city lights glinted, doubled, in the glass walls of the restaurant, the glass doors. Inside, people were beginning to take their seats at the long table, waiting for Grey and Ingrid to take their places. It looked like the beginning of a contemporary rendition of the Last Supper. Voices were raised now with wine and waiting, clothes rumpled, the music sounding louder, with Ingrid waiting to sit in the centre seat.

'I'll stay out here a moment longer,' I said, and let them go inside. The glass doors slid shut behind them with a sharp sense of finality. It felt like a heavily symbolic exit, even while it was happening: he took her inside, away from where I was, and shut the door, separating us. I watched her beautiful back retreating and wondered when I would ever see her in Sydney again.

What happened next had the odd distance of a dream, and it was all I had imagined in my fears about the event. I saw Mark inside talking to Ralph, who looked very drunk.

Mark's hand was on Ralph's sleeve, but he shook it off. Their words were unclear but I saw Ralph move away and towards Ingrid and Grey as they walked in. He stepped closer and addressed Grey. Grey looked at him with cautious concern, and whatever Ralph was saying made a crack in his expression, and Grey's hand went up to Ralph's chest. The violence in the motion, just restrained from turning into a blow, was surprising. Ralph threw his glass of wine at Grey. It mostly missed. It was red wine so it didn't show on his charcoal suit but it left a spot on the white shirt underneath and the silver tie, the colour of blood on snow.

I'd been transfixed by the sight of the argument, but the splash of wine snapped me into motion, driven by a desperate, hollow fear of what Ralph might do next. My grip faltered and slipped on the recessed handles of the sliding doors and they stuck as I pushed, juddering on their tracks, caked in harbour salt.

Ralph's arms were around Ingrid, his mouth on hers, and then Grey's hand was on Ralph's neck, pulling him away. The word 'scruff' made its way into my head. Ingrid's face was visible for a second, blank and tragic, before Mark dragged Ralph away – the doors opened smoothly for him as soon as he touched them – and outside to the balcony, up close to me where I could suddenly feel and smell their bodies, the smell of sweat and adrenaline. The doors closed and inside was a silent, sealed box where everyone was busily ignoring the scene and taking another drink, applauding the first course as it emerged, right on time, seconds after the bride, the wife, had taken her seat and raised her glass to the groom.

Mark's breathing sounded very loud, and so did the little waves smacking against the pier. Ralph looked sick and unhappy. Mark leaned over the balcony and for a moment it seemed as though he was going to vomit, but he didn't. He turned and started talking angrily to Ralph, who stayed quiet and met my eyes defiantly with his glittery, dark stare.

'Come on,' I said, 'there has to be a way out of here without going back through there.'

We made our way to the end of the balcony and back around the pier, wooden walls and walkway bleached out and blotchily lit in the fast approaching night. The road was deserted.

'Where are the fucking taxis?' Mark asked, scanning the street and zipping his fly. Again.

'What were you doing, Ralph?' I asked, furious, unable to help myself. My head hurt with the hangover already beginning.

He brushed a piece of ash away from his suit with one elegant hand. Apart from the tiny mark it left he was spotless, his face a ruined mask that broke into a grim smile. 'Don't start crying now,' he said flatly and began walking away.

I moved to follow him but Mark stopped me. He was strong, and held my struggling arms. Ralph kept going. His hands were in his pockets, his jacket creased up at the elbows the way it did when he bent his arms like that. I felt it all, the loss and anger, bile in the throat. Mark groaned and looked green, and a taxi cruised by, smooth and silent, and stopped to take us in.

On the ride home, the taxi seats squeaking and smelling of plastic, I thought about Ingrid's face when she had caught my eye across the room. The colour of the shadows under her eyes, little hollows beneath the thin skin, more iris showing. It had looked like a small second of fear. This was an emotion Ingrid never showed or seemed to feel. It was hard to imagine what fear would look like on her – would it be like that, the trace of a bruise under the eyes?

I thought about that expression from time to time over the next few years. It became so that whenever I summoned Ingrid's face, that look wasn't the first thing I saw – that was always the sunlit profile, the sculpted, gentle face of a Venus, smiling, hand pulling back the stray strands of hair – but it was always the next. The shadow of the first thing. I told myself it was jet lag and strain and later seemed to confirm that it was dread and fear and regret, and railed against the idea. It was only a second. I was imagining whatever it meant.

'What did Ralph say to him?' I asked Mark.

He shifted in his seat, reluctant. 'He was really drunk. He called him an arsehole.'

This sounded pretty unsophisticated, for Ralph, but I believed it.

'He said that he was an evil fucking bastard. That was it.' Mark was gathering steam.

'And something about someone being a bitch – Maeve, I think And –'

'Stop,' I told him. 'Stop.' I knew every word of it suddenly, the whole speech, the whole thing, and couldn't stand to imagine the sound of it in Ralph's voice.

The streets passed by, quiet, patches of brightness and dark. The lights of the clock showed on the dash. We had been at the party for just over an hour. The taxi stopped at a red light. 'Let me out,' I said, gripping the door handle. The locks clicked.

'What?' Mark asked. 'We're blocks away from your place.'

'Go home,' I said, and got out of the car.

II.

When the planes struck the towers that morning, it was late at night in Sydney. I spent the whole night in bed, re-reading *Middlemarch* for class the following week, eating shortbread straight from the packet. At that moment I was probably reading about the Lydgates arguing about whether to sell the furniture to cover their debts. When I woke up the next morning the book was squashed open next to me on the bed. I went out to the kitchen to make tea, and as I walked down the hall I could hear the radio. I wasn't paying attention to what the voices were saying, a news program. I could also, unusually, hear the sound of the television from the living room at the other end of the passageway.

Jenny was standing at the kitchen counter with her arms folded, looking down at the floor. I thought she might have been waiting for the kettle to boil, but could see that the stove wasn't on. She was listening. She must have heard me then, and lifted her head to face me.

'What's happened?' I asked when I saw her stricken expression.

'It's New York,' she said.

'What?' I frowned and rubbed my eyes. I started listening to the radio. As I started understanding what they were saying — ... *second tower collapsed ... blood donations ... missing and thousands presumed dead* … – I heard the phone start to ring. It went on ringing. I turned up the radio. My aunt went to answer the phone. I could hear the shriek of the kettle boiling, and then it stopped, an illusion. I blinked and picked it up and filled it with water from the tap.

My aunt held the phone in her hand. 'It's Ralph,' she said.

I took the receiver from her and put it to my ear. As I did, I remembered Ingrid. I hadn't thought of her until that moment, was thinking only of the planes and the buildings and the fifty thousand body bags the announcer said that Giuliani was ordering in.

'Ralph?'

There was silence for a moment. Then, 'I've tried calling Grey. I can't get through. The phone won't even ring. It's just dead.'

'She'll be OK, won't she?' I was trying to listen to the radio and get my thoughts straight. I needed tea. My aunt started making it, spooning leaves into the pot. 'It's just downtown, right? Ingrid's never that far downtown. What would she be doing there?' I started thinking it through. 'Why would she be at the Trade Center at – what – nine in the morning?'

'I know –'

'She lives uptown. That's far away. They're on the Upper West Side.'

'I know, Julia –'

'That's, like, a hundred blocks away. It's more than that, it's more than a hundred blocks.'

'I know, Julia, I know. I just want to know that she's OK.'

I started to think, then, of the other people I knew in the city. Were any of them still even living there? I didn't know.

'I just woke up, just half an hour ago, and just turned on the radio …' His voice was thick with panic.

'Call me, OK, when you've heard from Grey. When you get through to him,' I said.

I thought about offering to go over there. It was what I would have done six months earlier. But it wasn't like that anymore. The kettle started its screaming noise, for real this time. Jenny turned it off. Ralph and I said goodbye.

'I'm making tea,' Jenny said, as if to reassure me.

'Thanks.'

It was 9 am, just about the same time it had been there when the plane struck the first tower. Jenny poured the tea. We took it through to the living room and sat there for an hour watching the television, seeing the planes strike over and over again from different angles, the buildings crumbling slowly into a cloud of dust and smoke. I saw the dark plume rise and curve through the sky to fall down on Brooklyn across the water and waited for the phone to ring again. It didn't.

I called Ralph and the line was busy. I switched on my computer, impatient while it whirred and hummed into life, and sent an email to Ingrid – the folder showed that it had been six months since our last exchange. *Are you OK? Call me.* Send. The modem burbled away and onscreen the cursor blinked, a steady little machine pulse.

After two more hours and more attempts at calling Ralph, I went to my room and dug out my address book. Ingrid's name was there, and her number in New York. I called it. It rang out after what felt like endless minutes while my insides grew tight imagining the sound of Grey's voice on the other end.

My aunt looked at me. She was wearing her white straw hat and was heading out into the garden. The television was off but the radio was still going. 'I don't want to watch it anymore,' she said. I agreed. She rolled up the sleeves of her linen shirt. 'I'm sure he'll call again, won't he, if there's any news,' she said. 'If there's anything wrong. You'll find out.'

I nodded. I wanted to tell her to change shirts, not to wear that one outside to garden. It was one I liked, a soft pearl grey that once had been white but had gone through the wash with other colours too many times. But it seemed I didn't have much of a voice left. I went back to *Middlemarch* and the troubles of the Lydgates. The computer stayed silent, screen blank and asleep.

It was late afternoon and the chunk of sunlight in my room had travelled across the bed and onto the floor when the phone rang again. I put the book down quickly – my hand was stiff with holding it – and rose to answer the call. It wasn't Ralph on the other end, but Mark.

'Hi, Julia. I just heard, I just turned on the radio.'

How strange it was that we were all getting our first news of the event this way, I thought, like something out of World War II.

'How did you only hear about it just now?' I asked.

'I've been reading all day, working on this chapter at home.' He sounded defensive. 'Why didn't you call me? Christ.'

'I didn't think about it. Sorry.'

He sighed. 'No, sorry, I'm sorry. Look, is your friend OK? Ingrid – she's in New York, right?'

'I don't know. I don't know if she's OK, I can't get in touch – she's uptown though. I'm sure she'll be alright.'

'Right, right. OK. So. What are you doing?'

'Reading.' I brushed some crumbs off my lap.

'Are you coming over?'

'Well, alright.'

'I'm going ahead with dinner.'

'Dinner?' I had forgotten. Mark was having people over that night. 'I'll be right there.'

I tried Ralph and Grey again two or three more times before I left. No answer. The car started – it took a few tries – and I drove away. The streets seemed quieter than usual. Mark was only a couple of blocks from Ralph's old Kings Cross flat, and I thought about driving by but didn't.

Mark and I went to the shops together and bought mountains of food – long baguettes that stuck out of their paper bags like spears, damp parcels of fish and prawns, handfuls of pale green leeks and lettuces, bags of lemons and boxes of eggs. It felt necessary to be feeding people on some kind of larger-than-usual scale.

When we walked in the door of his flat Mark went right to the little television and turned it on. I stopped just inside the threshold and looked straight down the hallway at it. On screen the towers were falling again, again and again. I put down the bags carefully and stood still. Low sounds came out of the television, voices. I went to the phone and dialled Ralph. He still wasn't answering. Mark came and took the phone out of my hands.

He hated tears. He kissed me. The little towers on the screen crumbled and fell, burned and smoked and dissolved into dust. He switched the TV off.

I chopped and peeled and washed things in the kitchen while Mark cooked. He was good at it. The guests arrived early and more kept coming, neighbours from upstairs with bottles of wine, friends of the friends he had invited who wanted to come to be with somebody and wanted something to eat. There were ten people in his small kitchen-dining room by seven and we were all getting drunk fast. Plates piled up in the sink, on the tables.

I called Jenny just before we sat down to eat.

'Any news from Ralph?' I asked her.

'No, darling, sorry. I'll tell him to call you right away if he calls here.'

'Are you OK?'

'Oh, I'm fine. I'm sad about it – I'm afraid of what's going to happen next. The war that's about to start.' She sounded tired. 'Don't worry about me. Take care.'

'Bye.'

Mark was at his best in this environment, an expansive and generous host, opening wine, refilling glasses, humouring everyone. He refilled my glass and kissed me sloppily. I looked at him. If there was ever a time to say 'I love you' this would be it. An affirmation in the face of whatever it was over there behind the now-silent and dark television screen, all that way across the world, the smoking hole in the ground and pile of rubble.

'Why don't you move in here?' he asked.

I didn't even have a key. Well, I did, but not that he knew about.

'Wow.'

'Just think about it,' he said, and squeezed my waist, and

went back to being host, raising his eyebrows at a joke someone had just told, pouring wine into their glass.

We were all still stunned. The sense of crisis had the predictable effect of bringing us together, and more people from the building drifted in over the course of the night, and the crowd grew. It was an oddly distant sense of crisis though; already, there, across the world, it was morning again. It made New York and the whole United States seem at once closer and further away. The other side of the world, the other side of the day. Every now and again someone else would get up and go to the phone or open their mobile to call someone over there or a friend here to see what news there was. One of the upstairs neighbours was waiting for news of a friend of her brother's who was working in one of the financial companies that was in the towers. She went over to Mark's computer in the corner to check her email every half an hour. Her partner grew crankier over the course of the evening and got into a long argument with one of the original dinner party guests, a philosophy student like Mark, about what really happened in the Sudan and the Gulf War.

I don't know if my sense of the artificiality of that camaraderie was something I felt then, at the time, or whether I've back projected it, so that the whole scene of the evening seems like an elaborately designed film sequence with every character carefully choreographed in their movements. Someone lit the candles that sat on top of the bookshelves along the walls and along the windowsills. They didn't seem to burn down even as the night wore on. The light shone so that everyone's face was illumined softly.

It wasn't so much artificial, I suppose, as driven by a sense of self-consciousness and vague panic on everyone's part. Here we all were, seeking out company and comfort, afraid to be alone in our individual places. One of Mark's other friends tried to follow me into the bathroom after dessert.

'Come on, Julia,' he said, his hand reaching under my shirt. 'You've got to affirm life at a time like this, right?'

'You have to be kidding.' I slapped his hand away. 'And anyway, no. Fuck off. Go back out there.'

Horribly, I remembered then that it had been his knee in black jeans that I had grabbed years ago. The one who hadn't seen *Ben-Hur*, the movie. What had I been thinking? The dark hallway was lit with a frame of light falling from the bathroom door, our shadows in the way.

'OK, man.' He shrugged. 'Do you want some smack?'

'Derek, no. And don't hit up here. Go home.'

He went back to the table, and he was there, with Mark's vodka in his hand, chatting up one of the other guests when I got back from the bathroom. I wondered how close he was to becoming a real junkie. I thought twice about his offer of drugs and decided to stick with my red wine. I thought of Ralph, and wondered what he was doing. The remembered sound of the phone ringing and ringing at his end, unanswered, wouldn't go away. At the end of the table a man and a woman from upstairs had opened a CD case and were studying the lyrics printed on the leaflet inside. They seemed to be settling an argument. The man returned to his chair and shrugged defensively. 'I always thought it said "glue" not "hue", it makes more sense anyway.'

I thought of Ingrid, too, and for the first time in many

months wondered what she was doing with her morning; imagined her at home in the Upper West Side place that I had never seen. I hoped she was alive. Pain hit me then and I realised with a small shock that I had been numb all day. Most of it was familiar, mundane pain – Ralph, and Ingrid, and loss. I wondered what the next day would bring, and dreaded it. I wondered if the last glass of wine had been a mistake. I looked around for another.

Mark was slicing up two round lemon tarts. 'Can you start whipping some cream?' he asked me, eyes on his knife.

It looked like a boring job. 'No,' I said. 'I don't think so.'

He looked up at me. 'Why don't you go and sit down,' he said, softly, and took my arm and led me over to the couch.

I sat down in a small space between two other people who shifted over to make room. Mark was back in a couple of minutes with a plate of yellow tart and a fork. It was sweet and sour just like it ought to be. Every sense of feeling had concentrated in my tongue.

'She's waiting to hear about her friend,' the woman next to me said, half-whispering, to the man sitting on the armrest of the couch. He nodded, solemnly. I swallowed and found it strange to know that she was talking about me. The days ahead seemed to stretch out into the rest of the week, and next week. I'd hear from Ralph, he'd get in touch with Grey eventually, probably fight with him on the phone, and it would all have been a false alarm. Of course she was alright. They lived uptown. She didn't ever go down there, that far downtown. What was there for her down there? What did I know about her life anyway?

'She's not a close friend,' I heard myself say.

Right on cue, the phone rang. The sound was followed by a little ripple of silence that was quickly, steadily, filled by talk. By then I'd stopped attending to it, didn't imagine it would be for me. But whoever answered it stepped over to Mark, and he came over and stood behind me and put his hand on my shoulder.

'Julia,' he said. 'It's Eve.'

My ears filled with a rushing sound. It must have been my own blood. Eve's voice told me everything before I heard the details; it cut through the noise in my head enough to tell me that she'd heard, she'd heard from Grey, that there was no word, that they hadn't heard, and that Ingrid had been there.

The next hour. The screen goes dark, fades in and out into the next morning with quick, frozen images where I see myself as though in a dream: seated, listening, with the black plastic phone to my ear; standing in the bathroom, clinging to someone (is it Derek, or the woman from next to me on the couch?) with the taste of vomit and lemon in my mouth, sickly sweet now. Lying naked in bed, eyes red and throat sore, next to Mark, who rolls off me heavily. Still in bed, this time dressed in one of his blue striped shirts. It comes clear when I open my eyes and the room is dim with the blinds pulled down, mid-morning, and the sound of dishes being rinsed and stacked comes through from the kitchen, and the smell of coffee on the stove.

Mark was there in the kitchen, grey T-shirt and jeans, bare feet. One of the upstairs neighbours from the night before was there too, both of them standing at the sink. The radio was on. I looked at Mark cautiously.

'Is it true?' I asked him, because it was starting to come back. I was hoping it had been a bad dream without much sense of that being right.

'Bye, mate,' said the neighbour, and patted Mark on the shoulder. 'Sorry,' he mumbled to me as he passed.

I went to the bathroom and vomited again. There wasn't much to show for it but I felt better. Back in the kitchen Mark was still washing plates.

'OK,' I said to him.

'You're still in shock.'

'No, I'm alright now.'

'Alright.'

He poured me a cup of coffee. I drank it and sat down at the table. The surface was clean, pitted wood, all traces of last night gone. The radio was playing music: guitars and voices.

'Are you going to call Ralph?' Mark asked.

Some small, fine thread broke inside me, opening a yawning space. I closed it up and sat up straight on my chair.

'No.'

And I didn't.

Mark didn't mention the moving-in idea again for a while. It was a relief, although I was curious to see where he would go with it. His neighbours all met my eye with concern when they saw me now in the building or on the street nearby, even ones I was sure hadn't been at Mark's place that night. I had become the person they knew who knew someone … Sometimes one or another of them came into the bookshop – it was only a short walk away – and it got so that I would leave the counter and go out the back to Martin's cramped little office to avoid them, ashamed of myself and cross. I suppose it looked like overwhelming grief. Maybe it was. It felt the same as any kind of avoidance.

Ralph didn't call me, and I didn't call him. The days were much the same as they had been before, except now when I thought of Ingrid I had to make a sharp turn left or right, any direction, in my mind to avoid going there. Before then it had been a more lazy kind of manoeuvre. Sometimes I didn't turn quickly enough, and those times were sometimes very hard. Stupid little things would bring it on: someone buying a book in Latin (not many of those in the shop); catching a frame of *St Elmo's Fire* on TV late at night; the sound of fireworks in the sky. The first time I heard fireworks after the towers came down, I lost my breath on the street in a kind of panic attack and stepped inside the nearest doorway. It was a nasty, expensive hotel full of men in suits after work on Friday. I drank something fast, the sounds of distant explosions in my ears, in my nose the memory of salt air on the ferry at night.

Ten days after September 11, I received a mailing from the Classics department. In conjunction with the English department, they were holding a 'memorial gathering to celebrate the life of Ingrid Holburne-Grey'. It was a slim notice on thin paper with a date and time. I folded it in half so the words didn't show and left it on my desk where it sat, so light it looked ready to fly away with any breeze. I had wondered about the funeral in New York, the memorial service, whatever it was people did when they were left without an actual body. Grey hadn't sent me any word about it – I hadn't heard from him at all, only fragments once or twice from Eve in a couple of short phone messages. This was all we were going to get.

12.

The service was scheduled for four o'clock on a Thursday.
I decided that morning that I would go, and told Martin I
would need to leave early.

'Of course, of course,' he said, blinking and nodding
when I went into his office.

I lingered there at the shop after it was time to leave. The
afternoon had turned warm and dry. Traffic was sparse on
the street.

'Out you go,' Martin said in the end, emerging to take
over the till, and opened the door for me on the way out.

The 'celebration' was being held in the Classics department
common room. I could hear someone speaking as I walked
upstairs. It was Ingrid's honours supervisor, I saw when I
reached the glass-paned door and pushed it open. He looked
much older than I remembered him. There was a crowd of
about thirty people, all standing, and some tables at the side
with bottles of wine and trays of terrible-looking sandwiches.
The ancient head of the English department sat on a chair
near the front of the room, frowning darkly, a walking stick
held in his hand. I tried to focus on what Ingrid's supervisor
was saying – it was difficult to see him through all the
people, and his voice didn't carry well. I'd figured out that

he was talking about her honours thesis and how respected she had been by the department at Columbia when they had admitted her, when he stopped.

Ralph was standing towards the front of the group, shuffling some papers in his hand. He was wearing a corduroy jacket, I noticed with a pang, in mossy black. It had some soft, ironic-looking leather patches on the elbows. He didn't see me until he'd stepped up to the cleared space where Ingrid's supervisor had stood. Then, when he surveyed the audience, he looked right at me, right into my eyes. He didn't seem surprised to see me, and barely showed any recognition. His hairline was damp with sweat and he looked as ill as I'd ever seen him. He cleared his throat and raised his chin as he began to speak in his lovely, drawling voice.

He didn't talk for long. He thanked Classics, English, for holding the event and talked about how much Ingrid had loved both those disciplines. 'She was a luminous presence,' he said, 'as you all witnessed who knew her and taught her, and all of us who knew her could not but hold high hopes for her. We could not wait to see what she would do next.'

I remembered then with a blinding vividness his father, laughing and coughing and almost starting to choke, wheezing his words out. 'I can't wait to see what you'll do next, Ingrid!' He had always said her name with a vaguely musical intonation, so that it seemed to have more syllables than it really did. It had been a week before he died – or was it longer, a month? How long had he planned his bequest, his great contribution to her desire for an interesting life? I hung my head.

When I looked up Ralph was reading from the papers in his hand, but he didn't need them, and he folded them with one hand and continued speaking. I couldn't understand the Latin but somehow recognised the cadence and the words. People were looking down at little folded leaflets they held in their hands, where the poem was printed with a translation.

It was Apollo, chasing Daphne, and her plea for escape. The goddess heard her and changed her into a laurel tree. Ingrid had recited that passage to us, to Ralph and me, one afternoon on the lawn near the bar. Ralph had squinted at her when she paused. The sun was in his eyes and he shaded his face with his hand. Ingrid's eyes stayed on her book. He had taken a paperback out of his bag and leafed through it and read from it:

Apollo hunted Daphne so,
Only that she might laurel grow,
And Pan did after Syrinx speed,
Not as a nymph, but for a reed.

They were lines from Andrew Marvell's poem 'The Garden' – I knew because I'd sat through a lecture on it the day before with Ralph beside me. Ingrid had frowned and then smiled at him in her indulgent way. I couldn't tell what she thought. It was a chilling vision of the heartless gods chasing those poor nymphs, and I saw its cold logic of desire. The laurel of victory and the reed of the musical flute were not substitutes, after all, for the women who could not be caught. They were the ends of the chase all along, the women simply a sacrifice for that aim.

Whether Ralph was thinking of Marvell now or not, it seemed a strange choice even though Ingrid had loved Ovid. Daphne cried out in fear and despair, and felt herself turning into something else. It seemed a long time since I'd heard Ralph's voice. I closed my eyes for a second and was aware of how much I loved it and also how irritating it had sometimes been. Another compressed moment of mourning. I opened my eyes. His voice was very steady but his hand shook. He finished, and the previous speaker stepped back up briefly and asked everyone to stay and talk and have a drink and make a toast to Ingrid, our departed and cherished friend.

I moved as quickly as I could to the table of food and drink.

There were no photographs of her on display, thankfully. One of my fears in coming was that someone would arrange a slide show of pictures. Bach played softly on the stereo system. Ralph would have arranged it, made a CD mix especially for the occasion. The walls were unplastered old brick, a mix of rust and blood with seams of white. There was no air-conditioning in the rooms. Hanging from large exposed ceiling beams, two fans churned the air around. My black crepe dress clung to my back.

Ed stood a few feet away, a fierce look of grief in his eyes. His rower's body was still there but fading, and he was dressed in a severe pinstriped suit. He was working in banking. I wasn't even sure if I knew that for a fact or had made it up. He looked as though he hadn't slept well for a long time. Eve's profile appeared across the room, deep in conversation with a grey-haired academic. I looked again and she was gone.

A man in a white shirt addressed me. 'Excuse me. Are you Julia Alpers?'

'Yes.'

He had hair that had been red and now was mostly grey, and pale eyelashes. 'I'm Roger White. An old teacher – old friend – of Ingrid's.' He was shaking my hand, taking a long time about it. 'It's very good to meet you. I did hear a lot about you over the years.'

His smile was very sad. I remembered that he was Ingrid's high-school Latin and French teacher, the one who had mentored her and overseen her entrance to university. She had talked about him like a saviour. 'In this ... this wilderness, this high school,' – she said the words 'high school' as though they stood for a special circle of hell – 'he was just ... this beacon. Of intelligence, learning, that we weren't all there just to get prepared for our jobs as finance executives and business managers and doctors or doctors' wives. That there was something more to it.' She had been close to him, from what she said, and I had wondered sometimes if she had been in love with him, or he with her. Meeting him now I couldn't quite see it, but I could picture them together, going over translations in the library after class, making grand plans for her academic success.

I wasn't sure what to say. 'I heard a lot about you too.'

'It's such a tragedy – I was so happy to hear that she was going to Columbia, was pursuing those dreams. And now ...' He sighed. 'She was such a bright girl. But you know that.'

'Yes.'

'Well, it's good to finally meet you.'

He drifted away. He was the only representative there of her life before Sydney, her life in Perth. Before Ralph, before me, before any of it. Other people talked to me. No-one else touched me or shook my hand. Back to the table with the wine on it – my shoulders collided with Ralph's.

'Oh, hello,' I said.

'Hello.'

I remembered his voice on the phone that day: 'I know, Julia.'

'Eve called me,' I said.

'I know.'

He refilled my glass and his own. I drank quickly before he could propose a toast, then realised that it would be unlikely in these circumstances. It was a habit he used to have, of proposing a toast with every drink, random, exuberant, silly ideas. Drinking to whoever it was holding the party we were at, or the person who had just won the game of Trivial Pursuit, or the most obscure or depressing of the poets or film-makers we had studied in class that week. 'To good old George Meredith. And modern love!'

'I asked her to call you,' he said. 'I wasn't up to it.'

'She said that.'

We moved away from the table and back into the thinning crowd.

'I wasn't up to much of anything for a while there.' He gave a thin smile and wouldn't look at me. 'It's bizarre to be back here, isn't it?' he asked.

I looked around. I had been in the room maybe twice before, and maybe once with him and Ingrid. A public lecture, a retirement event for one of our professors.

'On campus, I mean. In the old building. The old place.'

'Yes. I suppose so.'

'The sandwiches are terrible. Not surprising, I suppose.'

'My wine is good though.' That was surprising.

'Oh, that.' He glanced away. 'I brought that,' he confessed. 'I couldn't bear to drink the stuff they would normally serve here at something like this. Sandwiches are one thing, but ...' He took a sip. 'I raided the old Kirribilli cellars for a few bottles of something.'

'That's good of you.'

'Yes, quite.'

There was a tiny glint of mischief and self-mockery in his voice – so small, a little speck, under the thick overlay of grief and desperation. He had taken off his jacket and his shirt looked loose on him; it was coming untucked at the back. He pushed his hand down into his pocket. I wanted to say 'I love you' as much as I ever had. It was alarming. I wanted to take his hand. I wanted to leave.

Ed came up to us. He looked hard at me, studying my face. 'Julia,' he said. 'It's been a while.'

He seemed years older than either Ralph or myself. His tie was too wide for the suit he was wearing.

He clapped Ralph on the back. 'Got to go. Back to the office.' His face was sombre and harsh. The two of them clasped hands for a moment and he was gone.

Everyone else was an academic or someone who had been a student with us. I recognised some faces from the lecture hall, classroom, bar. Somewhere I knew that the thing to do was to talk to those people and reminisce – wasn't that what these things were for? The prospect was unbearable. I remembered why I had thought of not coming.

Ralph's breath was hot and low against my cheek. 'Let's get out of here – can we – let's go for a drink.'

'I thought you'd never ask.'

There was a ghost there of how it used to be between us. We left the department and walked by the university bar. 'Not there,' Ralph said, not even turning his eyes towards the building. We kept walking, up the hill, into Newtown, and wound up in a small place where we sat at the very end of the bar in dim light. It was happy hour, two for one, and we drank tall red drinks made with berries and flavoured vodka.

For one happy hour we actually found things to laugh about. We were buoyed by our sense of escape from the funeral gathering. There was a pause after we got the second round of drinks. The place was filling up and at a table behind us a woman was telling a story that grew more and more hilarious to her friends. Ralph lit a cigarette and looked at me out of the corner of his eye, smiling.

'What do you think is so funny over there?' he asked, and exhaled.

'I don't know. All I could hear was something about her not being completely naked.'

He gave a pretend shudder. 'Let's be glad we can't hear the rest.'

We were pushed closer together at our end of the bar and more people crowded around us. My knees touched his. He recrossed his legs so that one of them touched mine.

We didn't talk about Ingrid. He told me a lot about what he was reading and listening to – too much opera, from the sound of it. I told him how it was going at the bookshop and my plans for law school the next year. He had plenty of his own ideas about what I should work on. We were a little pocket of intimacy there in the crowd. I couldn't stop reflecting on the strangeness and the familiarity of it – silently, to myself, not letting it show, not wanting to break the spell.

His hand brushed the flesh of my leg, just above the knee. It stayed there a second too long. My head swam. Behind the bar the blender whizzed, mashing up fruit. The two bartenders moved quickly, expressionless, filling glasses, pouring from bottles, taking money. It no longer felt like a bubble of intimacy around us. Instead I felt exposed to the air, as though every eye there could see straight through my skin to the wrestling blood inside. My breath was tight. I reflected with disgust on the conventional checklist of symptoms presented by my nervous system. The embarrassment came back too, of unrequited love gone on too long.

Ralph stood, crushed his cigarette out in an ashtray in front of him. 'I'll be back,' he said.

I finished my drink. When I rose and put my bag on my shoulder he was there again at my side. We left together, pushing our way out through a mass of people. The air outside was cool and sharp with smog, the sound of traffic loud on the street. Streetlights shone down.

'Are you alright?' he asked as he finished shrugging on his jacket. He rubbed his eyes, lifting his glasses up for a second, and looked at me. 'I've found that it hits me, sometimes – at different times ...' he said, haltingly.

It took me a moment to realise that he was talking

about Ingrid. He was talking about grief. Was he giving me an alibi? Was he serious? I despaired, and the rage in me went quiet.

'Sorry,' he offered.

'Just stop talking now.'

He stopped. He was never going to kiss me.

'I'll phone you. Here – are you going home?' His hand was in his wallet. 'Here – I'm sorry – let me get you a taxi.'

He was putting money in my hand, and turned away quickly, scanning the traffic, and raised his hand for a cab. It was like a bizarre rehearsal of old times. Putting me in a cab, quickly pressing a note into my hand the nights he didn't crash on my couch or I didn't end up at his flat. He always paid, for everything, once he knew that I didn't have money like he did. Always swiftly, money out for the food or drinks or fare or tickets before I could open my own purse. At first I had snapped at him about it, but it made him even more painfully embarrassed, which was worse, so I gave in and tried to be graceful about it. I had tried to make up for it by giving him books and other things when I had the chance. Free video rental.

It was all confusing, and for a moment I wanted to cross the street and walk down the several winding blocks to my old house, the terrace with the cool hallway. Home seemed a long way away.

Ralph looked close to tears. He put his arms around me, his mouth on my hair against my ear. His arms were thin. Oh, let this be the end, I thought. The taxi had driven on but a bus sighed to a stop beside us. He was about to say something. I pulled away from him and stepped onto the bus. The doors closed. There were two fifty-dollar notes clutched in my fingers.

'You'll need something smaller than that, love,' the driver said in a gravelly voice and turned the massive steering wheel around. I opened my bag, pushed the notes down inside and felt among the loose change settled there along the bottom for my fare.

Part Two

13.

The sky was a dirty grey as my cab drove through Brooklyn from the airport to the city, speeding along expressways lined with tenement apartment buildings, stalling for long minutes at the entrances to the bridge. There was a moment when the skyline came into focus – it hadn't been visible from my side of the plane as we had descended – and the line of skyscrapers seemed to reflect the grey of the sky with a darkly glittering sheen. I looked right down to the end of the island and saw the emptiness. It was the end of the day. It felt like night. The East River showed through the slats and cables of the bridge. Grey, grey. Banks of clouds seemed to lower themselves further. A ray of sunlight made its way through and hit the closed windows of a building as we passed over onto the island, turning them into squares of blinding gold.

Ralph had written the address of his uncle's apartment on a piece of paper, now folded into my pocket, a street just off Sixth Avenue in the Village. It was an area I knew well from the time I had spent here in the months after I finished high school, when I had practically lived for a while in the dorm room of a student at NYU. His room mate was rarely there, always staying with his girlfriend who had her own apartment in the East Village. When they finally broke up he was back at the dormitory, sulking and kicking cupboard doors closed. The student and I didn't last long after that.

The air smelled like evening – a soft dampness, grey like all the rest of it – when I got out of the cab. The apartment was in a tall, red-brick corner building set back from the street by a thin strip of garden, white blinds hanging closed in the ground-floor windows. I looked up and saw terraced levels on the higher floors. A delivery guy was coming out of the heavy glass front doors and he held one open for me. I dragged my suitcase through. The door of the first apartment inside to the left was open – the delivery guy had come from there – and a woman paused in the doorway, looking at me. She held a brown paper grocery bag in her arm.

'Hello,' she said. 'Welcome.'

It was hard to tell how old she was. Her hair was white. She was small, wearing a dark green dress. The interior of her apartment was hidden from view; it was her closed blinds I had seen from the street.

'Hi,' I replied. 'I'm staying … um … upstairs.'

'Good.' She sounded pleased. 'I'll see you later on then.'

'Sure.'

The floor started to tilt beneath me like the plane turning on its side as it came in over the city. Her door closed quietly. I wondered who she was and whether she'd known I was coming or was just being randomly welcoming. There were two lifts set into the far wall. The button glowed red and machinery creaked in the distance. After a long time waiting I looked over at the stairwell, speckled granite stairs. The apartment was on the fifth floor. The lift came.

The key slid into the lock on the apartment door easily

and turned. Relief. The door opened smoothly, a large slab of dark, solid wood.

The air inside the hallway felt stale and hot. There was a bedroom to my right. I heaved the suitcase in and set it down, glad to be rid of the weight. One corner of the room was filled with a bed made up with white sheets. White bed, white walls. Wooden floor. A tall, dark dresser. A square armchair, upholstered in a pastel colour. I waited as my eyes got used to the shape of the room in the growing dark. A small amount of light filtered in through French doors. When I opened them the sound of the street below poured in with a rush along with the damp, soft air. It felt like rain was waiting there.

The doors opened onto a small paved terrace scattered with plants growing in pots. There was a long cane lounge against the wall of the building and in front of it a long cane table, suffering from being outside. The varnished surfaces gleamed in places, joints painted deep red. I stepped out onto the terrace. Strings of Christmas lights hung around the walls in haphazard arrangements, unlit. I made a mental note to find the switch to turn them on later. Out here the air was alive with sound and a humidity that seemed to possess an energy of its own. A wave of fatigue hit me.

Through it there came a small sound of movement, closer than the distant noise that drifted up from the street. It came from the end of the terrace, a metallic tinkling. As my eyes adjusted I saw a large, elegant wire structure in the far corner, where the brick parapets reached up to just above waist height. A cage. I went and stood next to it; the top reached my shoulder. Various swings and mirrors hung down inside, a series of trapezes and bells. It was a little palace for a bird. Big enough, with toys that jangled. The strings of bells sounded in the faint breeze. There was no bird. The cage was empty except for the ornaments and mirrors.

It was 15 September. I wasn't sorry to have arrived after the anniversary of the eleventh had already passed. The date itself had been my last day at work in the bookshop before leaving, and I'd concentrated hard on staying busy. Dusting shelves. Alphabetising. Replacing, reorganising, rearranging. Counting out change very carefully after a sale. Double-checking the amount in the till, the list of sales, triple-checking. Neil had kept an eye on me and reached out, too quickly, to catch the stapler when I dropped it while fumbling with an exchange receipt towards the end of the afternoon, as though he'd been waiting for me to fuck up somehow. He didn't say anything, just handed it back to me and watched me set it back down on the counter, try again to make it work, open it, scratch my finger on a broken staple. I'd looked at the thin line of blood the staple had made when it scratched me, a drop pooling at one end. Neil had taken the stapler then and fixed it in one fluid movement, stapled the receipt and put it into the drawer. I'd taken a book that the next customer handed to me, keeping that one finger held away so it wouldn't bleed onto the jacket.

The sky beyond and over the terrace hung there, flat and uniform. A single pigeon flew by. Evening fell and I went back inside.

The passageway was lined with several doors I took to be closets – look later, I thought – and at the end of the passageway were two rooms: a living room and a kitchen. The walls were set at strange angles so there was only one right angle in each of the rooms; the other corners were either oddly wide or too narrow. A leather sofa and chairs took up most of the space in the living room, separated by a coffee table with its top piled with magazines in neat stacks. Plants in pots lined the deep windowsill. A square frame of butterflies hung on one wall, many small bodies pinned and lifeless. I was disgusted for a moment before I realised that it was only a photograph. Small watercolours hung beside it. A subway map was tacked up to the other wall. My eyes followed the familiar lines of colour. Blue A line. Orange F line. Red 1, 2, 3. I looked at the downtown section of the map and was surprised to see that it was complete, showing the lines and stops for the World Trade Center. I wondered why the Met hadn't printed a new map by now. Then it occurred to me that they must have, and this might be a souvenir. I pushed the corner of the map against the wall, securing it in place.

The overhead light in the kitchen revealed an alcove housing a 1950s era table – spearmint green laminex and chrome – with two matching chairs. A rack for wine was generously stacked with bottles of red and white. In the freezer there was ice and a half-full bottle of Absolut. It was tempting, but tiredness overcame me and I searched for a glass for water instead.

The cupboards seemed to contain only coffee and sugar, virtually no other food, but there were many glasses, bowls and plates. I checked the silverware drawers. The silver looked expensive. It looked like silver.

I returned to the bedroom and saw that there was a small ensuite bathroom attached, tiled in white and turquoise blue. The blue tiles, occasional tiny splashes, reminded me of the ocean and my body lurched towards Sydney with a wave-like rush. I left the bathroom light on to light the bedroom and searched for pyjamas. The birdcage outside sent in its tinkling sounds through the open doors. I pulled them closed.

The bed was firm. I lay on my back and thought about turning off the bathroom light. The doors were framed by long curtains pulled to each side. I thought about pulling them closed. A phone rang somewhere, rang and rang.

When I opened my eyes it was still dark and I wondered for a moment whether I had slept through the entire day and into the next night. It was hard to tell. A digital clock on a table next to the bed said it was 4:15 am. I thought again about closing the curtains, turning off the light, and lay there instead until light began to show in the sky, turning it pink and grey. As it turned into morning I slept again, a thick and dreamless slumber that took me through until the early afternoon.

I woke to see the sun again signalling a time of day different from what my body thought it was, though less brutally than before. The French doors glowed and the room was bright.

A noise came from the kitchen, shocking in the stillness. The tap had been turned on, hard. I froze, disoriented, forgetting for a frightened moment where I was, what room, what city. The noises continued: music started up from the direction of the living room and the sound of a male voice humming.

I quickly checked my clothes – pyjamas, blue, cotton, not obscene – and went into the hall.

'Hello?' My voice came out as a croak.

The owner of the humming voice stepped into the kitchen doorway. He looked to be in his late twenties with hair carefully styled to look tousled. He was wearing jeans and a white T-shirt. Both were very clean. He smiled.

'You're Judy? Hi. How are you?' He held a mug in one hand and was drying it with a checked towel. 'Mrs Bee downstairs told me to expect you,' he said. He turned back into the kitchen. 'I'm making coffee. Do you want some? I'm Matt, by the way. How was your trip? You're here from Australia? I would love to go there.'

I accepted coffee in a white mug and drank it gratefully.

'I didn't know that anyone actually lived here,' I said. The situation was confusing. Should I offer to leave? Why hadn't Ralph mentioned a person living in the apartment? 'I don't mean to come barging in. To your space here. I thought it was empty. My friend Ralph – do you know Ralph? No. He said it was empty, it's his uncle's –'

'No, no, it's no problem,' he assured me. 'Rob sends his friends to stay here from time to time. Friends, acquaintances, people he's met the night before, whatever. It's fine.'

Matt poured more coffee into my cup. 'It's not bad to have the company. And you have your own bathroom, thank god.' He flashed me a smile. 'I like my own bathroom.'

It turned out that Matt lived there in the apartment in some kind of arrangement with Uncle Robert where he watered the plants and sent on the mail in exchange for rent. It sounded like a very good deal.

'He's a very generous guy.' Matt shrugged. He had come in late last night. 'I looked in on you,' he said. 'You were out like a light.'

Matt slept in a bedroom between mine and the kitchen – one of the doors I'd thought was a closet. The proportions of the rooms kept surprising me, larger than they seemed they should be given the layout of the apartment. Matt's room was the same size as the one I had taken, but with walls painted robin's egg blue. Clothes lay strewn on the bed, the floor, the little desk in the corner. 'I really need to do laundry,' Matt said absently, and pulled the door closed.

He gave me a tour of the apartment, which I evidently hadn't explored very fully so far. A door across the hall from his opened to a gleaming bathroom in which all available surfaces were covered in jars and tubes of hair product and lotion, arranged in neat piles and rows. It smelled good, like oranges and mint. The mirror was misty around the edges from a recent shower.

Two other doors in the passageway revealed large closets, both filled with clothes, shoes and other objects. Two sets of skis lay on the floor of one. Several rolled-up rugs were propped up in the corner of the other. One appeared to contain mostly coats – old tweed overcoats, leather jackets, parkas, long puffy sleeping bags, a velvet cape, a floor-length coat of luxurious pale brown fur. I ran my hand over it. The fur felt cold and strangely liquid. I drew my hand away.

'Everyone leaves something behind,' said Matt, walking back to the kitchen. 'Put whatever you like in there. But there's a closet in your room too. And the drawers. Go ahead and use them.'

I sat down and put my hands around the coffee mug. It was cooling down. 'I don't know how long I'm staying,' I said.

'Well, welcome to New York anyway. Is this your first visit?'

'No. I was here a few years ago. A couple of times.' I didn't know what to say, about having been here before, about why I was here now. The jet lag came on with a slow tilt, the wave again.

'I think I'd like to go for a walk,' I said. 'I'd better have a shower.'

'Do you have any plans for tonight?' Matt asked.

'No. I don't have any plans.' No plans, period, I thought. 'I have to make some plans.' I sighed.

'OK.' Matt sounded very focused. 'Here's the plan. Go for a walk. Have a shower, whatever. We'll go out to eat later and you can tell me all about it.' He turned away and began to run water to wash the cups.

I looked around and noticed again the clean countertops and surfaces, free from dirt and crumbs. I understood now why it was that I had thought the apartment was empty.

'You're a clean freak,' I said, mainly to myself.

It was Matt's turn to sigh. 'Procrastinating,' he said, resignedly. He took my cup, just emptied, from the table.

'Wait,' I said. 'Tell you all about what?'

'Well. Whatever it is you're doing here.'

He had already washed the cups and cleaned down the clean counter. He folded the tea towel neatly over its rail on the oven.

I remembered before I went into my room. 'By the way. I'm Julia. Not Judy.'

Standing in the shower it occurred to me that I could be Judy. Why not? Judy in New York. What would Judy be like? It was impossible not to think of Judy Garland, heels clicking, red shoes sparkling. There's no place like home. There's no place like home.

The water fell hot and steady and had its own city smell, metallic and oddly deep. I washed the plane from my skin, layers sloughing invisibly down the drain.

There wasn't that much left of me in the city, I thought, but probably too much to make up Judy. Just Julia.

When I stepped out onto the street an hour later the full dislocation of my senses struck me hard. My head felt twice as big as it should be, and disconnected from my neck, as though it were a heavy balloon wanting to drift away – it would surely fall to the ground though, so large it felt on a weak string – I gathered determination and walked. The avenue was busy with cars and people.

I bought a bagel and coffee at a busy store around the corner, and ate and drank standing at a narrow bar in the shop window. The coffee was sweet and creamy and did something to unzip the film around my head. The sun shone down. It was the tail end of lunchtime, the street full of people hurrying more than usual.

Once outside, I turned and faced south. The avenue swooped down in a straight line. Summoning strength at every step, I walked south. If not today it would never happen, I thought. I would walk every day, as I liked to do, but if I didn't do it today then every next day would become an avoidance that would only get harder to face down. Blocks and corners passed until I reached the ragged snake of Broadway, the one affront to the symmetry of the grid. The further south I went the more conscious I was of the empty part in the sky where the towers should have been. The street filled with the smell of sweet roasting nuts from vendor carts on one block, pretzels on another. By the time Canal Street presented itself I was exhausted. The footpath was a throng of people jostling for space, drifting onto the road, cars honking. 'Excuse me,' someone said shortly as we bumped into one another, making it clear that I was at fault. There were a thousand different handbags in just one tiny shop, nothing more than a hole in a wall, and all the same bags in the shop next door. Colourful watches laid out on folding tables. Baby turtles in a plastic tank with a handle on top, noses pressed against the sides and tiny front arms spinning. More handbags. I turned around and walked back.

Matt came in the door just after seven to find me slumped on the couch in front of the television. Beautiful teenagers were behaving badly on the screen. 'Get up,' he said. 'It's just down the road.'

We went to a noodle place a few blocks away, and when my steaming bowl of soup arrived I was glad to be there. Matt ate some kind of stir-fried dish that smelled like chili and mint, sprinkled through with pieces of fluorescent red pork. He let me sketch a brief version of what I was doing in the city, the story of my lost friend.

'I thought I'd go down there, this afternoon, on my walk,' I said. 'I guess I forgot how far away it is.'

He nodded sympathetically. 'Take the subway.'

'Right.' I drank my soup.

'It's a letdown.'

'The site?'

'Yep. I go down there to Century 21' – a massive discount department store near where the World Trade Center had been. 'This shirt is from there – it's Prada, for thirty dollars. Anyway. There isn't much to see. A lot of tourists.'

Matt told me about himself. He worked at a gallery down in SoHo, a big space that showed a lot of sculpture. 'I'm one of the guys who move stuff around, set up the shows, you know. Hang the paintings, straighten the rails. Some heavy lifting. Some carpentry. Order in the wine. General running around.' At night he was doing a course in graphic design at the New School. He had a kind of likeable candour, and a self-deprecating tone from time to time that softened the edges of his confidence in himself. He seemed very honest and probably available. Exactly the kind of guy I would never fall for. In any case, I suspected that he was gay, and I was grateful that he was not attractive to me.

'What's on at the gallery now?' I asked. 'Anything worth seeing?'

'Oh, it's kind of interesting,' he said. 'A couple of installations. There's one with snails … I don't know. It's a little dull actually. Very conceptual.'

I asked if he knew Maeve and Grey. He looked at me more warily. 'Your friend was Ingrid Grey?' he asked. I'd said earlier only that she had been a student, hadn't said her last name.

'They're heavy players,' he said. 'Maeve's gallery is one of the most powerful in the city. She has a few big names. She and Grey together can make an artist.'

'Or break them?'

'That I've never seen. But they're a tough team.'

I nodded.

'Do you know her?' he asked. I said I did, a little. He shook his head. 'She's a ruthless gorgon,' he said mildly. 'Underneath it all.'

It was an image that clarified the menace I'd sensed under the surface when I'd seen her around Ingrid, the scheming brain inside.

When I asked if Matt had known Ingrid, he said no, but that he had seen her around. 'She would come to the openings sometimes, some of the art parties. Museum stuff. I always saw her with Fleur, you know, the girl. The artist. Haven't seen them for a while. Well, obviously.' He looked embarrassed and reached for his drink, a beer. 'Sorry.'

'It's OK,' I said.

'You look like you're about to fall over,' he told me with a smile.

I was so tired that I laughed, in way that felt almost like crying, and couldn't stop for a long minute.

We went back to the apartment, and the walk seemed so much longer than it had on the way there.

14.

When Friday came at the end of that first week it was a surprise. The haze of jet lag had put the days out of order, with no routine to give them meaning. But when I went out into the street that night there was no mistaking the aura in the air. The voices of people hurrying by all had an elevated pitch of excitement to them; women talked quickly to each other as they walked together, their tall heels hard on the concrete. There was a purpose to their stride distinct from the ordinary weekday walk – reaching forward an inch further, covering more pavement, a little faster. Others were slowed down, exhausted, or relieved that the week was over. The evening felt heavy with possibilities, but I was separate from it all and in a self-pitying kind of mood; those possibilities seemed to be reserved for others.

The jet lag had worn off by then but I still felt like an off-beat, slow and mangled, against the pacing of the street. People crowded the footpaths waiting for cabs and taking the steps up and down to the subway at a pace. My appetite disappeared and I walked on and crossed 14th Street, past the place I had been heading for, a little store I had taken to stopping at for food at the odd hours of the day when hunger struck. A turn around a corner took me to a street lined with several restaurants. The fast-walking women up ahead turned into one. Passing it a minute later I saw their legs seated on stools at the dimly lit bar inside. The whole block was full of people greeting each other, answering phones and laughing. A woman alone on the footpath, cheeks pinched in the cold, snapped open her phone. 'Where are you now?' she asked in a rush.

Halfway down the block there was a restaurant with a large window onto the street. A man was sitting alone at one of the tables inside. It was set only for one, with one elegant glass and a bottle of wine resting beside him. He was reading a book, which he held open with one hand while he drank from the glass in the other. I was transfixed by the same voyeuristic fascination that comes from watching someone through their living room window. He seemed quite comfortable, although that might have been an act.

I could be doing that, I thought, enjoying a nice meal and a drink on a Friday night in a restaurant on my own. I felt a pull inside, out of the cold. But I started to feel conspicuous standing there in clothes that were clearly not suitable for this calibre of restaurant – jeans and an oversized, black sheepskin jacket that I had found in the closet. It smelled faintly of cedarwood, a nice smell. The woman who had been talking into her cell phone walked past with a man at her side now, whereabouts known, and through the door into the vestibule and interior of the restaurant.

A wind pulled through and dropped the temperature on the street. It was too cold to stand still for long. The moment of identification with the man's comfortable solitude was gone, an illusion. My desire for company sickened me, and

I envied him. I went to find some food to take back to the apartment.

The lights were on inside the ground-floor apartment when I returned to the building with my arms full of gin in a brown paper bag, cigarettes and slices of pizza. The window was still, no curtains twitching, a light on inside.

I paused outside the door. There was a little peephole set into it, the kind that lets you see out from inside and shows whoever is there in a long, distorted fish-eye view. The piece of glass glinted inside its circular frame.

When I went out the next day I stopped outside a storefront crammed with images and small objects: souvenir versions of the Statue of Liberty; the Manhattan skyline in a snowdome. A magazine clipping was stuck to the inside of the shop window so that it showed onto the street: a picture of the New York, New York casino in Las Vegas with its replica of the Twin Towers made into a makeshift memorial after the attacks. The miniature towers stood there, backed by a fountain, their base surrounded by wreaths. The fountain sprayed behind them like the plastic snow in the snowdomes. One mourner was pictured sitting in a squat on the ground nearby, eyes cast low.

The shop entrance was blocked by racks of cards that spilled out onto the street. I turned one around. It teetered and spun with a creak. There was a glut of images of the city but hardly any of the towers, giving the impression that they were being tactfully avoided. Or maybe they were sold out. The United Nations building was a popular image, smooth and monolithic. The Empire State Building was there too.

There was a stack of cards at the bottom of the rack featuring the towers, just the towers, with the whole city a fuzz beneath them. Alone, they looked different. When they were shown as part of the old skyline the image drew attention to its transformed shape since then, the hole in the sky you could see from anywhere on the island.

There was another card, post-September 11. In this one a hand held up a picture of the towers in front of the camera, against the skyline, so the picture filled in the gap and repaired the view. The Brooklyn Bridge stood there in front of the towers in the picture, its two lovely vaults echoing the two buildings. Now the gap of space visible through the vaults anticipated their absence. The thin white edges of the held-up picture framed the sky around the buildings like a shield.

This was what my eyes had been doing, I realised, wanting to hold up a screen of memory against that impossible hole in the sky, blue and invisible. This hole was of a different order to the actual hole in the ground, which I'd only seen images of, which seemed to present such a clean wound. The hole in the ground was also somehow impossible, an affront to the imagination: it was impossible to believe that such a small-seeming foundation could have held up such buildings; impossible to believe that such a space could have contained all their wreckage. But the hole in the sky was just their size, their image filled it exactly, the blueness of that clear day closed around it. Their absence was so difficult to imagine that it had seemed to me sometimes since I'd arrived that they had not really gone at all but had been rendered invisible by magic, cloaked by the air around them like a spaceship in science fiction. The hole in the sky radiated so intensely that it had become presence.

I took the card, took three of them, another three. One to send to Jenny, one for Ralph, more for myself. I went to enter the shop to pay but paused on the threshold, stuck between the racks of cards. The interior of the shop burned with claustrophobia, crammed with cluttered shelves that towered up to the ceiling. Rows of little Lady Liberties met my eyes, red torches glowing in the dark inside. I readied my money, smoothed out the paper bills, and stepped inside.

Later on, I went out to get bagels and ran into Mrs Bee from downstairs in the vestibule inside the first set of front doors where the mailboxes were set into the wall. She was closing a mailbox and locking it with a small key, several envelopes in her hand. I said hello and she smiled warmly at me.

'Going out?' she asked. She looked immaculate, her white hair swept up in a comb, long linen dress.

'Just around the corner,' I replied. On impulse, I added, 'I'm getting bagels. From around the corner. Can I get you anything? Do you want a bagel?' It was hard to imagine her eating bagels.

'That's so kind of you,' she said. 'I've eaten. But I would love one for later. Can I offer you some tea? When you get back?'

I thanked her and said yes.

At the bagel shop I didn't know what kind she wanted and bought poppy seed, sesame, plain and raisin. The bagels were fat and shiny and warm. I ate mine, plain with cream cheese, on the way back to the building.

I knocked at her door, imagining the view through the peephole viewer. She let me in and took the brown paper bag from my hands.

'What's it like out there?' she asked.

'Warm,' I said. She nodded sagely.

The door opened directly onto a living room that had windows at one end onto the street. The floor was carpeted in a light mossy colour with a faint pattern of fern leaves. There was a fireplace against one wall with what looked like a gas-powered fire in it, unlit, just the fake coals sitting there, and a long, stone mantelpiece over it. The wide ledge was lined with photographs in frames and other objects: a ceramic rabbit, three glass vases, tall candlesticks, a crystal ball on a lacquered stand. On the opposite wall a gilt-framed mirror reflected back the whole array. A sofa with deep seats faced the window, a plain coffee table in front of it. Two armchairs sat across from the sofa, under the windows. In one corner there was a tree growing in a wide terracotta pot, its branches reaching almost to the ceiling. She saw me looking at it. 'It's a ficus tree,' she said. 'Sit down. I'll make us some tea.'

I sat on the sofa and she disappeared through an archway into the next room. A few minutes later she brought in a tray and rested it on the coffee table. The tray held a large, earthenware teapot, dark brown with rounded edges, and two china cups on saucers. They were white with a coloured stripe around the top edge, one jade green, the other pink.

'It's nice to finally meet you,' she said.

I wasn't sure what to say.

'Robert called to tell me you were coming,' she continued. 'He's an old friend. You're a friend of his nephew, is that right? And Matt's here, isn't he?'

I said that he was.

'That's good. He's lovely. I have a spare key to the apartment too.' I wondered if she was a caretaker of some kind. Then she said, 'There's a caretaker – he lives in the building across the road, takes care of both buildings.'

She poured the tea gracefully straight from the pot, no strainer, so that leaves drifted down and settled along the bottom of the cup. She offered milk but I drank the tea black, enjoying its smoky taste.

'How is your visit so far?' she asked.

'It's fine.'

She nodded again, knowingly. I didn't have a sense exactly of being scrutinised by her as much as an unsettling feeling of being already known, having already been read somehow, swiftly as a brief page of writing.

She took a long breath and pressed her lips together. 'Let's see,' she said, and made a small gesture with her hand. I had almost finished my tea, and thought that she was asking for my cup. I offered it to her, along with the saucer, but she said, 'No,' and smiled. My confusion must have shown. 'I'm going to read the leaves,' she explained.

I hesitated, but I was curious and didn't refuse. She asked me to turn the cup three times in its saucer, and then turn it upside down. I did. It clinked softly. We watched it sit there for a minute while the small amount of liquid left in it trickled away and pooled in the saucer.

The whole room smelled faintly of tea, like a canister of

good English Breakfast when it is first opened. There were no floral tones in the smell at all, just earthy, toasted, brown notes.

She picked up the cup and looked into it, turning it around in her fingers.

'What does it say?' I asked her.

She tilted the cup towards me so that I could see into it. Around her left wrist was a wide silver cuff covered with a delicate tracery of engraved, interlocking lines. Fine dots made a line around the middle of the cup.

'There's your journey,' she said, indicating it with a finger. 'It extends all the way around – but broken in points.'

Her eyes moved over the clumps of leaves. There were no shapes there I could see, no patterns. 'A flower,' she said, and gave me a quick, happy glance. 'When it's leaning towards the seeker like that – the standard meaning for the flower is that praise and compliments are coming your way.'

'The seeker?'

'The person seeking a reading. The person whose cup it is. In the cup, the handle is considered to represent you. Your direction.'

'What kind of flower is it?' I asked.

'Look,' she said. Her finger pointed to a gathering of leaves near the rim, near the handle. I could sort of see a flower – a stem; petals. 'There's another one,' she said, indicating a similar clump further down.

'I suppose it's a flower,' I said. 'A generic one.'

She shrugged.

'Wait – I see something,' I said. It had caught my eye, upside down, when I saw the second flower. 'A padlock.'

She raised her eyebrows and looked. Her mouth pursed a little. 'I see,' she said.

'Is it open or closed?' I asked.

She looked at me. 'What do you think?'

'What does it mean?'

She looked at the cup again. 'It could be open or closed. One way, a surprise for you. The other, a need for precaution.'

I looked at the flower, right there above the padlock, and thought of Fleur, the girl I'd never met. As I looked at the cup, shapes seemed to coalesce out of the gathered leaves all at once, in a rush: a cloud of crosses; birds in a dark V against the sky; a boat on the water; curling waves.

She was watching me, her expression inscrutable, somehow aloof and intimate all at once. It was a look I came to know well, and I came to think that it derived from having a lot of knowledge that she always had to hold back. The shapes lost their definition and became wet leaves again.

'You seem to know a lot about this,' I said.

She smiled. 'I've been doing it for a while.' I wondered again how old she was. 'It's what I do,' she explained. Her eyes strayed to the mirror, the crystal ball reflected there. 'Fortune-telling. Psychic readings.'

My eyes narrowed.

She smiled again. 'I know, I don't look like one.'

I thought of the many curtained shopfront windows in the East Village and scattered across the city with their ubiquitous neon signs advertising futures foretold, and the psychic hotlines advertised in the paper. She seemed so sane and rational with her genteel linen and understated decorative scheme, unlike all the junk and fakery I associated with the profession, if that's what it was. It reminded me too much of the crystal healing and spiritual arcana that my mother was obsessed with.

I stood and went to the mantel. 'Do you use this?' I asked, nodding at the crystal ball.

She gave a noncommittal kind of tilt of the head. 'Cards. Palms. People feel comfortable with different sorts of things.' She turned her own cup slowly on its saucer. 'You're a sceptic,' she said, neutrally.

I touched the crystal ball. It was cold under my fingers, and perfectly clear.

'That's healthy,' she said. 'I understand.'

There was a small stack of business cards next to the crystal ball, pale brown like weak tea. *M. Bee*, they said in raised black type. *Tasseography. Tarot. Predictions.* There was a phone number.

My empty cup sat on the table. I had the feeling that she wasn't telling me everything she saw there – she'd hardly told my fortune, after all, just pointed out the obvious sign of a journey, and observed that it was broken. As a sceptic I probably didn't warrant a fully fledged set of predictions.

The buzzer sounded and she answered it. Moments later came a quick knock at the door and, when she opened it, a man stood there with three full grocery bags in his arms. He came in and took the bags to the kitchen. She pressed a couple of dollars into his hand and thanked him and he left, wordlessly.

'Please excuse me,' she said. 'Some of this will need to be put away before it spoils.'

'Would you like a hand?' I offered.

She regarded me for a moment. 'No,' she said. 'Thanks. But you can come through and keep me company.'

She showed me through the archway to the kitchen. There was a square table set against one wall, big enough for three people to sit at. A hanging lamp cast light on the floor and the table. I brought in the tray with our tea things on it. The grocery bags were on the countertop. She went through them, packing food away into the fridge and cupboards. I sat at the table. The bags were printed with the name of a classy supermarket nearby.

'How do you like the neighbourhood?' she asked.

I said I liked it and told her that I'd lived here for a short time, not far away, a few years before.

'I suppose it's changed a little since then,' she said.

'Not that much,' I replied.

Her skin was pale under the yellowish light, against the light green counters and white tiled floor. Watching her unpack groceries – a collection of mundane items, bread, cans of tomatoes, milk, pasta in a box – some of the mystique of the fortune-teller evaporated and she seemed more like a normal person. I asked how long she had lived here.

'Oh, a long time,' she said with a little laugh. 'Forever.' She set the teacups into the sink.

I drank tea with Mrs Bee often after that. She didn't ever tell me her first name, or what to call her, and in her company I was able to get away without using her name at all. There had been a Mr Bee at some point, she revealed, but he was either dead or living far away; the way she put it made it ambiguous. There was a maternal edge in the way she treated me, an almost protective element in her attitude sometimes – never open – but something told me that she didn't have children of her own. Once or twice I saw people going into her apartment who might have been clients coming to have their fortunes told. A well-dressed woman in impossibly high heels and a style I didn't expect to see outside of the Upper East Side, two strings of pearls at her neck and a suit that looked like Chanel. A man with thinning hair, briefcase in his hand, nervous glances side to side before he went through the door. But mostly the people I saw coming and going from there were delivering something or other. Dinner, flowers, groceries, drycleaning, packages.

I came inside one afternoon and shucked off my coat as I sat on the couch. She was still in the kitchen putting the kettle on. 'Have you been outside today?' I called out. 'It's cold outside.'

'Winter's on the way,' she said, and didn't answer my question.

We started drinking tea and talked about something else. The buzzer sounded and she answered the door to another delivery person, who handed her a paper bag closed and stapled at the top. She took it into the kitchen and came back.

'You have it all worked out with this delivery system,' I commented.

'New York,' she said. 'You can have anything delivered here, to your door.'

When I was finished drinking my tea I asked her, 'Have you been down there? To the World Trade Center site?' I had still not made the trip to Ground Zero.

'Oh, no,' she said, as though we were talking about a visit to a very bad part of the Bronx.

There was a short silence.

'It holds no interest for me,' she said eventually, with all her usual Zen-like calm. 'But you'll get there.'

She had a way of peppering the conversation with little predictions like that, offhand, not portentous. Coming from anyone else they would have sounded just like reassurances or wishes, but from her mouth they had a different, oracular kind of tone.

I wanted to ask her how long it had been since she had gone outside the building, but it seemed to be overstepping some kind of boundary. By then I had come to the conclusion that she didn't go outside. She didn't seem to leave her apartment except to collect her mail from the vestibule inside the front set of doors. The big front window faced onto the street, blinds slanted down so that you could see out but it was hard to see in from the other side.

'I'll get there,' I echoed.

She had set out fingers of shortbread on a plate, crumbly and sweet. A piece fell apart in my hands, sending crumbs over my skirt and onto the floor.

'Don't worry about it,' she smiled.

She didn't read my cup that day. There were hardly any leaves in it at the end for some reason. I looked down into it before I stood to go. The whole thing was like a Rorschach blot test, the leaves presenting fuzzy shapes that your mind could make into anything. I said this to Mrs Bee once. 'That's true, in a way,' she had said. 'That's part of the whole thing. But you know. Sometimes you see a shape and you

know what it is – you know what that shape means to you.'
Today, the few leaves curled up in the bottom of the cup
looked just like a leaf that had fallen from a tree. There was
probably a meaning for that too.

When I told her at last, on my second or third visit,
something about what I was doing there in New York, she
nodded and didn't ask questions. I was on my way to visit
the Classics department up at Columbia. She listened to me
patiently. It was hard to escape the feeling that she already
knew everything I had to tell her, and was vaguely curious to
see what words I would use myself to describe it, how much
I would reveal or withhold. She would have made an
excellent psychologist. That was probably part of her work
too. I knew it was an aura that she cultivated – the quiet,
knowing look. She was good at her job. But it worked. It was
a powerful effect – the sense of being known, understood,
and not judged – and I believed that it was true.

15.

The professor's door was closed when I reached it. It was painted off-white like the walls around it, greying around the edges and the handle. The corridor was quiet as I considered knocking. The door opened suddenly: a girl burst out of it and walked away, her high sandals clopping. She didn't meet my eyes. I could see that she had been crying. Her dark hair was pulled back, a short black dress, pink scarf around her neck, a thin body clutching books to her chest. The corridor filled with students who poured out of a room two doors down, a horde of swinging hair and backpacks. The crying girl was quickly lost in the crowd.

Ralph had given me a name, Jones, Ingrid's adviser at Columbia. We had arranged the meeting over email, brief messages that had introduced me as a friend of Ingrid's and asked for a short meeting when I was passing through New York. It was the only appointment I had made in advance of leaving Sydney. When I turned back to the door he was standing in the middle of the frame. He was tall, and wearing a sienna-brown shirt. He didn't quite smile, but his look was not unfriendly for all that; curious, and challenging. His dark blond hair had been cut so that it fell into his eye. There was enough of it to show the dense beauty of the hair itself, its heavy straightness. I recognised the colour of wet sand and looked at the striking eyes, hazel green with their splinters of brown. The face in the Arms and Armor room at the museum.

'Julia Alpers.'

He said my name like an announcement, voice English, educated, as I remembered.

'Yes.' I paused. 'Have I come at a bad time?'

He looked confused for a second. 'No. No, this is the time we arranged. Please, come in.'

He stepped to the side and motioned me into the room. Two walls were covered in books, many of them fat volumes dating from at least the nineteenth century. I looked straight to them and thought of the bookshop back in Sydney. This one's spine was damaged slightly; the gold leaf on the title print was nicely intact. Titles in Latin and German and Greek. I took my eyes away.

The floor was covered in a Persian rug in tones of russet red, overlaying the institutional grey carpet underneath. One window looked down over the square below, full of sun and sharp shadows. I was wearing good clothes – my narrow black woollen pants and coat, a long top with chevron stripes in black and cream, red lipstick in place – but I wished that I had dressed up more, in heels.

The room was full of whatever had taken place just then to make the girl cry. His lack of embarrassment about the scene was unsettling. He took a seat at his desk and tilted back in his chair, a wide-legged pose with his hands clasped, fingers interlaced loosely. His features were softer than I remembered, but just as beautiful and distant-looking. The chair was old, polished wood, a teacher's chair. He gestured to another chair for me. It was out of place in the room, a cheap, plastic thing. I sat. His silence had begun to intimidate me. I began to recognise something in him, the power of a teacher who is hard to please, and too late I found something coming out of my mouth that was meant to be pleasing. I said something about the crying girl that made him laugh, about how she hadn't managed to convince him to give her a better grade. I felt bad then, sorry for making a joke of the girl's misery.

'So,' he sighed, 'you were a friend of Ingrid's?'

'Yes, we were friends in Australia, before she moved over here more permanently.'

'Ah, yes. We never heard much about her life there. She had a strange accent too, not one I would have recognised straight off as Australian. A little like yours.' It sounded vaguely like an accusation.

In my memory Ingrid's voice had a kind of precision along with phrasing that was sometimes a little off. 'Her father was … French? Swiss? Her voice had that sound.'

He looked doubtful. 'And are you visiting the Metropolitan Museum while you're in town?'

It was the first reference either of us had made to that earlier, accidental meeting, and I wondered whether he was actually recalling that experience, or whether he didn't remember at all and it was a casual question. It seemed to take a long time to process those various possibilities in my mind. His hands were spread on the desk in front of him, long and elegant, and he studied them as he spoke.

There was a knock at the door behind me, which he had left slightly open. He didn't respond, but looked into my face, still waiting for me to answer his question. A moment passed, and the door was pushed open a little. A girl half-stepped into the room, her face lit with apprehension, eyes wide with huge lashes and lines of kohl.

He looked at her irritably. 'Did I ask you to enter?'

Her eyes dropped and raised again.

'Why knock if you don't wait for a response?'

She stood still.

I cleared my throat. 'Maybe I have come at a bad time. You're very busy with your students. Sorry for the interruption. Perhaps I can make a time to see you later in the week.'

He was a little breathless when he turned, as though he was concentrating hard to focus on me and the girl at the same time.

'Maybe another time. But I don't know what you want to know. I don't know what I can tell you.' He sounded irritated, but he decided to give me something. 'You should talk to Trinh, you know. They were friends.'

'Trinh?'

'Another student here. You can get her number from the office. You might find her in the department if you wait.' He checked his watch briefly. 'She finishes teaching about now.'

The girl didn't say a word, she stood just inside the doorway, relaxed and expectant. As I left I caught a look from the side of her eyes, something like contempt. The door closed firmly behind me.

I started off down the hall, thinking about the crying girl, her red and tired face.

*

The department office was a long, narrow room connected to a small mailroom walled in with shelves, sectioned into slots for the faculty and students. Behind a glass partition a woman with glasses was typing at a computer behind a desk surrounded by filing cabinets.

'Excuse me,' I said. 'I'm looking for Trinh.'

'Yes?'

The voice came from the mailroom behind me, from a young woman standing in front of the rows of shelves against the wall. 'I'm Trinh.'

Her eyes were the startling grey-blue of coloured contact lenses. She was holding a stack of papers, student assignments. The blue-black line of a tattoo snaked out across her wrist from under the cuff of her shirt.

'Julia. I'm a friend of Ingrid Grey.'

The stack of papers slipped from her hands just then and they began to fall, sliding onto the floor. We both bent to collect them. Her hair was short, black and glossy. She had not spoken again.

'I was hoping to talk to you,' I offered. 'I was just speaking with Professor Jones and he said you were friends. With Ingrid. I'm here in New York looking for Ingrid – not looking for her – looking. Looking into what she was doing here.'

Trinh gave me a stare that was both injured and suspicious.

'You are looking for her?'

'No, just – I'm an old friend.'

Trinh reached down to the floor and picked up a leather briefcase. She slid the papers inside.

'OK, I'll talk to you. I'm busy now.'

She started walking. Her shoes made a loud clip on the floor, heels at least two inches high. I followed her.

'Can you meet me later?' she asked. 'Do you want to meet for a drink?'

'Sure.'

'Cool. Give me your hand.'

Her grip was light and smooth. With a pen she wrote the name and street of a bar on the back of my hand.

'It's down in Chinatown. Can you be there at about nine?'

'OK.'

'See you there.'

We stopped outside the lift. Trinh pressed the up button and the lift doors opened immediately. She stepped inside. As the doors closed she smiled, a transforming effect.

I pressed the button to go down and waited. The corridor was oppressive, low ceiling made of pocked, square white panels. The smile was a talisman to take me out of the building, away from crying and contemptuous girl students and into the air outside. I looked down at my right hand.

Lilac Lounge.

Already the ink had started to bleed into my skin, blurring the lettering.

When I finally descended the stairway to the Lilac Lounge, I had walked past the unmarked building at least twice in my search for the place. Finally I had made out a faded 'L' on a corner of the building's façade that could mean something. Layers of paint peeled off the front of the building, yellow and red and blue, each layer revealing a different set of indistinguishable letters. Stairs led down from the street to basement-level doors that opened onto a candle-lit interior. Couples and groups of people huddled in small alcoves around the room.

Trinh was sitting at the bar, clad in shining leather. She welcomed me and talked in low tones to the bartender, ordering me a drink.

'I hope you didn't have too much trouble finding the place.'

I shrugged.

My drink arrived, a squat tumbler filled with clear liquid and shattered blueberries. I asked her what it was and she said, 'Absinthe,' and laughed at the face I made. 'They don't make it so poisonous these days. Don't worry. Let's sit.'

We moved to a black vinyl booth under a panel of leadlight glass. The place was so shut off from the outside that it seemed as though no sunlight would ever make it into these corners during the day.

We went through questions and answers about how long I'd been in New York, whether it was my first time here.

'I lived here for a few months,' I explained. 'A few years ago.'

She nodded. 'Where have you been since then?'

'Sydney.'

Trinh pulled off her jacket. The vinyl seats squeaked as she moved. Her arms were traced all over with dark and intricate designs. I tried not to stare.

'So Jones told you to talk to me.'

'Yes, I met with him very briefly today.'

'Did he have anything to tell you?'

'No, not really. We were … interrupted before we really got talking.'

'Ah, yes. He is busy with the students.' She smiled. 'You might find it interesting to talk to him. I don't know. He was devastated when she disappeared, you know. She was one of his students. He doesn't take many on. And they don't tend to – well, nothing like this has ever happened before.'

'I'm sorry,' I said. 'I know this must seem a little strange. It has been – it had been – a long time since I heard from Ingrid. An old friend of mine – her cousin – asked me to come over here and find out a bit more about her life, about what was going on with her.' I wondered what to say. 'He's not able to travel.'

Trinh looked at her glass. 'I wasn't close to her. We were friends, sort of. She was a very private person. She was close to Fleur – her stepdaughter, you know – and I suppose she did have other friends.'

I nodded. It didn't sound like the Ingrid I used to know.

'Ingrid had dropped out of contact before September, but she surfaced occasionally. Very occasionally.' She drank and set down her glass. 'And now she is one of the "missing". I suppose they'll find a piece of her somewhere when they finish sifting through all that rubble and bone.' She regarded me with a neutral face. I could almost feel every bone in my body, inside, connected, not pulverised in a heap of ash.

'Another?' She indicated my empty glass. I nodded.

We drank on and I found myself telling her about myself – stories of the bookshop, the odd customers, the boredom of shelving, the pleasure of coming to understand the intricacies of rare book values, first editions. Plans for law school. Mark. I worked out the shapes of things in the stylised designs of her tattoos: a vine, or a vein. Flowers, or maybe hands.

She leaned back in her seat. 'So tell me about Ralph. I think I remember Ingrid mentioning him, maybe. He hadn't talked to Ingrid in a while?'

'They had a falling out. After the marriage. I mean, they fell out of touch.' I looked at Trinh's eyes, blue and plastic and shadowed in the semi-darkness.

'And you?'

'I want to know too. We were friends once. We were all friends. We just sort of drifted apart when she left.'

'That does happen, doesn't it?'

'I suppose it does.'

It made me think about Ingrid's last visit, the year after the wedding. Ralph and I didn't talk for a while after the party fiasco, and then we did, and he took to stopping by the bookshop again every so often. He took up drinking pretty seriously, drinking alone, at home and elsewhere. I talked to Ingrid maybe twice in that time; not long after she got back to New York, when she called me to say thank you for the wedding gift. A card arrived too, saying thank you from both her and Grey. And I called her once, a couple of weeks into the new year, feeling depressed and nostalgic. It was 2000, the new millennium. We didn't talk for long. She had been on her way to class, rushed and monosyllabic. It was just over a year after the wedding that Ralph wound up in hospital. A heart attack, an arrhythmia, a lot like his father. Ed called me, same as with George. It was an inherited disorder, he told me, and it had reached a crisis point. It was turning out to be a tough job to get him stabilised. Ralph had been with Eve when it happened.

Eve was there at the hospital when I went to see him, thinner than I'd seen her before, aged and strained in the face. Ralph looked terrible, frail against the sickly-coloured green sheets of the hospital bed. He asked me to bring him some cigarettes. I gave him some of mine when Eve wasn't looking. He complained that they weren't letting him drink, whining like a child.

I was furious with him for not telling me how bad his illness had become. 'I know you talked to Ingrid about it, didn't you?' I said, accusingly. 'It's not like you didn't know. You could have been taking better care of yourself. There's no point pretending this doesn't exist. You could be dead.' I had always indulged his refusal to talk about his health, not wanting myself to believe that anything was really wrong.

He didn't apologise or act defensive. He looked at me, his face composed and serious. 'Please tell Ingrid.'

I had already called her and left a message on the machine the day before, letting her know that he was in the hospital and giving her the number. I didn't tell him that.

The next day I called her again, with no luck. Ralph looked worse. They were trying new medicines to make his heart beat in a safer pattern.

'Do you think she'll come?' he asked me, wanting an answer, but I didn't know.

I finally got through to Ingrid the following day. Fleur answered the phone. It was the first time we had spoken. Her voice was like any teenager's.

'Julia,' she repeated after me when I'd said who I was. Long, silent seconds passed and Ingrid came to the phone.

'Julia?' she said.

'Ingrid — did you get my message?'

'No — no.' Her voice was fuzzy, as though she had just woken up. 'I didn't get any message. The machine sometimes plays up …'

'Ingrid, it's about Ralph.'

I told her. 'It's kind of serious,' I said. 'He's asking for you.'

She said that she would call. I waited for her to say she would come to Sydney, but she didn't.

When I next saw Ralph we didn't talk about it, but a few days later they had obviously spoken. He looked optimistic. The table beside his bed was piled with novels that I'd brought over the past week. I tried bringing him other things to read but he insisted on reading Thomas Hardy. It didn't seem like something that would do any good in the circumstances. She was going to come, he said. I didn't believe it, and I didn't talk to her again over the next week. Once they figured out the right combination of drugs Ralph got better quickly, enough to go home to his flat. He and Eve fought over it — she wanted him back at Kirribilli, but he said he wouldn't be treated like a child and did she want to give him another heart attack by arguing. That made her quiet, and furious.

I went around the next day to the flat with some more

books – the latest Booker winner, something else new. Ingrid was there, on the couch next to him. The scene had the look of a Vermeer painting with that morning light coming through the windows, still and silent. She was wearing light-coloured clothes, a crushed-looking white shirt, and the light struck her at an angle that made her glow like an angel, or a ghost. The face she turned to me was stricken, lips as pale as her skin. Her hair was a few inches shorter, and when she twisted it to the side and over her shoulder there was less of it to pull through her fingers. She had just arrived, straight from the airport. A silver suitcase sat inside the door.

Ralph smiled beatifically. 'Look,' he said. 'I told you.' Or am I remembering it wrongly – was that just what his expression said?

There was a fine layer of dust on the kettle when I lifted it from the stove and filled it from the tap to make tea. Ingrid didn't move from the couch. She looked sicker than Ralph. 'Horrible flight,' she said, and smiled thinly.

I gave her the tea and she sipped it slowly. 'It's just for a few days,' she said. 'It's hard to get away at this time of year.'

'I'm glad you came.'

'Thank you for calling me, Julia,' she said. 'I'm glad you reached me. Let me give you my cell phone number.' She grabbed a piece of paper and wrote down a string of numbers. 'It's easier to reach me that way.'

The moment I had interrupted between the two of them hung there in the air. I finished drinking my tea and left them just as they had been.

*

I called Ralph later that night. Ingrid had gone out to have dinner with Eve but would return.

'It's bad for her, over there,' he said. 'With him. It's worse than we thought.' I thought about her pale mouth and her drawn look and wasn't surprised.

Ralph had plans of talking her into staying in Sydney, proving to her that he'd been right about this whole thing being a mistake. 'Why should she go back?' he said. 'Why not just stay here in Sydney?'

'She's married,' I said. 'She lives there now.'

'It was all a mistake.'

'Maybe it was. Maybe it's like any marriage, any relationship. Ups and downs.'

'No. You don't understand. It was – he didn't want her to come out here.'

'To see you?'

'Yes.'

'She told you that?'

'I could tell.'

I waited. 'You two never liked each other. That doesn't mean that Ingrid's marriage is a failure.' That's what I said, impatient with him, but I knew in my heart that he was right.

'It's got nothing to do with me.'

'No, it doesn't.'

'No, I mean the problems – with him.' The urgency in his voice faded. 'She'll be back soon.'

We said goodbye.

Two days passed. And then late the next night he showed up at my house. It was raining and he stood in the hallway, soaked. He didn't say anything. He came inside. All I could think of was that he shouldn't be out in the rain, he was just out of hospital, and that he looked as though he needed brandy. I didn't have any brandy. We sat on the couch together. His face was the same as it had ever been, but it was empty. He leaned into the corner of the couch, his body stiff. I lit a cigarette and passed it to him. He held it in his fingers without smoking it. The smoke rose up through the air in a sheet, straight as a curtain.

I asked him, 'Is it Ingrid?'

He nodded, and he leaned in to me. I put my arm around his shoulders. His hair was damp when I rested my cheek against it briefly, and he smelled of rain and wet hair. There was another smell, too, that wasn't him, and I almost pulled away from him when I recognised it: it was her. She was all over him. I loosened my hold and we sat there. Minutes passed and my arm around him grew numb. The rain fell hard outside, glaze of water against the windows. It was strange the way his body spoke all at once of his possession of her, finally, and of his absolute loss. I thought of my yellow dress that morning months and months before, pulled over my head and stuck on my outstretched arms in my imagination. It had ended up at the bottom of a drawer, seldom worn.

Trinh's voice called me back to the present. 'A love triangle,' she said.

'It wasn't always terrible.'

'No. It must have been wonderful.'

She looked at me with low-lidded eyes. 'I have to go now. But I'd like to see you again.'

I finished my drink.

'I have an appointment, someone I have to meet. But why don't you come by the department tomorrow? My office is 520.'

We agreed to meet at two. She smiled again, the one I'd seen the time I'd left her in the corridor, and was gone.

I asked for another of what she was drinking, and sat at the bar.

At two the next afternoon I knocked on the door of room 520 in the Classics corridor. Several names on small pieces of paper were taped to the door with consultation times written alongside them. The door was opened by a man with curly dark hair, wearing a brown cardigan. 'Hello?'

'I'm looking for Trinh.'

'She's not in. She was working in here this morning, but I think she left a while ago. Can I help you?'

I was sure it was the right time. 'No, no, I'll catch up with her later.'

I looked around the room. It was an office crowded with furniture, desks and overflowing bookshelves. I wondered which desk belonged to Trinh. The space over each desk was filled with papers stuck to the wall: quotations in Latin and Greek and other languages, images of ancient temples and broken vases and jars, grainy pictures of inscriptions, clippings.

The man with the curly hair had sat down at one of the desks, a laptop computer open in front of him. The surface of the desk was littered with paper coffee cups.

I asked him, 'Did you know Ingrid?'

'Ingrid?'

'Holburne. Or Grey.'

'Not really – a little.' He shook his head. 'Gabriel.' He offered his hand. He had a South American accent.

'I'm Julia, I was a friend of Ingrid's …' I trailed off, unsure of what to say next.

'She was working with Jones, yes?'

'Yes, that's right. Well, I'll leave a note for Trinh in her mailbox.'

'OK. Goodbye.' He had a friendly smile.

I leaned on the counter near the wall of mailboxes to write my note. There was only a pencil in my bag, almost blunt at the point. No pen. I wrote a short message, and the phone number at the apartment. I wrote my email address and then crossed it out. The only computer in the apartment was in Matt's room – he let me use it but the modem was slow and unreliable so I rarely checked my mail. I was ready to put the note into Trinh's mailbox when I realised that I didn't know her second name. There were rows of slots in the shelves and no way of guessing. The woman with glasses at the desk in the adjoining room was talking on the phone, twirling a pen in her fingers. She was wearing a similar twinset to the one I had seen her in the day before, but in a slightly different colour.

Turning back around I saw that Jones had entered the mailroom. He was wearing a light-coloured suit that looked all wrong for the season. He gave me the same serious look as the previous day. 'Julia Alpers.'

'Hello. I was meeting Trinh. But she's not here.'

He said nothing.

'Do you know her name?' I asked, holding the note. Of course he knows, I thought, and felt stupider, and more frustrated.

He stepped forward and took the note from my hand and placed it into a slot. I couldn't see which one. He pulled a couple of letters from his own slot, glanced at them, put them back.

I remembered my conversation with Trinh the night before. 'Are you busy?' I asked him.

He inspected me, considering. 'Have you eaten lunch?'

'No,' I said.

'Then let's go.'

He was conventionally good-looking, arrogant, ambivalent, no doubt concealing a cache of psychic wounds or at least a few complexes. My heart plunged and I followed him anyway. Walking along the corridor we passed the crying girl from the day before. She wasn't crying now. He nodded at her. She gave a small nod in acknowledgement without meeting his eyes.

Once we were out of the building Jones walked fast, his eyes moving quickly across the faces we passed on the street. After several blocks he made a sudden turn into a crowded deli. He pressed through to the counter while I waited at the back of the crowd and studied the menu, a huge wall-mounted blackboard covered in writing, variations on sandwiches, bagels, heros, a thousand kinds of bread in slices and rolls. Behind the counter hands sliced and grabbed. I was working out something with tomato and basil and mozzarella when Jones appeared beside me, close enough to whisper, and held my elbow in a light grip.

'I've ordered you a sandwich,' he said, eyes over my head somewhere. 'I'll pick it up. Wait here.'

I waited. My elbow felt hot where he had held it. He came back with his hands full of food and motioned me to a table, magically empty in the busy space.

I kept seeing Ingrid in the place like a ghost, wondering if she had come here and stood there, and sat here, and ordered lunch, and chosen a cold drink.

'Wait,' I said, and squeezed past a throng of people to reach the fridge. I pulled out a cranberry juice, violent pink, and made my way back to the table.

The sandwich was good, a crusty baguette with bacon and avocado.

Jones asked a lot of questions about where I was staying, with that obsessive interest in location peculiar to New York. He knew the block, he knew the building, he knew the building across the road where his friends used to live. He was impressed by the terrace as I described it, and I told him about the empty cage. How big was the terrace, he wanted to know, and I couldn't put it into square feet.

'How many people could you fit there?'

I imagined the terrace full of people. The strings of lights on at dusk, men and women standing around and sitting on the low chairs. I wasn't sure how to count them: they grouped awkwardly in my mind into lots of two and four and five.

'About twenty? Thirty?' I guessed. 'I don't know.'

'You should have a party.'

'For what?'

'We'll think of something. Take advantage of that space in this city.'

We didn't talk about Ingrid. He had been in New York for six years, he revealed, after his doctorate at Oxford. His first name remained a mystery. The short silences while we ate were strangely casual and seemed to assume an intimacy shaped by long acquaintance. He ate a lot and drank my juice freely, taking in half of it in one swallow while I chewed.

'You're drinking my drink,' I said.

'I'll buy you another.'

My elbow burned. He touched it again lightly as he stood, and seemed almost to help me up from the table.

16.

The next day I decided to try again. I was standing in front of the closed door to 520, reading the names on it, when Trinh turned up beside me and said hello.

Her arms were full of papers again, maybe the same stack she was carrying the other day. It seemed larger now. There were red pen marks on one of the pages: a circle around a word, a question mark in the margin and some scribbled comments. It felt like spying. I looked away. Trinh struggled to balance the stack of papers as she unlocked the door.

'Come into my parlour.' She gave me a conspiratorial glance, eyes narrowed, over her shoulder.

'Did I make a mistake?' I asked. The rules of etiquette felt strained in that place, redolent of power imbalances among the people who inhabited it. The rooms and halls seemed designed to accommodate the rules of relationships between teachers and students and did not admit others easily. 'About yesterday, I mean.'

'I don't know,' she replied. 'Did you?'

Trinh busied herself arranging the stack of papers into several piles on her desk. She straightened up and smoothed the front of her clothes. Both her fitted, collared shirt and slim skirt were tailored with tight precision. They were a dark blue colour that was not navy. It suggested indigo as I looked at it. Or ink. I could taste the thick feeling of the word in my mouth.

Trinh seemed distracted. 'I have to meet with students soon so I can't see you for long. But I thought of something for you.'

She walked over to the tall bookshelf in the corner. Its shelves sagged under a chaos of objects: books, folders, papers, boxes, a mug, an ashtray showing traces of old ash. A small, ornate urn rested on its side on the top shelf.

'We cleared off Ingrid's desk weeks ago, then someone found this box when we were going through the desk drawers. Would you be interested in taking it?'

I nodded. 'Yes. Thanks.'

Trinh reached for a box that rested on one of the lower shelves and handed it to me. It was the size of a large shoebox, made of stiff brown cardboard.

'What was she working on?' I asked. 'I don't even know.'

'She was putting together a project on the Roman-British curse tablets.'

'Curse tablets?'

'She was concentrating on the tablets found at the shrine to Sulis Minerva in Bath.'

When Trinh looked up she saw the confusion on my face. 'Ancient writing tablets. Do you know what I mean?' She smiled.

'Yes, yes. I think so.' I remembered pictures of the Rosetta Stone, its huge slab face covered in lines of mysterious figures. 'Stone.' I rested the box on the desk.

'These ones are mostly lead.'

'And they're cursed?' I imagined the tombs of the

Pyramids in Egypt, the rumours of a curse that followed the Westerners involved in their opening.

Trinh laughed a little. 'No, they are not cursed. They are curses. Curses are written on them. They're thin scrolls of lead. If you wanted to curse someone, make bad fortune come to them, you would write down the curse, scratch it into the tablet, or hire a magician to do it for you, and roll it up. Sometimes people stuck them through with a nail to hold them together. And then you would leave it somewhere, a tomb, bury it. So the gods could read it. In this case people threw them into the water at this shrine, a spring.' She looked at the box. 'Sulis Minerva was one of those deities that Ingrid was interested in, a goddess that incorporated the Celtic Sulis with the Roman Minerva. The gatekeeper goddess. I think those tablets at Bath are all asking the goddess to curse the person who stole a pair of gloves, or a cloak, or money. Theft. All the British tablets are like that.' She sighed. 'Greek ones are so much more interesting. Look – why don't you read Ingrid's paper? There is a draft of it in there, I'm sure. It will tell you all about them.'

I took the box into my hands, and looked back to the shelf where it had left a gap, already filled now with books collapsing sideways into it. The box was heavy with the weight of paper, needing two hands to hold it.

Something shifted in Trinh's expression as she looked at me. She seemed nervous, as though she wanted to help, and as though she was uncomfortable with the feeling.

'So, Julia, are you doing anything tonight?' she asked.

I found myself wanting to lie. Not because I didn't want to see Trinh again. I did. I felt a little in awe of her glamour, as though I were back in early high school and Trinh was years ahead and ready to graduate, groomed and accomplished. My night seemed empty, and I wanted to hide it.

'Did you like the Lilac?' she continued. 'I could show you around a bit but I'm boring, I go to all the same places all the time.'

'Yes,' I said, abruptly.

'OK, I'll see you there. I'll be there at nine.'

I thanked her again for the box.

Back out in the hallway a student, a boy, was walking in my direction. I looked the other way and saw Jones. He flicked away the weight of hair that fell into his face with a horse-like snap of his head. It looked as though he was about to greet me when his eyes fell on the box in my hands. His steps grew faster. He let out a quick hello, opened the door with some force and entered Trinh's office, closing the door behind him. Muted voices were just audible from inside, no distinct words. The two voices sounded in quick succession.

The boy reached the door. He stood in front of it, sighed, and dropped to sit on the floor to the side in one disconsolate motion. No more sounds came through the door, and it remained closed.

I carried the box out of the campus and made my way to a coffee shop across the road. The tables were filled with undergraduates studying outsized textbooks and Victorian novels. I sat at a table and inspected the box. It had been my plan to sit with a drink and look through the contents, but as I looked at it I became more uncomfortable. The box appeared to grow in mass, absorbing energy from around itself. It reminded me again of the tomb-explorers. The box seemed like a coffin, a receptacle for the remains of the dead. I did not want to open it there.

The box fitted awkwardly under my arm, too heavy. I went to the counter and asked for a coffee to take away. Too late, I thought about how it would be to carry it back on the subway, hoping the carriage would not be too crowded, that there would be a seat for me and a seat next to me for the box. My coffee arrived and I hoisted the box to my hip a little more, picked up the Styrofoam cup with its plastic lid and left.

By the time I got back to the apartment most of the coffee was on my shirt, a wet stain against the white cotton. The street was hot and the building cool when I opened the front doors. I paused inside and considered Mrs Bee's door and thought about knocking. The box was heavy. I went up to the apartment and deposited it on the chair in the bedroom.

Matt was in the living room, snatching up his keys from the table and readying to leave. He was agitated.

'What's up?' I asked.

He gave a frustrated shrug. 'It's these fucking snails. In the piece – the installation I was telling you about – there's a bunch of snails crawling around on a couple pieces of Plexiglas – their trails are lit up – some of them have sort of strings attached to their shells – it's hard to describe. Anyway. Some animal rights activist has decided that we're oppressing the snails and keeps coming in and taking them. Setting them free.' He pulled on a frayed denim jacket. 'I think I know who it is. A woman.'

'What does she do with them?' I asked.

'I have no idea. But I have to go and find a bunch more snails right now. Do you want to come?'

I said no. 'Where do you get snails?'

'I have a friend who works in a restaurant who's doing me a favour. These things are fucking expensive, for snails.'

The phone rang and he answered it. The voice on the other end was loud. 'I'll take a cab,' he said after a minute, and hung up. He left and the door closed behind him.

In the kitchen there was a hot patch on the linoleum floor between the sink and the window where the sun shone in. I took off my shoes and stood there, pale feet in the strong light. I took a glass of water into the bedroom and sat on the bed and looked at the box. It didn't exude the same stern aura as it had earlier and instead looked quite demure, with its slightly battered and creased cardboard. The sense of aversion I felt was recognisable now as coming from myself rather than being projected by the box. I lifted the lid gingerly and saw a stack of pages inside, a couple of pages photocopied from a book and a page with its corner sticking out underneath them covered in Ingrid's writing in a heavy pencil. It was enough. I let the lid fall and, without thinking, went downstairs.

Mrs Bee opened the door and looked as though she were expecting me.

'Come in,' she said. 'I was just going to make some tea.'

She waited for several minutes after my tea was finished before examining the cup. She tilted it back and forth with little expression. Her eyes were shrewd when she looked at me. 'Well, you're making some progress,' she said evenly. She placed the cup back in the saucer.

I looked surreptitiously into it, not wanting to be seen showing too much interest in the contents. There was a scatter of leaves against one side of the cup. It reminded me of seaweed, browning against the rock of tidal pools as they dry in the sun. I thought of the brown stain on my white shirt, thrown onto the floor of the bedroom upstairs. The pale brown box on the chair came into my mind, the whiteness of the inside of the lid, the surprising heaviness of it, the fold of the cardboard around the edge of the lid. The taste of the black tea was strong in my mouth.

Half an hour later I looked through the box with more determination. The pages in Ingrid's writing appeared to be her notes on a book chapter or article. There was a printed draft of an essay titled 'Theft and Vengeance in Curse Tablets from Roman Britain'. It could have been an early or late draft; some twenty pages, lightly edited in Ingrid's hand, every page showing a word or two crossed out, a comma added, some whole sentences struck through and new phrases written into the margins. I skimmed it over and rifled cursorily through the rest of the contents. More drafts of papers, more photocopies. No more pages of Ingrid's writing. There were no revelations. It was disappointing.

What did I expect, I asked myself. A journal? A memoir?

I pulled out an image of Mercury, what looked like a reproduction of a fresco. He stood in profile, about to start running. The paper was worn and there were marks on the back of the page where the picture had been tacked up on the wall. I remembered the several desks in Ingrid's old office and the walls above them, covered in images and quotations and notices. From some deposit of memory I knew that Mercury was a messenger, a go-between, and also that he was one of the gods responsible for escorting the souls of the dead across to the underworld. What message was he carrying here, I wondered; who would he accompany across the river?

The next page in the pile, the title page of a book on Minerva and other goddesses, showed a single faint print against the paper, the trace of a finger marked with toner from the photocopier or printer. Something gave way then and the impact of the tragedy struck me without warning. I remembered Ingrid's fingers pulling her mass of hair back into a braid, the sun in it, the colour of it against the tortoiseshell clip she wore. It seemed long ago, another life.

I suddenly wanted to call Ingrid and hear her voice on the phone, forgetting for a short instant that this was impossible. She would have pushed her hair back with one hand as she brought the phone to her ear. I looked at the black phone on the dresser next to the bed. When was the last time we had spoken?

I didn't want to call anyone else. I piled the pages back on top of the fingerprint, closed the lid, left the room and turned on the shower.

Under the hot water I scrubbed my whole body and washed my hair, wringing the water out of it more fiercely than usual. Steam billowed out in clouds to fill the small room. Water beaded on the tiles. I thought of Jones in the corridor today, the flick of his head as the hair fell into his eyes – I saw now how much it was like Ingrid's, that dark blond colour, straw in the sun and shade, or how that might look since I had never actually seen such a thing, only imagined it by how it looked like something else. One of my hairs had stuck to the tiled shower wall, a straight dark line. Dead already, I thought, and washed it down the drain.

When I met Trinh that night we didn't talk about Ingrid, or the box. As she was ordering us another round of drinks Jones showed up at her side, folding his arms and leaning on the bar. He gave me a nod and a smile but kept his attention on Trinh. They shared a joke, a minute of talk, and he walked away to a table behind us. A while later when I came back from the bathroom he was there again, sitting in my seat this time. The place had filled up by then. He stood up when he saw me and said, 'Saving it for you.'

Trinh got talking to a friend of hers who had showed up not long after Jones, Darryl or Cameron, a woman with a name that sounded to me like it belonged to a man. When I rose to leave Jones said he was leaving too. Trinh looked at us, from one to the other, and wavered for a second, as though she wanted to say something to me, but thought better of it, or couldn't, with him standing right there. She just said that she would see me soon.

Jones and I took the stairs up to the street. 'Can I get you a taxi?' he asked.

'No,' I said. The night was warm and my head was fuzzy from being underground for so long. I wanted to walk. He seemed pleased, and said that he'd walk with me. It was hard to tell how late it was. The streets and bars were still busy, still a few people in the small restaurants we passed. We crossed Broadway and walked together back up to the

Village. He didn't walk as fast as he had the other day, when he'd taken me to lunch. We passed the dorm where my NYU student boyfriend had lived and I told him the story. He laughed. As we went he pointed out a storefront here and there, explaining that this boarded-up place was once a restaurant, this restaurant was once a pharmacy, this was where his old friend had made cabinets in a studio upstairs. When we reached my building we stopped and stood there outside.

'This terrace of yours,' he said. 'I'd love to see it.'

I took him upstairs, through the French doors and back out into the cold. He looked around, inspecting the birdcage, assessing the space. I stayed by the door and watched him, then went to him when he stopped at the tall parapet for a while and leaned his arms on it. We looked down at the street below, and south to the sky full of lights. He smiled in a very contented way, as though he had arrived somewhere he wanted to be. Or maybe he was just a little drunk. After a time he walked back towards the doors and I followed him.

Just before we reached the doors he took my arms, both arms above the elbows, and pushed me back against the wall. The strings of coloured lights across the terrace glowed faintly but we were in shadow. He kissed me roughly. His hand was under my skirt quickly and I felt myself making a sound as my throat tightened. It didn't sound like my voice. One arm was still pinned against the wall, and the other fell slack by my side. He should have tasted like cigarettes but he didn't. He withdrew his hand and took his face away so that he could see me, a cool, appraising look. I wanted to keep looking at him. We were both breathing fast. He said something like 'Hummm'. Very softly. I wanted him to say it again. I was about to force my hands from their place by my side to touch him when he moved, very subtly, in another direction. He pressed his cheek against mine and said 'Goodnight'. My face burned. I stayed where I was in the shadow as he walked back through my room and to the front door. It closed behind him with a neat click.

In the room the box was still there on the bed, Mercury inside, poised and ready to run. I put it on the floor and lay down in the depression it had left on the mattress.

My dreams were filled with ringing phones trailing coiled, snaking cords. Whole banks of phones ringing and ringing, and me too afraid to answer any of them, knowing it is Ingrid on the line, and afraid of where she is calling from. At the end of the dream, Ingrid sitting patiently at the end of the bed, waiting for me to answer.

The next morning I called Ralph. Aaron answered. Ralph couldn't come to the phone, he told me. He was resting.

'How is he?' I asked.

'He's resting a lot. He's fine. It's … you know. He's tired a lot.'

I waited. 'Please ask him to call me when he's feeling better,' I said.

'OK. Can I give him any message, Julia?'

'I'm through here,' I said. 'That's the message.'

'I'll let him know,' Aaron told me in his sweet, neutral voice. The sound of a bird calling somewhere in the distance came through on his side of the line in the faint rustle of the heat. I put the receiver down.

'I'm through here,' I said to myself, as though it were a line I was practising. 'I'm done.' I sighed and knew it wasn't true.

Without thinking, I showered and dressed and got on the subway all the way to the university uptown, and knocked on Jones's door and walked right in without waiting for him to respond. It was still early and the halls were almost empty. He raised his eyes from his desk calmly as though he was expecting me, and said my full name. I closed the door and moved the plastic chair so that it jammed under the handle. I couldn't see how to lock the door without a key. He checked his watch.

I stood just near the door, a few feet away from him, and we looked at each other. A whole conversation seemed to take place between us in the silent seconds that passed, which felt like long minutes. Questions, explanations, prevarications, invitations. By the time he drew breath and spoke it felt as though we had come to some kind of agreement.

'Later?' he said, completing the dialogue we hadn't been having. Casually, in that voice I remembered from the museum.

I nodded. As I turned to unjam the chair and open the door he moved swiftly to my side. One hand circled my wrist, gentler than before but still deliberate, and the other held my face and lifted it up, thumb against a vulnerable part of my throat, so that he could kiss me. My arms were alive this time, and I pulled my hand free from his grip to touch him, the warmth of skin through his shirt. Voices sounded in the corridor outside, no words audible, the sound of an irritated explanation and a laugh that sounded wrong in response. Jones didn't seem to notice or to mind and kept his mouth on me. I pulled away soon after, unnerved by the presence of others beyond the door.

'Later,' I said, and he stepped back quietly.

There was a long strand of hair on the red carpet, I saw as I was leaving, an S shape against the geometric lozenge shapes of the rug, glowing gold in a shaft of sunlight. It could have been anyone's.

Matt sized everything up in one long look when I arrived back at the apartment carrying bags of groceries.

'Your hair's a mess,' he said, folding his arms and leaning back against the kitchen sink. 'You look great.'

The radio was on, and he hummed along. I unpacked the contents of the bags: bread, butter, mustard, four kinds of ham, lettuce. He helped me make a salad and sandwiches but in the end neither of us ate much. We drank a fizzy drink made with the juice of a berry with an unpronounceable name – Matt was crazy about it – and he asked me dumb questions about Australia. He'd seen a tourist special on TV the night before.

'So are the koalas really cute?' he asked. 'Or are they pests?' He had some idea that they were everywhere in the city, infesting all the trees like squirrels.

'It's not like that in Sydney,' I explained. 'No koalas.' He looked at me doubtfully. 'No kangaroos.'

'I didn't think there were kangaroos in the city,' he said defensively.

'Right.'

'So … Sydney is not rich in wildlife.'

'Not where I'm from. There are lots of cockroaches.'

Matt was disappointed.

He disappeared into his room to make a phone call and I went to lie down and read a book but fell asleep instead. The lettuce was wilted when I came back out a couple of hours later, bread dried out around the edges. Matt was gone and the place was quiet, and it felt like mine at last.

17.

It was mid-morning a few days later when I went to see Grey at the apartment he had bought with Ingrid on Central Park West. A thin fog hung in the air, paling the buildings and obscuring the view down the long avenues. It was a light-coloured brick building from the 1920s, the front flat against the street, border of dark hedges neatly clipped. An intimidating display of flowers rested on a table just inside the front set of doors, in the centre of the passageway so that you had to walk around it. Birds of paradise turned their spiky heads out to the side, in profile, and sharp green leaves fanned out from the centre of the arrangement.

All the surfaces were polished but not shiny, grey and tones of sage green. The doorman stood behind a granite desk, dressed in a navy blue suit. He nodded at me gravely and let me through. As I passed I saw him raise a telephone handset to his ear. A mirrored lift took me up to the fifteenth floor and opened directly across from the apartment door. When Grey opened it the smell of coffee tinged the air, beans freshly ground. He gripped my hand gently with both hands, a gesture of consolation, or blessing. His hands were cool.

'Welcome.' He gestured me through the door.

We stood together in the kitchen, all marble countertops and stainless steel, while he made the coffee and poured it into white cups. From another room the sound of classical music came through faintly, piano, melodies weaving around one another, in and out of hearing, in counterpoint. I looked for the blue teapot and saw it set up on a high shelf, squat and handsome. A pile of pomegranates sat in a crackled gold bowl on an island in the middle of the room. There was a large sink in the centre of the island, three stools at the other end. The espresso machine steamed and shone, little dials quivering. I thought of the spit and hiss of my own battered coffee maker, never quite balancing on the gas burner, and missed it.

Grey was wearing a black sweater with a round neck, the colour of mourning, with charcoal pants and black shoes. I looked at his grey eyes, the skin around them more lined than I remembered, his lean body, watching for signs of grief. He projected the same imposing presence, the same compressed elegance. He moved quietly between the counter, sink, fridge. This was the first time we had been together, just the two of us. It was as though Ingrid had just left the room and we were waiting silently for her to return in a moment, not bothering to find our own point of conversation.

'Come on through.' He led me to the living room and motioned for me to sit.

Everything – the walls, carpet, furniture – was shades of light grey, ivory and white, eggshell and cream, except for a black baby grand piano set into one corner. Behind it a folded screen leaned against the wall, a Japanese scene in faded silver and gold with lacquered edges. The proportions of the room and windows had a classical, balanced aspect: tall ceilings and tall windows hung with long, fine curtains, the one aspect of excess in the room. They fell from their high rail like the pleats in Ingrid's wedding dress and hit the floor in a tumble, lengths of extra fabric crushed in peaks and waves, a bride's train. I held my coffee carefully, imagining the stain a drop would make on the cover of the deep armchair Grey had offered me.

There was a curious lack of expectancy in the way he sat there drinking his coffee. On my way over it had been impossible to think through what I might have to say to him or ask him, and now my mind was a similar blank, flattened by the expanse of pale linen on the sofa across from me, the colour of new concrete.

Across the room, glossy white stairs led up to a small mezzanine level. It was lined with built-in bookshelves stacked with books, the floor yellowish oak. From there more stairs led to another level, a passageway filled with white doors.

'I've got this for you,' Grey said, and handed me a slick leaflet. *The Grey Room: American Abstract* it was headed, with the logo of the Whitney Museum at the bottom. It unfolded to a page of text and some images of paintings. I took in words here and there: ... *generous donation from family ... showcase American abstract art ... legacy.*

In memory of Ingrid Grey.

At the end of the leaflet was the briefest description of Ingrid's life: born and raised in Australia, promising Classical scholar, Columbia, dedicated patron of the arts.

'We'd been planning on adding to our other gifts to the Whitney,' Grey said, 'and this was ... well, an opportunity –' He stopped. 'They'll open the room later next year.'

I re-read the text. The room would showcase acquisitions purchased with the assistance of funds provided by the Grey family.

'It seemed like the right thing to do with the money. With some of the money.'

'The money,' I repeated. I thought at first he was talking about Ingrid's money.

'The compensation is quite substantial,' he said. He cleared his throat. I realised he was talking about September 11, the money that went to the victims' relatives. 'I thought you might like to know about this project.'

'Thank you.'

Would he mistake my lack of words for a symptom of grief, I wondered. Was it grief? Was this another aspect of what that felt like – dumbness, tongue bound in my mouth? I didn't exactly feel a sense of loss sitting here in the pale grey room. I didn't feel Ingrid at all in this place, and it was hard to imagine her in this grown-up environment of expensive coffee makers and well-made bookshelves and light-coloured sofas. Ralph's family home had always exuded a sense of wealth, but in a way completely different to this – rooms filled with antiques and beautiful side tables and carpets, so many carpets that they were all laid over the edges of another, and one old couch sat in a room upstairs with many rugs piled up on it. It was careless and disorderly. But this was a refined environment of sophistication and the careful display of taste.

I asked him the one question that was suddenly clear in my mind. 'What was she doing down there? Downtown?'

His face betrayed – what? Sympathy; horror?

'Sorry,' I said. 'I just wanted to ask.'

'It's perfectly alright,' he said, composed again. 'I believe she was keeping an appointment with her financial adviser. She used a firm based ... down there.'

I looked down at the coffee table between us, a stack of art books carefully placed to one side. One of the paintings hanging on the wall right across from me, a roughly painted red triangle with more coloured marks at the bottom of the frame, was reproduced on the cover of the book on the top of the stack. I recognised the image.

Grey noticed me looking and smiled his slightly predatory smile. 'That's the book of Fleur's work from the Whitney.' Steam rose faintly from his cup. 'She's the youngest artist to have had her own show there. Of course – you remember. You saw the show with Ingrid.'

There had been stacks of the books in the bookstore just inside the entrance to the museum that day. I lifted the book and opened it. There was a photograph of Fleur on the inside back jacket, a sullen child standing against a window. One of her hands hung down limply at her side, holding a paintbrush as if it were about to slide out of her grip. The ends of the brush were dark with paint. I flipped through the first pages and saw another picture, a tiny girl kneeling and holding up two hands in front of her, both covered in paint, head lifted up and laughing, eyes squeezed almost shut. In front of her, on the floor, was a large canvas showing the beginnings of a painting.

'How old is she here?'

Grey looked for a moment. 'Four.' He drank his coffee. 'That was her most productive year. And the year she incorporated brush and hand painting into the single canvas.'

The photograph faced the first page of an introductory essay written by Grey himself, followed by several others.

'Does she still paint?' I asked.

He shifted slightly in his chair, and his face tightened. 'You'll have to ask her that yourself,' he said. 'Not as far as I know – she certainly doesn't paint to show.' He paused, and continued, obviously pained. 'She started taking … photographs,' he admitted, embarrassed, as though he were explaining that she had taken up thieving as a profession, 'and also video.'

'That's interesting.'

A quick scan of the walls revealed no photographs on display, only paintings. There were a few small photographs in silver frames resting on bookshelves; a different order of image.

'She has a great talent,' he said, with a sound of having said it often. 'I hope she will return to painting. She developed as an artist so young – I imagine that she's still developing her vision in her own way, and she will return to the canvas as the most truthful medium of that vision.' It was a carefully considered statement.

'Do you own many of her paintings?' I asked. 'Are any more of these hers?'

Grey straightened keenly, and nodded towards a canvas on the wall behind me. It showed the characteristic triangular shapes I had noticed in the painting on the cover of the book and other images in it. He took this as a cue to give me a tour of the apartment and his art collection, and led me over to the side of the room.

'Now, this artist – very underrated – this is a study for his most famous work ...' He stood with his arms folded low, hand raised now and again to gesture towards some aspect of the painting, a wash of tones in grey and blue. A smaller version of what looked like the same image, only with more pink in it, was next to it on the same wall. 'And an earlier one,' he said, nodding towards it. He went on, and I began to really understand what it was that Ingrid had seen in him. He was a natural teacher. He talked about the works and the artists with real feeling, explaining without giving the sense that he was talking down to me. I felt that he assumed in me an intelligence and capacity for appreciation, and it was flattering; that sense would have been powerful for Ingrid, the eager student.

He showed me his office on the same floor, a stark room with a desk in the centre and just one painting on the wall facing the door. 'De Kooning,' he said simply, and I saw a shadow of that possessive expression he wore in the photograph I remembered from the wedding, holding Ingrid's hand. 'A gift from Ingrid.'

There was a framed photograph set low down on one of the bookshelves behind the desk: a woman with her face turned away from the camera so that only a fraction of her profile was visible. It looked as though she was sitting in an artist's studio. Her shirt had paint marks on the sleeves and her dark hair was pulled back. Paintings were a blur, slightly out of focus on the wall behind her, and sketches. She was familiar in a half-remembered way.

Grey left the room and I followed him. Across the hall, a door to another room was half open, and the mountainous piles of clothes that covered the floor – jeans in black and denim and white, t-shirts, red sweaters, pink scarves – suggested that it was Fleur's. We reached the stairs and I noticed that he had passed over one picture, hung out of the way under the staircase. The image contrasted with the rest of the collection in the house, which were all abstract. I recognised it with surprise as one I had seen hanging in Ralph's house at Kirribilli, a small, hazy painting of the Thames river in an ornate gold frame that swallowed the image. It was a valuable object, a study by Turner. George had been fond of it. 'Worth more than this house,' he said proudly to me once. 'Can you believe that?' He'd sighed. 'I love it though.' I couldn't remember Ingrid ever noticing it.

Grey saw me looking at it.

'A wedding present,' he said brusquely, and started up the shallow stairs, his back to me. 'I've wondered if I ought to return the thing.'

I guessed that this had been Ralph's gift.

'Would you like to see her room?' he offered when we came to the top of the stairs.

He led the way and we walked down a short, carpeted hallway. I glimpsed a bedroom to my left, the door half-open, and we passed other doors. At the end of the passageway we turned and reached another door. It was white, like the others, and like them it had a heavy glass knob. It stood just ajar. Grey stood and held out his arm, directing me in.

'Go on,' he said.

I stepped past him and pushed the door. It opened silently. I took a step inside.

'What's it like – what's it been like – without her?' I asked, inspired by a sudden breath of courage and curiosity about what lay beneath his smooth exterior. As I spoke an awareness of her absence came over me again, a vague tingling sensation on my skin as though ghostly fingers had brushed past and withdrawn. I could sense the space of the apartment around me, the building, the whole city, extending in all directions, everywhere, all empty of her.

His face didn't betray any feeling but his eyes held mine in a questioning gaze that made me feel presumptuous for asking. Eventually he gave me a small, sad smile. 'This place feels so much darker without her,' he said. 'You'll forgive me if I don't feel like talking about it.' 'With you,' he might have added, but didn't.

'Perhaps you would like to take a moment here?' He hovered just inside the doorway. I nodded.

He hesitated, as though reluctant to leave. 'Yes. Well.' His hand rested on the door frame. 'I'll be downstairs when you're ready.'

He left, footsteps silenced by the carpet.

My eyes were drawn to the only picture on the walls of the room. It was a version of the painting I remembered from Ingrid's room in Sydney. I always thought of the woman as the Lady of Shalott, and the Tennyson poem came into my mind again now as it always had when I looked at the image, but I knew that it was Ophelia, as Ingrid had told me, by Millais. On Ingrid's Sydney walls it had been a print of the painting, a poster from an exhibition of Pre-Raphaelite paintings, framed behind Perspex. It had sagged a little in one corner, the plastic coming away slightly from the paper behind it. The image I saw now was the same, but looked as though it had been put through a kind of digital process, like a photograph of the painting that had been enlarged to show the coloured pixels. Minute coloured dots made up the picture, the colours dulled towards grey apart from the flowers that surrounded the woman's head, bright fuchsia pink, and her hair floating in the water, a brilliant yellow. The woman's face was a collection of points, and as I looked the picture seemed to lose shape and grow in randomness: a mess of disconnected spots. Examining it closer I was unable to tell whether I was seeing paint on canvas or a photograph. I could see the grain of the canvas and wanted to touch it to tell if it was actually canvas, or engineered to look that way, but the surface of the image repelled me. I looked away.

The room had the same pleasing proportions as the rest of the apartment. Shelves had been built into one wall, on either side of a tall panel surrounded by a Grecian-looking decorative plaster motif. The shelves were filled with books relating to Ingrid's studies, carefully organised and neatly set back from the edge. There were titles on ancient Rome, writing, orthography. One half-shelf was dedicated to books on magic in the ancient world. Against the adjacent wall there was a wide chest of drawers covered in a walnut veneer. The slightly curved design of the body stood out, at odds in the room and the apartment, with its classical proportions and linear features.

Each drawer in the dresser had a small brass keyhole set into it. I tried the first drawer on the right. It opened stiffly, empty except for a handful of coloured pencils. The sight of them – blunt and worn – prompted a sudden self-consciousness, a sense of acting without permission. The pencils rattled as I tried to close the drawer, and it stuck. I felt sweat begin to break. The drawer gave way suddenly and slid home.

Several objects sat on the chest of drawers: five or six tiny wooden elephants painted in bright colours; some coloured glass bottles; a jewellery box made of inlaid wood and mother-of-pearl. I recognised all these things from Ingrid's old room in Sydney. There was one unfamiliar thing: a small brass key. It seemed to be made to fit the keyhole in the drawers. I picked it up and felt the familiar stirrings of desire. I wondered if Grey came in here much. The room had an untouched feeling about it, as though it had been empty for a long time. He had seemed so reluctant to enter, reluctant to leave. It was impossible to know whether he came in here or not, or how often, or how well he knew the collection of objects on the chest. Taking the key would be a risk. I decided against it, but held the key in my hand anyway as I inspected the rest of the room.

A large chaise longue sat at an angle at one end of the room, solid and wide as a single bed. It was covered in light green linen, with one short armrest and a back support at one end. A cushion of the same fabric rested against the back. More than anything else in the room this spoke of Ingrid's body: she had sat and lain here. It was a perfect chair for reading, long enough to stretch out and put feet up and fall asleep. A soft mohair blanket was folded across the seat. I felt an urge to cover the whole thing with a sheet, to blanket it like a corpse.

The only other things in the room were a desk and chair, set against the wall between two windows that reached almost to the ceiling. The room presented at first as a study, dominated by desk, books, chaise longue for reading, but the chaise looked as though it could equally be used for sleeping, and the dresser added another note, personalising the room. I wondered if the other drawers held clothes. It was a room that could be lived in, slept in, not just studied in, but didn't want to proclaim itself openly that way.

I sat down at the desk, my back to the picture of Ophelia and the chest of drawers. The desk was a simple construction, beech stained with a transparent white wash. No drawers. A miniature, hollowed-out classical column held some pens and pencils, and there was a glazed ceramic dish with paperclips in it, a spiral notebook open to a blank page, and a small amphora. The amphora looked old, its surface slightly pitted.

I leaned over and raised the shade on one of the windows, fine white canvas that lifted easily on its ropes. Sunlight fell against the window now in a way that blanked out the glass in a golden slant and lit the desk brilliant white. Sounds of traffic rose faintly and I had a sudden sense of how far I was above the ground, how many storeys lay below, how much distance to the street beneath the window. Dust particles danced in the light, tiny galaxies shifting.

On one side of the desk sat a stack of manila folders filled with papers, and on top of the stack a black pocket diary. I paused, then decided to look. A quick glance at the folders showed them to be filled with photocopied articles and book chapters for Ingrid's research on Roman culture and writing. I put them to one side and picked up the diary, held closed by a brass clasp. I turned the clasp softly and opened it. It fell open to the page marked by a ribbon set into the cover of the book. The page was divided into days of the week and the words *Paul, 9* were there in Ingrid's hand. I skipped to the next piece of writing, what looked like a short list of book titles and author names, with *Labyrinth* written at the top, the name of a bookstore near the Columbia campus. I looked back at *Paul, 9* and saw that the date was 11 September. I dropped the diary and felt my lungs constrict. The little book fell and landed on the carpet without a sound.

There was the same self-consciousness and guilt as when I had opened the drawer, but I retrieved the diary anyway and studied the writing on the page, the familiar shape of it. Neat round letters, a large hand. I turned the pages back and saw the writing on other pages, other days. Names, events. Dinner. Lunch. Coffee. Parties. Book titles. Websites. Numbers. I turned the pages forward, through each week of the empty months that followed. Blank. Blank. Blank.

On the note pages at the end of the diary there were more lists, more titles, shopping lists, random words I couldn't make sense of. It wasn't until I found my own name that I realised that I had been looking for it, looking at all these other words without retaining a single one of them, waiting for my own name to occur. It was there in a list with names and dates. Birthdays. Julia: 28 May. Ralph was there. Fleur. Gil. Victoria. I recognised one or two other names and not others. The list did not quite fill the page.

It had been a couple of years since Ingrid had sent me a birthday greeting. I remembered Ingrid's birthday, 3 October, and the last time we had celebrated it, in Sydney with a crate of champagne. Sadness came over me and I thought resentfully of Ralph. He would want a full report on this: Ingrid's room, her books, the place in the house that was hers, the list that included his name. The sun shifted its angle and the window cleared, showing the walls and windows of the buildings across the street and a generous patch of sky.

I closed the book and tried to rearrange the pile of papers as I had found it. It was time to leave. What time was it in Sydney? What time was it here? There was no clock in the room.

I took the key back to the chest of drawers and tried it briefly in the lock of the second drawer. No movement. I put it back on the chest and snatched up one of the tiny elephants quickly, before I had time to think. Its shape was firm and sharp in my palm and then dull in my pocket. I looked at Ophelia before leaving the room and her face was whole again, dead and empty against the water up on the wall.

Grey gave me a postcard before he showed me out. It advertised a show at Maeve's gallery, with the artist's name and the words *New Work* on one side, black capitals on white, and the address and details for the gallery on the other. 'It's opening on Thursday,' he said. 'Maeve would love to see you. Come and have a glass of wine.'

I said I would see him there.

18.

When I thought about Ingrid, her actual dying was the part I tried not to picture, but it was the part that featured in my dreams every night for those first weeks in New York. The dream would always be both different and the same, with her smiling, or turning her head, or presenting simply her enigmatic, smooth-skinned back, with its shoulder bones rounding and lengthening into the shape of wings. But always, then, dying. Suffocating, her eyes wild and pleading like Desdemona on stage, hair matted against the sheet, face disappearing beneath the pillow. Or drugged, her body slumped in a chair. The overstuffed armchair in the off-white living room, the one I sat in across from Grey that morning there.

In one version of this drugged death her hand drapes over the arm of the chair, fingers catching the light like a Vermeer maiden, nails the eerie colour of death. So white that I know, when I understand the colour, that she's gone. The nails are telling me, the white of the poisonous powder that killed her, in the dream.

The night after that one, the dead white nails, she sits up in another dream in the same chair with a glass of wine, regarding me with an amused look on her face. The windows are bright, opaque, impossible to see through to what's outside, the view obscured like it was that day in her room with the sun hitting the glass at a blinding angle.

Where do you think I am, she asks me, with a look – or in words, I can't remember, though it must be words because her cadence is there in the word 'think', tongue soft on the 'k'.

Her glass is bubbling now. It's champagne, or fizzing with bubbles from tablets dropped into it, white foam.

The dream stayed in my mind like a photograph the next morning, and I held it like I held the photographs that were to come later, examining it from every angle I could remember. What was through those windows?

There were versions where her dying was less elegant. Some nights I simply saw the towers burning and falling. They appeared from a distance, tiny structures made of matchsticks, and at other times huge monoliths of concrete and stone that collapsed before me, falling miles down into the earth.

She fell. From a cliff; down a long flight of stairs; down a grassy hill. She floated downriver like the Ophelia she loved, flowers around her. She drowned in a lake, and presented a faceless, pale body recognisable only by the necklace around her neck, the empty cameo frame on a chain.

I walked from the Village to Fleur's studio in SoHo along the cobbled streets and past iron-clad storefronts. The shops were fewer to the block as the street went south towards Chinatown. I stopped in front of a place that sold either shoes or chairs, or both, and maybe lamps. All these things were artfully arranged on the floor space of the shop. It could have been an art gallery.

Fleur's place was on the top floor of the building. I pressed the button next to her name – a handwritten label reading simply *Grey*. The button didn't seem to make contact with anything much. I wondered if it worked. After a little while the buzzer sounded and I pushed open the heavy iron door and climbed the painted iron stairs. Light came through skylights and windows into the stairwell and by the third floor the space was bright with sun. Fleur opened a wide iron door, painted red, and held it while I stepped through.

The door opened onto an expansive loft, half the floor of the building at least. Large windows let the sun spill in onto the floor, making slanted shapes of light on the white floorboards. A small kitchen fitted into a corner around from the door, and four black corduroy beanbags slouched around under the windows.

Fleur looked her seventeen years: her feet were bare and she wore black jeans with a T-shirt and a grey hooded sweatshirt over it. Her hair had the appearance of blonde dyed black, pulled back into a high ponytail. She wore a lot of eyeliner. She smiled a sweet smile, and I half-expected to see metal braces, then reminded myself that girls like Fleur probably wore the new invisible braces. Her face was older but vaguely recognisable from the picture I'd seen of her and Maeve that had been stuck to Maeve's fridge on that night when Fleur hadn't made it to dinner; the same elfin shape, pointed chin.

I recognised a Nan Goldin photograph on the wall, an unhealthy-looking couple on a bed, and a few others, all portraits or photographs with people in the frame. There was one that looked like a picture of a slightly younger Fleur: she wore heavy lipstick and a dark velvet dress, pearls around her neck. Another figure stood in the frame, a woman with her back to the camera and one hand on Fleur's neck. They glowed in the diffuse light. In the picture Fleur looked a little towards the woman, whose head was inclined slightly as though listening. Suddenly the shape of the woman's back cohered in my mind and I recognised Ingrid, and knew the dark blonde hair tied back from the neck.

Fleur watched me looking at the photograph with her observant eyes. She asked me if I'd found the place OK, all politeness, and I said yes.

'Would you excuse me for a second?' she asked. 'I was in the middle of setting up a shot.'

'Sure.'

'I'll just be a second.'

One large corner of the space had been made into a kind of set, with a video camera on a tripod and two tall bright lights with cords that snaked across the floor. The lights shone on a small set where two dolls appeared to be undressing each other. Some photographs hung on the wall nearby that seemed to be Fleur's own work: two black-and-white and two colour photographs of dolls posed as classical statues, painted white. All were missing parts of or entire limbs. Their remaining hands held little doll accessories as they would urns or spears or other classical props. They were photographed against a painted background of leafy landscape, familiar from eighteenth-century portraits.

'Are these Barbies?' I asked.

'No, I use Sindy mostly. And other cheaper models.' Fleur stayed focused on the dolls, her back to me. 'Barbies look too generic. I try to use older dolls when I can. And I like them fatter than Barbie.' She dragged on her cigarette.

The dolls being filmed were posed against a curtain tacked onto the wall behind them, a garish fabric that looked like sparkly astroturf. They didn't look too healthy. One appeared to be wearing extra black eyeliner and a miniskirt. The other was missing some of her blonde hair and had on only a bra top and fishnets painted on her plastic legs. The similarity to the Nan Goldin photograph on the other wall was striking.

'What's happening here?' I enquired.

Fleur regarded the dolls for a while and smoked with one hand crossed in front, resting on her hip.

'Can't give it away.' She paused. 'Haven't worked out the story yet.'

'How do you work it out?'

'Well, I can't work it out as I film,' she said, turning to face me, 'although that's what I'd most like to do. It's too slow with the stop-motion. So usually I sit with them for a while, and play through a scene, and film that, and then I reconstruct a sort of script from that. Although there's no words so it's not really a script. It's a sort of storyboard.' She kept on smoking. 'There will be music though. Actually, I just got a request to make a music video. But I don't know. I'm not sure if I want to do that. Of course, Dad would say that music video is about all this amounts to.'

'He doesn't like your new work, does he?'

'No, it's not really art, blah blah. Not like painting, the hand holding the brush, etcetera.'

She was smiling, and didn't sound too upset. I wondered if she was doing this stuff with dolls and video just as rebellion, but that didn't seem right. It wasn't clear how much this all had to do with him, or not, or whether it would be possible to break down this image of the dolls undressing to explain it all that way.

'I didn't grow up with dolls much,' Fleur volunteered. 'Apart from Cynthia here.' She picked up a doll from a small alcove set into the wall near where the photographs hung, stroked her hair, and replaced her gently.

The photographs and stories on video seemed like a deliberate kind of return to childhood, but one with any sense of innocence evacuated or transformed. Whatever play she was engaged in here was intently serious, troubling beyond the usual forms of mutilation that little girls sometimes visited upon their dolls. The humour in the work quickly slipped away into something more ironic and disturbing. Fleur couldn't have had much of a normal childhood, whatever that meant, with her celebrity and the expectations that success brought with it. I hoped she was finding some kind of catharsis in the project.

There was only one of her paintings in the place, and I was surprised to see that it was a print, laminated onto cheap board. It was the red triangle painting from the catalogue cover on Grey's coffee table. Fleur noticed me looking at it.

'The museum owns that one.'

'Is this your favourite?'

Fleur smiled, but her eyes stayed flat. She shook out

another cigarette from the packet in her sweatshirt pocket, and lit it from the one she had finished smoking. She looked too young to be smoking so much.

'It could be my favourite,' she said when she had lit it. 'Ingrid didn't like it though.'

Seconds passed.

'Tell me about her,' I said.

'What do you want to know?' Fleur asked tiredly.

I waited again.

'OK,' Fleur said. She walked to the half-sized fridge over in the corner and squatted in front of it, pulling out two beers. She gestured to a beanbag. 'Sit.' She handed me a bottle, and sat on the the other and started drinking.

In my dream that night Ingrid showed me a curse tablet, pulled out of a drawer. At first it seemed tiny, smaller than the palm of my hand, but when I started to prise apart the scroll of lead it grew so that it was suddenly very large, and Ingrid took it and held it out before me in two hands. When it was fully open I could see that it was not lead after all, but a canvas. I was looking at Fleur's painting, the red triangle a gash on the surface.

I look to Ingrid to ask her what it means, but she only smiles, then turns her back and appears like the portrait with her and Fleur on the wall in Fleur's studio. I look again and Ingrid's right hand is gone, and she stands like a disfigured classical statue, or one of Fleur's white dolls.

A large painting greeted me as I walked into Maeve's gallery that Thursday night, hung so that it faced the open door.

It looked like Sargent's painting of a woman in a dress with shoe-string straps, *Madame X.* It was life-size like that, just to the proportion of a body. The woman stood straight and tall, one foot slightly in front of the other, in a strapless gown made of velvet or thick satin. One pale hand rested on her thigh, while the other held lightly to the corner of a small table. A plant on the table trailed its fronds down towards the floor. She wore a silver chain around one wrist. Her neck was bare, and stones gleamed in her one visible ear, itself shining and perfect as a shell. The entire painting was dark and heavily glazed, as though the Sargent was there underneath a layer of brackish, distorting water. It wasn't quite the same woman, nor quite the same dress or body. She gazed off in another direction. Her feet were strangely bare, like small white fish under the weight of her long gown.

I continued in. The walls were hung with paintings in a similar style, all portraits. Some showed the whole body and others only the head and shoulders. Mostly women, except for one portrait of a child and one of two men, both wearing tuxedos, heads leaning in as if sharing a private joke.

Grey and Fleur were standing together in a smaller room just beyond the main space of the gallery, through an archway that was half closed off by a heavy black curtain. It was my only glimpse of the two of them together, a short, silent tableau. Grey stood with his hands on his hips, pushing his jacket to the sides, and Fleur was half-turned away from him, arms folded, her shoulders a little hunched over. She was wearing black pants and sneakers and a long-sleeved shirt with some kind of colourful design on it, letters and pictures, and a heavy red cardigan. Grey's stance was tense and exasperated. Fleur tossed her hair back over her shoulder with one hand in a petulant gesture.

Someone walked by carrying a tray arranged with plastic cups of wine. The room was filled with men and women dressed expensively in dark clothes. One woman trailed peacock feathers from her gathered black hair. The woman from the Sargent-like painting materialised in front of me, dressed in a gown almost identical to the one in the painting, pointed shoes on her white feet. She stood there with a drink in one hand listening to a grey-haired man in black. He gestured to the painting closest to them. I wanted to hear her voice. The man kept talking. The woman laughed at something he said, a giggle, high-pitched and tinkling. She started talking and her voice wasn't how I'd expected it at all, but high and breathy, a girl's voice. It felt disappointing. I took a cup of white wine from a tray that paused at my side.

The black curtain across the entrance to the back room had fallen closed, and Maeve emerged from behind it. She came straight to me with silent steps through the long, narrow space of the room, in that gliding way she had. She was the same, regal and elegant; she was even wearing the same pelt-like dress I'd first seen her in, or so I thought. When she got closer I could see that it was different, a lighter colour, a newer cut. She kissed me on the cheek and gripped my shoulder briefly with her hand. 'Oh, Julia,' she said, expressively. Her eyes were heavily made-up but the pale concealer underneath didn't disguise the dark shadows there. The longer I looked at her the older she seemed.

'Tell me how Ralph is doing. Eve says he's very fragile.'

'I suppose so.'

Seeing Maeve here, in this place of hers, it was hard not to remember that it was Maeve's connections with them both that had helped to cement the relationship between Grey and Ingrid. I wondered if she ever regretted it.

'It's so wonderful that you could make it. Let's catch up later. You're staying at Robert's? Eve told me,' she explained.

She drifted away to greet some people who were just arriving. It was her element, her space. The artist was the real focus of attention, the star of the show – a calm-looking guy in the other corner, younger than I expected him to be – but Maeve was a force of gravity with a deeper kind of power. Many of the guests showed a kind of a deference or wariness towards her and she moved among them gracefully, an attentive host.

Grey was standing across the room now, talking to a man and a woman, shaking hands and moving away as they went to look at the paintings. A young man with dark hair and black-framed glasses was standing nearby, alone, and they almost collided as Grey backed into him. They appeared to know each other and spoke briefly. I couldn't hear what they were saying. The noise in the room had grown louder, voices bouncing off the concrete walls. They seemed to be arguing. For a moment I saw Ralph at Ingrid and Grey's Sydney wedding party, Grey's hand on Ralph's chest. Now Grey lifted his hand, but didn't touch the other man, who seemed to stand expectantly, waiting for the push or strike that didn't come. Grey lowered his hand and turned away. It looked a lot like he had told the other guy to fuck off. The dark-haired guy had a drink in his hand, red wine in a plastic cup, and he drained it. He looked in my direction and met my eye as he lowered the cup. I looked away. Trinh turned up then. I had invited her a few days before with all the nervousness of asking someone out on a first date, but hadn't been sure if she would actually show up. She was holding a real glass with white wine in it.

'Where did you get that?' I asked.

'Oh, those plastic cups are awful,' she laughed.

She stepped over and caught the arm of the guy with glasses. I cursed the elegant way she had of avoiding questions.

'Richard,' she said. 'What are you doing here?'

'I'm just about to leave,' he said.

She was still for a second and then reached her arm around behind me, as if presenting me to him.

'Have you met Julia?'

'No.'

We shook hands. He put his back in his pockets, nervously.

'Julia's an old friend of Ingrid's.'

He swallowed.

'Did you know her?' I asked.

'Richard was in the program, in Ingrid's year,' Trinh said, before he could speak.

He nodded and pushed his glasses back with one finger. Light reflected off the lenses so that I couldn't see his eyes well, and then he moved a little to the side, and his eyes were dark blue.

He shifted his weight from one foot to the other.

Trinh spoke to him softly. 'How are you, Richard?'

'Good, good.'

They talked briefly. Richard knew the artist from college. That's what he was doing here. They both thought the show was stronger than the last one. His eyes strayed towards the door.

'Well, if you have to go ...' Trinh said, obviously not anxious for him to stay. 'Let's get together soon. I know Julia would love to chat to you more. Right, Julia?'

He took a small step back, as though I might be carrying something contagious. Then he paused and pulled out a wallet from the back pocket of his jeans, and took a card from it and handed it to me. 'Call me if you like,' he said, and didn't look at me, and grasped Trinh's arm for a moment. He left. Trinh watched him sadly.

'It's been hard on Richard,' she said.

I nodded. I could see Grey watching Richard from the corner of his eye, looking away as he moved out through the door.

'I haven't seen him around. I think he's taking a year off. Anyway.' She smiled firmly in a way that suggested a change of subject, and I put away my questions about how well Richard had known Ingrid. 'Here you are. Let's look at these paintings. Do you think anyone else is?' She linked her arm into mine. With her high heels on she almost made it to my height.

We looked at all the paintings, one by one. When we reached the last one on the walls and found ourselves in the corner, furthest from the door, we stood there for a minute and watched the crowd. The room was full by now. Trinh turned to me with a resigned, apologetic face.

'Look, sorry,' she said. 'It's none of my business.'

I waited. 'What?' I asked, eventually.

'Jones,' she said, and focused her eyes on the painting next to us, a woman in profile, collarbones showing, in a red, sleeveless dress. 'He doesn't often mention that he's married.'

'Oh, that,' I said. Somehow I'd already known.

'She's away a lot,' Trinh admitted, as if that explained everything.

'Why do you call him that?' I asked, looking for a way to change the subject, not sure how. I'd seen the spines of his books on the shelf in his office, the ones he'd authored and edited, but they didn't show a first name or initial.

'Call him what?'

'Jones. What's his name? His other name.'

'Philip,' she told me, her eyes serious. 'Don't mention it to him. He hates it.'

When I got home it was late, probably too late to call, but I got Richard's card out from my pocket anyway. It was a plain white card with his name in capitals and a 212 phone number. Richard Evans. I dialled it, thinking of that moment between him and Grey at the gallery when Grey's hand had risen. My curiosity grew, and I held my breath, waiting for his voice. A machine answered.

By the time a week had passed I'd left two messages with Richard Evans and hung up on his machine once. That step back he had taken before he had given me his card rankled with me somehow, and intrigued me. The shape of his eyes, the way they disappeared and shone behind his glasses, was very sharp in my mind and I wanted to see them again.

I stood by the phone, thinking about calling him again, when the yellow phone book caught my eye, sitting in the shelves under the phone. There were a lot of Richard Evanses but with his phone number I was able to find his address. I wrote it on the back of his card. Uptown. The phone book flapped shut. It was mid-morning. I rinsed out my coffee cup and left.

The front door of Richard Evans's building was not in great shape; it looked as though someone had taken a small axe to the lock. It had once been a nice door, stained wood with a recessed glass panel. There was no answer when I pressed the black button next to 14B. The battered door swung open with a push and I climbed the four flights of stairs to his apartment. I wrote a note, crumpled it up, wrote another one and pushed it under the door. By then it was getting towards afternoon. I went downstairs and called Jones at his office from the payphone at the end of the street. He answered right away.

'Yes?'

'It's me. Do you want to get lunch?'

He paused. 'No.'

'OK.'

'I don't have time. But I'll see you tonight.'

'I'm busy.'

I hung up.

I called Richard again the next day, deciding that it would be my last attempt. It was early. He answered after only two rings.

'You're persistent,' he said when he heard my name. It didn't sound like a compliment.

We arranged to have coffee. He sounded reluctant. I remembered my missed meeting with Trinh.

'If you don't show up, I know where you live,' I told him.

He sighed. 'Apparently so.'

Riding up there on the subway I thought about my conversation with Fleur at her studio, sitting on the beanbags with bottles of beer in our hands. Her asking me to sit had seemed like the prelude to a sharing of confidences, but it hadn't really worked out that way. She had started out telling me about what it had been like to meet Ingrid in Venice, and how she had hoped from the first that her father would like her. 'I'd never met anyone from Australia before,' she said. Her nose wrinkled. 'Except for artists there at the Biennale. But Ingrid was a real person.' Something of her opinion of other artists came through in this reflection.

Ingrid was probably closer to Fleur's age than to Grey's, but when they first met Fleur would have been barely a teenager and Ingrid a grown woman – a huge gap. But thinking about it, looking at Fleur, it was hard to imagine her ever really being a child. Her way of holding herself – sitting there on the beanbag, knees together, long shins splayed out, sneakered feet pointed in – declared how young she was, but the look in her eyes every now and again – watchful, unsmiling, calculating, intelligent – made me wonder if the teenage act was mostly just a useful mask.

'I was glad they got married,' she said with a shrug.

'How did Ingrid like it here, in New York?' I asked.

She stared at the floor without seeming to see it, and a smile played around her mouth. 'She helped me find this place,' she said, happily. 'Well, she was with me when I came to look at it the first time. It was that summer she was here, when her and Dad got engaged. She would always bring me croissants from Balthazar when she came to visit. The chocolate ones.' She was talking about a restaurant and pastry shop not too far away from the studio. Ingrid had always loved sweet things.

'I suppose you'd say that we were good friends,' she continued. 'My friends – some of them have stepmothers who are real bitches, you know? Ingrid wasn't like that. She never tried to be my mother. She never told me what to do, what to wear, all that crap.'

This was the most Fleur said about what her relationship with Ingrid was like, and she wouldn't be drawn out about how Ingrid had really liked living here, in the city, with her, with her father. I wanted to know about the rest of it, the triangle of Fleur and Maeve and Grey and how Ingrid had reshaped it, but there was no asking those questions. There was a subtly guarded aspect to the way Fleur talked, and held back some things and offered others in their place. She didn't ask me about my own friendship with Ingrid. I was glad of it.

'I miss her,' she said at the end, quietly, resignedly, and I knew that the conversation was over.

As she opened the front door for me, I took a look back around the studio. There was a small room sectioned off right towards the back of the space. The door was half-open, and offered a glimpse of a futon bed, low off the ground, covered in a rumpled Indian cotton bedspread. Seeing the bed there made me wonder if she actually lived here, or spent more time here than she did at home uptown. I was suddenly curious. 'Who has the lease on this place?' I asked. Fleur must have been not even fourteen when she took it.

The usual wariness wasn't there in Fleur's face as she looked at me. 'Maeve,' she said, simply, as though she were surprised I needed to ask. 'Maeve has the lease. Jointly.'

Heavy rain clouds had massed low over the sky so that it looked almost like evening when I left the building. Thunder sounded, far away. Or a truck rumbling. Up ahead, a long, vertical sign on the side of a building glowed bright red against the grey of the sky and street. *Parking* the letters formed with little light bulbs, one blinking on the 'P'. The wide entranceway to the garage smelled like grease and smoke.

The train had stalled in its tunnel as I was thinking about this, and the overhead lights flickered. Most of the passengers stared ahead, some glanced nervously from side to side. The gears ground into action and we moved again.

Richard had agreed to meet me at a coffee shop not far from his house. When I arrived he was already there, a coffee and an open book sitting in front of him, forehead resting in his hand, elbow on the table. He poured sugar into his cup from a glass dispenser and stirred it while he read.

He rose to stand when he saw me, and sat down again. I ordered coffee and a slice of cherry pie.

'I'm sorry for stalking you,' I said.

He gave me a hard stare. 'You're a friend of Ingrid's? You were a friend of hers?'

'That's right.'

He looked down at his coffee. The surface of it was flat as a mirror. The pie came with two forks. I offered him one and he looked embarrassed and refused. He shifted in his seat uncomfortably. The pie was good.

'Look, I probably shouldn't have given you my card,' he said. 'If it's OK with you – I'm dealing with this in my own time. I'm really not ready to have a big conversation about Ingrid.'

His tense face, the tightness in his voice around the sound of her name – wanting to say it, not wanting to say it – reminded me to always begin with the assumption that any man who knew her had probably been in love with her.

'Well, OK then,' I said. 'You could have said that on the phone.'

He tilted his head in a gesture that wasn't a nod or a shake. He had a nice face and I wanted to see that lovesick look go away from it. There was a shadow on his jaw, as though he hadn't shaved that day, but he appeared like the kind of person who usually did. He was wearing a buttoned shirt that looked as though it should have a tie worn with it but there was no tie.

'So, what do you want to talk about?' I asked.

He didn't say anything. I remembered the way he and Grey had stood there at the gallery in their little stand-off, and I liked him, probably because Grey obviously didn't.

'Do you want to tell me about that fight you were having with Grey at the gallery that night?'

His eyes were dark with anger when he met mine, and he shook his head.

'Some other time then.'

His look softened.

'Tell me about you,' I said. 'Are you still a student there at Columbia? What are you working on?'

'No, no,' he replied. 'I'm taking a year off. I was working on Greek inscriptions.'

'So what are you doing now?'

He drank his coffee. 'Do you always ask this many questions?'

I laughed.

'Are you like a professional sleuth?' he asked.

'That sounds very glamorous. No. It's nothing like that. I work in a bookstore, or I did – I still do – and I'm going to law school. It's all very boring. I was at university with Ingrid.'

He gave a little flinch when I said her name.

'OK, sorry. No talking about her.'

'I'm a graphologist,' he offered. 'And I do some translation work. From French and German.'

I didn't know what being a graphologist meant. He explained that it had to do with the analysis of handwriting. It was some kind of 'consulting work' he said, for a couple of companies.

'When they're hiring people, or sometimes when they're promoting someone, they bring me in to look over the materials of their job candidates. Forms they've filled in. It's a kind of human resources thing.'

'So you analyse the writing of people applying for jobs.'

'Yes.'

It was still confusing.

'Look,' he said. 'I'll show you. Write something.' He pushed a paper napkin towards me. 'Do you have a pen?' There was one in my bag.

'What should I write?' I asked.

'Anything.'

Cherry Pie, I wrote. *Caffe Latte.*

He almost smiled. 'Write your name. Your address,' he said.

I wrote it down.

'You have my phone number already,' I said. He flushed slightly.

'No,' he said. 'I meant – it's for the numbers. How you write numbers. Never mind.'

He took my paper napkin and pen and dissected my handwriting for me.

'First we look at the overall shape of the writing,' he said. 'Does it sit on a straight line – are the letters big, small, evenly shaped, formed consistently or not, and so on.' His hand hovered over the writing, holding the pen. 'The baseline is mostly straight, writing has a strong slant. Hmm. Passionate.' He gave a little smirk. 'Your writing is slow – you might be stubborn. But maybe it's the surface you're working with.' The pen had snagged on the thin surface of the napkin. 'Interesting arcade connection in this one place … so much space between words. You keep people at a distance. But there's a possessive streak too.' He pointed to a loop in my letter 'S'.

'You can tell that from my writing?'

'It's not one hundred per cent reliable. But there's a lot of information there.'

'Do you actually believe in it?'

He took his time thinking about it. 'It started out as just a curiosity for me. Something else to learn. I liked the idea of it at the time. Sometimes I see things that make me think it has some interpretive power. Other times it's just an exercise. I don't know.'

'I guess you must be good at it.'

He shrugged. 'I was well trained. I work fast.'

'How do these people feel about baring their soul to you in their job applications?'

'Oh, they never know about it,' he said, studying the formation of my capital letters. 'It's all very discreet. I get paid a lot because it's all pretty hush-hush. Graphology – well, it's not exactly regarded as being scientific these days. It's not something that these companies want to advertise that they do.'

'Because it's kind of creepy,' I said.

'No,' he said calmly. 'It's unfashionable, I suppose.'

'No-one writes anymore anyway. Everyone uses computers.'

'I know.' He sounded regretful.

'You must hate signing your name. Giving away everything about yourself.'

'I manage to avoid it fairly successfully.'

His face was serious and distant once more. He took some money out of his wallet and put it on the table. We left, and on the street he pulled up the collar of his dark overcoat.

'Let's do this again,' I said.

He almost smiled, same as before. 'You know where I live.' He walked away.

The subway platform was oddly deserted when I descended to catch my train back downtown. Dark trickles of mud ran down the white tiled walls across the tracks, around posters that warned of 'rodenticide' in the area, complete with a drawing of a healthy-looking rat. On cue, a long tail flicked away underneath the tracks. The train arrived.

I recognised Gabriel sitting in a seat near the door when I entered, the graduate student who had opened the door to Trinh's office that day. He was reading a book with a worn red cloth cover; an old edition of a Greek text. I sat down in the orange plastic seat across from him. The carriage swayed.

'Gabriel?' I said. He looked up and blinked and recognised me.

'Hello. Sorry – I forget your name – Trinh's friend?'

I told him.

'I'm sorry about your friend Ingrid,' he offered.

It was hard to know what the etiquette was around the event. So many people had died that I assumed that anyone I met could have lost a friend or family member. It felt not quite right to count myself among them.

He seemed to understand my thoughts.

'She's the only one I knew. Not that I knew her that well – we had one class together, last year, my first year. But she's the only person.'

'Where were you?' It was the first time I'd asked anyone this question.

The book he'd been reading was still open, his hands relaxed around it. They shifted now, but didn't close the book.

'Yes, I saw it, a lot of it. I was on my way to the Center for a meeting downtown there. Lawyers.' His eyes wandered. 'I walked up out of the subway station at Fulton Street and there at the top of the stairs was a piece of an aeroplane, a huge fuselage, just a few feet away from the subway entrance.' He rested the book in his lap and moved his hands up and out to describe the outlandish size of the aeroplane fragment. 'It was surreal.'

I could picture it, the fuselage sitting fatly – singed at the edges, perhaps, burnt? – at the top of the stairs, blocking the entrance to the street like a misplaced object in a Magritte painting. It was hard to read his expression. He didn't sound disturbed.

'But no-one was looking at the fuselage, this enormous piece of a plane right there in the street. I could see that everyone was looking up. I looked up, and I saw the building, the tower. It was melting.'

Now he swallowed, and his skin seemed to take on a different sheen. Or perhaps the lights in the subway car became stronger, whiter, to my eyes as I tried to imagine the thing he was describing. A woman muffled in a scarf a couple of seats from me had become very still as he was talking, and she rose abruptly now, not looking at us, and moved to the other end of the car where she stood and held onto the metal pole.

'The metal on the outside of the building – the supporting struts, whatever they were – it was melting. It was sliding down, the outside of the building was sliding, like liquid.'

Now his hands were lost for a way to signal what he had seen. The carriage lurched a little, an arrhythmic side to side as we turned a corner. The lights were bright, and all the shadows seemed to have disappeared.

His tone grew tired, and he talked a little about growing up in Bogotá. The difference of this from the terror there. The sameness.

We were both quiet for a while before the train came to my station. We said goodbye. Speakers blared. The walls across the platform were almost identical to the ones at the station I'd come from, right down to the dribbles of mud and the rodenticide warnings, only these ones were emblazoned with neon pink tags in spray-paint, unreadable names and messages.

I took the stairs and thought about the street that would be there another three flights up. The tubular metal rail on the side of the stairway felt very solid under my hand. It shone and reflected all the tiles and colour around it in a thin kaleidoscope. I couldn't help thinking of all its solidity melting away. The difference between the cool hardness I felt and its potential other state, pouring away in a rush of heat, seemed suddenly both very small and horribly alien. I pulled my hand away and wanted to run up all the rest of the steps to the street, feet clacking against the tiles, but my legs felt heavy and I had to drag myself up, step by step, without the support of the treacherous rail, arms wrapped around my body.

19.

Back at the apartment the hallway was dark but there was a light on in the living room. Jones was sitting there on the couch. There was music playing, minimalist tones with so much silence between them it took a moment to realise it was music.

'How did you get in here?' I asked him.

'Don't be ridiculous,' he said.

I guessed that Matt had let him in. He wanted to take me out for dinner. But first he asked coyly for another tour of the terrace.

I turned on the strings of lights and we went out through the doors. He walked to the edge of the terrace again and leaned on the ledge. The dusk fell until it was night on one side of the sky and a smudge of sunset on the other. We spent a while with my body pressed up against that same wall where he had kissed me before. The air grew dark around us.

He lifted his face away from mine. 'I don't love you,' he said casually, without stopping what he was doing with his hands, as though he were reminding me of an important detail I might forget, a detour we had to make along the way to our final destination. It was hard to make words, part of my brain detached from language. I swallowed. Anywhere we weren't touching or clothed – small areas of skin – felt invaded by cold.

His face was back in my neck. 'I don't love you too,' I said, his mouth against the place my voice came from. He threw his head back then and laughed with real delight. I smiled.

'Now ...' he said.

Desire was thick in my throat, I was lost in it, and I pulled him inside through the doors; he fell heavily onto the bed when I pushed his chest.

'No,' he said when I started to undo the buttons at my neck. 'Leave them on.'

I was all rush and wanting to go faster; he let me for a minute and smiled at me. Then he pinned my wrists above my head against the bed and gave me a cool, hungry look. He found a weak point in the seam of my skirt at the waist where the stitching had started to come undone and tore hard, a practised motion, so that the whole thing came apart in one jagged movement down my hips and thighs. A long, liquid breath went through me and I felt my body relax at last, surrendered.

'That's better,' he said, and touched me just as slow and as fast as he wanted to.

The rest of our clothes came off with varying degrees of force and speed. We struggled and pushed and pulled each other with a kind of desperation that shaded quickly into play; he held me down, and did what I said, and made me laugh and cry out, fight and give up.

We lay exhausted afterwards on the bed in my room with the French doors open. He rolled over and mumbled something that ended with 'go'. A short moment later he was snoring lightly, lying on his stomach with his face pressed on its side into the pillow.

I shrugged my body up the bed and let my head fall back on the pillow behind me. The room was still in the darkness, and the shapes of things in the air around us seemed to grow more precise. Jones breathed heavily, his unguarded face half-lit by a glow from the street. Ingrid's box sat on the chair across from the bed, filling the seat with its bulk. Jones hadn't seemed to notice it. I wanted to hide it, to throw a blanket or a towel across it.

The thought was still with me when I opened my eyes, with no memory of having closed them. The room was filled with the thin light of morning. There was no sign of Jones, the pillow lying flat and silent on the bed next to me. I slapped it with my open hand, feeling the feathers collapse, the pillowcase inflate and sink again. Sounds of early morning on the street outside penetrated the room: grates rolling up on the fronts of shops, trucks idling, traffic stalled and starting. The roar of a motorcycle passed through and faded. I imagined the scene of his departure, and felt uncomfortable, picturing him awake and dressing while I lay sleeping. I remembered watching him fall into sleep the night before.

In the bathroom my naked torso was pale in the mirror, a small red cloud of a bruise forming on the side of one breast. His mouth there – hands, gripping – I swallowed, unsteady. Having slept in front of him provoked far worse feelings of vulnerability than having slept with him. I crossed my arms against the sight and yawned.

Coming back into the bedroom after a shower I noticed the remains of my skirt on the end of the bed, halfway to the floor. The sight of it sent a hot, heady rush through me. I eased it off with one toe and pushed it under the bed. Part of me distantly regretted its loss – it had been old, made in the 1940s, with a high waist and a faded silk label stitched onto the inside, embroidered with a little flower. I had bought it years before at a market stall one Saturday. The tearing feeling crossed my body again, a pleasant shiver that passed out of me with a sigh.

Wrapped in a towel, I made myself a mug of strong coffee. It cleared my head, chased the taste of the night before from my mouth. I sat on the bed and placed the box in front of me, opened the lid and started reading again.

It was afternoon when I came to the end, having skimmed through most and read carefully through some of the contents. A plate lay on the bed covered with toast crumbs. I finished looking through an article copied from a journal, a piece about the storage of lead curse tablets, the kind of conditions they required, the fragility of the material. An important cache of tablets had been destroyed, years ago, just by storing them in a drawer made of the wrong stuff. The air had been made too acidic by the wood, and gradually the tablets decayed. They had been in bad shape to begin with. By then the writing on them had been transcribed, but now it would be impossible to check any possible errors of transcription.

Even looking so briefly into Ingrid's field, it was clear that the whole discipline of recovery was a complex tragedy of loss, a salvage operation whose finds, however stunning they might be, were random, piecemeal, tiny – small bits of a larger, unrecoverable picture. What survived. What died. What made it. What didn't. Who lived. Who died unknown. Who left behind two lines quoted by someone quoted by someone. A game of whispers. A graffitist who attacked their lover in writing on the walls of a street in a dead city could be preserved and quoted endlessly, while poets renowned in their time left nothing behind in their own hand.

I turned the pages and added them to the pile of paper next to the box, its emptied contents. The last piece of paper lay alone at the bottom of the box. I looked at it for a while before picking it up.

It wasn't a piece about the curse tablets or ancient Roman writing. It was a page of a letter from a medical insurance company, a statement of account. It was dated from August 2001, and it mentioned an emergency room visit and orthopaedic services. The reverse side of the page was blank; it seemed to be a photocopy of the original. I looked at the page again but could see no pen marks, no notes. I put it back in the box then thought again and took it out. I put the rest of the papers back in, and laid the medical account on top. The room was growing dark. A sudden breeze came up and swept across the terrace, making the birdcage tinkle and lifting the edges of the pages on top of the pile. The French doors slammed shut. I replaced the lid.

When I woke up the box was on the floor beside the bed, although I couldn't remember putting it down there, and the plate and coffee mugs were gone. Matt. The clock showed 8 pm. I felt hungry and thought about the last piece of toast before I had fallen asleep. I got up and turned on all the lamps, and the lights out on the terrace.

In the kitchen Matt was drying dishes and looking more tanned than usual. I suspected that he used a tanning salon. We talked about ordering dinner.

'Matt,' I asked, 'an orthopaedic surgeon works on bones, right?'

He smiled archly. 'I saw one once about a broken nose. Don't ask.'

I stared at him, and at the table.

'OK, it's a long story,' he started, enthusiastic. 'It also involves a fractured hand and a contusion or two. Let's wait for the food. In the meantime you can tell me all about the racket coming from your room last night.'

His nose was handsome, a slight bump evident now that I knew about the break.

'Over dinner?' I said.

After we ate he helped me choose an outfit, a dark shirt with a gauzy sheen and a pair of black jeans. I found myself inspecting the integrity of the material with a new kind of interest, testing the solid feel of the denim in my fingers as I pulled up the zip. He also found a pair of boots in one of the hallway closets.

'I've been waiting for someone to make use of these,' he said. They looked like tall motorcycle boots, harness and buckle around the foot, heels worn down on one side. 'They've been here for at least a year.'

When I was dressed and lipsticked he looked at my face critically. 'Great shirt. Great boots. Now let me fix your eyebrows.'

I allowed him to spend five minutes pulling my eyebrows into shape with little tweezers. It hurt less than I had imagined it would. This position of compliance, standing with my face to the bathroom light, felt strangely relaxing. My eyes watered.

'OK,' he said finally.

My eyebrows had been almost straight lines; now they had the suggestion of an elegant arch. I raised one for him.

'You're beautiful. Go.'

I thought I would get there before Trinh – wasn't even sure if she would come, but was counting on the fact that she drank there most nights. But Trinh was already standing at the bar, talking to the bartender, when I entered the Lilac. She was wearing a leather jacket zipped up to the neck, and a short skirt. Her cheeks were flushed as though she'd just stepped in out of the cold. She smiled when she saw me, and said something to the bartender, and he nodded and started mixing a drink.

'Hi,' Trinh said, as though she'd been expecting me, and touched her hand lightly to my waist. 'Ben's mixing some mean martinis tonight.'

Ben smiled and put two glasses on the bar, filled them from a shaker.

With the first few mouthfuls of my drink I glowed with a sudden sense of belonging: to walk into a bar and find a friend there. This was what it meant to be at home in a city. Wasn't it? I remembered Thursday afternoons in that last spring on campus, when I would walk upstairs to the bar and count on finding Ingrid and Ralph there, huddled on the battered red leather sofa. They would be drinking gin and beer and playing board games on the coffee table littered with ashtrays and cigarettes.

Then I remembered what I had come here to talk to Trinh about. The glow faded.

We sat together at the same booth of black vinyl. Trinh unzipped her jacket. My drink was very strong. I told her that I had looked through Ingrid's box.

Trinh raised her eyebrows. 'Did you find anything interesting? I don't think there was much in there very personal.'

'There wasn't. But I know a lot about magic in the ancient world now. More than I used to, which isn't saying much.'

Trinh smiled. 'Ingrid's work was very promising. She was a good student.'

'There was something else in there.'

Trinh's eyebrows stayed where they were.

'It was a medical bill. Not a bill – an account. It was from the emergency room.'

The table was lit by a small votive candle in a cloudy glass holder. Trinh passed her hand over it, back and forth once, absently. 'There were all kinds of papers in her drawer and on the shelf. To tell you the truth I didn't look through them very closely.'

I waited.

'The account must have been from when she broke her hand at the end of 2000 – no, the year before last,' she said.

'She broke her hand?'

'Yes. She fell down those stairs in the flat. You've seen

them. Broke her fall badly, broke … some bones, I don't remember how many, those little bones in the hand. She was so cross about it – she wore a bandage for a couple of weeks and couldn't type, had to type with one hand.'

I pictured Ingrid, bandaged, and thought of Fleur's doll statuettes with their missing hands. Something didn't fit.

'The bill is from 2001,' I said. 'Not 2000.'

Trinh frowned gently. 'I might be remembering it wrong. I thought it was the year before. Maybe they were sending the account later …' Her eyes strayed across the room.

'The visit is from August.'

'God, I hardly saw her all that summer. She must have been in and out of the office. I don't know what that might have been about. It's been a while since I saw her. It was a while – is that right? I hadn't seen her for a while. Anyway.'

Her eyes came back to me and her expression was concerned. She leaned forward. 'I'm sorry, Julia. I wasn't thinking. How awful for you to come across things like that, so personal, something from her life. I didn't think, when I gave you the box, about how upsetting that would be.' She looked down. 'I just wanted to get it out of the room. I thought you might like to see some of her work …'

I looked at my own hand holding my glass, other hand in my lap. 'It was good to see her work. Thanks.'

'Why don't I come and get that stuff back from you? Take it out of your hands?'

'No – no, it's OK. I'll hold onto it.'

Trinh looked as though she wanted to argue.

I spoke instead. 'So, this person Richard Evans. What was the story there?'

She thought for a moment, a cautious look in her eyes. 'Ingrid was very … attractive,' she said.

'Yes,' I agreed, waiting.

'Richard and she were good friends,' she said reluctantly. 'But that's it.'

It made sense with what I'd seen of him.

'He's taken it all very hard. Have you seen him again?' she asked.

'Yes,' I said. 'But he didn't want to talk about Ingrid.'

Trinh nodded thoughtfully. Then she looked up over my head and smiled. I turned around. Jones stood behind me, his hand resting on the edge of the booth. He was holding a drink in one hand and a cigarette in the other. He slid in beside me and touched his glass to Trinh's, then to mine, and drank.

'Good evening,' he said. He drew on his cigarette and looked at me briefly. 'Good to see you getting along so well.' He leaned back in his seat.

Trinh gave him a smile that was friendly and knowing and somehow ironic. 'To your good health,' she said, 'and to our departed friends.'

I raised my glass to my mouth.

Jones's hand strayed down to my leg now and again. I stayed still, giving nothing away.

Trinh checked her watch at some point around ten.

'Working?' Jones asked.

She nodded.

'Where do you work?' I asked, imagining her behind a bar.

She looked back and forth for a second or two between me and Jones.

'I work downtown, not that far from here. Basically – how should I put this – I tell people what to do.'

'So you're some kind of manager?'

'No, not exactly.'

Jones watched her silently.

'People pay me to tell them what to do.'

I waited. She held her glass. Consultant, I thought; instructor?

'I'm, like, a dominatrix, I suppose you call it.'

Jones gave a small smile and lifted his glass to drink.

'It's not sex,' she said. 'Some of that goes on at the place I work at – not much – but it's mainly, you know, discipline and so on. It's all about power.'

'Like bondage? S & M?' I asked, feeling slow and ignorant.

'That's the idea.'

'And you're the one brandishing the whip?'

'Exactly.' She smiled. 'And issuing instructions. It's great money and great benefits. It's putting me through school. Usually I tell people that I teach dance.'

She pulled out a card and handed it to me. Salon Réage, it said, with a design of a wheel in the centre, five spokes, and a phone number, and the name Verity.

'It's better to be the one holding the whip than on the other end, in terms of which end you work. There's much more work on the other side of things for the Asian girls, you know, but I do OK. The girls who work as bottoms at our place work hard. Make a lot of money but for me it wasn't worth it.'

I didn't like what I was imagining. It was easier to think of Trinh holding a whip than being struck by one.

'Some students in the department do that medical testing stuff to make money – you know, where they pay you to take an experimental drug or get a piece cut out of your mouth, see how it heals.' She grimaced. 'It's too gross. The pay can be really good. But this is a lot better. For me at least.'

'What are the guys like?' I asked. 'Is it all guys?'

'Oh, it's all guys. Lawyers. They are our best clientele. And politicians. A judge or two. No surprise. It's expensive.'

'Trinh has a sixth sense for this,' Jones said. 'She can tell – in much the same way some people guess your star sign – she'll know whether you're the S or the M, the top or the bottom. Some people surprise you.' He looked at Trinh admiringly.

'So which one am I?' I asked her.

She laughed. 'You're too easy.' She drank her drink. 'Ask him – his sense is as good as mine. And by the way, you're a Gemini.'

She eased her way out from behind the table and stood. 'I'm off to dominate for a few hours. Have fun, kids.' She squeezed Jones's hand for a second before she left.

He looked at me. 'Can I buy you that drink?'

We walked later up Sixth Avenue, past the shops with windows full of sex toys and bongs. I stopped outside one with a display of handcuffs and looked at Jones, raised my eyebrows.

'Not for me,' he said, with a barely perceptible shake of his head. 'So literal.'

We kept on walking, back to the apartment.

There was something about this air of detachment he had, the way part of him remained dispassionate and contained even while his whole body was engaged in sex, that both enraged and excited me; the cooler he was, the more furiously I wanted to see him lose control, studying him intently to make sure I caught the moment when it might happen, listening for his breathing to change, his voice to collapse. Even when it seemed that the moment would never arrive, I chased it more and more helplessly, like an animal throwing itself against the bars of a cage. He seemed to know it, and not to care, and let me wear myself out. And so I gave up, and had forgotten to keep watch for it when it finally came, not with his eyes shut as I would have expected, but with them open and distantly unfocused, suddenly vulnerable. It didn't last long. His eyes closed and he was intact again. I lowered my body to his and turned my face away, buried it in his chest, and felt not triumphant as I had thought I would, but uncertain and drained.

The sheets were cold when I woke in the early hours of the morning, alone in the bed, driven awake by a dream. There had been rows of drawers, like the sliding cabinets in a morgue wall, or specimen drawers, some shallow and some deep. They were all made of wood, filled with tablets and papers and other, more disturbing artifacts. I didn't want to look. Ingrid opened them expertly one by one and turned to me, her face close and troubled. Her hand rested on a drawer's handle at hip height. She was talking about those destroyed tablets kept in the wrong kind of case. 'Even lead decays,' she told me. 'The drawings,' she said, or was it 'drawers'? 'The case was wrong.' I thought she was talking about Latin grammatical cases, and laughed; in this dream world I imagined them as capacious, invisible containers, cases, for meaning. 'There were problems with transcription,' she insisted urgently. 'Transcription.'

The room was dark. An argument was happening down on the street below, a long, wheedling voice against an angry shout. The clock showed its bright red digital numbers and I pushed it away. The darkness started to lift and lighten. The sheets were no longer as cold. The voices outside grew more distant. I willed the drawers shut in my mind and fell back asleep.

Jones talked about Ingrid just one time, a week or two after that night. We were in his office. I'd picked a book off the shelf, his most recent one, an edited collection. There it was on the title page – Philip R. Jones, the hated first name. Opening the book dislodged a piece of notepaper inside with Ingrid's writing on it – the title of an article, a reference she had copied out from his bibliography. Page numbers. A word below, crossed over so it was illegible.

Jones took the book out of my hands almost roughly and looked at it for a minute. 'She borrowed it,' he said, and handed it back to me, keeping hold of the note. He folded the piece of paper in half and held it, as though not sure what to do with it, and sat there on the edge of his desk. There were several copies of his book on the shelf on the wall, and he looked at them without seeming to really see them.

'I didn't see much of Ingrid in the six months, year, before that September,' he said eventually. This was becoming a common refrain among the people she had known. 'I've been sorry about that. You know, I was on the admissions committee the year she applied. So I knew her from the start of her time here. From before the start of it. She changed so much in that time.' He seemed to be looking for how to describe it. 'It was subtle. Her work was excellent but she had a lot of trouble choosing a topic. She seemed to lose faith in her own ideas about things, to have trouble maintaining her confidence about her work. And, of course, she was very unhappy, after the first six months or so. But you know that.' He gave a small, bitter smile.

I remembered how Ed had seen Ingrid here once in that time, in New York, a few months after she had come to Sydney for those few days to visit Ralph. It had been a business trip of some kind for him. I had met him for a drink with Ralph after he got back. He was drinking a lot that night and when he spoke about Ingrid he was furious. At first she hadn't agreed to see him at all, and then she did, and they went out to eat. 'She looked just the same,' he said, 'but it wasn't her at all. You wouldn't know her.' Ed had blamed Grey, said that he was trying to run her life and had to know where she was every minute of the day. 'She's just pretending,' he said. 'It's all an act. Very careful. It's like he's replaced her with a robot. A good robot.'

Ralph had said something in reply about Grey being like Pygmalion, taking Ingrid and shaping her according to his own desires. I mentioned that to Jones, and he thought for a moment then he shook his head.

'No,' he said. 'Pygmalion started out with a statue – he made one himself – and the gods turned it into a living woman. Grey is something like the opposite of that. He started with a living woman and turned her into ...' He paused. I waited for him to finish. He shook his head again.

I thought I understood.

He nodded towards the book in my hands. 'It's yours,' he said. 'Take it. There are ten copies here. It's embarrassing.'

I hesitated.

'If you don't want it ...' he started. 'Some of the pieces are quite good. But it might not be your kind of thing.' He held out his hand, ready to take it back.

I held on to it. 'You're giving it to me?' I asked.

'Yes,' Jones said, becoming impatient. He pulled the book out of my hands and opened it to the title page, *Perspectives on Tribute in the Late Roman Empire*, took a pen out of his shirt pocket. His hand hovered over the page, preparing to write an inscription. He seemed to almost change his mind, clicked the top of the pen up and down, then wrote quickly for a second. He smiled apologetically, closed the book and handed it to me again. I took it, uncertain, and thanked him.

20.

At my first visit to her studio, Fleur had invited me to a party
there, two weeks from the day. I had asked if there was a
special occasion. She had looked confused and thought for
a second, and said, 'It's Theo's birthday,' but that seemed
like a statement of fact and not the reason for the party.

When I got there the place was filled with people,
everywhere from Fleur's age to my own and older, a few
heads of greying hair, everyone in black and denim
punctuated with spots of metallic sparkle. Sheets of coloured
gel had been placed over the standing lamps so that the
space was dimly lit in red. Candles dripped wax onto the
floor from a tall, branched candelabrum in one corner. As I
watched it, a teenage boy took a candle that had almost
burnt down and tilted it so that a drop of wax fell onto his
hand, impressing the girl sitting next to him. He held it over
her hand and another drop fell onto her skin. She giggled,
and he held the candle there, smiling at her.

Fleur saw me and pulled me into a huddle of people in
the small kitchen area. The air was thick with smoke.
Someone put a clear plastic cup in my hand and said,
'Punch,' into my ear over the loud music. It tasted like red
cordial and bourbon. A piece of fruit floated in the pinkish-
brown liquid. Fleur was wearing a silver, sleeveless shirt

with her hair down, pushed back behind her ears. There was glitter on her cheekbones. Her eyes were paler than ever under black and silver make-up.

I found my way out of the crowded area. The corner of the room that was used as a video set was closed off by a tall folding screen of wood and paper. I stepped behind it. The music sounded softer in this corner, as though the screen had a greater power as a sound barrier than it ought to. There was a work table against the far wall, papers and plastic pages full of slides strewn across it, two drawers underneath. There wasn't much light. The drawers opened easily. They were full of pens and paperclips, snapshots, postcards, rolls of tape, coins. In a small stack of photographs at the back of the second drawer there was one of Ingrid, taken outside somewhere on a sunny day. It looked relatively recent. She was smiling at the camera. I saw that much when there was a noise behind me and I quickly slipped it into my back pocket.

I looked around and saw Richard Evans standing there with a beer in his hand.

'Hello,' he said. He looked over at the desk. I had shut the drawers. My cup of punch was leaving a wet puddle on the white laminate surface. 'Sleuthing?' he asked.

The photograph of Fleur and Ingrid with her back turned was on the wall between us, and both our gazes drifted towards it silently. I had the feeling that he had come here to the screened-off corner to see it.

'I'm off,' he said, glancing towards the screen. 'Just passing through.' He flattened down a piece of his dark, straight hair with the heel of his hand.

'Don't go,' I said. 'You're the only person I know here apart from Fleur.'

He glanced towards the screen and then to me, hesitating. 'I don't have to go right away.'

Neither of us looked back at the photograph. He settled himself on the floor, against the wall. Cynthia sat in her alcove above him. I stayed in the flimsy chair at the desk.

'What's in your drink?' he asked.

I grimaced. 'Punch. Would you like to try it? It tasted terrible at first but it grows on you.'

He shook his head and drank from his bottle. 'It's quieter here,' he said. I nodded.

His face was clean-shaven and the light glinted here and there off his glasses. The piece of hair he had tried to smooth wouldn't stay down. His features were very average-looking but his eyes gave something more special to his face. They were iron-blue, serious, scrutinising. We stayed there like that, not talking much, for a little while. Soon my drink was finished, thin slice of strawberry stuck to the side of the cup. Just as I was about to suggest that we go together to find me another drink he stood up and stretched his legs, stiff from sitting. Suddenly it was hard to make the suggestion; I felt shy, and when it became clear that he was leaving I was disappointed. We went around the screen to the main room together.

'See you later then,' he said, and smiled.

'That would be nice,' I said.

His smile turned into a questioning look; it was tentative but not uninterested. My heel caught on something, a hole in the floor; I looked down. He went over to a group of people talking and spoke to one of them, a man I recognised as the artist from the opening at Maeve's gallery the previous week, wearing the same brown and green argyle vest as he had before. They put their heads together for a moment and then said their goodbyes to the others. Richard skimmed the room quickly before they left. His eyes met Fleur's briefly as she happened to turn towards the door and looked away without any sign of recognition. I went to look for more punch.

Jones and I were leaving the building one evening a few days later and went past a man in a brown jacket outside Mrs Bee's door, waiting for her to answer. The look of recognition between the man and Jones was unmistakeable; they finished it with a nod. We pushed through the front set of doors and left him standing there for a moment, until I looked back and saw her door open. The man smiled tenderly at her and passed through whatever it was he had to deliver.

There could have been a small smile at the edge of Jones's mouth, or not; he was playing the straight face for me. A strong breeze came up. Gum wrappers skittered across the footpath and he did a quick one-two to avoid them. A paper bag slapped into my leg and I shook it off. I didn't want to ask; it annoyed me that he wouldn't say. The breeze was cold around my ankles. I tried to let the question drop from my mind but it stayed there, banging around like the garbage on the windy street. Quite how Mrs Bee's sphere of acquaintance might cross with Jones's was unclear but in New York any connection seemed possible.

In the end it was Jones who raised it. The pleasure of

withholding information must have become outweighed by the enjoyment of revelation.

'Your Mrs Bee is a dark horse,' he said, apparently addressing his whisky, looking at the meniscus as it tilted, fingers rocking the glass. His eyes were liquid bright. His fingers distracted me, long and evenly shaped, the cleanest of nails. He set the glass down.

I tried to play that straight face of his, but I got impatient. 'So who was that guy earlier?'

'He's a delivery guy,' he answered, with a knowing smile.

'Yeah. I guessed that.'

'You guessed what?'

By then I was sick of the conversation, and my glass was nearly empty. Jones stood. 'Sad face. I'll get you another. Sam, the delivery guy, he delivers, you know, drugs.' He said the last word in a secretive, ironic whisper in my ear, leaning down over me as he passed.

He walked away to the bar with a slow, lazy stride.

Back again, he set the drinks on the table. He had bought me a martini.

'Classy,' I said.

'I guessed you for a twist rather than olive,' he said, and took a substantial sip from the glass. 'Not bad.'

The gin smelled sharp against my nose.

He leaned towards me, elbows on the table. 'So I guess your Mrs Bee is one of those upscale William Burroughs-style junkies – live forever on the good stuff as long as they find holes in their arms.'

Why not, I thought. But it was hard to put the idea of heroin addiction together with Mrs Bee. I decided that he was probably delivering other kinds of drugs, something she used to induce psychic visions.

'Drink up, baby,' he told me.

It sounded dirty and a little absurd in his clipped, English voice. He waited for me to complain and seemed disappointed when I didn't. I knew what he'd be looking for: the chance to point out that I'd never complained before, when he'd called me that in other, more private circumstances. Instead I just smiled and wished there was an olive in the glass to chew on. My body went a little soft at the joints. He raised his glass in a half-hearted toast.

> *Jenny – The sky here looks weird without the towers.*
> *Missing you.*

I had finally got around to mailing one of the postcards. The stamp was an image of the Statue of Liberty; the other option at the post office had been an American flag. Reaching to drop it into the mailbox on the corner, I stopped, disturbed. I looked down at the card, the short note, my writing. It was suddenly unfamiliar, the handwriting of someone else. What was I giving away, I wondered, seeing the marks and strokes and lines that would mean a whole range of things to Richard Evans the graphologist, things I couldn't see in my own writing.

There was someone waiting behind me with her own things to post, a woman wearing a brown fur coat and big sunglasses. I glanced over. She made small sighs and noises of irritation and shifted her weight from one foot to another on kitten heels. In one hand, raised to her waist, she held a miniature dog, a chihuahua with big, wet eyes. It tilted its little head to the side and bared a set of tiny teeth at me.

I stepped aside, let the woman post her several letters.

When she was done, I pushed my card through the slot. It didn't make a sound falling in.

There was a message on the notepad next to the phone when I got back to the apartment.

Julia: Peter pls call

Friday pm

Peter and I hadn't spoken since I'd been in New York. Before I left he had started his residency at a hospital out in Sydney's western suburbs, the same place he had been working as an intern. I called. His phone rang and then went to an answering machine. I left a brief message. Was there a birthday that I had forgotten? No – his birthday was in May, a week before my own. I tried calling my aunt. The phone rang out.

I tried again the next day, calling Jenny first this time. Again there was no answer. The phone rang almost as soon as I had set it down, and it was Peter. His voice was tired. The news was bad.

'It's Jenny. She's had a stroke. A serious one. We think she's going to be OK but recovery could take some time. It took a while to find your number.'

I stared at the clock on the wall and absorbed its details. The two hands, one longer than the other – by how much, I wondered. Two centimetres? How many centimetres in an inch again? Little black lines around the edges marked the seconds, and the numerals were all bold, finished off with just a little curlicue. This is shock, I thought, the idea floating. This absorption in the details.

My hand felt numb against the plastic of the phone. How many seconds had gone by? The thin little ticking third hand didn't help me decide.

'I'll come back as soon as I can,' I told him. Peter's voice was so familiar, and my own now sounded so strange.

'I think she'd like to see you.'

'She's awake?' I asked.

The distance between us sounded like the backwash of a wave. Seconds passed, although my eyes were having trouble now focusing on the thin black lines of the clock. Peter's voice brought me back from deep underwater.

'So when will you be able to get here?'

'I don't know. Soon. The time difference ... I don't know how long it will take. I'll get a ticket as soon as I can.' My brain started to wrap around the logistics of airlines, times, travel.

I watched the dirty-looking sunset finish. When the door buzzed later it was dark and the room was lit by just one lamp. A second later the buzzer sounded again, a long ring. I rose to answer it.

Jones's voice crackled through the box. I pressed the button to open the downstairs door and went to open the latch. He was there quickly and inside. He almost lifted me from the ground, arms squeezing out the breath, and then he stepped back. He looked at me strangely.

'What is it?' I asked.

'What is it with you?' he countered. 'You're pale.' He touched my arms. 'You're freezing.' He began to pull off his jacket.

I told him. 'My aunt had a stroke.'

'Your aunt?'

'We were close. We live – I lived with her in Sydney.'

He became suddenly solicitous and kind and ushered me inside and through to the couch with a steady arm, opened wine and poured me a drink. 'Have you eaten?' he asked. I shook my head. He went into the kitchen and used the phone. 'Food's on the way,' he said as he came back in.

'Now,' he said, looking at me as though he were about to explain a complicated concept. 'You don't have a seat booked already, do you?'

I shook my head again.

'Alright,' he said, and turned on the television. I stared at it. He changed the channels until a black-and-white film appeared. He went to use the phone. When he came back a little while later he handed me a sheet of notepaper with an address written on it and some sets of numbers. 'You can pick up the ticket from there in the morning.'

I looked at the notepaper.

'It isn't far,' he said.

I was confused, thinking for a moment that he meant Sydney. 'Oh, you mean this place,' I said eventually. The address belonged to a travel agent. It was a shopfront a few blocks away, always filled with students. The numbers on the paper were dates and times and flight numbers but I read them without real understanding.

Food arrived at the door then and I ate the noodle soup straight from the plastic container. Jones cleared the table when we were done and came back. The television was still on, a different movie that looked the same as the one before.

'There was a flight tomorrow or not till next week. So you're leaving tomorrow,' he said. 'Now come to bed.'

I was half-afraid that he would try to take me out of the semi-present state I was hovering in, but he seemed to understand that oblivion was what I was looking for. And when had it been any different really, ever, I wondered, as a long breath left me, and the question dissolved. He was rough and deliberate. I wondered what a concussion felt like. I slept.

The light came through the doors at a strange angle the next morning. It was too early. The knowledge of Jenny's stroke was perfectly present in my mind when I woke; there was no moment of not remembering, no sense of it coming back slowly. It was just there.

Jones's jacket rested on the armchair at the other side of the room, flung across so that the crooked arms suggested a fallen person. This was odd. I imagined that he had forgotten it when he left in the night. The buzzer rang. I pulled on a shirt and went to the hall, pressed the button, croaked out hello.

'It's me,' a voice replied.

'Jones?'

Nothing. I buzzed him in.

He walked in with coffee and doughnuts in his hand, six in a flimsy cardboard box. I pulled it open and took it out of his hands and chose one with chocolate icing. It seemed to be made of chocolate cake.

'You eat utter crap,' I told him with my mouth full.

He grinned and made his way into the apartment. 'You're welcome. Good morning.'

'What are you doing here anyway?' I asked.

He didn't reply, stood in the bedroom facing the French doors, pushing his hair back, drinking coffee. I sat on the bed and chewed my doughnut. He watched me eating, undoing the buttons of his shirt.

'This is good,' I said.

'I thought you said it was crap.'

'No, good. Thanks.'

'Hmm.'

Jones's and Matt's voices drifted in from the living room when I came out of the shower a while later. I dressed and went in there. Matt was gazing at Jones with eyes full of adoration and dragged his gaze away to look at me.

'Did Jones tell you?' I asked.

'Tell me what?' Matt glanced back at him quickly.

'My aunt's had a stroke. In Sydney. I'm leaving today.'

'Oh, god,' he said, and put his arms around me. 'I'll help you pack. And we can talk about when you're coming back. Don't think about staying there.'

I looked at Jones, but couldn't catch his eye.

'I'm off,' he said. 'Don't forget the ticket. Your flight's this afternoon.'

The note with all the details was still there on the coffee table. He pushed it in my direction with his finger. He and Matt exchanged a look and a nod that seemed to convey something about making sure I made it to the airport in one piece.

I walked Jones to the door and he held me close for a short moment, and put his hand in my wet hair and squeezed so that it almost hurt.

My suitcase didn't take long to pack. When it was done I went downstairs and knocked on Mrs Bee's door. She opened it and let me in. Her hand was warm on my arm and she looked at my face, my eyes. 'Sit down,' she said.

She filled the kettle and set it on the stove. The sounds were a reminder of Jenny, and I felt myself lose steadiness inside.

Mrs Bee brought the tea out on the usual wooden tray, which rattled as it came to rest on the low table. She poured the tea into two cups. It smelled delicate and earthy, and I imagined a flower on its stem freshly pulled out of the ground, dirt clinging to the threadlike roots. Black leaves floated down through the liquid.

'Men carrying doughnuts and coffee can be a portent of many things,' she said with a smile. 'I don't know what it signifies in this case but you look as though you've had a shock.'

'My aunt's had a stroke. In Sydney.' I put my hand to my hair, smoothed it down.

Mrs Bee nodded slowly, listening.

I sipped my tea, waiting for her to say something. I saw my arrival in the city and my imminent departure, bracketed by the loss of one person and now, almost, another. The feeling of Ingrid's loss was refreshed by this new brush with grief, and I knew that it would deepen and change now.

'So you were right, at my last visit,' I said. 'The search is coming to an end.' She'd made this prediction, unusually specific, while inspecting the dregs of my tea a few days before.

Mrs Bee smiled gently. 'All searches end one way or another. Yours was bound to end one day. But you can return to it, if you feel as though it's not finished here.'

She reached for my cup, now almost empty. I turned it, the gesture now automatic. The liquid drained out as I rested it upside down on its saucer. She looked into it casually, and tilted it so that the inside of the cup was visible to me. The leaves made a rough circle, broken in one place. I looked again and saw an hourglass, or a cloud. I closed my eyes and saw a brown, clear river, old leaves and branches resting at the bottom.

I opened my eyes. 'Did you see it?' I asked her.

Mrs Bee placed the cup back in the saucer.

'The last time I was here – did you see it?'

'No,' she said, meeting my eyes. 'But think about it. What would I do with knowledge like that, even if I had it?'

She leaned back against the sofa, tiredness in her face, a new expression.

Part Three

21.

The plane was still sitting on the runway when I took out my book, knowing I wouldn't start reading it yet but wanting to have something in my hands, some words ready to distract me when the take-off began. Removing the book required some subsequent rearrangement of the things inside my bag; bags within bags within bags; things I looked at now and couldn't imagine needing. At least ten pens. Why were all these receipts in here? I took out a Valium pill and swallowed it, struggled to do the zip back up and fitted the bag under the seat. The seat next to me was still empty. In the aisle seat was a middle-aged man in a suit. He had taken off his tie as soon as he sat down and squashed it cruelly into the mesh pocket in the seat in front. Wrinkles were beginning to form around the bottom of his jacket. Neither of us ventured to put anything on the seat between us. I thought about it and decided to wait.

The book rested squarish and large on my lap, a mystery novel with a jacket dominated by raised silver lettering. An envelope packet of photographs had got stuck inside the cover while it was in my bag, and I took it into my hands. I had borrowed Matt's camera, a lightweight Nikon, a few times in the past weeks, and had the snapshots developed. The cover of the envelope, provided by the photo shop, showed a generic Alpine scene with snowy peaks and improbably shaded sky.

The plane's wheels started to move slowly, slowly, crawling out along the runway. I removed the photographs and studied them: the first one was a snap of that picture on Fleur's wall, with Ingrid's back and Fleur's young, made-up face. Ingrid seemed very solid in this image, and alive. Something in it made me think of my aunt; I remembered her standing at the stove as the kettle boiled, her back to me, steam on the windows and the lamplight soft as I sat at the table waiting for tea to be made. There was a longing for home in this memory, and I wondered if there would be any return to that kind of moment, her standing there like that, both of us waiting. I moved the photograph to the back of the pack.

The next one was the picture of Ingrid I had taken from Fleur's drawer, stowed in here with my own pictures. It looked as though it had been taken on the Brooklyn Promenade, a wide walkway in Brooklyn Heights that ran for a mile along the East River, lined with playgrounds and mansions looking over to the southern end of Manhattan. The city was a blur behind her across the water. Her hair had come loose in strands and blew around her head, a blonde corona. One hand was raised to shade her face or keep the hair away, obscuring one of her eyes. She smiled her Mona Lisa smile, no teeth showing, lips soft. I moved to the next photograph, and the plane moved a little faster. I concentrated on the photographs – of SoHo, of the apartment, the birdcage on the roof, rooftops beyond it, the skyline, the sky – and came back around to the Promenade.

This time I saw something different. It was as though the angle of the photographer had shifted. Perhaps my change of perspective came from viewing these dozen other pictures, many of them skylines, but the photograph seemed to show the city beyond Ingrid's figure in a new way. Where was she standing? The wheels moved faster, and the feeling in the pit of my stomach grew more troubling as they gained in speed. But now the feeling was attached equally to the photograph. I tried to imagine myself there again on the Promenade, the wide pavement, the people walking and laughing, sitting on the benches, the generous trees overhanging and laying their spotted shade on the grey path, the roar of the expressway below, a monster beneath. The way the island looked from there, from the start of the walk – here the pretty old skyscraper, there the stepped pyramid roof of that other building, the bridge swinging down all the way over there. But where was she standing? I strained to remember the place and where she could be. Behind her head the sky was palest grey or blue. But it was empty, I realised with growing wonder. Above the stepped skyline of downtown the fingers of the towers did not reach into the air. The towers were not there. Where was she standing? When was she there?

She continued to smile, and it had never seemed so mocking, or mysterious, or aggravating. The photograph was smaller than the other ones by half an inch around the edges. I had always imagined that Fleur had taken the picture but now I wondered. The plane hurtled along the runway, walls shuddering. I suppressed an urge to shout, Stop! Let me off.

I wanted to run through the airport and all the way back to the SoHo loft and ask Fleur about the photograph – when was it taken? Who took it? What does it show?

I looked down and saw that I had unfastened my seatbelt, ready to rise. I couldn't, of course, I told myself. It would wait, for a phone call. I fastened the buckle again. The man in the aisle seat slept, his head tilting to an awkward angle as the plane lifted off and left the ground.

The turbulence began as we approached the clouds. The city, the water, all the shrinking freeways and buildings and little islands disappeared slowly below. I looked from the square window back down to the photograph. The contours of the city behind Ingrid seemed fuzzier somehow now, and the angle even less clear, as the drug entered my bloodstream.

A few rows ahead a small child's scream cut the mechanical buzz of the aircraft, a thin, reedy note right on pitch. After a long minute it dropped away to sobbing, responding to a mother's voice almost inaudible above the other noise. I heard the child crying and had a second of displacement where I wondered fearfully if it might be my own voice. The crying continued. Was it a boy, a girl? Through the Valium haze the shudders of the plane felt like rocking by a huge, unseen hand.

My brother Peter met me at Sydney airport in his nice black car.

'Where am I taking you?' he asked.

'To the house. Mosman.' It didn't feel right to call it home somehow.

By the time we were halfway there we were fighting traffic.

'How's Leonora?' I asked.

Peter had been having a secret affair with one of the other doctors at the hospital, a woman in a senior position, for months. The secrecy was something to do with their relationship at work; it had never quite made sense the one or two times when he had tried to explain it to me. Jenny disapproved in a silent, resigned kind of way.

Peter shrugged and made a show of focusing hard on the road.

He walked up to the front door with me, and I went to my room while he wandered back out to the verandah. The house felt empty as a tomb, and I thought again of the chambers in the Pyramids and the curse tablets that Ingrid had been working with. Tiny, rolled-up pieces of metal, some of them stuck under a corpse's tongue. What would it have taken to have found them – prying open the old bones?

The air in my room was cool and still. I dropped my bag and went through to the studio. It was filled with the direct light that Jenny liked to work with. Canvases sat stacked against the wall. One was standing up on an easel towards the back of the room. The blue of it was immense, swathes of colour swept through with white strokes. Clouds; the foam on waves. The bright whiteness of sunlight through a window in a strip against the floor.

Something in me answered to the long, white line cut through the blue – sorrow, guilt, relief. Then it receded, flattened back against the canvas.

Peter stood at the door. 'There's tea in the kitchen,' he said quietly, his suit hanging awkwardly on his body. 'Should I bring it –'

'No,' I cut him off. 'I'll come.'

We finished the tea. Peter had used a strainer, so the cups were free of leaves, just a faint smudge of wet fragments around the bottom. He put the cups into the sink and ran water over them.

We drove to the hospital and Peter filled me in on Jenny's condition. She would recover – but for now she was having trouble speaking. Impaired movement on the left side of the body. Difficulty walking. It would be a lengthy process: more time in hospital, and then weeks in a rehabilitation facility. Once he'd explained it to me we drove in silence the rest of the way. He parked the car and seemed to come awake somehow once he'd pulled the handbrake on, before he switched the engine off, and glanced at me and then quickly away.

'Shit,' he said. 'I didn't tell you.'

'Tell me what?'

He gave a short sigh. 'Mum's here. Sorry, I should have said.'

I sighed in turn. He flipped the key and the car shut down.

My mother, Rachel, was sitting by the bedside in my aunt's hospital room. She wore a purple cotton dress with a brown print, little boxy shapes like misshapen Mayan characters. Her hair was long and straight, grey mixed equally with brown. She was reading a book, and she wore purple-rimmed glasses that I had never seen before. When my brother said hello she looked up quickly and folded them away in a swift motion. They seemed to disappear into an invisible pocket in her dress.

She embraced me with her wiry arms, leaning in so that the rest of her body didn't touch me. 'Julia,' she said. 'It's so good of you to come.'

I felt a flame of resentment then. I had been away for just weeks, while she hadn't seen Jenny for years. Peter caught my eye with a warning look.

Jenny looked small in the hospital bed, the starched sheets with their stiff folds around her. She smiled at me with half her face. There was a spiral-bound notebook on the bed beside her with a ballpoint pen next to it.

My mother had moved quickly into a conversation with my brother about my aunt's status and the doctor's comments from the day before.

'I came as soon as I could,' I said to Jenny.

She picked up the pen and slowly wrote *good to see you J*.

I took the chair that my mother had been sitting in. Her book was on the bedside table now: the latest instalment in a self-help series that promised 'A Course in Miracles'.

The room was dominated by a huge television screen set up high in the corner, now switched off. The sounds of others in the rooms next door came faintly through the walls. There was a big, square window across from the bed with a tree pressed right up against it, dark green leaves touching the glass.

Peter and my mother talked and the moments of silence between their exchanges grew longer. Eventually Rachel came over to the bed and inclined her head sympathetically at me.

'Let's get some coffee,' she said.

'You're drinking actual coffee?' I asked.

Her brow creased. 'Well,' she said firmly, 'I'll have tea. You have whatever you like.' Her smile returned.

Peter came down with us to the hospital caféteria. We passed through the fluorescent-lit aisles, holding plastic trays that we filled with bad pastries, and sat down finally near a window. Peter brushed a pile of crumbs from the table and mopped up a small puddle of brown liquid that might have been tea.

He watched Rachel carefully, as though ready to intercede in the conversation if necessary. She sipped at her peppermint tea and explained that she had been thinking about moving back to Sydney again in any case and that this was perfect timing. I looked at Peter nervously.

He cleared his throat. 'Jenny's going to need quite a bit of support, initially at least,' he said. 'Rehabilitation. She'll need someone around.'

'Where are you staying?' I asked Rachel.

She smiled. 'I'm staying with a good friend. In Rozelle. For the time being. Jenny will be out of hospital before too long. We'll take it from there.' The look on her face told me that the good friend was more than just a good friend. But it was typical of her to be enigmatic, even with us, about this kind of thing.

The unspoken issue was there between us — she would be moving into the Mosman house. I caught Peter's eye. He sat back in his chair, checked his watch. His hair was the same brown as Rachel's, straight like mine, short and badly cut around his ears.

'I have to be going,' he said.

We said goodbye and he left, walking quickly, straightening his jacket. Rachel and I were alone together. We both seemed equally uncomfortable about it. She kept her hands around her cup. Our talk was all about her: she had moved on from doing astrological charts and crystal healing and was now qualified as a Reiki practitioner. It had something to do with energy emanating from the hands. Everything was happening with perfect timing – 'convergence,' she said – there was an opening at a natural healing centre in Balmain that she was exploring. I didn't like the idea of my aunt's near-death experience being structured into my mother's view of serendipity or whatever it was that was being timed so well. I wondered what had gone bad for her on the north coast that had really inspired her move, if that was what this was, but didn't ask.

Her blue eyes, lighter than mine, just like Jenny's, were rimmed with blue eyeliner that had a kind of metallic sheen to it. Her hands went to the chunk of amethyst she wore on a cord around her neck, pointed at one end like the crystalline tooth of an animal. It had some kind of mystical significance I didn't understand.

'I'm glad we could have this little chat,' she said. 'I can see that you and Jenny have such a strong connection. It's very powerful.'

I swirled the last of my tea around in its paper cup. The room lurched. Rachel left and went off to Balmain and I went back upstairs to Jenny.

22.

I went over to Ralph's a few days after that first hospital visit. The conservatory was warmer than ever. Aaron was still wearing his sarong, a long-sleeved white shirt with it this time. He poured me a brandy with lime and soda. Ralph sat in the same place, the same chair, but looked a little brighter than the last time. His black shirt was one I remembered from Paris. For a brief moment I wanted to take it into my hands, holding the cuffs so that my knuckles would graze against his chest, but it passed. A surprising sense of stillness took its place.

He asked about Jenny. I didn't want to talk about it. 'My mother's here,' I told him. He looked concerned and allowed us to change the subject.

'Have you seen Mark?' he wanted to know.

I shook my head. 'That's well and truly over,' I told him firmly. 'For the best.' Our breakup before my departure had been quiet and formulaic, both of us almost embarrassed by our lack of feeling about it.

Ralph sighed. 'I told you to stay away from the Philosophy students.'

'You did. Thanks for that.'

He bit his lip with a little smile.

'So,' he said, with something of his old tone. 'Tell me.'

So I told him what I could: Fleur and her video doll dramas and parties; the off-white apartment full of art; Ingrid's room with the chaise longue and the elephants on the dresser (leaving out the fact that one of them was still with me, now in a pocket in my suitcase). Ingrid's office, her research, the curse tablets. Trinh and her glamorous style. Much of it came easily. I skipped over Jones, saying only that her teachers admired and liked her and seemed pretty smart themselves.

Ralph listened, stopping me only occasionally to ask me to further explain something – more information about what the apartment was like, how it was laid out, the view from Ingrid's windows.

The photograph was there with me, in my bag, still in that book with the others. I thought about showing it to Ralph but didn't. The light was morning-pale through the glass, yellow from the lamps in the corners of the room. Aaron came in with a bottle in his hands and starting spraying the plants, sending a fine mist over the dark green leaves.

'There's something you're not telling me,' Ralph said.

I hesitated. 'I slept with one of Ingrid's teachers,' I said. It was the first thing that came into my mind – I didn't want to talk about the photo, or the emergency room report.

He looked faintly disappointed. It was nothing to do with her, really. 'Oh.' He raised his eyebrows and his eyes drifted off to the side, up towards the ceiling. 'Is he good-looking?'

'I suppose so.'

He grew more interested. 'Wait – is it that English one?'

'Yes.'

'Do you think she –'

'No.' I cut him off and shook my head. 'Apparently not.' His disappointment returned.

'What are you going to do now?'

I dropped my eyes to the floor. Dark slate.

'If you want to go back …' he began.

I looked back up at him. 'I don't know.'

'Well. Go ahead, if that's what you want to do.'

I thought about it. 'Ralph, what do you do with yourself here all day?'

He smiled at me gently, almost peacefully, but I could see the lines of tension around his eyes. 'You know me. I'm good at doing nothing. Next week I think I'll have another go at Proust.'

Ingrid was here with us in a way that I hadn't felt her in New York – she had been barely there at all in that bleached-out room I'd sat in with Grey, only a ghost in her room and Fleur's studio – but here in the Kirribilli house the imprint of her presence was strong. I half-expected to see her white silhouette behind a layer of foliage towards the back of the room. Plants rustled softly in my peripheral vision. She was alive for him here too. Whatever trace she had left behind was given more life by his grieving desire, the nostalgia that he somehow thrived on. Of course he was reading Proust, I thought – in search of lost time.

Aaron appeared at Ralph's side with a china plate in his hand filled with bottles of pills, four or five of them, and a glass of water. He brought a small breath of cool, refreshing air with him from elsewhere in the house, and I wanted to be outside.

I stood up. 'I'll see myself out.'

Aaron regarded me silently.

'Ring me,' Ralph's voice called out as I was in the hallway, towards the door.

The Sydney spring passed in a haze, numb and warm. Peter visited and drove me to the hospital and the rehab place to visit Jenny. I took her novels and read to her sometimes from them, or from a book of Elizabeth Bishop's poetry she kept by the bed.

I did call Ralph, and he called me; we spoke on the phone every week, short conversations that included a lot of long silences and repetitive exchanges. Something of our old intimacy resurfaced in those phone calls; we seemed to be feeling our way back, very slowly, to somewhere we could talk again.

My mother floated in to see me at Mosman every now and again in her badly printed dresses and leggings and expensive sandals. Whenever she came it was to drink the last of the tea or finish the loaf of bread, the last of the biscuits or the remainder of a piece of cheese. 'Darling, sorry,' she would say. 'Next time I'll bring something.' The one time she did it was a loaf of panettone in a dusty yellow box tied with a ribbon. It wasn't clear how the box actually opened, the thin cardboard folded in a complicated kind of aperture around the bottom. I could imagine that the bread inside would taste just like the yellow cardboard. We didn't try it, and the box stayed on the kitchen counter, getting pushed further into the corner as the days went by.

Her visits were never long, although they drained me of energy as though she had stayed for hours every time.

I would fall straight onto the couch when she was gone, television on loud for the rest of the afternoon and night.

My postcard arrived at the house with the mail one morning, the one I had sent from New York. My own writing on it was still uncanny. It had got beaten up in the journey over, several big creases and a little tear in one corner. A wavy red stamp covered the Statue of Liberty, and on the front, across the image of the skyline and the towers, was a long, thin sticker printed with an obscure set of numbers. When I started to peel it off, the paper underneath came off with it, so I left it there.

I took the card over when I next went to visit Jenny and propped it up against a glass jug of flowers next to her bed. Her hair had grown longer, past her shoulders, and was pulled back in a plastic slide clip. She was wearing a lavender V-neck shirt with short sleeves that reminded me uncomfortably of the clothes that the nurses wore, serviceable, starchy cotton. She turned slowly from the flowers and the card and looked at me with concern for long seconds.

'This card arrived the other day,' I said. 'I sent it just before I left.' I told her the story of buying it, settled back in my chair and talked on.

I saw Victoria, Ingrid's sister, once, one weekday morning on the street in Mosman where the shops and cafés were. I was standing outside the grocer's, an old-fashioned kind of shop with tilted boxes and crates of fruit set outside the doors. There were mandarins on display, bright, waxy orange in their rows and piles. Victoria came out of the chemist's next door. She was wearing a little black dress like a slip, and her legs were slim and long in flat, strappy shoes that slapped along the concrete path. There was a short second where I wasn't sure what to do, and she had only just passed me when I called her name.

She stopped and turned to look at me. Her face showed no recognition. Large round sunglasses hid her eyes, and her mouth was expressionless, unsmiling under its sheer gloss. It seemed for a moment as though she were going to pretend that she didn't know me and turn back around, and it occurred to me that I wouldn't be sorry. But I'd stepped towards her without thinking.

'How are you?' I asked.

Her hair was pulled back from her face by a band. She chewed the inside of her lip.

I hadn't seen her since that party, Ingrid and Grey's wedding party on the water.

'Hi. How are you?' she said reluctantly.

'OK.'

She raised her chin in a defiant kind of gesture. I was holding a mandarin; it was surprisingly light, the fruit loose inside the skin. The citrus smell mixed with exhaust fumes from a car idling next to us on the street. The morning sun was harsh and bright on the pavement. I was inside the shade cast by the shop's awning but Victoria was in the full sun, skin glowing with a deep tan. She shifted her weight from one foot to the other, ready to walk away.

'I've just got back from New York,' I said.

'What?' she asked, her nose wrinkling in seeming disgust and incredulity. 'What were you doing there?'

Her eyes were invisible behind the shaded lenses. I was sorry that I'd said anything, sorry I'd called her name.

'Oh, just passing through,' I said. 'I met Grey. And Fleur.'

Her body stilled to attention. 'Both of them?' she asked.

I pulled a plastic bag from the roll next to the crate and started filling it with mandarins.

Victoria folded her arms. 'Who else? What were you doing there?' she asked again. Two diamond studs glinted in her ears, and when she uncrossed her arms a diamond glittered on her finger. It was large, cut with many sharp facets, in a shiny platinum ring.

'Are you engaged?' I asked.

She nodded and pursed her lips.

'Congratulations. Are you seeing Eve while you're in town?'

She nodded, looking past me to inside the grocer's. 'Yeah. For lunch on Sunday. At her flat.' She frowned suddenly. 'Will you be there?'

'Victoria,' I said, 'I'm so sorry about Ingrid.'

She looked at me resentfully for a second, and then relented.

'OK. Thanks. Bye, Julia.'

Her phone rang as she said it, a musical jangle from inside the leather bag on her shoulder. She didn't answer it right away, and I thought she was going to ask me something else, then she turned and reached for the phone. I watched her walk away, phone held to her ear, other hand readjusting the thin leather strap of the bag. She paused a few shops down and half-turned back to look at me, still talking, then turned and kept walking, more quickly, down the street.

Keith came over once or twice. The gallery was going to go ahead with the show of Jenny's paintings they had planned. He came in the late afternoon and would bring a bottle of wine to drink with me when he was done sorting and packing the paintings or papers. The spring sun was treating him well, adding new, pretty freckles to the ones already there on his face and arms. On his second visit I poured the last of the bottle and thought about opening another.

'So, Julia,' he said. 'Are you still planning on law school?'

I frowned. 'I don't know.'

'Or going back to the bookshop? I know Martin misses you.'

'Oh.'

He leaned across the table towards me. 'You've got as much time as you need. But I think you'll feel better if you start – you know – doing something with your time.'

'Feel better?'

'Less depressed.'

It hadn't occurred to me that I was depressed, but now it seemed obvious. I wondered if I should care, or do something about it. This seemed like a pretty typical sign of depression.

'You're probably right.'

'Or were you thinking of going back to New York?' He sipped his wine. 'It's a great city – I know you love it.'

I thought about the apartment, Matt and the birdcage on the terrace. The terrace made me think about Jones. I hadn't spoken to him since I'd been back. The phone had rung late one night, three or four in the morning, and I had felt sure that it was him. I'd listened to it, and had just sat up in bed, thinking of going to answer it, when it stopped.

'I don't want to leave Jenny,' I said.

'She's doing alright, you know,' he replied. 'Your mother's around quite a bit. I think they've had some kind of ...' He smiled, searching for a word. 'Rapprochement?'

'I suppose that's good.'

'It is.'

I hadn't looked at the photograph of Ingrid since coming back. It was still inside the book, which was on a shelf in the wardrobe in my room. I'd felt such an urgency about it on that flight back, and it had all drained away. I had called Fleur several times, never able to get through to her, and had decided it was something to talk to her about when I saw her next, always assuming that I was going back. But then there was the hospital, and my mother, a series of waves that had crushed me into a whole other state of mind by the end of that first week. It had opened up a new kind of rawness about Ingrid, so that I had avoided thinking about her.

Keith looked at me. 'Grey's doing very well. So I hear. There was a rumour that he was going to split from Maeve, from the gallery, but I think that's all sorted out now.'

He started to get that guilty look that he wore when he talked about Grey. I didn't say anything.

I stood in the kitchen after he left and looked at the calendar on the wall. It showed the month of October, when I'd come back to Sydney. I knew it wasn't October anymore, but wasn't sure if it was the next month, or the one after that. I had to think hard to figure out what day of the week it was.

I was scaring myself. Rain fell steadily outside, running off the verandah roof. The night was cool but the day had been warm. It seemed like the end of November. October on the calendar was a picture of an old church somewhere in France. November was a French farmhouse with a sea of coloured flowers out the front of it. This seemed like a wrong kind of image for a European November. The flowers looked like the tiny purple ones that were coming out now along the side of the house near the verandah.

Back in my room I looked at the books on the shelf in the wardrobe, the novel with the photo inside its jacket, and *Perspectives on Tribute in the Late Roman Empire*. The spine of Jones's book was still fresh and uncracked. I opened it now to the only page I had really looked at, the title page he had inscribed to me that afternoon in his office. His writing was a swift, level dash across the page, sharply angled. *For Julia – Yours, Jones.* It was the simplest of inscriptions and I couldn't tell if it was impersonal or intimate in its brevity. It had nothing to say, or was loaded with things unsaid. The dash after my name was long, so much that it looked as though the line indicated a blank space that had yet to be filled in.

The phone rang. It was Peter.

'Just checking in,' he said.

'Peter,' I began, 'Keith came over today. He says that Mum's been around. And that she's getting on well with Jenny.'

'Yes,' he replied, sounding surprised – at what I'd said, or the situation, I couldn't tell. 'I thought you knew that. Mum seems to be entering some sort of responsible phase.' He laughed, a dry, ironic sound.

'Keith said they'd had a rapprochement.'

'I suppose you could call it that. They never exactly fell out, did they? They just didn't get along. Not that they're exactly good friends now. But it's getting to be that way.'

'I'm thinking of taking another trip.'

'By all means. I'm here too, you know. I know Jenny loves having you around. But ...'

'It's not going to happen again, is it?' I asked. 'Another stroke.'

He breathed out heavily. 'It's possible. But not that likely. If that's what you're worried about ...'

'I don't know what I'm worried about.'

'Well, don't worry about that. There's nothing you can do about it.'

There was a brief silence.

'Are you breaking your heart over someone over there?' he asked impatiently. 'I thought it would be good for you to get away from Mark – that wasn't going anywhere – but it doesn't seem that way.'

I sighed. The only time Peter asked about my personal life was in contexts like this, acting from some kind of intermittent frustrated desire to protect me from my own unwise impulses. I knew better than he did that my love object choices were unfailingly bad.

'It's so self-destructive,' he said.

We had had this conversation before.

'You don't know anything about it,' I said. 'And no, I'm not breaking my heart.'

'No, that would involve actually getting involved, I suppose.'

'You can talk. Is that why you're checking up on me?' I asked.

'You're so fucking prickly,' he said.

'Sorry.'

'Checking in. Just saying hi. I thought you'd want to know that Jenny's doing well this week. I'm going to be there Sunday if you want to stop by, get some lunch.'

'OK.'

'Mum won't be there.'

I breathed with relief. 'Alright.'

'I won't hassle you about the guy, whoever he is. You can tell me about it if you want to.'

'As if.' But the irritation had fled.

The next morning the garden was green and freshened by the rainfall. I took my tea outside to the verandah and sat in a chair watching the sun break through patches of thin cloud. The sound of the radio came through from the kitchen and told me the day and the date. I had taken the little elephant out of my suitcase and held it in my hand now. The radio told me what time it was: too early to call anyone. I walked to the local shops and bought the paper, took it back, read it in the shade. The sun rose higher. I called Ralph. Aaron answered, as usual, and Ralph took a long time getting to the phone.

'Ralph? I think I want to go back to New York.'

'Thank god. I knew you would eventually. You're turning into a fucking corpse here in Sydney. Giving me a run for my money.'

'I didn't realise it was that bad.'

'No, I know. OK. When do you want to leave? I'll get Aaron to arrange the flight.'

'It's OK – there's no need –'

'No, Julia.'

I was silent.

'You're going back for her, aren't you?' he asked.

I thought again of the picture, her mysterious smile. 'I suppose so. There are a few more things to look into.'

'Let me pay. I want you to feel obligated to me. That way I can feel justified in getting you to tell me everything.'

'I'll tell you everything anyway.'

'I know you're really going back for that cruelly beautiful professor of yours. Good luck with that.'

'Oh, him.' I tried to sound casual. But it was Richard's face that came to my mind, bent over the table, explaining my own writing to me.

'And whatever else you get up to. Oh, I'm seeing Victoria for lunch tomorrow.' He started coughing and it went on for a disconcertingly long time. 'Sorry,' he said eventually, his voice still harsh. 'Do you want to come?'

'Are you kidding?'

'Well. She called me up yesterday and said she'd run into you.'

'In Mosman.'

'She's curious about your visit to New York.'

'She's engaged.'

'I know – Eve told me. Gold Coast money, a developer. Now we know why she wasn't that upset about her sister becoming a multimillionaire.'

'Are we too hard on her?'

354

'Probably. Yes. No. It *is* sad – she's lost everyone now. All her immediate family. Eve's tried to be supportive.' He paused, and said painfully, 'She looks so like Ingrid.'

I couldn't tell whether he was about to say that he loved seeing her, or hated it.

'But Ingrid never talked about her,' I said.

'No. But they were close in their own weird way.'

Were they? I supposed that Ralph would know better than me.

It was late November. I could get a flight the following week. Aaron booked it.

23.

I waited a long time for a taxi at the airport in New York, and the sky darkened quickly into night during the drive. The driver talked into his phone the whole way in a language I couldn't identify. A word that here and there sounded Spanish. I pressed myself into the corner of the seat and watched the buildings go past, the dark, glowing hulk of the skyline as we travelled towards the island.

The downtown streets were strangely empty and we drove for blocks with barely another car on the street, catching every green light. It was cold when I got out of the cab, patches of dirty water hardening to ice on the pavement. No light showed from Mrs Bee's window onto the street. There was a coldness inside the building too; winter had stolen in while I was gone. The whole city seemed to have gone into hibernation, closing its doors, closing down.

The apartment was empty. I looked through the rooms but there was no sign of Matt. His bed was rumpled, with three pairs of identical-looking jeans strewn across it and a black scarf thrown down in a folded zigzag against the dark red bedcover. The fridge held several takeout containers that could have been days or weeks old. My room – I thought of it as mine, and it still felt that way – looked emptier than before, and silent. I tugged open the curtains across the French doors and breathed dust as they moved. The bed was bare, no sheets, showing the mattress with a couple of faint stains on the quilted cover. The place had an abandoned, sad feeling.

I looked into one of the closets in the hallway, the one I'd found the boots in weeks ago, thinking it might hold some linen or blankets. It was still mainly full of coats and rugs rolled up at the end of the space. I looked through the coats, thinking of the cold night outside, and borrowed Matt's scarf instead.

The place was just as empty when I came back half an hour later with orange juice and pizza. I took a glass from the kitchen and sat down in front of the TV. *Friends* was on. It quickly went to a commercial. I took the book from my bag, the one with the photos still tucked inside it in their envelope, and looked at the pictures again, and put them away.

I called Ralph. Aaron answered after a few rings. I was prepared to give him a message, but he said, 'I'll get Ralph for you.'

Long seconds passed, then Ralph's voice.

'Julia.'

Keep talking, I wanted to say. Say anything. That longing I'd felt when I had seen him last in Sydney, the desire to clutch his shirt between my fingers, became a wild undulation in my chest right where I thought it had gone to sleep forever, filling up the silence.

It calmed down as soon as I heard his tired, expectant tone again. 'You're there?'

'I'm here.'

'OK.'

Laughter from the television.

'It's, like, winter here.'

He didn't respond.

'I just wanted to let you know I'm here.'

'Thanks.'

'Are you OK?'

'Oh, yeah.' I could hear a smile. 'Well …'

'Ralph,' I said. 'Have you heard from Victoria?'

'Victoria?'

I thought of her long legs and tense back walking quickly away from me on the street that day; her hostile response to my statement that I'd been to New York.

'Not since that lunch. I guess she's back to sunning herself to death in Queensland. Why?'

'It's nothing. I'll call again, later.'

'Good.'

'Goodnight.'

'Right. Goodnight.'

That thing in my chest gave a restless twitch and subsided. I tried reading the novel again but by the end of the chapter I'd forgotten the beginning and had to re-start; after two times I gave up. Another episode of *Friends* started, and another.

I woke up on the bare mattress with the down cover from Matt's bed wrapped around me. It took a while to remember that I'd taken it in with me when I'd gone to bed, brain slowed by sleeping pills. The room was frigid. There was no radiator that I could see. Instead there were vents in the floor that seemed to be letting out no heat at all. I shivered and ran the shower as hot as I could stand.

It was a hazy morning when I got out of the subway in Brooklyn and walked down through Brooklyn Heights along Montague Street to the Promenade, stopping on the way to buy coffee and doughnuts. The coffee tasted faintly of hazelnuts and artificial milk. At the Promenade I walked down the footpath until I had almost reached the south end and sat on a bench. Nannies and mothers wheeled blanketed babies in strollers and the shouts of children sounded from the playgrounds behind. Joggers ran past. Down the other end of the walkway a small film crew was setting up with cameras and large foil umbrellas. I shaded my eyes against the glare of the sky and took out the envelope packet, removed the photograph of Ingrid. It seemed very small in my hand. I looked across at the city, the cascading shapes of the buildings. The mirrored sides of glass-walled structures reflected and distorted the buildings next to them, making ghostly twins of their neighbours.

Ingrid smiled out at me, a half-smile. I looked closer at her mouth and thought I saw the shadow of a bruise on her lower lip, one side more swollen than the other. The blue of her eyes was barely there in the picture, all the colours bleached out. I could see the stepped shape of a building behind her and I looked up to match it with my view. It looked sort of like one building I could see, and sort of like another. I tried to remember the placement of the towers and where they would stand next to and behind these other buildings. It seemed like they should be there, in the picture, whether it was one building I thought I was seeing, or another. I went to the railing and walked down the Promenade, holding the photograph, checking. By the time I left, the sky was taking on the glare of noon.

I pressed the buzzer next to Fleur's name and waited. There was no response. I tried again. I had tried calling her from a payphone in Brooklyn with no luck. There was a phone at the end of her block but the mouthpiece was missing from the receiver, the plastic shattered. I stepped back from the door.

The storefront on the street level of the building had changed its display but was no less ambiguous than before. A single red velvet sofa sat in the window, a book lying open on the seat and a pair of high-heeled boots on the floor at one end. The laces were undone and the right boot had fallen over on its side. A tall lamp lit the arrangement. Velvet hangings blocked the view of what was inside and a sign on the door said *Closed.* Shoes? Furniture? Lamps? Art? I wondered. Books? A pair of opera glasses rested on the seat of the sofa.

The day had turned into afternoon. Fleur was probably at school.

I went to find something to eat. A couple of hours later I pressed the buzzer again with not much hope of success, and a second time. The opera glasses were gone from the sofa in the window. The front door clunked open and Fleur's face appeared, pinched and cold-looking.

'Hi,' she said. 'The fucking intercom is broken. The whole thing. I can hear you but I can't buzz the door from upstairs ...'

Her eyes were light greenish-grey against silver and black eyeliner.

'Come in,' she said and held open the door.

It was warm inside. She was wearing jeans and a heavy, white, cable-knit jumper that came halfway down her thighs. The sleeves were too long, rolled up and pushed up her forearms. She had sheepskin boots on her feet.

'What is that place downstairs?' I asked on the way up.

Fleur shrugged. 'It's always changing. Right now I think they sell underwear.' We came to her door. 'Or maybe it's still a gallery. I don't know.'

There was music playing in the loft, and two teenagers, a boy and a girl, sitting on the beanbags and looking at a camera. The girl had one of Fleur's dolls in her lap. They both had black hair and black fingernails, the polish chipped.

'Hi.' I waved at them. They smiled back.

'They're helping me with a shoot,' Fleur said. A couple of tall lights stood over in the corner where I'd seen her photographing the dolls the last time, looking as though they were waiting to be put into action. The astroturf surface was gone and the set was covered in shag-pile carpet on the floor and peeling gilt paper on the walls. Over on the beanbag the black-haired girl lifted the doll and moved its arms up and down in a series of gestures, displaying it for the boy. He nodded and they talked in low, serious voices.

'So, here you are,' Fleur said. 'Haven't heard from you in a while.'

'I was back in Sydney.'

'Oh, right.'

'My aunt had a stroke.'

'God, I'm sorry. You know, Dad mentioned that. That's awful.'

'Thanks. It's OK.'

'So you came back over here to get away from all that?'

'I suppose so.'

She watched her friends with the doll for a while.

'Fleur. I wanted to talk to you about this photo.'

I held it out and her face changed when she saw it. Her arms remained folded.

'That's mine.'

'I know – I'm sorry.'

'Well, thanks for bringing it back.'

'Would you mind – I don't have many photos of Ingrid ...'

She studied my face, and looked at the floor for a second, calculating, and looked back up at me decisively. 'OK, for now. But I'll dig out some others for you. I'd like that one back. Come round again in a few days and I'll see what I have.'

She looked at her friends and back at me. 'Do you want to hang out? We're going to start setting up – but I don't know, if you want to help, you could help me with these lights.'

'Thanks. But, Fleur, I wanted to ask you about the photo.'

'What about it?' she demanded briskly.

'I've just been down to the Promenade.'

She frowned.

'Where's it taken from?' I asked.

'Right – the Promenade – you've just been down there. What did you want to ask?'

'It's just that – I couldn't see – the angle – where it was taken from ...'

She glanced down at it. 'It's hard to tell.'

She refolded her arms and then unfolded them and took a cigarette from a pack on a bench behind her, and a lighter from her pocket. Her hands were slim; her father's hands. She lit the cigarette and blew smoke away from me.

'What?' She gave an enquiring smile. 'You look like you've seen a ghost.'

'Did you take it?'

'The photo? Yeah.'

'I was looking for the spot – where it might have been taken from …' I could feel myself beginning to repeat words, not able to form a question.

'Is this part of your mission or whatever it is? Tracing Ingrid's last steps?' She wasn't smiling now. 'I took the photo. It was in the summer sometime. Ingrid loved the Promenade. She loved the view you get of the city from there. She liked to walk across the Brooklyn Bridge. And there was a place over there where she liked to get muffins.' She drew on her cigarette. 'I don't know. Those muffins never seemed that special to me. Anyway.'

She glanced down at the photo again and for a second I thought she was going to take it from my hand. I could sense that she regretted having agreed to lend it to me.

'The towers aren't there,' I said. 'In the photo.'

'It's the angle. I'm telling you, I took the photo.'

'That's what I thought. That's why I went down there. To see.'

'Well, maybe you should check again. Or maybe you should just get a life.'

The ash had burnt down to a long, curving cinder at the end of her cigarette. Her voice was softer when she spoke again. 'Sorry. You're dealing with this in your own way, I can tell. But it's kind of upsetting for me to talk about. Do you mind if we change the subject?'

'Sure – sure,' I said.

She stepped over to the sink and let the ash fall into it. 'I know what it's like when you're feeling that sad,' she said. 'Nothing makes sense.' Her face was turned in profile, mouth set, and I had a sudden sense of her grief. She had never really known her own mother, and now Ingrid was gone too.

'I'm sorry, Fleur.'

'That's OK.'

At that point I badly wanted to bury all my doubts about the photograph. Coming here to question Fleur seemed to me then like a pointless and cruel thing to do. She went over to where the lights were waiting and picked up a video camera from a shelf, inspecting it. Her friends looked at me with suspicion.

Fleur looked over at me. 'Stay if you like,' she said, neutral, conciliatory. 'I could do with a hand.'

'Well, OK.' I hung up my coat and bag on a peg near the door, next to a dozen other pegs all hung with jackets and coats and bags.

'We're just playing around with the lighting today,' she said. 'Seeing how it looks with the different dolls, how the new set looks.'

The lights were heavy. I dragged one over to a place on the floor that she marked with chalk.

'Good.' She flicked a switch and the set flooded with light. I stayed for an hour or so, watching as Fleur and the boy and girl, Eric and Erika, stood around and posed the dolls in various combinations and positions. Fleur took still photographs and some video. There were dolls I hadn't seen last time, a couple of Kens, one naked with a suit painted onto his body, and some new girl dolls. Halfway through, Fleur pulled out a robot from a box. It was about the height of the dolls. She wound it up and watched it trudge across the floor, crouching down to see it move. Its little motor whirred, face a mechanical blank. It came to rest after knocking over a Sindy in a minidress. Fleur picked her up and stood her with the other dolls. She sat the robot down on the edge of a chair near the set. Seated there with its legs bent at the knees, expectant somehow, it seemed more pathetically lifelike than the dolls. Fleur stood, thinking. 'Not sure yet how the robot fits in,' she said. 'Costuming is an issue.'

It was turning to evening outside when I made to leave, and when Fleur switched off the big lights the loft was dark except for one fluorescent tube that buzzed fitfully over the kitchen sink. She turned on some lamps.

'OK, Julia?' she asked, eyes assessing me.

'I'm good. See you soon,' I said. I felt her gaze follow me out the door.

I went back to the Promenade the next morning, which broke hazy and cold like the day before. This time felt different, knowing something about Ingrid's relationship to the place. On my way from the subway I passed at least seven places that sold muffins and stopped at the last one at the end of the street. I bought a coffee and a blueberry muffin, taking a guess.

The photograph was in my bag. I sat on a bench near where I had been the previous day, and took out the book it had been tucked inside. I made it through several chapters and they mostly made sense, although there seemed to be a vital piece of information earlier in the story that I'd forgotten. Boats passed across the water, and the expressway under the walkway roared. A sombre couple stopped close by and took photos of one another, unsmiling, with the city in the background, and walked on.

The muffin was average. I looked over at the skyline. A helicopter flew noisily overhead. It was difficult to conjure up an image of Ingrid here with Fleur. I'd never seen them together, and I tried to imagine their trips here, to this place. The bricks beneath my feet were a pattern that looked like honeycomb. I walked down to the end of the Promenade and around through to the entrance to the pathway over the Brooklyn Bridge. I had done this walk once already, in the last days before I had left the city my first time, years ago. The great blue arches of the bridge framed the buildings, midtown skyscrapers glittering against the sky. That day had been hot, the tail end of summer, the bridge and the streets smelling of burning bitumen and garbage.

As I walked I had the feeling of going against a current, tracing steps facing the wrong way. Halfway across I turned and looked back at Brooklyn, the railings and pathway and trees of the Promenade, the mansions with their windows looking out to the city. The glint of a blonde-haired head against a red coat made me catch my breath; it was only a small girl, leaning against the Promenade railing, a woman standing next to her who could have been her mother. The girl stretched her elbows along the rail, chin resting on her hands. People pushed past me. The bridge was crowded. Ingrid's absence had never felt so close to complete. Was it because there was no body to be found, I wondered, that Ralph was driven, and now I was too, to know more about the life? It would have been different if I had been able to visit a gravestone or look at an urn filled with ash. But her ashes had been scattered here, in a way; I remembered seeing images of the plume of smoke and burnt debris that arched through the sky after the towers had fallen, to disperse in the air and land, some of it, in Brooklyn. The only kind of grave to be visited was that hole in the ground downtown. I kept walking, over the bridge to the city, and turned away from that direction as soon as I could.

Back at the apartment it was still cold. I was thinking about taking the sheets off Matt's bed and putting them on mine when I saw the laundry basket on his floor, just behind the door, clean sheets folded on top. I took them into my room and sat on the bed. Tiredness overcame me, the sickly pull of jet lag, and I lay down.

When I woke, hours later, it was night and I could hear Matt in the kitchen, humming, much like it had been the first time I visited. He put his arms around me in a half-embrace when I came into the kitchen, a bottle in one hand and a glass in the other.

He poured me some wine and we talked. He seemed tense and preoccupied, half-listening, drinking fast. As he finished his glass he looked at his watch. 'I'm off.'

'Have fun.'

I had no idea what time it was. I turned on the television. *Friends* was on again, the sound down low. Limbo would be like this, I thought, or hell in some version of it. Another episode followed, and another. I woke up again on the unmade bed. It seemed to be sometime in the afternoon; it was day anyway.

The birdcage was still there on the terrace and I walked out in my socks. Today was warmer, less chill in the air. The bells tinkled gently. I pushed my fingers through the bars but couldn't reach the little swings.

Matt joined me, a cup of coffee in each hand. He gave me one and we stood leaning against the ledge.

'Work's busy,' he said, frowning out into the distance. 'Really complicated pieces going up this week and the artist keeps coming in and telling us to rehang it, rearrange it, and then the curator comes in and tells us to put it back. They're heavy pieces. It's a shit.'

'I'll have to think about getting a job myself pretty soon,' I said. I'd taken this second trip without much thought about how to afford it; the prior weeks in the city had come close to exhausting my savings.

'Really?' Matt asked.

'Well …' I backtracked. 'I'm not really sure how long I'm staying this time. So I don't know. Maybe.'

He peered at me, scrutinising for a moment. 'One of these artists, the one we're showing next, he might be needing a new assistant. The one he has now is leaving.'

'Why?'

He chewed his lip and gave a half-shrug.

'Well, maybe,' I said. 'I mean, thanks, let me know.'

He looked at me, frowning. 'This has all been kind of hard on you, hasn't it?' He put one arm around me. 'I hope you get some closure soon,' he said. 'Isn't that what they call it?'

'I believe so,' I said. 'That's what they call it.'

'Huh,' he said.

'Yeah.'

Back inside the room I looked through my suitcase, the jumble of papers packed inside the pocket in the top. I pulled out a set of stapled pages: a graduate student directory for the Classics department that I had taken from Jones's desk one afternoon. Ingrid's address was still there, her phone number and email. I looked through until I found Trinh's name.

24.

Trinh's house was an old four-storey brownstone that had been long converted into apartments. I climbed the stoop and pressed the buzzer. Her voice came out through the black plastic grille of the speaker. 'Yes?'

'It's Julia.'

I waited for two seconds, three, four, five, and then the door vibrated as the lock buzzed open. Her apartment was on the top floor. The stairwell echoed with my steps, a hollow sound. She pulled back the door, a heavy rectangle of steel, and held it half-open for a second, looking at me, and then stood back to let me in. Her face was pale. One of her eyes was brown, the other plastic blue. She saw me looking from one to the other.

'I was in the middle of taking out my contacts,' she said. 'So, you're back. Sit down.' She showed me to a table in a room that was both kitchen and living room, and I sat down. 'I'll be back in a second.' She was wearing a long white T-shirt, and bare feet with toenails painted silver. A stylised vine with heart-shaped leaves snaked around one leg.

I looked at the black kettle sitting on the stove across from me and wished for tea. Matchstick blinds hung in the window, half-closed. An unfinished game of mahjong was laid out on the table next to a black-covered Greek lexicon.

There was a vase with stems of purple freesias in it on a bookcase over on the far wall, next to a sofa. Otherwise every surface was clear. A painted metal radiator on the wall behind me clanked softly and pushed out heat.

Trinh came back with both eyes brown, wearing wire-framed glasses and a stretchy black skirt. In her hands was a large manila envelope. I recognised it from every noir movie I'd ever seen, photographs inside, saying blackmail just like that.

I hadn't said anything to her about why I was there. I hadn't said anything at all.

'It's nice to see you,' she said with a smile. Her face looked naked without make-up. I looked down at the envelope, now sitting on the table between us.

She gave a short sigh. 'I probably should have given you these when you were here before.' She rose and took two glasses down from a cupboard, poured us water from a pitcher she took from the fridge. 'You know, I didn't think of it until after the first time you came around to the department. And then there was the box, and then I thought about these and I didn't know what you would want with them in any case.'

Neither of us drank our cold water.

'Go on, have a look if you like. This is the last thing I have to give you.' She stood up again and poured her water down the sink, leaving the glass in there. 'You're here about Ingrid, aren't you?' she asked.

'Yes,' I said. 'I suppose so.'

I had the same feeling about this envelope as I'd had about the box when Trinh first handed it to me, an aversion to opening it. Trinh picked it up and pulled out some papers – charcoal drawings and small paintings on thick paper, and a few photographs.

The drawings were not recent – how old, I couldn't tell. The paper had yellowed. One showed a spindly tree in spare, simple lines, almost abstract. The first painting was familiar: purple and white lines, some of them crosshatched unevenly. The second painting I recognised right away. There were several colours and shapes in it, a blur of pastel layers in one corner, but the biggest shape was striking: a red triangle, crudely painted, off-centre, a white shadow of paint behind it. The paper had warped from the original moisture in the paint.

'Are these old drawings of Fleur's?' I asked Trinh.

She paused. 'No,' she said. 'I don't think so.'

I looked at the photographs. The first one, too, was familiar. In this one I knew the face immediately that had been half-turned away, just hazily familiar, when I'd seen it in almost the same pose in Grey's study, photographed in the same room, the same studio. The depth of field was different in this photo from the one on his shelf and I could more clearly see the images tacked up on the wall behind Maeve, and the canvas on its easel. Spindly trees; crude squares; a triangle. She looked straight into the camera in this picture, a level intimacy in her gaze. The streak of grey was there even on this much younger head. She looked to be in her early twenties, if that.

The angle of the next photograph was different, but it was the same room. There was a deep-set window with thin curtains drawn across it and a low ledge, a window seat. A man sat in the seat, his form made dark by the brightness of the light behind him so that he was almost a silhouette. The way his legs were crossed at the knee and his arms crossed over them, his slimness, a cigarette in one hand, reminded me of Ralph for a moment and my heart contracted. I did know the hands, but they weren't Ralph's. The blood seemed to draw away from the surface of my skin and hurry inward, like it did in the cold outdoors.

Trinh switched on a standing lamp next to us to add to the lights recessed under the kitchen cupboards. Outside, night had fallen. The room felt very silent. She seemed to notice at the same time and turned on a radio that sat on the kitchen counter. The sound of jazz music came out of it, softly, almost atonal. A trumpet, an answering piano.

I had several questions about the contents of the envelope and I didn't expect that Trinh would be able to answer many of them, or want to. She sat back in her chair.

I started with questions that I knew she could answer. 'When did you get these?'

She lit a cigarette slowly and exhaled smoke. 'Sometime before the end of summer last year. I wasn't seeing much of Ingrid then – she wasn't around much – I told you that. Anyway, she came over here one day. I was getting ready to go to work.' She cleared her throat.

'She was kind of agitated. And she'd broken her hand – you remember, you saw the emergency report. The second time. So, she came over, and we sat for a while, and I made some coffee. It seemed kind of strange – she wasn't in the habit of doing that, you know, dropping over – we used to go out for a drink or whatever, but it wasn't really a dropping-over kind of friendship. I had to go to work. I think she had almost decided not to, then just before she left she pulled this out of her bag and gave it to me.'

'What did she say about it?'

Trinh thought for a moment. 'She said she had some documents that she wanted to keep safe and she wanted me to hang on to them for her for a while. I think she knew how weird it sounded and she was sort of embarrassed.' She frowned. 'You know her – you knew, I mean, you knew her – she didn't lose her cool, you know?'

'No,' I said.

'I asked her about getting a safety deposit box at the bank – what was wrong with that idea – and she said she was getting around to doing that. She was kind of vague about it.'

She stubbed out her cigarette in a round porcelain ashtray. 'Look, I know it sounds weird, but I didn't even look inside the envelope for a while. For a week or two after that – after we had a break-in here, and I remember thinking that it was kind of ironic that she had left these documents here with me and never got around to putting them in her safety deposit box and here we were, getting burgled.

'There wasn't much here to take – well, I did have a nice stereo, and that went – but besides that nothing was taken – everything messed up. I don't have a lot of jewellery or anything like that.' She smiled wryly. 'What I do have they didn't want, and they didn't want my shoes. That would have set me back. Anyway, it was after that happened, just a couple of days, and I was unpacking my bag and the envelope was in there. I must have picked it up with some other folders from my desk here and it sat there in my bag for who knows how long. That's when I had a look at it.'

She picked up her packet of cigarettes and put it back down again.

'Ingrid didn't ask me to open it and I felt kind of bad doing it at all.'

'What did you think about it, when you saw these – what did you think it was all about?'

'I didn't want to think about it,' she said flatly. 'Like I said, I felt bad about looking at it at all. If she had wanted to tell me what it was all about she would have. We weren't exactly close. It was private.' She looked at me. 'Whatever it was – between her and Gil – whatever this is – it was private. We all have our secrets, our issues, things we want to keep private. I get to see a lot of that in my work, the things that people usually keep private. I'm used to just … putting that away, in a way.'

'But you're showing me.'

She leaned forward, and then back again. 'It's all over now,' she said. 'I don't want to have this … stuff anymore.'

'But why are you giving this to me – why didn't you give it back to Grey?'

She almost snorted. 'You don't need to ask me that. You can figure that out for yourself.'

'No.'

'Look – I don't know. I don't want to give it to Gil – if you want to give it to him, fine, it's all probably his somehow. But if you do, don't tell him it came from me.'

'I'm not giving it to him.'

'I'm serious.' Her voice was stern now. 'Seriously. I don't want him to know it came from me. When you take it away, as far as I'm concerned I didn't have it and it was something you found in Ingrid's office. Julia, I mean it.'

'I'm not going to give it to him.'

'OK.'

She breathed sharply.

'You're afraid of him,' I said.

She looked hard at a corner of the ceiling. I thought of Grey's cool demeanour, the sense of rigid self-control he presented and seemed to want to hide. I wondered for a crazy moment if he might be one of Trinh's clients. Or a client on the other side of the business, the one who paid to hold a whip. That seemed to fit better. It was still unlikely, and I knew that Trinh would never tell me if it was true.

'Trinh –'

'Julia.' She interrupted me. 'I've met him, and I wasn't blind about how things were for Ingrid. He's a scary guy. But whatever was going on between them – like I told you, it was private. If Ingrid had wanted me to know she would have told me. But why would she have told me?'

'Why did she give this to you?'

She considered the question. It probably wasn't one she could completely answer.

'She knew I didn't ask questions and that I was good at keeping things quiet. That might not be the answer to your question but it's true all the same.'

'Did Grey ever ask you if you had this?'

'Not exactly.'

'Alright – did he ever ask you if you had anything that belonged to Ingrid?'

'I gave him everything that we knew we had from her office – I told you, the box I gave you was something we found after all that, and I wasn't in the mood for more catching up with him.'

I persisted. 'Did he know Ingrid had this? Was he looking for it?'

'I can't tell you that. I mean, I don't know.'

'Why are you giving this to me?'

'I already told you – I don't want it anymore. I don't want anything to do with it. You do what you want with it. If I were you, I'd burn it up.'

'You could have done that.'

'Well, you're saving me the trouble, aren't you?' She smiled.

The paper in my hand was brittle with dried paint, as though it could crumble under any force at all. I felt a terrible sense of sadness and constriction.

'Listen, Julia,' Trinh said quietly. 'Think carefully about what you want to do with this. I mean it when I say it would be the best idea to put it away, get rid of it, whatever. I like you. I liked Ingrid too. I'm sorry about what happened to her.'

'She was so unhappy, wasn't she?' It wasn't really a question.

'She was unhappy, like everybody else.' Trinh sighed, irritation in her voice. 'But to Ingrid, unhappiness seemed like the world's biggest injustice.' She shook her head. 'Like I told you, I liked her. No-one deserved to be that unhappy.

She was really miserable towards the end there – I thought so anyway. She seemed to have so much ...' She hesitated. 'Potential? In the beginning. It was appealing. She seemed more shocked than anyone else at how it all turned out.'

I wondered how much Trinh had really seen and intuited – probably everything, if she had wanted to, but I wasn't sure that she had. Her arms were folded and it looked like she was finished talking for the night. I pushed the papers together, the drawings, the paintings, the photographs, and tapped the edges on the table so they were sitting evenly, and put them back into the envelope. It just fitted into my shoulder bag.

'Please think about it, Trinh,' I said.

She looked at me. 'About what?'

'Telling me. Whatever it is you aren't telling me.' I waited.

'Look, I'm trusting you here,' she said.

'I won't tell Grey it came from you,' I said. 'I promise.'

'OK. Good.'

She saw me to the door.

'It's up to you. But I think you'd be fucking out of your mind to go to Gil with this. Do whatever you want to gather up her stuff, put it all to rest, but leave him alone.'

She lifted her arm to the door, a tracery of black lines. For the first time I wondered if the tattoo had hurt – of course it had – the soft skin of the underneath of her forearms looked taut and thin.

'Let's get a drink soon,' she said. 'You know where to find me. If you can agree to not talk about this.' She moved one bare foot so that it was on top of the other one, resting it lightly there. 'I'd like to catch up,' she said.

I was halfway out the door. It smelled as though someone in the building was cooking bread.

'OK. That would be great.'

'Take care.'

I didn't hear the door close until I was all the way down the stairs.

The subway was crowded almost to standing room even this late in the evening and I stood and held on to the strap swinging from the high rail, feeling more and more confused about the contents of my bag. When I arrived at the apartment building there was a light in Mrs Bee's window and I thought about knocking but changed my mind. Her door was closed. The apartment upstairs was dark and I switched on the light and set my bag down just inside the door. I thought about calling Richard. I thought about getting something to eat and forgetting about the envelope in my bag. The kitchen smelled like stale coffee and there was a stack of glasses in the sink. The buzzer sounded.

I pressed the button and spoke. 'Hello?'

'Hello.' It was Jones.

'What are you doing here?'

'Well, ask me up and I'll tell you.'

He was upstairs quickly and before I knew it we were on the stripped mattress, the front door barely closed, and on the floor.

'So what are you doing here?' I asked afterwards.

'Isn't it obvious?'

'I mean, how did you know I was back?'

'Talked to Trinh just now,' he said. 'And I was in the neighbourhood. Passing by. Good timing.'

'Good timing,' I repeated.

'It's a bit … spartan, isn't it?' he asked, looking at the bed.

My back was getting stiff from lying on the floor. I sat up. 'I just got here,' I said.

'Are you hungry?' he asked.

'You know me too well.'

He pulled on some clothes and left the room. I thought about my bag inside the front door and the cardboard box under the dresser. I wondered what Trinh had told him, and waited for him to ask me about the envelope. He didn't.

We ate Chinese food that he took out of takeaway containers when it arrived and put onto plates, and he left. I took the envelope from my bag and put it into the second drawer of the dresser, and then started unpacking my suitcase, putting clothes on top of it. Underwear, shirts, jeans. I made the bed with the sheets from Matt's laundry basket and lay down. The sheets smelled like rain and paint and reminded me of the Paris hotel.

The envelope was still there in the morning. I'd half-expected it to be gone, half-hoping it was a dream, but it was there, blank and yellow at the bottom of the drawer.

I spent the next few days going out for coffee, walking to the bookshop down the avenue, buying a novel or a magazine, reading it on the couch, going out for more food, reading, sleeping, letting the thoughts about the envelope tick away in a part of my mind that I pushed back from consciousness. Peter called with news of Jenny – no news at all really, just to tell me that she was improving as expected. Matt dropped in and out quickly, always rushed.

'More snail trouble?' I asked him one night when he came inside looking harried, grabbed something from his room and made to leave again.

'No,' he said. 'I wish. Fucking artists.'

I wasn't sure if he was sleeping at the apartment or not.

Jones was back again at around the same time the next night, and the night after that, and that time we went out for a drink later, down to the Lilac.

'Are you keeping an eye on me?' I asked him as we walked downtown.

He gave me a questioning, critical stare. 'What are you talking about?'

'Oh, forget it.' I pulled my coat tighter. 'Where's your wife anyway?' The only thing I knew about her, from Trinh, was that she travelled a lot for work.

'Berlin,' he said briefly, without looking at me.

We came to a traffic light and stopped. We didn't talk the rest of the way there, and when we arrived he pulled me by the wrist into the one of the bathrooms and shut the door.

I looked at the lock, which he hadn't turned, but he just stood and leaned his back against the door and kept his grip on me.

'Don't worry. And don't talk.'

I stayed standing, looking into his eyes for a moment, challenging. He lost patience and broke the gaze, an irritated smile on his face before he moved one hand to my shoulder, pushing me down. I was addicted by now to that sense of surrender he inspired in me, even as a faint worry about it floated beside and past me at these moments. The floor was cold and hard against my knees, bringing me completely into my body. We had perfected this particular tableau and we both played it well that night, conditioned by touches of tenderness where I wouldn't have expected them and a shared, mournful sense that it would soon be over.

Trinh was there at the bar when we came out a few minutes later, and she smiled at me as I straightened my skirt. We all sat at the bar together, and more people arrived that she knew, and I drank my drinks and forgot about the envelope. Trinh was at her most charming and introduced me to her friends. Jones was soon surrounded by three women who hung on his words. 'New students,' Trinh whispered in my ear, and raised her eyebrows. I caught something from their conversation about diplomacy in the Roman empire that made it sound like an elaborate sexual game.

'He never actually sleeps with them, you know,' she said. 'It's all foreplay.'

I must have looked sceptical.

'It's some twisted ethical thing he has.' She sucked the last of her drink through the thin straw so that it made a slurping sound. 'No students.' She rolled her eyes. 'Just hope you get to avoid the lecture on the subject. Very unoriginal.'

It was hard to imagine him feeling the need to give me that particular lecture. But it did clarify the sense I had that his relationship with Ingrid had not involved sex; it had been intense in its own teacher–student way, but not like that. Somehow the thought of her there in his office, talking over her work, discussing her next brilliant project, was just as hard to bear in the intimacy it implied as it would have been to think of her half-dressed on his desk. I remembered the strand of long, gold hair caught in the carpet on the floor that morning and blinked it away.

'How's work for you?' I asked.

'Oh, fine, you know,' she said. 'Down to a couple of shifts a week. Less.' Her gaze wandered around the room. 'I'm getting really bored to tell you the truth. So.' Her eyes met mine. 'No news?'

'I thought you didn't want to talk about it,' I said.

'Just checking in.'

'No news.'

'Good.'

'Did you send Jones to keep an eye on me?'

She looked exasperated and sorry for me. 'Your paranoia really is kind of charming, up to a point,' she said. 'It's neurotic in a cute way. But don't let it get out of hand.'

She looked me over. 'Anyway. It's pretty obvious that Jones doesn't need to be asked.'

He didn't show up the next night. When it got past 9 pm I went downstairs and knocked on Mrs Bee's door.

She answered right away.

'There you are,' she said, and showed me in. She was wearing layers of dark green clothes, the colour of ivy and pine needles.

I told her a bit about the hospital, the time in Sydney. I wasn't sure what to say about the photographs I'd seen on the plane, or my visit to Fleur, the envelope upstairs in my room, any of it. Part of me thought that she guessed everything in her psychic way; part of me wanted to keep it from her just because of that.

'Let me know when you want to read the cards,' she said just before I left.

'I forgot you did cards.'

She shrugged. 'Sometimes.'

'Tarot cards.'

'That's right.'

'Maybe next time. But I'm a sceptic, remember?'

'Just let me know. I'll see you for tea tomorrow.'

'See you then.'

I went down the next afternoon. I had just finished my fourth novel since I had arrived, an Agatha Christie.

She looked at my cup and tilted it around for a while.

'What are you going to do?' she asked.

'I don't know,' I said. 'It's a complicated situation.'

'Yes, I can see that.' She put the cup down.

She saw me eyeing a Scrabble box on the bookshelf against the wall. 'Do you play?' she asked. I said that I used to play. She took it out and we played a game. Art. Part. Apart. Apartment. Lie. Lied. Applied.

'Don't use any psychic cheating on me,' I said. 'Can you tell what letters I have?'

She laughed and didn't say. I won.

'You'd better get back up,' she said as I cleared the letters off the board. 'He'll be around soon.'

I poured the letters from my hand into their little velvet sack. 'I hate it when you do that.'

I thought about the bed; Jones liked it unmade now,

stripped the sheets off and twisted them into coiled ropes on the floor. The mattress was making graze marks on my skin.

'Sorry,' she said. She paused and her eyes refocused. 'It's not who you think I mean.'

The letter pieces clinked together. Fear fell through me. The envelope, still there in the drawer, seemed like a bright, dangerous beacon in the apartment. For a moment it occurred to me to leave it with Mrs Bee but I dropped the thought.

Upstairs, I rummaged it out of the drawer and sat down on the bed, spilling the contents next to me. The paintings and drawings were unsigned. They were similar, but not identical, to the images behind Maeve in the photograph. She looked like the artist in this picture, paint stains on her sleeve, but it wasn't clear whether it was her studio or not, whether these were her paintings or not. Grey seemed to be an equal candidate for frustrated or failed artist, and there he was in the window, arms and legs elegantly crossed. I put the images back into the envelope and put it into my bag. The photograph I had taken from Fleur was inside its book on top of the dresser, the book I had been reading on the plane that time and had never finished. That went into the bag as well. By the time I left I was rushing, dropping my keys as I went to lock the door, waiting impatiently for the lift to arrive.

The afternoon was already freezing and the street seemed less crowded than usual. Only a couple of people passed me on the walk to the subway. I wanted to get off the street, out of sight. Everyone on the train was reading a newspaper or a book, except for one couple locked in a slow-moving embrace in the middle seat.

The sides of the cars were lined with posters. The one that faced me was a picture taken from inside a room with a window looking out, someone's living room perhaps. Two green shrubs in pots had been clipped and shaped into tall rectangles and placed in the window frame so they filled the view, taking the place of the Twin Towers. One was slightly taller than the other so they created a perspective effect, the towers seen from an angle, from a distance. The writing at the bottom advertised an art school.

On the other side of the doors was another poster, an enlarged image of a handwritten note. It was signed by a woman, Maria, 36, Queens. The note briefly described her depression after September 11 and how she had recovered with the help of her friends and family. The poster provided a telephone counselling number at the bottom. There was a similar one further down the car, this one in Spanish, signed by Johnny, 24, Brooklyn.

Maria's writing had a sharp slant, narrow loops on her letter 'G'. I found myself wondering if she might be left-handed. My conversation about handwriting with Richard Evans must have had more impact that it seemed at the time. I told myself to stop it, straightened up, moved my hand to a new grip on the pole. The train rattled around a corner. I turned away from Maria's note and the topiary towers, but now Johnny's round and even numerals and letters looked back at me. Information, telephone numbers, the MTA logo were printed at the bottom of the poster in type, and my eyes pulled down to that, absorbing the shape of the machine-made words. The type had a personality of its own, the friendly roundness of the official MTA lettering; the imperious serifs and thin stalks of the ad above it, advertising expensive beer, or cider, something. But handwriting was different from this. It held traces of the person who'd made it. To the eyes of someone like Richard it could reveal secrets. I wondered what he would make of Maria and her possibly left-handed slant.

The train pulled into the station and I stepped out through the sliding doors as the speakers mumbled the station's name. It was one stop too soon but the walk wasn't long. I was walking uptown, but it felt as though the sunset-lit sky behind me would still be showing the hole. Once night fell it always seemed to diminish in intensity, swallowed up into the emptiness of the dark sky.

25.

I walked fast to Richard's building and pressed the buzzer.

'It's Julia.'

'Don't you ever use the phone?'

'Just — let me up.'

I took the stairs quickly. There were four sets of locks in the door but only one slid back before the door opened. Richard looked me over and put his arm on my shoulder to steer me inside.

'What's the big hurry?' he asked. 'I didn't even know you were back in New York.' He held half a sandwich in his hand and was chewing.

'Is that peanut butter?'

'Yes.' He swallowed. 'Yes. Do you want one?'

'Please.' The entrance hallway was cramped and narrow, a low bookshelf against the wall and over it a print of the Eiffel Tower, a black-and-white photograph. 'Paris,' I said.

He made a dismissive gesture with his hand. 'That was here when I moved in.'

I took off my coat and held on to my bag.

'I suppose you'll want a drink.'

'What do you have?'

We sat down on the dark green couch together, my

sandwich on a plate on the coffee table and my bag still on my shoulder and a glass of whisky in my hand. I laid the bag on the couch and drew out the manila envelope and the book with the packet of photographs still stowed in its cover.

'Did you call me the other day?' Richard asked.

I nodded.

'You didn't leave a message.'

I lifted my shoulders and dropped them again.

'What are you doing back in New York? I mean, it's good to see you.'

He was drinking coffee from a black mug. There were papers out on his desk across the room. The desk lamp cast a pool of light on them. He followed my eyes and rose and straightened the papers, placing them back in a white folder. A manual typewriter sat in the corner of the desk, shrouded in a neat grey cover. Looking back to the filing cabinets along the wall, he hesitated, then placed the folder back on the desk and sat down again next to me on the couch.

There was a plant over on the windowsill next to the desk, an African violet with three purple flowers. I thought about the image on the subway of the two plants trimmed into the shapes of the towers. Richard had brought an apple from the kitchen, a green Granny Smith, and he held it in one hand. He was wearing a black vest of thin wool over a finely striped shirt, his square-rimmed glasses, the whole Clark Kent look.

'Sorry, I should have asked. How did it go in Sydney? How's your aunt – did you have much to take care of?'

I sighed. 'Oh, it was alright. She'll be OK.' I thought of my room in Jenny's house, the light coming through the window and the coolness of the bed that settled quickly into warmth. I wanted to be there. 'My brother's taking care of a lot of things. He's very organised, very together.'

Richard bit into his apple.

'Have you seen those posters on the subway?' I asked him. 'The statements from people after 9-11?'

'Oh, yes.'

Why was I asking him, I wondered. Was I really going to ask if he thought 36-year-old Maria was left-handed? Was I trying to impress him as a good student? I was getting ready to change the subject when he replied.

'They're very interesting. I'm fairly sure they are actually authentic.'

'Authentic?'

'They look as though they may have been written by those people, the ones who signed them. Of course they're too neat to be first drafts, they're too polished, but they might be a copy by them of something they wrote.'

He took another bite.

It seemed obvious now to think that the notes would be fabricated. A range of sentiments and situations, carefully distilled from life, from some kind of record, arranged to reflect the right range of age and ethnic background and gender. Maria's statement had probably been written by the copy guy from whatever design company had produced them.

'You think so? Why? How do you know?'

'They just seem real. The writing is right, you know, for a

person of the age and gender. There's one by someone called Carl –'

'But what about what they say?' I interrupted him. 'The things they say they've experienced, what's in the statements? Do you think they're describing something that really happened to that person?'

He paused. 'Um …'

It was a hopeless question. The truth of the statements for him was not connected to the content of the words, what they said as words. It was all in the line, the form. Anyone could lie convincingly about themselves in what they said, in the substance of what they wrote. But their writing would always give them away in some sense, dropping unconscious clues. Or that was the idea of graphology as I understood it. To those trained to understand it, writing would always speak the truth, despite itself; the truth that Richard looked for, at least. One layer of it.

'It doesn't matter,' I said.

But he had already started to think about it, and explained that it was hard to tell in this case because the notes seemed so carefully revised and neat; it was hard to tell if the sentiments matched the writing because they looked as though they'd been copied out from an earlier version.

'So sentiments can match writing? Can you tell if a person is, say, really sad when they write that they are?'

'Maybe,' he said. 'Noah – the person who trained me – said that he could spot honesty or deception in someone's line, he said it was somewhere in the upstroke, the pressure marks there … I don't think I can do that though, I'm not that good. The overall shape of the writing reveals tendencies like that but not matched to the specific statement.'

He stood and took his carefully shaped apple core to the bin in the kitchen. When he came back I turned to the manila envelope and the book.

'I found this at Fleur's place before I left.' I pulled the photograph out, of Ingrid on the Promenade, and passed it to him.

He looked at it. 'You found it?'

I shrugged. 'I found it in a drawer. At that party you were at. I took it.'

He was still looking at it.

'I wanted –'

'It's OK, I understand,' he said, turning it over to look at the blank back, turning it to the picture again. His expression settled into something sad and hard as he looked at Ingrid's face, and he handed it back to me.

'But look – look at where she is.' My fingers held one side of the picture, and his the other. He looked.

'Where – oh, is this taken from the Promenade?'

'Yes, yes.'

He looked at me, puzzled.

'Richard, the towers aren't there.'

'It's the angle.'

'No, I've been down there, I went the day I arrived, and the next morning. I can't see how you could find that angle without having the towers in the shot.'

'Well, it's hard to judge when you're not looking through a camera. Maybe it's taken from somewhere else – the buildings in the background are pretty blurry.'

'Well – I suppose so.'

We were silent for a while.

'Look, I know as much as anyone that it's hard to accept. Those stages of grieving – I found out all about those. Had them pointed out to me rather forcefully.' He smiled, a grimace. 'Denial. It's the big one. It's the most painful one, when it finally goes.'

'I thought you would understand,' I protested.

'You thought I'd tell you that you were right? That you're seeing a ghost? In a photograph? Julia, she's dead.'

'Come down there with me.'

He sighed. 'It wouldn't help.'

'Maybe it would.'

He looked troubled.

'I'll think about it.'

'Not a ghost. Alive. I thought you'd want her to be alive.'

His eyes closed.

'I thought you'd want to figure it out.'

He opened his eyes, studied me, weighing something up. Whatever it was, I could see that it didn't get fully decided.

'What else have you got there?'

I handed him the envelope. He pulled out the drawings, the painting, the photographs, and looked through them one by one. His face grew pale. I picked up his cup and took it to the kitchen and poured more coffee into it from the glass jug in the coffee maker. It didn't smell like anything. I handed it back to him.

There was a ghost of anger in his face when he met my eyes, but not with me. 'Did you go to see Grey?' he asked. 'How did you get these out of there? Or Maeve –'

'No. I didn't get them from there. I didn't get them from either of those two.'

'So …?'

'They're …' I wasn't sure whether to mention Trinh. 'Ingrid left these with – with a friend. And now I have them. Now they're with me.'

'Ingrid had these?' he asked, his eyes a flash of colour.

I nodded. He drew a deep breath, and then didn't breathe again for so long that I found myself holding my own breath, waiting for his lungs to start again.

I decided there was little to risk with him. 'She left them with Trinh.'

He lowered his chin in a kind of nod. 'When?'

'Late summer.'

'Of course.'

'Look, Richard, I don't know what to do with these things or what to make of them. I've been sitting on them for days not knowing what to do.'

Part of me wanted to leave them with him, the drawings, the painting, the photographs, leave and walk out and go straight to the airport and wait until a plane could take me home. But I knew that if I was going to do that anytime soon I would have done it already.

He put his hands on his knees, suddenly animated and business-like. 'OK. Tell me everything. Does Grey know you're in town? Does he know you have these? Does he know Ingrid took them?'

'I haven't called Grey but I've talked to Fleur – I've tried to talk to Fleur. But not since this.' I remembered Mrs Bee's words to me earlier – 'It's not who you think I mean' – and the chill went through me again. 'He probably knows by now that I'm in town if he's talked to her. But I don't know why she would tell him.

'And the rest of it – I don't know, only what Trinh would tell me. She didn't really want to say very much – I'm not sure how much she even knew. She said Ingrid was obviously stressed out when she gave her the envelope – Trinh didn't even look in it for weeks.'

Richard raised his eyebrows.

'OK. Whatever. She says Ingrid didn't say anything about what was in it or what it was about, where she'd got the pictures, anything. Just that she wanted to keep them safe and was getting around to putting them in a safety deposit box, but she never did.'

'He'd have access to everything, all those places, after she died.'

'I guess so.' I went through his words. 'But she didn't know that she was going to die – it wasn't like she knew, she was just putting them out of the way, just ...'

This was further than I had made it myself in any kind of straight line of thinking about the pictures. The past few days whenever I felt them coming to the surface of my thoughts I had pushed them right down, not able to bear the image of Ingrid there in Trinh's kitchen, the thought of her anxiety, which it would have pained her so much to display. It hurt to think about it now.

'How could she have known?' I asked, knowing as I asked it that there was an answer and I didn't want to hear it.

He started to speak. 'No,' I said. He stopped.

We sat there for a while. Whatever it was he had been deciding earlier seemed to be figured out in those moments. He stood and went to the filing cabinets, opened one and went straight to a file at the back of a drawer. He took out something, a Polaroid photograph, and held it out to me. I looked at his face without really seeing it. I didn't want to look at what was in his hand.

I remembered the nausea after the phone call on that 12 September – or was it the thirteenth by then – and it rose again in my stomach. Richard's hand dropped to his side. I looked down. The bruise in the photograph was a bloody purple, its colour made unnatural by the Polaroid film. Next to it and under it the shape of ribs showed through skin. The background of the picture was dark.

Looking away, my eyes fell on the Polaroid camera itself, high up on a bookshelf next to the desk, folded away, a blue foil packet of film next to it.

I thought about those stairs in Grey's apartment, white and sharp as bone. His feet in their black shoes, stepping up quickly ahead of me.

'You look a little green,' Richard said. 'Maybe it was a bad idea,' – he indicated the photograph, holding it in both hands – 'but I wasn't sure what to say. I wasn't even sure if you knew.'

'I knew about the broken hand. Was that part of it too?'

He shrugged. 'I can't say for sure. She never said.'

I could see only half her face in the photograph; it was turned away, her whole body twisting slightly. One arm pulled her shirt across to show her bruised waist. Her hair was tied back. A greenish blotch spread out from the lower corner of the image as though a finger had pressed too hard while it was developing.

Richard turned and placed the picture back in the file and closed the drawer.

'Sit down,' he said. I had risen without realising. The room was black around the edges like the photograph. I sat down. 'Put your head between your knees,' he ordered.

'No, I'm OK now.' I straightened up, or tried to, but was seemingly stuck, bent forward at the waist.

'Are you saying he killed her?' I asked eventually. 'Or that he was going to kill her?'

He pressed his lips together. 'Well, that's what I thought at first,' he said, very matter of fact. 'You can imagine the reception I got with the police.' He smiled ruefully. 'The city was full of people denying that their friends, their lovers, their wives, had really been killed in the towers. Those posters for people "missing" stayed up all over the place for weeks.' He took my glass and finished off the whisky that was in it. 'And there I was saying that this missing woman's husband had bumped her off.'

'You went to the police.'

He nodded. 'I didn't tell you this before, when you were here before — I'd kind of put it away — it was useless — well, I didn't want to see you at first because you were a friend of hers and I was doing my best to forget all about it. I'd, uh, filed it away. Closed the drawer.' He sighed heavily. 'But I suppose you can hear about it now. You brought these with you after all.' He cast his eyes briefly to the drawings.

'At the time, you know, I was distraught. I thought I'd lost another friend too — someone who worked in the restaurant in the towers. Turned out he wasn't at work that day. Anyway. As soon as I heard that Ingrid hadn't come home that day I thought, he's finally done it. That July I'd been away in Maine – my family has a house on a lake there. I was with them for a few weeks and I called Ingrid after I got back.' He took a deep breath again. 'We talked a little. She agreed to meet me for coffee.' He passed his hand across his eyes. 'It was a horrible summer. I went away just a few weeks after I took that,' – he nodded towards the filing cabinet – 'and we'd been fighting. We'd had a couple of arguments, I mean.'

I waited.

'I was trying to talk her into leaving him,' he said.

'That's the part I don't really understand. Why she didn't.'

He looked at me. 'Really? I thought you'd understand, knowing her for so long.'

I thought about it.

'She couldn't stand to fail at anything,' he said. 'Couldn't stand to be wrong. She was still playing out this – idea – this idea of the perfect marriage. And she hated being shamed more than anything.'

I tried to imagine it, and I could, although it made my stomach turn. The shame of being a beaten wife, or of admitting it hadn't worked. Could that be worse than the violence? This image more than any other made her seem so much older than she had been when she left. I remembered how much her face had aged when I'd seen her in Sydney that last time.

'But you took the picture,' I said. 'You saw the bruise.'

'But, see, she hadn't said anything that night. She hadn't

denied it – she'd just hardly said anything, the whole time she was here. I'd tried to get her to go to the hospital, but she wouldn't go. I was worried that one of her ribs was broken – you saw, did you?'

I nodded. 'The bruise looked really bad.'

'Yeah. It was. But she didn't want to talk, just wanted to stay here, didn't want to go home. Fleur wasn't there – she was away somewhere. A friend from school? I don't know. Maybe that's why she came here.' Ingrid and Grey's apartment wasn't far from Richard's, only a short ride in a taxi. 'She had been here before a few times. We became … friends, I guess you'd say,' his voice caught, 'in that first year at Columbia. It was still a surprise, seeing her that night.' He sighed. 'She wasn't crying. But she was really shaken up. It was my idea to take the picture. Evidence, since she didn't want to go to the hospital and get it looked at. She wanted to take it away with her at first but then she seemed to just forget about it. I suppose she was in shock. Anyway, later, when I tried to talk to her about it over the next couple of weeks, she had this story about falling down the stairs. Literally, falling down the stairs. She wouldn't talk about it, wouldn't say why she had come here. She wanted the picture back.' He stopped, exasperated with the memory of it.

'It just started to seem like if we wanted to stay friends I had to agree not to talk about it, not to push it.'

I remembered the visit to New York with Ralph, the silence that had formed then around the topic of Grey. I wondered if Richard had become a friend to Ingrid in the way Ralph had once been – an admirer, a confidant held always at a calculated distance.

'I found that really hard.' He paused. His elbows rested on his knees, hands together. 'We didn't talk while I was in Maine. And when I saw her in the summer, after I'd got back, there was something different. She just refused point-blank to talk about Grey, the relationship, anything to do with it. She was going up to the place on the Hudson every now and again. I pressed it one more time, just before she left – she was going up there again, and I was really worried about what might be happening up there, you know, in the country.'

I nodded.

'I swear – I saw a burn on her arm. Jesus.' He rested his forehead in his hand. 'But she said I didn't need to worry. She had gone into this mode – she had a plan for something, but she wouldn't say what it was. It wasn't for leaving him – at least I didn't think so – she just said I didn't need to worry, that she was going to sort it all out. I wondered if she'd been trying to talk him into spending more time up at the house, less time in the city, just so he would be around less.'

He got up suddenly, and went to the kitchen and came back with the bottle of whisky. There wasn't much left. He poured it all out into the glass and drank some and handed the glass to me. 'And that was the last time I saw her. August.'

'So when she disappeared you thought that Grey had – that he'd killed her.'

It was difficult to get my mind around this idea, even after seeing the bruise. People hit people – that was different to killing them. I remembered the feel of Jones's thumb against my jaw, his hand against my neck, my face, pushing. A whole series of images passed across my mind in quick succession – the pomegranates in their golden bowl on the granite island – Grey's delicate hand against Ingrid's back – his feet again, stepping up the stairs – Ingrid in my dream, hands opening to show me the scroll that was a painting.

Richard was thinking, choosing his words. 'I thought there was a possibility that he'd killed her, yes, that he'd gone really out of control.' He looked down at the glass in his hand.

'What did Grey say about it?'

'Well, our conversations about it – they weren't really conversations. The police got involved right away. He's very convincing, the grieving husband, I'm the raving mad rejected lover, you can imagine. Pretty soon I was legally restrained from going within a whole city block of him.' He interlaced his fingers, parted them again. 'It sounds paranoid, I know. In grief, you know – everything starts to look strange. I don't know why it was easier to believe that than to believe the other thing, that she just died like everyone else.'

That was it – her special, exceptional quality, that brilliant thing we held on to. It hit me like a stone. He looked up at me.

'It was that strange edginess she had that last time. Like I could see all the fear that she had been trying not to show for so long, but only because it was over, and it had been replaced by a new kind of fear, a new kind that she hadn't figured out yet how to hide. She was on the verge of something.'

He looked at the envelope. 'And now I think that this was it.'

'Do you think she was blackmailing him?' I wanted to listen to Richard's thoughts about it, my own ideas too dark to open, starting to unfurl.

'Here's what I think,' he said, leaning towards me. 'She must have figured out at some stage that something wasn't quite right with Fleur, with the paintings.'

I recalled the dinner party at Maeve's the night it started snowing, after we'd seen Fleur's work at the Whitney, the phone call and how Fleur hadn't shown up. It had been right after that show that she had stopped painting. Had the pressure of the Whitney show made it all unbearable, whatever secret was encoded in the pictures Trinh had given me?

'Ingrid must have figured it out,' Richard said. 'She could have known something, whatever, for a long time and let it lie to protect Fleur. She loved her, you know. They really were close. But when it got worse with Grey – maybe she'd been digging around at the Hudson house that summer and found these.'

'But what for?' I asked. 'What would she have blackmailed him for if she didn't want to leave him?'

'Maybe she was going to leave him and just didn't want to tell me. Or just to stop him hitting her,' Richard said bluntly, 'and let her live a little bit.'

'But if she broke the secret it would hurt Fleur too.'

'That's what could have made it impossible to really wield it for all that time.'

'But what would Fleur have thought about it?' I persisted.

'They were pretty loyal to each other,' he said. 'Maybe she decided to go along.'

'Or maybe she didn't.'

'Who knows.'

'But the pictures ...' I began. 'What do they actually show?'

He looked at them. 'There's no signature on them. But they are clearly the pictures on the wall in this photograph, or ones very much like them, studies or versions. And you can see Maeve in this one – you can see how young she is – and Grey in the other – it's before Fleur was born. Or before she started painting.' He pulled out one edge of the photograph of Maeve. Her eye looked out at me in black and white.

'It raises a lot of questions about the process behind Fleur's painting,' he said. 'Who was really behind the paintings in the first place.'

'I can see that,' I said. 'But it doesn't show whose they really are. Are those Maeve's paintings, or drawings,' – I looked at the drawing of the spindly tree on top of the pile – 'or Grey's?' The paintings in the picture seemed to have signature marks on them, too small to make out.

'I don't know. But my money's on Maeve. I've seen Grey's writing, and I don't think it's his hand.'

'Drawing's different though, isn't it, from writing?'

'Yes.'

Maeve's level gaze in the photograph seemed tragic now and conspiratorial all at once. She had made such a neutral, dispassionate dismissal when I had asked her if she herself was an artist, back in Kirribilli, years ago. No talent, she had said. Eve had taken me aside later that afternoon and told me the rumour that Maeve had been a painter once – she denied now that she'd ever taken it seriously – and had been devastated by her initial failure. She had sworn off it and buried all evidence of her early work. 'None of her paintings survive,' Eve had said, 'except one or two I've seen at her house – she says that they didn't deserve to.'

I pitied her, and Grey – what frustrated ambitions had gone into the production of their child prodigy, the talented girl? But I remembered the look that had passed between them at her house that night, before the snow fell, and began to allow myself to develop a glimpse of the secrets and bonds that underlay it, and I hated them both.

'It doesn't matter, exactly, whose these are,' Richard said. 'Whoever they're by, if not Fleur, it would bring them all down – Maeve and Fleur and Grey.' He looked strangely satisfied. 'It was never really clear to me before, what could have made him snap – I thought it was something to do with this new thing with Ingrid, this new fear she had. Now I think it's clear – she confronted him with these, or he found out that she had taken them, and he couldn't risk it – he had to find a way to silence her. And then the towers came down – it was the perfect opportunity, the perfect cover, I've always thought so – that's what I tried to explain to the police. If you were planning a murder and were just waiting for the right time, wouldn't you just try to seize that when it happened? It's so convenient – she disappears, and it's the one day ever when you will never, ever have to explain someone's disappearance.'

He was talking faster and faster, and I was starting to see some of the manic edge that might have convinced the police that he was a little unhinged.

'But, Richard,' I said. The purple of the bruise wouldn't go away, a coloured blur over part of my vision. I blinked.

'He's clearly a horrible, violent man and I suppose I can believe that he would think about that and want to do that. But she was there. She was downtown, she was at the Trade Center.'

'He always claimed that she was.'

'But I've seen her diary. I've seen the appointment.'

'What appointment?'

'The appointment at nine. At 9 am, with her financial adviser downtown.' *Paul, 9.*

Richard was silent.

'How – where did you see it?'

'It's on her desk. It was on her desk when I went there, when I was here before, when I went to see Grey at the apartment. I was in her room. I looked through it ...' My cheeks flushed. 'I was looking through the things on her desk – I was just glancing – anyway, I saw the diary – the calendar – there and I looked at it. It's written in there: 9 am, Paul.' I recalled the single line of writing on that date, the blue ink, the length of the line on the page.

'Was it her writing?'

I paused. 'It looked like her writing.'

He made an impatient sound. 'But that's just it – how easy it would be for him to write that in there afterwards, it's perfect – to make up proof that she was there. How do you even know she had an accountant down there?'

'I imagine that it wouldn't be too hard to check. Why would he make up a lie that obvious?'

Richard looked unsettled. He stood and paced behind the couch.

'Can you get hold of it?'

'What?'

'The calendar. I'd like to see it.'

'I told you – it's at Grey's place. It's in Ingrid's room there.'

'Right, so you know where it is.'

'You think I'm going back there to take it?'

He stopped pacing. 'Come on, Julia.'

I swallowed.

'I know how good you are. I saw you take that photo from Fleur's drawer. I couldn't see the picture, but I saw you slip it in your pocket. Very smooth.'

My mouth was dry. 'Oh.'

He started pacing again.

'I'm not that good,' I said. 'It's a big thing, it's obvious – it would be obvious if I took it. I don't even know how I'd get in there.'

'We'll figure that out.'

'You have to be joking.'

'No.'

His presence was somehow larger and heavier than I'd seen it before, more strength in his body than I had realised.

'Richard – you've been telling me that you think Grey killed Ingrid. Bludgeoned her to death or whatever you think he did. Now you're asking me to go and get evidence – if that's what it is – from his house.'

He looked at me blankly. 'But he doesn't know you have any of this.' He motioned to the pictures. 'Or know that we've spoken about this. Why couldn't you just ask to go and pay another visit to your old friend's room? Why would he care?'

'We weren't that close towards the end, you know.'

There it was again – this feeling that I wasn't quite entitled to this position of grieving, intimate friend.

'Would Fleur let you in?' he asked.

'I don't know.'

He waited.

'Let me use your phone,' I said.

I called Mrs Bee.

'It's Julia.'

'Yes, how are you?'

'I'm OK. Look – can you tell me – the person you said was on his way – did he show up?'

She was quiet for a moment. 'No,' she said. 'I believe you took it into your own hands and went to see him instead.'

'When? Just now?'

She laughed softly. 'Sorry, I can't tell – it's just not clear. It may have happened – has it? Or it may be still waiting to happen.'

'That isn't very specific.'

'No. Are you alright, dear?'

'Did you mean Gil, or Richard?'

'I'm sorry. I can't help you. I oughtn't to have said anything. I didn't realise it would be so unsettling.'

I hung up. I thought of Jones – the one I had been thinking of at Mrs Bee's place earlier, the one who wasn't coming. According to her. I wondered if he had been more angered or put out by my question about his wife the other night than he had shown. We hadn't spoken to each other that night much at all, and he hadn't been around since. Something told me he wouldn't be around again for a while.

It was late. Half the windows were dark in the buildings opposite. The few cars on the street below drove slowly by.

Richard joined me at the window. 'If you'd like to stay, you're welcome.'

'Thanks.'

I stayed there at the window for a while and heard him quietly treading around the small apartment, putting things in the sink and moving around. Sounds of water running from the bathroom, doors opening and closing. When I turned around there were pillows and covers on the couch, which was long enough to lie down on comfortably. A toothbrush still in its plastic wrapping was set on the pillow. I imagined a neat collection of them in a cupboard somewhere.

The envelope was on his desk. I went over and put it back inside my bag and rested it next to the couch. The lights were off except for the desk lamp and a light in Richard's bedroom. He stood in the doorway, wearing a T-shirt now and long, dark pyjama pants, his glasses still on. 'Please, use anything you need,' he said. 'Goodnight.' He turned and pulled the door almost closed without shutting it.

I brushed my teeth in the bathroom, white tiled walls and pink, black and white tiles on the floor. A light shone down from above the mirrored cabinet on the wall. My face was pale in the mirror against my dark hair, faint traces of lipstick left on my mouth, and the reflected walls were smooth and white. The cabinet had three mirrored doors that opened so that one surface would reflect the other. I pulled the two outer ones open and looked at the side of my face reflected the wrong way around, the multiple walls and corners that appeared. I thought about the photograph of Ingrid and how I'd tried to find that angle from the Promenade.

I sat down on the edge of the bathtub. The tap for hot water was warm to my touch but it was stiff in my fingers when I tried to turn it and my desire for a bath disappeared. My legs felt cold against the tub, feet bare against the tiles.

Richard's door was at a right angle to the bathroom door. It was still almost closed, the door's latch not quite touching the edge of the jamb. The handle was long, the kind you pushed down to open rather than a knob that turned. It looked like brass. I looked at it for a while, and put my hand to it, white in the dark against the brass, and pushed it. The room was larger than I had expected it to be. His bed was set under a window across from the door with a white shade pulled all the way down. He was lying on his back, and raised himself up on his elbows slowly when he saw me open the door. His face was a blur in the dark. The shapes of an elegant chair in the corner and mirrored closet doors emerged. He stayed still.

I shut the door so that the latch caught, but it was noiseless. I stepped to the bed, my feet making no sound, and the quietness was so absolute that my own breath was silent when it should have been loud. His head turned to follow me. The echo of a light from a passing car or truck passed quickly across the window for a moment, leaving the room darker than ever when it was gone. Sound seemed to return then, and a floorboard creaked under my foot. I thought I heard him say my name, but it was strangely muffled, and I wondered if I was dreaming after all. He was motionless as a statue. The desire that filled my body was for proximity and I wanted to lie in the bed just to know that I was not alone. My name echoed in my head, his voice, not his voice. I was about to turn around and leave when he spoke, and it was his voice this time.

'Don't go.'

It was the same thing I had said to him at Fleur's party. I slipped under the covers and we lay there, side by side, not touching. The sheets felt stiff and newly laundered, the down cover light and soft. I glanced over at his face in the dark and his profile was turned away to the side, neck exposed. A pulse beat there somewhere in the throat, under the skin, and I wanted to lift my fingers to that place under the jaw just like you see people doing when they're checking to see if a person is really dead, to feel the proof of life there.

The next morning the room was dim, no direct sunlight. The detailed scrolls of the ornate bed frame were visible that had been shadowed in darkness in the night, metal painted glossy black, chipped in places to reveal old layers of colour underneath – leaden white, pale blue. On the floor next to the bed was a glass of water, almost empty, and a newspaper folded to the crossword. Every clue was filled in except for one.

The walls were empty like the rest of the flat apart from that one poster in the hallway, saying nothing.

The silence of last night had lifted but the apartment was still quiet. I stayed in bed, half-sitting up, listening for him, but there was no sound. After a few minutes the front door opened, keys in each of the four locks, one by one, and brought the sound of footsteps entering, paper bags being set down, the faint slap of a newspaper on the counter. Other noises followed, and then the jerky bubbling of the coffee maker.

I pulled myself out of bed and left the room. My jeans were still there, thrown over the back of the armchair, the only sign of disorder. The covers and pillows were gone from the couch. Richard didn't say anything. I took the jeans and went into the bathroom to shower. The water came on with a shudder, fast and scalding hot. The yellow shampoo had the smell of grapefruit that had been on the pillow last night.

Richard was standing at the kitchen counter, looking at the paper, drinking coffee, when I came in, dressed, my hair wet. The look he gave me was a combination of hostility and desire, and he quickly looked back down at the paper and flattened out the page he was reading.

'There's coffee,' he said, his voice neutral.

I poured some.

He sat down with the paper. There was a small, square, black table under the window, separated from the kitchen by a high ledge. The tension was something like what I would have expected if we had slept together and regretted it, but we hadn't. His bed was wide and we had managed to fall asleep with a body's worth of distance between us, though when I woke up I was almost over on his side of the bed.

He leafed through the paper.

'I'm sorry about last night,' I said. 'I didn't mean to intrude.'

'Oh, no,' he said quickly, and his voice was warm. 'That's alright.' He looked up at me.

'So, the Promenade,' he said, conciliatory. 'It's a nice day for it.' The sky outside was blue.

'OK.'

He looked pleased.

'Let me go and run an errand first. I won't be long.'

'Sure,' he said. 'I'll be here.'

The copy shop was several blocks away; I'd passed it on the way to Richard's building from the subway the previous evening. A row of Xerox machines stood against the glass wall in front. It was empty when I walked in apart from what looked like a college student making multiple copies of pages from her spiral-bound notebook. Her face was pale under the bright lights except for her cheeks, an apricot cosmetic flush made brighter by the glare.

I chose the machine furthest away from her and fed coins into it, fished out the photograph of Maeve in the studio and placed it on the glass. The buttons on the machine were grimy. I pressed 'Enlarge'. The original photograph was fine-grained. The enlargement that came out of the copier was grainier, but showed more detail. It was still too small. I put the enlarged copy on the glass and pressed the button again. After repeating this process one more time the paintings in the background and on the easel had almost dissolved into pixelated dots, but I was pretty sure that I could read a signature at the bottom of two of them – the tree and one of the crosshatched ones that looked like the purple and white painting of Fleur's that I'd seen hanging in the Whitney. The corner of the one with the triangle was obscured.

MW. Two letters down at the bottom right corner,

reversed mirror images of one another. Maeve Wheeler. Or perhaps she called herself something different back in those days, whenever those days were. I wondered where this studio was, where the light came from that filtered through the thin curtains at the window. Eve had told me that Maeve came from somewhere in the Midwest – 'Somewhere surprising,' she had said, with a look of concern. I had imagined Idaho or Nebraska, one of those big, square, flat states where the wind could rush for miles with nothing much to stand in its way.

Someone coughed, startling me. It was only the guy behind the counter. He ignored me. There was a small pile of pages by then on top of the machine, copies of these pieces of the photograph. It felt wrong to leave them in the waste basket. I folded them into a messy bundle. There was one colour copy machine in the place. I opened its lid and saw that the glass was covered with some kind of stain, like spilt coffee that had dried. The guy behind the counter spoke to me without looking up. 'No idea what that is. It won't come off.'

I returned to my original machine and pulled out the photograph of Ingrid. The copy of it that slid out was a contrasty translation of the original, all the gentle blue and yellow turned into black and white. It looked as rough as the enlarged enlargements of the other image, a small rectangle placed high up on the white page. The distant buildings behind Ingrid receded into a faint tracery of grey. It wasn't the same thing at all. I knew the time would come when I would have to return the photo to Fleur. This was a poor replacement.

'There's a Kinko's a few blocks away,' the guy offered as I was putting everything away. He was still staring at the screen of his computer. 'They might have a colour machine.'

'Don't worry about it,' I said.

'What?' he asked, glancing up finally. Was it an accent thing, or was it just weird to have responded to his comment? I didn't know.

'Forget it. Thanks.'

26.

In the end I couldn't think of what to say on the phone or in an email, so I just showed up at Grey's place a few days later. It was the same time of morning as the first time I had visited there, similar kind of cold sunlight chasing away traces of fog, different seasonal angle. I announced myself again with the same doorman behind the massive granite desk in the foyer. As he was calling up to the apartment, I wondered what I would do if Grey said he wouldn't see me – but then, I told myself, there would be no reason for him to do that. The conversation that gave me entrance was very short and I went to the lifts and straight on up.

'Julia. This is an unexpected pleasure.' Grey was dressed in a dark grey suit, black tie pulled loose. 'Come in, please.'

The apartment was quiet. The lid on the piano keys was shut; had it been open the other time?

He was so light on his feet – those delicate hands, never a sharp movement, all smoothness and considered motion – it was impossible to reconcile the person in front of me with the Polaroid in Richard's filing cabinet. The heavy brutality of the bruise, the dark substance of it. Watching him move around the kitchen from the other side of the room I found myself drifting fast into doubt. Ingrid had said that she'd fallen; what if Richard was wrong about everything? With Grey right there it felt like an offence to hospitality to imagine him in any act of physical violence. The thought made me flinch and I buried it.

Grey didn't ask why I was there or seem to care; it was as though, like the last time, he had been expecting me. Without asking he poured me a glass of sparkling water from a blue bottle in the fridge. It tasted salty, the bubbles tiny and harsh. We sat in the living room in the same position as last time. He checked his watch with an incline of his head.

'I'm due at the museum for a meeting early this afternoon. But not for a little while.' He looked down at the arm of his chair. 'Julia, I was so sorry to hear about your aunt.' His eyes met mine, and the look of compassion in his face was surprising. He gave a small smile. 'And glad to hear that she's doing OK now. My own mother died when I was about the age you are now. It was a devastating event.'

'Yes.'

'And so soon after …' His voice trailed off.

The words I hadn't been able to think of ahead of time or rehearse came easily now. 'I suppose it brought it all back, in a way.' And it was true. I tried to find Ingrid again in the bloodless room. It seemed darker than it had been last time. She wasn't there.

Grey looked at me, but not with the sickening pity that had made me avoid Mark's neighbours after September 11. It was a form of sympathy that I found I could handle. No 'you must feel …'; instead, surprisingly, an alertness to what I did feel, but one so remote it was almost cold. For the first time I felt something in common with him, and envied the way he was so practised at guarding his own feelings that the action was close to invisible.

'I was on my way to the museum. To the Met.' This was what I had prepared to say, vaguely, if he asked what I was doing there.

'Oh, yes.' He cleared his throat. 'Ingrid left some money there, it turns out.'

For a moment his words conjured an image of Ingrid's purse lying abandoned on a bench to the side of one of those numberless rooms, bills and coins falling out of it.

'A bequest to the antiquities department,' he said.

'Do they have curse scrolls there?' I asked. But then all I could think of was the statue of the figure spearing the stag, the helpless animal, the way the whitening light had fallen that day on Jones's hair when he had taken out his black book. I blinked.

Grey's eyes had met mine very sharply and it was a few seconds before he spoke. 'It's a general bequest to the department.' He paused. 'I didn't realise you were so intimate with her research. I suppose I should have known.'

'I did talk with some people in the department at Columbia – who had been students with her. Teachers.'

He nodded. 'It's a wonderful department. Such a loss for them.' He didn't ask who it was I'd been speaking to.

'I know it's a strange request and I don't want to intrude, I'm sorry – I was just wondering – Ingrid's room – would you mind – could I see it again?'

His face was expressionless as he rose. 'Of course.'

'It's been hard to … let go …'

I stood, awkwardly. It was true, again, but everything was a lie, an affront to hospitality and sympathy. Guilt slowed me. He waited at the foot of the stairs, one hand on the railings.

'Of course,' he said again. I was there, about to take the first step. 'It's so sad, I've always thought, that the two of you weren't closer after we married.'

I stilled.

'It's sad, but inevitable, isn't it, how such a great distance necessarily ...' – he searched for a word – 'erodes relationships.' He smiled kindly, with a maddening, faultless sincerity. His eyes were as cold and sharp as they had ever been. 'We don't think of these things at the time – so hard to foresee. But I know you meant a great deal to Ingrid.'

It was the challenge I had feared and faced only in my imagination until then. I took the stairs slowly, eyes down. They seemed to go on forever, sharp-edged and white as before. Chiselled bone. Easy to slip and break a wrist, crack a rib. I didn't look back at Grey; I heard him walking quietly towards his study once I had reached the landing.

The room was different. The dresser was gone and there was no sign at first glance of the objects that had stood on it. The desk was still there against the window, but a different pile of notebooks and textbooks sat on it now, and a pile of magazines. The little amphora was there, leaning on its side, and a cobalt blue porcelain ashtray. The room smelled faintly of cigarettes. I pulled up the shade. The chaise longue was there at a slightly different angle, its green linen covered with a patched, beautiful Indian textile in maroons and purples, tiny mirrors shining here and there on the surface. Ingrid's books were still there on the bookshelf, from what I could remember, and on the first shelf down near the floor were the papers that had been on her desk before. The diary was there, sandwiched between some folders. I kneeled, quickly pulled it out and pushed it to the bottom of my shoulder bag under a book, my gloves and wallet.

Richard had wanted me to bring a replacement, a book the same style and colour that would match the diary and so mask the fact that it had been taken. 'You could probably buy a similar model,' he'd said, 'it sounds just like a Filofax or one of those things.'

It seemed like a good idea – I knew how important it was to leave the scene looking like it had before – but I didn't want to have to take it back and switch them again. 'What if they do notice it's gone, that it's not the same book?' I had asked. 'Wouldn't it look worse to find a decoy, a fake book? If it's just not there, it could be lost. But an empty diary – that would prove it had been taken.' He agreed in the end.

The shelf didn't look so different without the diary. I had counted on the fact that Grey didn't go into the room, thinking of his hesitancy to enter last time, but now it seemed like a strong possibility that the room was being used by Fleur. I sat at the desk and looked out the window and waited for a few minutes before leaving.

Grey heard me coming downstairs and came out of his study to meet me.

'Is Fleur using the room now?' I asked him.

'Oh, yes. I forgot to mention.' He raised his hands to his hips, pushing his jacket aside. 'I wasn't sure what to do with the room.' He grimaced faintly. 'It seemed odd to leave it there like that – it couldn't stay that way forever. And Fleur said she'd like to use it as a study room. It seemed like a good idea.'

I nodded.

'Not that much studying is happening, from what I can see. A lot of talking on the phone. That never seems to end.'

His smile was graceful and self-deprecating, the smile I remembered from that first dinner when he'd talked about Fleur. Proud, exasperated, adoring. It could have all been an act, or it could have existed alongside the rest of it: the exploitation and expert opportunism. He could have imagined that the fame and reputation he and Maeve had created for her was an invaluable gift, an act of love.

If he had once looked at me with real warmth, I might have fallen for the charm of his good manners and nice looks. In a way I wanted to, to put a real stop to Richard's suspicions, to go along with the version that Ingrid had tried to pass off. She was clumsy indoors, after all, for all her athleticism and strength once she started throwing a tennis ball around outside; any place with stairs was a potential danger zone to her. But his gaze stayed cool and his hands, resting there on his hips, filled me with dread when I thought about the uses to which they might have been put.

'Thanks, Gil.' It was not the first time I had said his first name, but it still felt wrong.

'I'll see you again, I hope.'

Before we reached the front door I asked him, 'How's Maeve?'

'She's well.' He paused. 'It's been terribly hard on her.

Ingrid was like a daughter to her …' He hesitated, perhaps seeing the oddness in his wife being like a daughter to his friend and contemporary. 'Or a sister,' he continued, 'or a niece – you would know that. I think she's, well, finding some kind of closure now. I'm sure she'd love to see you.'

He opened the door for me. 'Goodbye, then. I hope you enjoy your visit to the museum. It's a lovely walk across the park.'

The fear and anxiety that I had managed to keep at bay in Ingrid's room came flooding in, a wave of sweat, as soon as I stepped into the lift. Someone had sucked all the oxygen out of the box. The floors ticked by and air entered again when the doors opened.

The park was lovely to walk through, just as Grey had said, transitioning to winter grey, the grass losing its green and the trees showing their half-bare branches. It wasn't until I saw the back of the Metropolitan Museum that I stopped and thought about where I was actually going. I turned and walked back west, not ready for a wander through Antiquities or Arms and Armor. Richard was at the New York Public Library that day, something to do with the translation he was working on, consulting some editions. We had a plan to meet at his apartment later, but seeing him was the only thing I could think of to do.

At 42nd Street, the library station, I walked from the platform to the exit through a tunnel decorated with a recent mosaic. Tree roots reached down the white walls in fragments of gold and bronze tile, like an unfurled tendril from a Klimt painting. Shining green leaves trailed down across the other side. A thin slab of granite grey was etched with a line from Ovid, and it was Ingrid's voice I heard intoning the words: *gutta cavat lapidem*: dripping water hollows out stone. All the tiles looked impossibly clean next to the concrete pathway littered with paper and plastic.

The library's stone and marble bulk stretched the whole block from 41st to 42nd Street on Fifth Avenue. Shallow puddles were drying in patches on the stairs leading up to the doors: water hollowing out stone. I was inside the main hall before I remembered that it was a big library and Richard hadn't said where he would be, in which one of the many rooms and restricted collections. I went upstairs, long flights of shallow stone steps, and through to the Rose Reading Room. It seemed like the best place to start, or to look at least, and if he wasn't there I could go and find some coffee and sit in Bryant Park.

The echoing space of the reading room opened up through the wooden entranceway, rows of desks and gleaming lamps, oak and gold. Around me people stood or sat, all watching the digital screen of numbers at the front of the room that would announce when their requested book had arrived from the stacks below. The industry of thinking and reading and waiting was soothing. I walked slowly down the middle aisle, looking for Richard's dark head among the numbers of readers seated at the long desks. The Chrysler Building was framed by one enormous, arched window, a piece of it with its points and curves like a broken crown. I was looking at it, having forgotten about the stolen diary in my bag, when I heard a familiar voice at my side.

It was Jones. His hand touched my elbow for a second, and I wasn't sure if it was the touch or the voice that told me it was him. We stood looking at each other.

'Well,' he said eventually. 'It's nice of you to come by and see me here.'

I frowned at him.

He looked at the clock on the far wall. 'Let's eat. Are you hungry? Just give me a minute.' He was holding a large volume with worn leather binding that looked too old to be out of a protective box. 'Returning this.'

He picked up his black case from a place at the desk a few rows down, leaving a pile of notes and books and pens, and came back to me. I looked around quickly for Richard. He didn't seem to be there. I imagined him in some smaller, darkened room down the hall – where they fetched the books using ladders that ran along the floor on wheels, and possibly provided gloves – reading at a desk with five different editions in front of him.

Jones had put on a woollen coat over his light-coloured suit. He saw me looking at it. Fawn was the colour. A deer's pale underside. 'What are you looking at?' he asked. I shook my head.

The baroque ceiling recessed forever, lined with naked golden women holding banners high, empty of words. Cupid, blank-eyed under a satyr's face. We walked the length of the aisle and out through the doors, past the readers at their desks, our way lit by chandeliers and the painted sky above our heads blazing.

We ate at a small café a block away from the library, huddled around a little table in the crowd. He was charming all through lunch and insisted at the end on ordering a large piece of chocolate cake, refusing to share it. Instead he watched me eat it with openly erotic fascination. It was rich and dark and not sweet enough.

'You're awfully quiet,' he said when we were outside on the street, and he lit a cigarette. He glanced at me out of the corner of his eye and started walking back towards the library. I went with him. 'I hope everything is alright.'

I nodded. I seemed to have made it through an entire forty minutes in his company without saying anything much at all. It was oddly calming. Speech felt as though it was waiting somewhere just adjacent to where I was, holding its breath ever since that suffocating lift ride down from Grey's apartment.

I stopped when we had just started up the monumental stairs at the front of the library. He stopped too. 'Listen, I'm busy tonight,' he said, apologetically. 'But tomorrow – a drink maybe.'

We stood next to one of the pair of giant stone lions that guarded the entrance, handsome and impassive. I looked over at the other lion across from us. A girl was having her photograph taken in front of it, and she roared and raised her hands in a clawing gesture. 'Raaarrr!' Her friend with the camera stood still and attentive and pressed the button.

Jones looked at me and raised one corner of his mouth in a smile. He touched my arm and I felt it through to the bone. I thought about Richard inside somewhere, but didn't want to follow Jones. He turned away and stepped briskly up the stairs to the door. I walked slowly the other way and headed down the avenue.

*

Richard found me waiting outside his building when he finally got home. It was an hour earlier than we had agreed to meet.

'Hello,' he said, his face composed.

I still didn't feel like talking.

The flat was darkening in the early evening and he switched on lights. The manila folder was nowhere to be seen, although I had left it with him. Our trip to the Promenade a few days earlier had been inconclusive; once we got there, Richard had shown little interest in comparing the photograph with the view, and just said, 'Maybe,' and 'Possibly,' or nothing to anything I suggested. He had spent a long time standing at the railing, looking up towards the glittering buildings of midtown and the bridge. I'd given him my set of enlarged photocopies as we stood there looking towards the city and he paged through them expressionlessly. 'It's as I expected,' he'd said.

We sat at the table in the lamplight. I pulled the diary out of my bag and pushed it across to him. He opened it, turned over a few pages and found the entry for 11 September. He looked at it for a while, and turned the page back, once, twice, examining other entries, and looked back at the original page.

'She's used a few different pens, but she seems to like this blue one, quite a thick line. It's written in the same pen as a lot of the other entries.'

I nodded.

'I don't know if I'd want to swear to this in court,' he said. 'But I'm not sure it's her writing.'

'But – do you think it is or not?' My voice was creaky.

He shrugged. 'There's an inconsistency – it could be an inconsistency – with the formation of the letter "a", lower case.'

He turned the book and held his finger to the page to show me. I looked at it and looked back at some of the entries written on earlier days. In some of them the circle of the 'a' closed up with the down stroke; in some of them it didn't quite seem to.

'I should have thought of it,' he said to himself, leaning back in his chair. 'Grey's writing. I need something to compare it with.'

'Well, I'm not going back there to steal something else, if that's on your mind.'

'No. OK. There would be other ways. I suppose.'

'I don't like this.'

He looked up at me.

'Reading through her diary like this. It feels wrong.'

'It's not like it's a personal memoir – this is just a list of times and dates.'

'I know. But it still feels wrong.'

He didn't say anything.

'You do this all the time – this is your job, reading things that weren't intended for you and subjecting it all to analysis. Figuring out people's secrets. But I'm not used to it.'

The diary looked small on the counter but Ingrid's death gave it a kind of heaviness, a greater mass than it should have held.

'You can leave it with me if you like.'

'No, that's not what I meant,' I said.

'You know what's at stake here,' he responded.

The bruise was there again, overlaying my vision, purple and dark. I screwed shut my eyes, and opened them. It wouldn't go away.

'What do I know about you anyway?' I asked.

His face clouded.

'This is a completely insane idea that you have. You've got me to help you – you've pulled me into this whole crazy thing.'

'You brought me the stuff from Trinh, the drawings. What did you want out of that?'

'I don't know. I don't know what I was thinking.' I forgot about the one thought that had been with me when I left the apartment that night and caught the subway here: that I trusted him for some reason, absolutely. Now there seemed to be no way of making sense of what I was doing. I think that even then I knew somewhere that I just didn't want it to be true, what Richard was thinking, and the anger at him was misdirected. But the words came from somewhere, my voice having come back somewhat alien from that adjacent place. 'I don't know anything about you, except that you had a restraining order taken out against you. And you – you probably think you know everything about me, don't you?'

'No.'

'You've probably still got that note I wrote, haven't you? The one I left here on your door? Filed away somewhere?' He shifted in his seat. 'I thought so. And I suppose you ran up a full personality profile on me with it.'

He closed the diary.

'But you don't know anything,' I continued. 'And I don't know anything about you. Look at this place – it's like a hotel, or an office. I don't know …' I struggled to think of something. 'All I know is that you drink whisky, and even that might be a decoy. Maybe there's a stash of something else, some secret red wine in the locked cabinet. I don't know who you are, where you came from, what your favourite colour is –'

'My favourite colour?' he asked. 'What are you, five?'

'Don't patronise me,' I said.

'It's true,' he said after a while. He spoke very formally. 'I don't let people in easily.'

'But you loved her. Ingrid.'

He put his forehead in one hand, eyes down, elbow resting on the table. I picked up my bag and left, leaving it all behind, the envelope, the pictures, the diary.

Matt was home, on the couch watching TV. 'Hi,' he called out. 'There's leftovers on the counter.'

I filled a bowl from a bucket-like plastic container of fried rice in a paper bag and sat down next to him. *Rear Window* was playing; I recognised the shot of the apartment building that is the scene of the crime, rows of windows, one of them showing a woman with a blonde ponytail practising ballet in her room. James Stewart looked on longingly from his wheelchair across the way.

'Look,' Matt said, pointing to the television.

'Great,' I replied, thinking the opposite.

'I know,' Matt said happily. 'It's a Hitchcock marathon. I've just watched *The Birds. Vertigo* is next.'

I settled in reluctantly.

'What have you been up to?' he asked.

'Don't ask,' I said.

'Haven't seen the divine Mister Jones for a few nights.'

'No. His wife's in town.'

'No way. Hey, if you're still interested, that artist is still looking for an assistant. Carson. I think he'd like you. He's a bit, you know, temperamental, but you're good with people.'

I stared at him.

'OK. You could handle him. You'd start next month. Think about it.'

I said I would.

The idea of a job was appealing, although I doubted the wisdom of entangling myself further with the art world. It wasn't a career opportunity, I told myself; it would be a way to remain in New York on my own terms.

'If you stick around much longer, you'll have to start doing your share of watering the plants,' Matt smiled at me.

'Whatever you do, don't ask me to do that.'

'Sure. I'm going to tell Carson that you're interested. He'll be happy that you're not an aspiring artist.'

I laughed. 'But seriously. Can I keep living here?' When did it become living, I wondered, instead of staying?

He shrugged. 'As long as you like.'

Grace Kelly swept us both into silence then as she made her entrance on screen.

I crawled into bed after *Vertigo* finished and met a dream of Ingrid, her face the face of the doomed Carlotta that looks down on Kim Novak from the wall of the museum, a posy of flowers in her hand, lavender dress hiding her injured side. Her hands were white and the bunch of flowers she held looked too small, as though it were missing some. Violets?

Pansies? They were purple and yellow and green, the colour of blood when it has pooled under skin in an old bruise. She smiled at me sadly.

There was an envelope pushed under the front door when I got up in the morning, an ordinary letter-sized white envelope with my name written on it in blue ink. It looked like the ink that Ingrid used when she wrote *Paul, 9.* If she wrote it. Of course she wrote it, I scolded myself, and shook my head to clear it and picked up the envelope. There was one piece of notepaper inside with just one word written there. His writing wasn't quite what I had expected. The letters weren't very regular and didn't sit exactly in a straight line. I noticed the small loop of the letter 'e'.

Blue.

I found his card in my wallet and called his number.

'OK,' I said. 'I'm sorry about last night.'

'Don't mention it.'

'I'll buy you lunch.'

'Alright. I'll be at the library.'

'Where can I find you?'

'In the reading room. The left side. 650.'

I met him there and we ate sandwiches in Bryant Park. It was getting too cold to sit outside comfortably and we both sat hunched with our coats wrapped around our bodies, perched on two chairs at the edge of the grassy square in the middle of the park. The grass was fenced off. The paved space around the lawn was filled with chairs and tables like ours in random assortments, light enough to be moved around, half of them filled with people eating and reading.

'You don't need to keep on with this if you don't want to,' he said. 'I understand. It's painful stuff. In fact, it might be better if you leave it.'

'No, I'm with you,' I said. 'For now.'

'I saw how upset you were last night.'

I chewed. I'd found it hard to look at him since seeing him in the library just now, head bent over four books laid out on the desk under a lamp, pretty close to how I'd imagined it before. His hair had shone darkly in the lamplight and I'd stood there watching him for a moment.

'It's important to me to know the truth about what happened,' he said. 'But I realise that might be a little … obsessive.'

'Obsessive,' I repeated. 'As long as you're not just obsessed with getting this one version of the story that you've fixed on.'

'I don't want it to be true,' he said. 'That was why I gave it up before. Apart from the fact that I couldn't get anywhere with it. I decided that it was more horrible than the thought of the accident.'

'So why don't you give it up now?' I asked. But he didn't say anything and I didn't need the answer.

I offered to talk to Fleur.

'She might be able to get some of his handwriting for us,' Richard said.

'I don't want to ask her that,' I said. 'I just want to talk to her.'

'Watch out for her,' he said. 'She's no fan of mine.'

'What do you mean?' I asked, but he shook his head and didn't reply.

Neither of us mentioned Richard's note. I could only guess at how much of himself he felt he had betrayed. I wondered how many other instances there were, all over the city, of his handwriting. There were no credit cards in his wallet, I'd noticed, when he had left it open on the counter the morning after I had spent the night. He paid cash, never needed to sign. On the desk beside him when I had collected him before lunch just then had been a well-ordered pile of yellow library call slips for books, neatly filled out on the typewriter at home in advance so that he wouldn't have to write in the details in his own hand.

I had left the note on my unmade bed that morning, inside its envelope.

Richard went back inside the library and I went down to the Village. I thought about calling Ralph and wondered what time it was there. I picked up some things at the mini-supermarket and the deli on the way, and knocked on Mrs Bee's door. She opened it.

'I brought you some things,' I said, handing her a paper bag. Inside was milk and bread and some of the shortbread she liked.

'Thanks,' she said. 'Actually, I just got a delivery.'

'Didn't you know I was coming?' I smiled at her, teasing.

'You surprised me,' she said.

The tea she made was hot and strong. It scalded my lips and I set the cup down to cool.

27.

Fleur let me up to the studio and eyed me reproachfully, one arm leaning against the bench next to the kitchen sink. She was holding a bottle of Coke, the small, old-fashioned kind in glass, and set it down sharply after taking a drink.

'Look,' she said, hardness in her voice, 'I want that photo back. I want you to bring it back.'

'I want to show you something.'

I took the diary from my bag. She stayed still but looked as though she were holding in a flinch.

'Put that away.'

'Please –'

'No! I know what that is.'

'It's about that day.'

She relented. 'OK.'

I opened the diary to the page and handed it to her. She looked at it briefly.

'Dad said you had been around. Is this what you were doing? Julia,' her voice was compassionate now, 'if it would really mean something to you to have something of Ingrid's – I can find something for you.'

I cleared my throat. 'It's about the appointment that Ingrid has listed for that day.'

'Paul was her accountant, her financial adviser. She met with him every once in a while. His offices were in the

433

Trade Center. It's because of that appointment that she was downtown that day.'

'I know.'

'He was killed,' she said, flatly. 'Along with everyone in his company, everyone who was there in the office that morning. Is that what you wanted to know?'

'I waited a second. I just was wondering – does that look like her writing to you?'

'Yeah – she kept her own diary. Sometimes Dad's secretary helped her out with organising, you know, responding to invitations and all that, but she wrote everything into this herself.'

'So you don't think – you don't think someone else might have written this in?'

She frowned.

'I'm not talking about a secretary,' I explained. 'I'm talking about it being added in … well, later.'

We stood there for a while.

'Where are you going with this?' she asked eventually.

I put the diary back in my bag. 'Can I just talk to you about it? Fleur, I'm not sure – I just wanted to talk to you.'

'What do you think you're doing?'

What was it Richard had said? 'I suppose – finding the truth?' It didn't sound right, even to me.

She stared at me, disbelieving, and then the anger returned.

'Don't you think it's hard enough that she's gone? What do you think you're going to get out of this? When you were here before – that was different – now you're seeing ghosts – you're carrying her diary around? And making up big conspiracy theories?'

I was silent.

'Richard's crazy, you know. He's just mad because she wouldn't sleep with him. Jesus. I thought he had stopped with all this shit.'

She paced and smoked and finished her Coke and pulled out a beer from the fridge. She didn't offer one to me. The dolls were propped up in a corner of the little video set on the other side of the room; the furniture I'd seen there before was gone and there was a miniature television set and recliner chair in front of it. I wondered what story was being played out there now.

'I don't know why you're … prying into her life like this.'

I could have said that she was my friend, but it would have sounded worse than the earlier truth comment.

'And my life,' Fleur went on. 'All of our lives. She's gone.'

I still wasn't sure how much she knew – about the envelope Trinh had given me, whether she knew that Ingrid had it, that I had it, what understanding she had reached with Ingrid about the whole thing, if any. I didn't know what to say. I felt doubtful and ashamed.

She met my eyes and hers seemed so much older than her face; they were lightless and stony, older than I'd ever felt.

'Don't you just think …' She paused, stuck for words, unable to go on. She seemed to give up trying, and the tension in her body ebbed a little. I waited.

'Just give me back that photograph,' she said. 'If you want some kind of – memento – tell me what you want. I've got plenty of other photos of her. I'll send you one. That one's special to me. That's all. She's gone, Julia,' she repeated. 'Now go.'

She came to the door with me, and surprised me when we got there. She put her arms around me tightly, clamping my own arms to my side, and buried her face in my neck. 'Sorry,' she whispered. I tried to move, to put my hands on her back, to respond, but she let go and turned away.

She called me the next night.

'Do you want to get a drink? Anywhere you like.'

I met her at a bar on Bleecker Street that she suggested in the end. It was just one small room lined with red booths, red lampshades hanging from the ceiling. The bartender carried on a long, impassioned conversation in Russian with a customer while I waited for Fleur to arrive. The exit sign over the door flickered. There was a sticker over it, covering half the word, that said EXPLODING.

Fleur was wearing a coat with a hood that framed her delicate face, and pushed the hood back when she came in. We sat down at a booth in a corner. She drank a Coke through a thin straw.

'I might have got a little carried away when I talked to you before,' she said. She swept her hair back behind one ear. She looked young again and she opened and closed her eyes in a way that made her eyelashes look pretty. 'It's just still so hard, and I miss her a lot sometimes.'

'I know. I'm sorry.'

She looked at me. 'I know it's hard for you too – I can imagine. I just think – for your sake too – it would be better if you let it go.'

She was all calmness and persuasion. I drank my drink.

'I've seen the bruises,' I said. 'I've seen a photo.'

She smiled at me curiously, but with a knowing look on her face that showed me her intelligence and something of the strange life she'd lived so far. 'You've seen a photo,' she said. 'You've seen plenty of photos.'

I thought about the bruise and the white stairs and the pale carpet that absorbed so much sound.

'Look,' she said. 'It was her life.'

And one conversation with Ingrid, one of the last ones face to face before she left for New York for good, came to my mind.

'It's my life,' she had said angrily. 'Not Ralph's. He's acting as though — as though he paid for it,' she spat the words out, 'as if he *bought it*, so it's his — but he didn't.'

'That's not it,' I said. 'He just wants you to be happy.'

She had sighed. 'Then he'll see. I'll give him time. But stop acting like his stupid messenger.'

Fleur held my gaze, her expression serious. 'Photos tell all kinds of stories. I should know.' I thought of the dolls, acting out their dramas in the damaged interiors she made for them. 'You've seen enough,' she said, 'that you should know by now: let it go.'

I looked away. It sounded like a warning. I wondered how much I ought to fear Grey, and thought about the envelope somewhere in Richard's cabinets.

'What are you doing here anyway? Why don't you go home?' Her voice was gentle, a subtle blade. 'Trust me,' she said. 'Listen. Ingrid wouldn't want all this.' She faced me, her eyes still young and now filled with something like panic. 'Please let it go.'

'Are you protecting him?' I asked. 'Are you trying to protect me? From what?'

She gave me that disbelieving look again, and then forced it away. Her face went blank. 'Do you have the photo?' she asked. 'I want the diary back too.'

'No,' I said.

She stared at me. 'I want it back. Look – I've got others.'

She took out an envelope and opened it. I caught sight of a few pictures of Ingrid in Fleur's studio, smiling, and sitting at her desk, the light behind her, mouth serious. It was unbearable to see her face. Fleur leaned closer.

I asked her, 'Don't you have the negative, another print, whatever?'

She shoved the envelope into my hand. 'You are not helping,' she said. She was almost whispering. 'You could ruin everything.'

I put the photos she had just given me back on the table in front of us. 'I'm not interested in your secrets – in the paintings,' I said.

She frowned. I could see, in the second before she rearranged her face, that she hadn't been thinking about the paintings. I held her gaze with difficulty, the room suddenly close. She swallowed.

'I don't know what you think you know about the paintings,' she said. 'Or what Ingrid knew. I don't care.'

'Fleur –'

But she was gone, out the door, her face filled with rebuke and fear and something else: determination.

*

At Richard's the next night I described my two conversations with Fleur. He asked me to repeat what she had said, with as many of the actual words as I could remember.

I had gone over it in my own mind since then, her half-whispered comment about my ruining everything, and the look that told me she wasn't thinking about the paintings. It had the clarity and strangeness of a dream with a significance I hadn't yet understood.

But Richard was busily working through the possibility that Fleur could have known about the envelope that Trinh had given to me, and that she wanted to cover up any evidence.

'I don't think so,' I said.

'But what else could she have meant?' he asked. 'If you leave out the idea that she was a conspirator in the actual murder. And I don't think she was. Or that she's just trying to protect her father after the fact. And that's a possibility. She doesn't seem to like him much but she is loyal to him.'

Her face had been so worried at the bar, her arms tight around me when I'd left her apartment. *Sorry.*

Richard's voice pulled my attention back. 'Are you still seeing Philip Jones?' he asked me, suddenly.

I didn't ask how he knew about that.

'It's hard to say.'

He looked down at the newspaper open on the table in front of him. He seemed to read a whole story, following it from the front page through to its finish at the end of the paper.

*

'I dislike him,' he said eventually.

'Jones.'

'Yes.'

'Was he your teacher?'

'Yes.' He looked up at me. 'He's smart,' he added grudgingly. 'Ingrid idolised him.'

'So he had more luck than you then?' I asked, bitter. It was about Ingrid, of course it was, whatever jealous drama was playing out here.

'No, I don't think so.' His voice was calm. 'No more luck than me.'

He folded the paper once across. 'Forget it. I'm sorry I asked. It's none of my business.'

'That's OK.'

'I used to know his wife. At college.'

'Oh.' I felt suddenly naked, and pushed my hair back from my face. It was the first time he had spoken about his past.

'She's as bad as him. They deserve each other.'

I pulled a bagel out of the paper bag on the counter and chewed on it.

'He's not so bad, at times. He has his moments.'

'He's —' He stopped. 'It doesn't matter. I'm sure you're right.'

Days passed. I tried to call Jenny at the rehab centre but she wasn't yet able to speak. Peter said she was doing OK when I spoke with him. Rachel was living in the Mosman house now. Whatever it was she had going with her good friend over in Rozelle hadn't worked out.

'Where is she sleeping?' I asked.

'I don't know,' he said. 'Jenny's room? Our old room? What does it matter?'

The phone rang one afternoon and I answered it after listening to it ring for a while. It was Ralph.

'What time is it there?' I asked.

'I don't know. Late. Early. Look, how is it going?'

I sighed. 'It's so complicated.'

'Complicated?'

I waited. 'There have been … developments.'

'You're being very mysterious.'

'Sorry.'

'How's your professor?'

It took me a moment. 'Married, I guess.'

We chatted awkwardly. I told him I'd been seeing a bit of Richard, and Ralph's voice grew envious and tight. I couldn't understand why. It could have been just that Richard had been a friend of Ingrid's, connected with her by association. Finally I told him that I would call him in a few days' time. He seemed satisfied.

Matt came and went grumpily. I went for long walks around the area, winding streets to the west, starkly straight avenues to the east. When I wasn't walking I was reading books about New York architecture and the buildings of the East and West Villages. The skyscrapers didn't interest me so much, with all their chrome and steel, but I loved the apartment buildings, the tenements and tall, high-ceilinged buildings of flats with their rows of windows onto other people's lives. Many writers and artists and musicians had lived in the buildings along these streets. Matt seemed to know all their addresses, especially the ones still living. 'Elvis Costello's old place is there,' he'd say when I told him the street I'd walked by that day. Or, 'Didn't Philip Glass live on that block? I swear I saw him taking out his trash one day right there.' These minor celebrities weren't interesting to me but I came to be something of an expert on the shape of brickwork around windows and doors between the wars.

Richard phoned one morning, saying that he'd seen some of Grey's writing – I didn't ask how he came by it – and that he still wasn't sure about the writing in the diary, whether it was Ingrid's or not. His voice was anxious and preoccupied. He was calling from the library. He was having trouble with the translation he was working on. It was a novel by a dead German writer. I could picture him standing in a quiet corner, hand running nervously through his hair.

'I don't know if I'm going to be able to figure it out,' he said.

'The translation? Don't you have, you know, dictionaries – other translations?'

'No,' he said, and I realised my mistake. 'The writing. I don't know if I'll be able to decide, conclusively, if it's his, or hers. Or by someone else. I thought about taking it to an expert, a friend of mine who does some forensic work along this line.'

'You should do whatever you need to do,' I told him, but the prospect was depressing. 'But maybe it's not something that can be proved, or resolved.'

'I don't know if I can accept that,' he said.

'You might have to. Acceptance. Isn't that one of the five stages?'

He snorted. 'Don't think I've made it to that stage yet.'

'Well, hurry along. It's the final one.'

'I know.'

There was a silence that felt long. Since leaving the diary at his house it had taken me a while to feel really clean again. I didn't want to go back into it. We said goodbye.

I found myself in a bookshop that afternoon, in front of a table full of notebooks and diaries, stacks of little books identical to Ingrid's diary in a rainbow of colours – pink, blue, yellow, pebbled white leather, all with the same shape and clasp. They seemed to multiply in front of my eyes. I blinked and turned away.

There were shelves of books on architecture and I bought a couple on the buildings in the West Village and the Lower East Side. Back at the apartment I looked through them. Our building was there in the corner of one photograph, taken chiefly to display a building a few doors down. The edges of the terraces were visible, pieces of greenery showing over the ledges.

When Richard came to the door that night, the first thing that struck me was that he was drunk, a thing I'd never seen or imagined before.

'You'd better come in,' I said.

He lurched silently through the doorway. I stepped aside to let him pass and a cold halo of air came with him, as though it had stuck around his clothes all the way from the freezing street. I felt it on my face and it passed through to my skin. The cold and its passing over me seemed to take long, liquid seconds, during which he stopped, still and dark against the paleness of the walls. He was poised, deeply unsteady, about to spill.

When he moved, he just about fell against me so I crashed into the wall. The door was still open, I saw out of the corner of my eye. It began its slow swing closed. His face was cold, cold against my neck, the hulk of his body a blackness beyond that, and then in seconds hot, a quicksilver interchange of temperature between our bodies.

'Richard,' I said. 'Richard.'

I wanted him to be there. But I thought in bitterness of those other times when Ingrid had indirectly driven a wanted man to me. Ralph, on my bed, hand on my leg; sitting on the couch, wet with rain.

I knew what Richard was going to say before he said it: 'I can't bear it.'

'I know,' I sighed.

28.

I took a cup of coffee onto the terrace the next day, even though it was cold out there. My book was open on my lap, the pages fluttering in the breeze, and my coffee cooled quickly. The light was alternately soft and hard, fading in and out of bright sun as small clouds drifted over and across the sky. The bells in the birdcage tinkled. A pigeon came to sit on the high brick ledge that ran around the edge of the terrace. It was grey and blue with a baleful, red-rimmed eye; an ordinary kind of pigeon. It hopped up on top of the birdcage, pecked it once or twice. I wondered how the cage looked to the bird, and whether the bird understood what it was, that it was meant to cage a bird like itself. Not exactly like itself; a more glamorous cousin of some kind. I had invented an imaginary inhabitant for the cage: a green and gold finch with a sweet, chirping voice. The pigeon tottered around awkwardly on its feet, twitching its head to one side and another, then it took off in flight, made graceful for a second by that motion. I stood to see it fly. It disappeared over the ledge and was gone; a few seconds later it landed on a windowsill on a building across the road and stayed there for a moment, greeting a couple of other pigeons, or that's what it looked like. Then it flew away again, out of sight. I looked down at the empty cage. It didn't show any rust, which seemed odd. The mirrors twinkled in the light.

The sensation I felt was a bit like drinking a very cold drink and feeling the chill suffuse quickly through your stomach and into your body, leaving you just a little colder, or sometimes, somehow, hotter than before. Seeing the pigeon fly away from the cage made it all seem somehow more possible and more obvious than it had before. It must be true, I thought. She escaped. The metaphor was so conventional that I felt disappointed in myself. The clouds cleared so that the sun shone clear and bright, casting my shadow across the concrete ground.

The sun kept shining. I walked down in the direction of Fleur's studio. As it turned out we ran into each other on the street halfway between my place and hers.

'I was on my way to see you,' she said.

Her hair was tied back from her face and she was wearing what looked like a school backpack on her shoulder and carrying a shopping bag from Toys R Us in one hand. The big schoolbag looked out of place on her thin body. She held a cigarette and smoked it quickly, finished it, threw it away. We walked downtown in the direction of her street and stopped outside a café not far from her studio. 'Let's go here,' she said, and I followed her in. It was a cavernous space lit with a huge set of skylights in the back of the room, tall trees in pots along the side and back walls. We bought coffee and sat at a table.

I pulled the photograph out of my bag and put it on the table between us. She took it quickly, covering it with her hand, as though hiding it from sight. I saw her glance at it before she unzipped her bag and put it inside. As soon as it disappeared I regretted having given it back to her, but it seemed like an important gesture of good faith.

'And the calendar?' she asked.

'I'll get that to you later,' I said.

She was visibly anxious, her small hands moving nervously on the table from her coffee cup to her lap.

'I think I understand,' I said.

She looked at me with a mix of condescension and impatience.

'I meant it when I said I didn't care about the paintings,' I told her. 'I don't.'

She glanced around us. The place was fairly quiet. The sound of a blender started up from behind the counter at the front, and the coffee machine hissed.

'I don't want to talk about it,' she said. 'Not here.'

We stood up.

'Can we talk at your place?' I asked.

She wanted to refuse. 'OK,' she said, unwillingly, and we left.

Once inside her studio she shut the door and stood with her arms crossed in front of her. The Toys R Us bag clunked heavily on the floor as its contents came to rest. 'Look,' she said. 'For a start, you can't prove anything.' I didn't know whether she was talking about Ingrid or the paintings, or both.

She went to the room at the back, the one with the futon bed, and came back out carrying a wide, black portfolio case. I followed her to the beanbags under the window, where she kneeled on the floor. She opened the case, and I saw that it was full of paintings on paper. She pulled one out and laid it in front of me, closing the case. There were purple handprints on the painting, the hands of a little girl, as well as marks made by fingers and a brush, a smudged cloud in the corner, a triangle that looked like a lightning bolt folded back on itself.

There had been handprints like these on some of the paintings at the Whitney. They served, I saw now, as some kind of sign of authenticity – the actual mark of the artist's hand on the work. But who had laid down all the paint that surrounded them – who had held the paintbrush? She had been so dismissive of her father's romantic concept of art – 'the hand holding the brush' – before. Her photography seemed more clearly than ever to be a statement refuting everything the paintings had stood for. The pathos and fury of the white-washed, dismembered little dolls on the walls nearby encoded something unspeakable. The triangle that appeared in almost every painting looked now like a silent gesture towards the trinity behind the work: Fleur, Maeve and Grey.

'This is yours, isn't it?' I asked.

'This one's mine,' she said, meditatively, gazing at the painting. 'All mine.' She looked up at me. 'But they're not – I think you know – they're not all all mine, exactly,' emphasising the repeated words.

There was agony in her expression, although her voice was level and steady, and I looked away. It was as close as she would come to actually admitting anything. The long weight that she had carried, caught up in the intricacies of Maeve and Grey's deception, was almost visible in the strain of her shoulders, the careful carriage of her head and body that was at times, like now, too mature, too knowing.

Fleur put the painting back inside the case, but didn't zip it shut. She stood up. One hand on her waist, she was again like any other passive–aggressive teenager.

'There's been speculation in the past,' she said, dismissively. 'It never went anywhere. It usually came from people who were jealous. There's a lot of that in the whole art world.' I could only imagine what lengths Grey and Maeve would go to in order to squash those kinds of questions. 'Ingrid figured it out. And you say you don't care?'

'I'm curious. But no, I don't care.'

She eyed me suspiciously.

'I'm not going to … blackmail you,' I said.

Her laugh was hard. 'I don't think you would. So. There you go. Are you all through here?'

'Just about.' I paused. 'So, Fleur. Hypothetically. It occurred to me that if someone – if someone wanted to leave town – hypothetically – without anyone knowing – September 11 would be a good day to choose. To leave.'

She was very still, and met my eyes, expressionless.

'Of course, everyone you left behind would have to believe that you were dead,' I said.

We looked at each other.

'Everyone,' she echoed, eventually. 'It would only work if everyone believed that you were dead. This hypothetical person.'

I waited.

'I can't help you,' she said. 'You can't make sense of it. You need to stop now.' Her words came out stilted, as though she were making a conscious effort to use as few as possible to convey what she needed to say.

'Can you just tell me –' I started.

'No.' Her voice was firm. She went and sat down on a beanbag under the window and pulled out her cigarettes. Her hands were steady as she lit one.

'You can't tell me where she went.'

When she faced me she was innocent-looking, eyebrows lifted and knitted just slightly in concern, and her eyes were unreadable.

'I don't know. I don't know what you're talking about,' she said flatly, quietly.

'Did you help her?' I asked.

But she had said everything she was going to say to me.

If I wanted to make her tell me whatever she knew, the things in my manila envelope would provide some leverage. But she had a steadfast look about her and I wondered what choice she would make in the end, whether the leverage would be effective. Something told me it might not work. I understood why Ingrid had trusted her.

'OK,' I said.

And why would Ingrid have trusted me? And why should Fleur trust me now? That little stone, the secret pebble in my chest, pressed hard against me, its compressed currency of resentment and envy grown hollow over the years. I felt transparent as water in front of her, and ashamed.

Her expression was blank in its studied way and I saw

everything there I looked for, and probably imagined it all: fear; relief; anger; guilt.

Downstairs the velvet sofa was still there in the shopfront window, pair of unlaced boots on the floor beside it. A woman coming out of the door of the shop almost collided with me. She was carrying two large shopping bags in each hand and wearing high heels that made a scratching noise on the pavement as she stopped. She smiled, embarrassed, and swung her bags out of the way. Her face was familiar: she was the woman in the painting at Maeve's gallery, the updated Madame X. She continued down the block, purposeful, a little unsteady in her heels, walking north. I paused, and turned around, and walked downtown.

By the time I reached Ground Zero it was late afternoon, the air grey with smoke rising from the grates and holes in the street, and evening waited, almost there. The sky in the west had a yellowish tinge. Getting there had been trickier than I had expected; without the landmarks of the towers to guide me, my sense of direction got turned around and I had circled back once or twice before reaching the site. As I turned onto Church Street it was there in front of me very suddenly, and I walked past the little chapel and the tall, black, glass Hilton until I was standing there at the wire fence. There were people all around, some looking at the site, most on their way somewhere, as usual. Someone tried to give me a leaflet with a heading that was something to do with Bush and Osama bin Laden and Iraq, a conspiracy. I raised my hand and refused. Glimpses of the hole in the ground showed through the fence, the chalky concrete white and grey. It was pitifully small, and empty. I looked back at the chapel across the road, St Paul's, still standing there in its green surround of lawn and trees. *Paul, 9*, I remembered, and wondered if she had been indicating this place in her brief note for that day.

Shoppers poured out of the solid bulk of the department store opposite, red-and-white bags in hand. The footpath felt very narrow, congested with people. I had carried away a sense of loneliness from Fleur's apartment that sank and grew within me. I thought of the manila envelope and the secrets in it that Fleur had carried around for so long, and the burden of whatever Ingrid had entrusted her with before her departure, as I had decided now to call it.

Other people stood next to me at the fence, visitors at a gravesite. A man paused a few feet away, a bunch of roses in his hand, red roses, and looked uncertain what to do with them. I moved away. I did not know how I felt, or what it was I thought I had understood, ever, about Ingrid's life or death. Or departure. Evening fell and I walked back uptown.

Horrible doubts circled me, walking those blocks. I'd wanted to imagine that she could have escaped, that she might have, from the life she had made with Grey. Even when I'd expected her to, she hadn't. Was I reframing her story to make it more consonant with what I wanted to believe of her – the bravery and brilliance that I had admired as her friend? It was romantic to believe that she had escaped after all, and fooled us all, and made a new life for herself somewhere unknown, like a person in a witness protection program. Maybe that was real freedom. It was easier to bear than the thought that she had meant to continue her life as it was, refusing help and understanding and any other way out. It was easier to bear than imagining her face in Richard's Polaroid photograph, and the bruise, and whatever violent death he thought that she had faced in the end. I thought of the picture of her on the Promenade, my black-and-white copy, and again regretted having returned it. And then, as I approached SoHo, the blocks close to Fleur's studio, I wondered if Fleur had seen this desire of mine to believe in Ingrid's escape, and manipulated and fed it. It was the secret, cherished hope of everyone who had lost someone on that day, after all – that she was not dead but missing, just as it said in the few remaining notices posted by relatives that still fluttered from telegraph poles and the walls of phone boxes here and there downtown. I saw Fleur as Ingrid's secret champion but there was every reason to think that she was also protecting her father, Maeve, herself. Her face when I left had been unreadable – had there been triumph in there as well, the sense of her own escape, her own success?

My mind ran again and again to thoughts of where Ingrid would have gone, if she could have escaped. It was difficult to imagine Victoria entering into the picture, and I couldn't imagine her wanting to talk to me. Aside from her I couldn't think of anywhere or anyone; I didn't know Ingrid's early life well enough to know what places there might be that were truly secret from Grey, from Fleur. I believed now that Ingrid would have kept the details of her plan secret even if Fleur had known about the escape itself and had been there with her after that first departure from the island, over the bridge to Brooklyn, to the Promenade where Fleur had taken that last picture. Where to from there? JFK? A rental car? A Greyhound bus? Now the skyline from that photograph grew hazier as I tried to remember it, and it seemed as though it could have been taken from any city, any place. It looked like a solid thing that dissolved into particles of air under any pressure, any touch; a mirror that reflected back to me my own unrecognised desire.

The decision that was hardest, that I put off and came back to, was whether to tell anyone else, and who to tell. If it was true that Ingrid had escaped, then it seemed as though I ought to keep it to myself. I saw myself and Fleur as lone secret keepers, guarding a dangerous truth. Grey lurked on the edge of this vision, prowling, patient, threatening. Fleur had counted somehow on the fact that I wouldn't tell anyone and that I would stop asking questions. But more questions pulled at me and I battled the need to share my thoughts with someone else. If Richard really started to believe that Ingrid might be alive then he would surely go tearing off to find her. Ralph would not rest until he found out the truth, and his expectations of me might never end. I thought of Richard's cold face against my neck the night before, his broken voice, and I knew that I would keep everything to myself, for now.

My feet began to hurt and the pavement felt harder and harder. I found myself on Bleecker Street, passed the place I had visited with Fleur, and walked into another bar one block away. Jones's fair hair appeared at the end of the room, behind a brightly coloured jukebox; I saw the angle of his arm resting on a table, then he moved and it wasn't him at all. Someone younger, with an American accent I could hear from my seat at the bar. He caught my eye and I looked away. Little illuminated plastic skulls hung on a cord across the mirror behind the bar, glowing green and black. The American voices around me talked on, here and there another accent, an unplaceable one pitched lower than the others. I missed Jones's ability to show up when I didn't expect it, when I needed it. I half-expected him to walk in now, but he didn't. The jukebox was playing a track that had been everywhere in the city over the past weeks, a song by Wilco about a heavy metal drummer, innocence, the river. I thought about calling Eve but couldn't think of how to ask the questions I wanted to in a way that would make sense.

I had been chasing this story half-heartedly in pieces and fits and starts for months now, and I let myself wonder for the first time what it had all been for. I had been acting as Ralph's surrogate in the beginning and now, unhappily, held information and suspicions that I didn't want to share with him. I was a hopeless detective. Nothing felt the way it did in stories about private investigators or hard-boiled journalists who would risk everything to know the last piece of truth. The burning desire in me now was not to know, but to forget; not to go on digging, but to stop and rest, especially if, as I suspected, Ingrid had calculated the risk herself and decided to stay hidden from everyone – me, Ralph, Richard. If Richard wanted to pursue his version of the story, he could. My turning away from that was probably a form of cowardice, but I could live with that. If Ingrid was out there somewhere and wanted to come back in one day, she would know where to find me.

A vista of infinite patience seemed to open up before me. It had only been a year, just over a year, since it all happened; a year from now, Fleur might decide to tell me more. Things could change. It might seem less important to her by then.

In all the places and scenes of my life I saw myself having drifted slowly to the margins: on the edge of the conversation, overhearing; playing at being Jones's bit on the side; downstage in shadow, with Ingrid in the spotlight. But I wanted my part in it to be finished, for the script to change. There was something else here for me, if I could find my way to it without Ingrid.

Back at the apartment in the early hours of the morning there were messages scrawled next to the phone in Matt's writing. Richard. Jones. Trinh. The freezer was empty, nothing left to drink.

In the bedroom Ingrid's tiny red elephant stood on the chest of drawers, half-buried by a scarf and a folded newspaper from days before. I took it in my hand. Something about it looked wrong. The red wasn't quite what I remembered when I pictured it on the dresser in Ingrid's room at Kirribilli. It might have been the light. Was it a replacement, a decoy? The real one could be with her now, perhaps the one thing she had decided she couldn't leave behind. I was good at spotting small differences, or so I liked to think. There were little black marks for eyes and tail, and the legs and trunk weren't quite symmetrical, carved carefully but not with absolute precision. The elephant looked much like it always had, but the more I looked at it the less it seemed to be the same. It now looked like an impostor. But my memory wasn't good enough; I couldn't be sure. In the end I decided it didn't matter.

I went to bed and prayed for a dreamless sleep.

The dreams of Ingrid's death that had forced themselves on me those first few weeks in the city had gone since I'd come back, replaced by occasional visions of her as the menacing Carlotta. But that night, after I'd looked at the elephant and crashed in bed, was different. I woke up to the sound of an impossible bird call, a mournful Sydney sound that I'd never heard in New York, unsure if what I'd seen was a dream or a vision, a premonition or a wish, future, past or present. It could have been an image of heaven or hell or that strange afterlife of the ancients where spirits live on in a sorry half-existence, deprived of the ability to touch.

As it sometimes is in dreams, I wasn't sure if I was myself or her or some other being entirely; it was both my body and not my body, and it carried itself forward with an exhausted determination, all other feeling spent. I had arrived at this place after a long drive, after several wrong turns that had led only to gullies and dead ends. The house that appeared through the trees was as I had expected it to be: wooden shingles, old paint, a casement window opened at the side that seemed to promise that someone was home.

The cars on the distant highway sounded like the roar of waves, and then the break of actual waves sounded. They broke and tore at the edge of hearing, another set following in their wake.

The front door was wide and painted eggshell white, chipped in places. Six high squares of mottled glass showed a white-walled hallway inside; a framed photograph hung just opposite. I recognised the two girls in it, one laughing and looking into the camera, eyes squinted in a smile, the other looking at the laughing girl, just smiling, one hand raised to her mouth.

The keys were light and cold in my hand. All my patience left me and I longed for the journey to be over.

'Are you there?' The words disappeared into the space, no echo back.

I opened my eyes; the mournful cry of the bird dissolved into a siren's wail. My hand shook when I lifted it to my face but my eyes and cheeks were dry.

There was quite a story to tell Ralph in the end, woven from pieces of the actual or possible versions. We stayed on the phone for hours, with him listening and me patiently sharing with him a carefully constructed edition of the past weeks. Fleur fascinated him, the child genius, and I told him more about how sweet and grown-up she was, the privilege of being shown some of her early works on paper, the disturbing brilliance of her photographs and videos and how she had let me assist in a photo shoot at her studio.

'It seemed as though she and Ingrid had a special kind of relationship from the beginning,' I told him. 'I think she probably did see Ingrid as a kind of mother, or a sister, a friend. They loved each other.'

'She said that,' he said. 'Ingrid said how much she loved her.'

Hearing about Fleur seemed to calm some of Ralph's anguish, the idea of her being there as a positive presence in Ingrid's life, so that it wasn't all defined by her miserable subjection to Grey. 'I'll send you pictures,' I said, thinking of a snapshot I had from my earlier visit, of Fleur in the studio near the astroturf set. This made him happy.

He was scandalised and fascinated by the story of Trinh's secret working life as a masked dominatrix. It injected a frisson of sex and danger into the dull conservatism he had expected of a Classics department.

'Does she like doing it?' he asked.

'I don't know,' I said. 'It's hard to tell. It seems like the best option for her.'

'What does she wear? Does she have to provide her own outfits?'

I made it up.

I embellished my own tale of heartbreak too, the inevitable fate of the discarded mistress. Ralph pushed me again, insensitively, on the question of whether Jones had slept with Ingrid, but I told him that it was very unlikely. Richard I left out of it and he didn't ask.

The conversation ended formally, like the conclusion of a presentation. I wondered whether Ralph was taking notes. 'So,' he said, 'you're all finished up there?'

'I'm all finished with Ingrid,' I said.

And with you, I thought – feeling treacherous, proud, sad, relieved. I pictured him there in the conservatory – but something told me he was in another room, perhaps at the dining table or on the sofa facing Ingrid's velvet chair. Would her presence in the house slowly drain away, or would it persist, for him? What difference would it make, being able to know the story as he now did? If there was going to be some kind of process of moving on, it wasn't clear where he would go from here. I thought about his medicated heart struggling to stay in time and turned away from the thought as surely as if I had removed my hand decisively from his skin. Empty air filled the gap.

'I might stay on for a while anyway. I could find some work — of the non-dominatrix variety. There's a show of Bonnard's late interiors coming on at the Met next month. I'd like to see it.'

He didn't seem to mind. My obligations were discharged. I was a liar and a thief. We said goodbye.

After that conversation I wanted to leave the apartment, get out of sight of the phone that seemed to look at me accusingly, knowing all the words I hadn't said. The day was cold and sharp, early afternoon sky the pearly whitish-grey of a dove's wing. A couple of subway changes brought me to Brooklyn Heights and I started off down Montague Street, intending, I suppose, a kind of farewell to the Promenade and all the questions and doubts that had come to inhabit that few feet of pavement, the empty miles of view. A few days earlier the first snow had fallen, just an inch or two that hadn't stuck anywhere much, but here and there a few frozen, grey lumps of it sat on the pavement, pushed into shady corners and pressed up against garbage cans on the street. I turned into a shop a couple of blocks down the streets incongruously called

Manhattan Muffins, the name in faded green capitals on the awning next to a simple rendering of the city skyline. It was both shabbier and more busy than the muffin shop I had visited before, the last one on Montague before the Promenade. Waiting in line for my coffee and bagel I noticed a picture tacked to the wall – one of those commemorative images of the Twin Towers, a photograph that seemed to distort the buildings so that they stood even taller and more apart from the others than they ever really had. A red banner unfurled across the bottom of the image with *9-11 – Never Forget* inscribed in machine-made cursive letters.

Fuck, I thought, and almost said it, so strong was my own desire to forget and escape these reminders. Muffins of all varieties were arranged on the shelves of the glass case in front of me when I reached the counter. I asked for a coffee and a bagel with cream cheese. The dark-haired guy in a clean white uniform turned around to call the order across to the others and turned back for my money. By then I was holding the photograph, the black-and-white copy of the photograph that was still sitting in my bag. One last try, I thought. My throat wanted to close over but I held it out to him.

'Do you know her?' I asked. My weeks in the city had already trained me out of the use of any unnecessary preliminary words.

He looked at it. His whole body seemed to nod very slightly, as though he were rocking back and forth on his toes. 'Joe!' he called out suddenly, whipping his head around to the three men behind him who were pouring coffee and spreading cream cheese on bagels. 'Someone's asking about your girlfriend.' He looked back at me and met my eyes for a short second, neutral shading into something else – contempt, resentment, pity – and held out his hand for money. I paid him and he passed me my change and my bagel in a white paper bag.

Another man passed me a white paper cup of coffee and said, 'I'm Joe.' He exchanged a few muttered words with the guy at the register and then squeezed out from behind the counter to meet me. His eyes flicked quickly to the picture in my hand and then he nodded towards the door.

He was thin and young, a few years older than Fleur maybe, with a beautiful, serious face. He wore the white uniform with a diffident slouch. It looked as though he was experimenting with growing a moustache. I wanted to tell him to give that up. We stood on the street just outside the shop doorway. He lit a cigarette, cupping his hands around the lighter. The smell of the smoke was acrid, poisonous and tempting, and everything around us seemed to grow dirtier and more toxic as I waited, all of it becoming solid and determined in a new way by what I felt I was about to discover. A stubborn patch of snow near the kerb was fast becoming ice, trapping like fossils all the cigarette ash and pieces of dirt that had got stuck in it over the past day.

'Did Ingrid come here?' I asked him.

He nodded. 'Ingrid? That was her name, yeah.' It was a Brooklyn accent, born and bred. I guessed that he hadn't been sure of her name before and I could see him attaching it to the woman in his mind.

'When did you see her last?'

'That was a long time ago, lady.'

'How long?' I was persistent. My feet had turned to ice, my heart to stone and metal.

He shrugged. 'Last summer.' He gave me a long, sad look. 'I saw her picture in the paper. In the *Times*, you know, the pictures they ran of all the victims.' He dragged on his cigarette. 'I had to look at all those pictures. Saw them all.'

'So you didn't see her after that?' I asked.

'I was surprised – to see her picture with all those, you know.' He glanced up and down the street nervously, probably anxious to get back to work, and nodded towards the store. 'The guys. They knew I liked her.' He smiled half-heartedly. 'She used to come in every now and again. I always took her order.'

'When did you last see her?' I repeated.

He shrugged again. 'It was a few days later. Not quite a week. After 9/11, after that. It wasn't her that came in. It was her little sister.'

The word 'sister' tore across my hearing – Victoria, with her big sunglasses and flashy ring, out of place inside the little shop in her summery black dress. Here. A few days later.

Then he said, 'You know, the young one. With the dark hair.'

He was talking about Fleur. I breathed out. 'That was her stepdaughter.'

He blinked. 'Whatever. You know who I mean? Skinny girl, make-up on her eyes. They were usually here together.'

I nodded.

'She came in. She ordered Ingrid's order. I knew it was for her, she always had the same thing, this kind of weird thing — a blueberry muffin warmed up in the microwave, sliced in half, butter on it.'

Yes, I thought. There it was, a memory of Ingrid's hands, their short fingers, spreading butter on a muffin, waiting while it melted in. A thick, old china plate. A dented Sydney table.

'She came in by herself, the girl. But she ordered her own thing too, her own bagel, her own coffee. Two coffees.' He looked at the long, wooden bench on the street in front of the shop window. One leg of it was chained to a heavy link set into the cement pavement. No-one was sitting there now in the cold. 'I noticed it because, you know, I liked seeing her. Ingrid — that was her name.' He blinked slowly. 'I guess she was waiting outside here on the bench. I looked out — I saw her from behind. She had that blonde hair.' He looked at me, and his gaze was intelligent and direct. 'So what was her picture doing in the paper that day? I wondered about that.'

One eyebrow lifted and lowered. His mouth was thin and handsome under the ridiculous short moustache. He ground his cigarette out with the heel of a steel-toed boot. It joined all the other crap dredging into the cracks in the concrete path, the ice, the gutters. My coffee cup was warm against my hands and I took a sip, scalding my lips and tongue.

'So where is she now?' he asked me.

'That's the big question,' I said.

He nodded slowly.

'Well. Thanks,' I said eventually.

He shoved his hands down into his pockets and pushed the door open with his shoulder, disappearing back inside.

I lifted my coffee to my mouth more warily this time and

sipped at it. The sky above had grown denser, more pearlescent. I looked down the hill towards the Promenade, knowing that if I went down there I would find a changed landscape; my steps would lead irresistibly to that formerly elusive spot where Fleur had stood and taken the picture; the buildings in the skyline would align themselves as if by magic to match the pattern of shapes in the background of the photograph.

I looked down at the picture in my hands, at Ingrid's mocking smile. With one layer of mystery stripped away her look was somehow more silent, more inscrutable even than before.

That narrative of escape I had wished for seemed to be true. So why didn't I feel more elation? I was glad to know that Richard was wrong, that Grey hadn't murdered her. It felt good to give up that image of him as a killer, which had never sat quite comfortably with me. But a guilty, resentful part of me was sorry to give up the possibility that Ingrid had died in the terrible events of that day just like all those other, ordinary hundreds and thousands, all her promise and exceptionality turned to that sudden end. I grudgingly admired the fact that she had chosen that to be her known and accepted fate. But it wasn't so ordinary after all, when I considered it: to join the martyred mass of people – heroes – whose names would be read out at memorials for a long time to come, whose pictures had appeared with an obituary in the *Times* in those big spreads.

I remembered the feeling I had experienced at Fleur's apartment that last time, knowing and accepting that Ingrid had not trusted me with any of this information, any of these secrets. I tried to turn my mind to wondering about her whereabouts. I pictured an overnight bag, already packed and prepared for weeks, waiting for the right moment to leave, the grip of a hand on it – and that was as far as I could get. My imagination stopped and baulked, just like a horse refusing to jump over an obstacle too high, a river too wide. It was enough for the moment to know that she *was* somewhere; not there, across the river, in particles of dust. It was a secret that, for now, still belonged to her.

I went back inside the store and grabbed a card from a stack next to the fridge full of juices and Coca-Cola. Manhattan Muffins. The little green line drawing of the skyline stretched across the card. I took another. I had my manila envelope; now I had a witness, of sorts. At the stationery store a few doors down I bought a stamp and an envelope, borrowed their pen and wrote Fleur's address on it, wrote my name and email address on the back of one of the cards, sealed the card inside. By now I was familiar with all the signs of dissembling that marked my handwriting, in Richard's estimation: the uneven slant, the give-away 'shark's tooth' sharp angle of the upstroke of the letters *r, n, m.* I let them be.

That vista of patience I had found at the end of my long walk from the Trade Center site a few days earlier opened up in front of me again and softened the new hardness I saw all around, with everything now too sharply defined. There was no forgetting; I would never need the imperative reminder of the memorial picture inside the muffin shop. The ancient residue of smog and ash shadowed the bricks of the building behind me, the corners of the mailbox, and I closed my hand over the dirty lever, opened it, pushed the letter in, and walked away. Then I remembered my recent dream, the sense of arrival at a journey's end, and felt a renewed certainty that I had glimpsed a piece of reality. The frozen street gave way to another landscape altogether, a blurry, brilliant blue horizon in the distance, fringed with green and warmth.

Richard sat across from me in the coffee shop where we had arranged to meet that first time, when I was playing at stalking him. After I had told him I was through with it, that I wanted to get on with mourning, he hadn't called me back for a couple of weeks. I had relied on my store of forbearance, knowing it was a risk to wait but part of me knowing it would pay off. His voice on the phone had sent a surge of relief through my veins, along with something else. Hope, a delicate shaft of light. Now we sat at the same table, only on different sides than we had before. When we first met it had been Richard who had banned her name from the conversation; now it was me. He poured sugar into his coffee and stirred it.

'Trinh won the fellowship she was applying for,' he said. 'I heard from her the other day. So she's going to Rome.'

'Good,' I said.

'And Jones is spending his sabbatical in London, I hear.' He didn't look at me. I didn't reply.

My cherry pie arrived, two forks on the plate.

'And where are you off to?' I asked.

'Me? Nowhere. I have a lot of work to do. And I'm getting very attached to my seat at the New York Public.'

The ice cream next to the pie had started to melt and puddle, black flecks of vanilla dust against the white. 'I suppose I should be off home again soon myself,' I said. Money was running out. I had pretty much decided to take Matt up on the offer of working for the artist Carson, whoever he was. When I thought about Sydney, now, it felt somehow less substantial than before, and it was becoming harder to imagine a place for myself there. Here in New York it was easier to imagine – not a place, exactly, yet, but a way of making one. A lot, not everything, depended on what Richard had to say. Something rattled for a moment way down in there behind my ribs – a brief, guilty, excited flutter like a bird's wings against my back, and then quieted into silence.

He picked up the other fork and turned it over in his fingers. Flip, flip. It caught the light gently. 'But you've only just arrived.'

I let myself smile.

Acknowledgments

Thanks firstly to my mother Lyn, a fantastic agent and a great reader, and to my father John, for their unstinting support and encouragement. I am indebted to the brilliant Bruce Gardiner, who inadvertently inspired this story years ago in a tutorial on Henry James and George Eliot. Thanks also to Debra Adelaide, one of the earliest and best readers of this book; my editors, Nicola O'Shea and Linda Funnell; my fabulous agent in New York, Claudia Ballard; my friends Tanya Agathocleous, Yelena Baraz, Bridget Crone, Heather Furnas and Tina Lupton; and my patient husband, Danny Fisher.

Many thanks to Faber and Faber Ltd for kind permission to include an extract from 'Portrait of a Lady' by T.S. Eliot, published in full in his *Collected Poems 1909–1962*.